Sasha vs the Whole Wide World (and Dragons)

(and Dragons)

Rachel Taylor Thompson

Chapter One

It should've been an entirely normal, early morning, absolutely nothing-unusual-happens run on the beach.

I left the house at 5:37 a.m., the sun a hazy reflection behind the horizon. I wore my usual outfit—long hair in a pony, light hoodie, jogger shorts, and high-end Saucony Endorphin running shoes.

No, my family wasn't rich.

We were more endlessly-on-the-verge-of-foreclosure, worry-instead-of-sleep, dead-but-unburied-due-to-costs broke. Dad, Gramps, my brother, and my brother-in-law went in on the Sauconys as a combination Christmas and graduation gift. Yes, I'm that girl who graduated from high school a semester early.

The drive to my favorite beach took ten minutes. I parked in the sand-strewn lot, hid my keys under my seat, and stretched my upper body as I hiked over the dunes to the water. Running in the mornings was pretty much the only quiet time I got, and I cherished it like most people my age did their cellphones. Okay, I totally cherished that as well, even if mine was six years old and had the crappiest cell service on the planet.

I knew the moment I left the dunes that something was off about the bay. No salty breeze. No morning bird calls. Even the surf seemed muted.

Meh. Enjoy the peace. I had a small window here.

I had the timing of my runs down perfect. If I began at six a.m. sharp and kept my pace, I'd finish at 6:54. This gave me twenty-eight minutes to get back to my car, drive to Carmel, and arrive for my Job #1 only two minutes late. Any later than that and Mrs. Lee gave me a bruising lecture on punctuality and threatened to fire me. Yes, it was a weird motivational tactic. Yes, it worked.

The moment my phone chirped six a.m., I shoved it into my pocket and took off across the damp sand.

Only then did I notice what was wrong.

Something in the distance blocked the beach. An overturned boat hull maybe, half out of the rolling tide.

That happened sometimes. A boat would get loose during a storm, drift down the coast, and show up somewhere else beat-to-death. But it was April and this was California. Whale, then?

That happened too. A couple years ago, my dad and brother had taken me with them to get pictures of a partially eaten whale calf. Gross.

This was much bigger than the calf. Much, much bigger. "Fourteen hours," I complained to the object, the ocean, my dad and brother who couldn't hear me anyway, "That's how much I worked yesterday. Fourteen very long, very tiring, very doing-ten-more-today hours. I deserved to get to run. I earned this."

I slowed to a walk anyway, pulling my phone back out and setting it to video. My dad had a minorly successful social media channel, meaning he made enough money to not quite cover his expenses. My brother, Antony, was his producer. While the platform was exotic car parts, they could work in pretty much anything that might get views. A recently deceased whale was a no-brainer, especially as Ant would find a way to blame cruiseships or fishermen or someone like that for the death.

"This isn't likely to make any financial difference," I grumbled to myself. (Nothing ever did.)

I hit Record. "Oh, wow," I exclaimed in a hopefully-not-too-fake tone for the benefit of the channel's audience. "Upside-down sailing boat? Gray whale? Giant squid? What could it be?" I panned my phone, watching the screen to make sure I framed it well. Weirdly, the boat/whale/squid didn't end where it should've but continued on and on and on and on into the water like it had a massively thick, extremely long tail. Also, the whole thing appeared to be purple.

"Mother of Dog, no way." My pulse leaped so hard a quiver ran through my body. I lowered my phone. "I think it's a seadragon."

The thing's front end was blunt with a wide mouth and enormous eyes. Very whale-like, really. That was the end of the resemblance, though. The curve of the body was longer and more serpentine. Instead of fins, it had water wings, long, thin appendages that were currently limp and crushed against the sand but underwater supposedly floated like rippling gossamer webbing.

Supposedly, because no one had ever photographed a seadragon underwater. Magical-creatures were rare. Seadragons were . . . well, whatever "rare" was divided by a hundred thousand.

They were also valuable. Pricelessly valuable.

I jerked my phone back up and continued filming. "No one's seen a dead seadragon since . . ." My voice hitched. Not fake this time either. "Since . . . that one they made the movie about before I was born."

I walked forward again, describing what I saw, my voice ragged with excitement, my pulse still in high-gear. This dead seadragon had to be worth an easy hundred million. And I was the only person who currently knew it existed.

There was an opportunity here.

However . . .

Seadragons were protected under every single international law on the planet, and the Monterey Bay was a marine sanctuary. Removing anything, touching anything, was likely to get me into serious trouble, possibly even arrested.

Right.

I wouldn't touch it.

I was totally going to touch it.

A single scale would pay for four years of college without my living at home and holding down multiple jobs. Two scales would cover my brother's school debt. Four would pay off my dad's credit cards. Five (maybe more like nine) would save our house from the never-ending threat of foreclosure.

Yeah. No way was I not going to pilfer as many scales as I could carry. I'd just snag some quick and hightail it back to my car. No one would ever know.

The sun cracked over the dunes, splitting the shadows and lighting the carcass in iridescent purple and green and black. I froze mid-step, momentarily awed.

"It's . . ."

The perfect word to describe the resplendence in front of me lost itself halfway up my throat. It wasn't just the richness of the color, either, but the sinewy shape and texture of the hide. Everything about it was just so stunning, gorgeous, amazing . . .

" . . . dead." I finished softly.

I headed to the seadragon's blunted head, trying to be respectful while still filming and gauging how I was going to remove the scales. (Because admiration didn't pay the bills and nothing I did now would bring it back to life anyway. Gotta be practical about these things.)

"I'm so sorry," I whispered as I neared. "I hope you weren't in pain."

The head was twice my height. Its huge eye had a hazy, dead cast to it. The scales were even more colorful and gorgeous up close, pearly and reflective and gleaming all at once. Each scale was twice the size of a piece of binder paper and lay smooth against the hide.

After taking some close-up photos, I tucked my phone under my arm and ran my fingers under the edge of a glossy scale. It lifted easily, as if meant to flare out. "Please, don't hate me for doing this," I said to the dragon as I gave the scale a tug. "I really, really need the money, and I promise not to waste what I take." The scale didn't budge, so I put a foot on the side of the dead creature, leveraged my weight backward, and pulled as hard as I could.

My hands slipped down the velvety smoothness, and I toppled backward, landing on my butt in the sand. The massive eye blinked at me.

I screamed and clawed backward, my hands digging wrist-deep into the sand as I panic-pushed myself away as fast as I could. I flipped over and jumped to my feet, running up the beach faster than I'd ever run before.

It wasn't supposed to be alive.

How could it be alive? Was it now going to kill me? I had, after all, been attempting to tear a piece of it off. A small piece, but still. How salty would I be if someone tried to steal one of my fingernails while I watched?

Since it made no move to chase me, I slowed and glanced back.

Seadragons weren't thought of as killers, not like the desert fire-lizards of Africa or the eel-like-things that lived in Norway, but all magical-creatures had better-than-cow intelligence. It blinked a second time. The milkiness I'd assumed was the cast of death was some kinda inner lid.

Before I could do more than recognize this, it threw its head in the air, and I threw my arms over my head as I was peppered by sand. The seadragon thrashed against the beach. Great thumping thrashes, head up and down, body back and forth, salt water and grit flying everywhere. A screeching flock of gulls broke from the dunes for the safety of the sky. The surf crashed violently against the shore. I bolted backward again.

At the same time, I could just hear my father's voice when I told him I'd witnessed the death throes of a seadragon, and I hadn't filmed it for his channel. *Sasha Beth Clems, Have. You. Learned. Nothing?!*

I stopped again and hit Record right as the creature lunged backward cobra-like and threw its upper body fifty feet in the air, revealing a pale underside.

And an anchor-sized harpoon jammed into its scales.

"Holy freaking not-a-cow. Someone shot it?"

The seadragon fell back to the sand with the loudest thump I'd ever heard, making the ground shake way worse than the 6.3 earthquake we'd had when I was ten. The wind disappeared and the ocean waves stopped waving for a long, held breath.

I kept filming.

The creature had come down crooked and facing me. Its eyes narrowed to slits and its face wrinkled as if it were in horrible pain. Pain so strong the sand under my running shoes shivered with it. Or maybe that was actually me shivering in reaction.

This was so wrong.

The seadragon was beautiful and it was in pain and it didn't deserve this. Regardless of my family's financial needs, I was an animal lover and I truly, deeply, didn't want the creature in front of me to die.

The wide grimace of a mouth parted, showing huge ice-pick teeth. My pity dove behind my liver and I bolted backward a third time.

The creature made a wet popping sound as if blowing the world's largest kiss. Then its entire body shuddered, teeth to tail. The surrounding sand shook in response, for-real-this-time. The seadragon went still. Slack. Limp. Dead. (Again, for-real-this-time.)

I stared at it for a long moment, silent, sick, somber. I glanced at my phone to be respectful. "6:07 a.m."

Only then did I notice what the seadragon had expelled onto the sand with that kiss.

Oh. My. Dog.

What a complete and utter idiot I'd been. Dumbest of the dumb. Too stupid to own a phone, smart or not. There was only one group of people with the gall, the resources, and the desire to kill a seadragon, and especially to do so within a marine sanctuary.

"The magic-handlers," I whispered and then frantically scanned the bay as if saying their name might call them.

Magic-handlers wouldn't care about the scales or the value of the creature itself. They had more money than many small nations (Lucky!) and were said to have their fingers in the economies of half the planet (Unfairly lucky!). Nope, the magic-handlers didn't care about the creature's value or beauty or pain. They cared about the thing that made magical-creatures alive, the thing magical-creatures gave up when they died.

The raw magic.

The seadragon's magic sat half-buried in the sand in front of its slack mouth. A basketball-sized sphere glowing with internal swirls of blue and purple and black like something from a trendy glassblower shop.

Semis. That's what raw magic was called. A Latin word that rhymed with "freebies" (or "feces").

If a handful of scales would solve all my family's financial problems, a Semis would make us gazillionaires.

Chapter Two

The movie about the last time a seadragon's Semis had been found included an international manhunt, several buildings blowing up, and the sun disappearing for four days while the hero raced to the only auction house with a vault strong enough to keep out magic-handlers. The storyline had been more focused on cataclysmic chaos than accuracy, but a seadragon had died, a Semis had been found, and the finder had auctioned it off for an insane amount of money to a magic-handling family.

What most of us normal people knew about magic-handling came from movies. Magic-handlers existed in a shadow world and interacted with normal people in the same way as billionaire internet magnates. (I wouldn't mind being one of those.)

Magic-handlers took the magic from dead magical-creatures and used their special, genetically passed, super-secret handling skills to turn the magic into highly prized, even more secret spellbooks. Then they hid the spellbooks in quadruple-secret libraries that existed in some kinda fourth dimension only they could access to draw on the magic.

Or at least that was the common understanding. Journalists and such were all quick to add phrases like "to the best of our knowledge," "simplified down," "allegorically speaking," whenever these topics came up.

What *was* universally agreed upon was that magic-handlers were secretly running the universe.

I currently had $4,277.34 in my checking account and $532.07 in cash. This plus an additional $1,000 would just barely cover my first quarter tuition at UC Santa Cruz if I lived at home and continued working two of my four jobs to help my Dad with the mortgage. (No way would I be stupid enough to get student loans like my brother. Members of the Clems family just didn't do debt well.)

If I took and sold that Semis, I could skip the work step, the struggling step, the worry step, and jump to the college step while never again thinking of things like late bills, foreclosure notices, or interest rates.

There was also the morality of the situation. If I left the Semis just sitting here, someone way worse than me might find it. I, at least, would be very careful with what happened to it. I wouldn't sell the Semis to the highest bidder, but only to someone who deserved it. (I mean, someone who deserved it and had enough funds to pay me off.)

"I swear, I'll do good by you," I said to the carcass, which was getting brighter and brighter in color as the sun rose. I put my hand over my heart as if pledging allegiance.

Which was all very good, but if I took it, I'd have to keep the magic-handlers from stealing it from me while also finding a safe way to auction it off to them. Not exactly an easy problem.

My Gramps had a favorite saying about not worrying about over-salting the soup if no one had yet RSVP'd for dinner.

Or, in other words, take life one step at a time.

Step One: Collect the Semis.

(Apparently, I *was* doing this.)

I walked over to where it lay just past the dead creature's mouth. Considering the size of the creature, the Semis wasn't particularly large. I'd be able to carry it, but the idea of touching it grossed me out. I leaned over to look more closely, and my stomach shot bile up my esophagus, kinda like if I'd just left the vet's office after having our old cat Banjo put to sleep and the vet insisted I take home Banjo's spleen. So gross.

The Semis itself wasn't gross. The inner strands of purple and darkest blue shimmered with their own internal light.

I took off my hoodie and threw it over the top, then scooped the whole thing up without touching it directly. It lifted from the sand easily and wasn't a full sphere, but only half, as if the basketball had been sliced down the center by a ninja's sword. It felt quite glass-like, or maybe a particularly high grade of plastic. In the movie, the Semis had looked like a glowing squishy ball.

"I'm really sorry," I said to the blunted front of the seadragon's head. "When I end up rich, I'll make a donation to the marine sanctuary on your behalf. I swear, I will."

I walked over to a driftwood log, keeping my arms outstretched and the Semis as far from my body as possible.

Step Two: Return to the seadragon, erase any obvious footprints, and refilm finding the carcass sans Semis to throw off anyone who came after me. Because guaranteed someone would connect me to the morning, the beach, and the dead dragon. My best bet for short-term protection was denial. (Which I was excellent at.)

My dad's favorite Clems-ism was *To make them eat the cake, frost the bread thick.* Or in other words, make the lie look like the truth through sheer effort. My Gramps had been a culinary specialist in the Navy before turning into a chef-to-the-wealthy. He and my dad used to pick up side income through small-time cons. We had *lots* of food-based, graft-friendly Clems-isms.

I did a good job of it. I didn't even have to fake feeling both excited and entirely freaked out on the audio.

Step Three: Act normal to perpetrate my lie. I stashed the Semis on the floor of Gladys, my 2005 Hyundai, and drove back to town while considering what would be the obvious, expected thing for me to do next.

Easy enough—report the carcass.

The landward side of the dunes was artichoke fields, meaning no cell service, so I drove to the She Sells Seashells Coffee Shack. The She Sells Shack was across the street from my old high school and had free wi-fi. With that thought, an entire plan struck me all at once.

It happened that way sometimes. All the best ideas did, according to Gramps. Not that I planned elaborate cons regularly, or at all really. That was Dad's and Gramps's life rather than mine and even then, it was mostly their former lives, Thank Dog. The last thing we needed was one of them going to jail again.

Ordinarily, I might've bumped into a friend or two at the She Sells Shack, but today was the first Friday of spring break. Campus and the coffee shop would be empty of anyone who knew me. Perfect.

When I arrived, I parked Gladys in the gravel lot around back where there were no cameras.

Step Four: Text my brother, Antony, that I was sending the "greatest thing I'd ever seen" to the online server he kept available for such moments. Then I uploaded the re-created version of finding the seadragon. The original I considered deleting but decided against it. Once the Semis was safely sold to someone rich, I'd publish the death throes video. I owed it to the seadragon.

My phone said the upload would take seven minutes. Experience said I could count on twice that.

I slid my phone under the front seat of Gladys. The upload would confirm my location while I snuck across the street. (It was well known that the handlers had the entire cell system bugged.)

Clever me, I had a key to the backstage of the high school theater, courtesy of me filling in as a stagehand for Paige Lymon my freshman year after Paige broke her leg. We'd traded three weeks of me moving props for her lending me the key to the prop storage room so that Zachary Stults and I could use it to make out. I'd made a copy.

Of the key that was. Zachary, *The Faithless Schmuck*, hadn't been worth duplicating.

The school didn't have cameras, but I still crept stealthily over to the storage room door, the Semis wrapped in my hoodie. I snuck in no problem and hid the Semis under a stack of bedding from last year's production of *Once Upon a Mattress*. Seemed appropriate somehow.

Back at Gladys, my phone still said *uploading* in blue letters, so I went into the She Sells Shack and splurged on a skinny decaf latte for myself and a cappuccino for Mrs. Lee. I did that occasionally, for which she gave me a curt thank you as long as I arrived on time. If I was late, she added a lesson on bribery to my lecture on punctuality. She was a total peach.

The upload finished right as I returned to the car.

Step Five: Text my fifty closest friends and post to several social media sites, telling everyone to monitor my dad's channel for something crazy good. Everyone who has ever met him knows about the channel.

Once done, I turned to look in the general direction of the ocean. "Rest in peace," I murmured to the poor, dead creature out somewhere on the sand. "I'll do my best by you." (And makes lots of money too.)

Step Six: Tell the magic-handlers of my find and see who shows up. I googled their magical-creature reporting website.

Chapter Three

I finished up at Mrs. Lee's at 9:55 a.m. Having arrived ten minutes early, I not only didn't get yelled at, but she graciously accepted the coffee and awkwardly asked after my morning.

Going just fine, thank you very much.

While I'd walked her cutie pie dogs and scooped poop in her yard, Ant called three times and my Dad once. I didn't call either of them back. Since Job #2 didn't start until the afternoon, and it was my day off from Job #3, and Job #4 was only on weekends, I was heading home anyway. I tended to think the magic-handlers would arrive quickly, and I wanted to be ready.

Everything looked normal when I pulled Gladys into the driveway of the Clems family residence, officially titled *The Blue Castle*. It was robin's egg blue in color, but rather than being made of brick or turrets, it was a rundown 1930s ranch house shaped like the first two steps of a staircase. Gramps had added on the back second story in the 1980s.

My long-deceased Grams had insisted on the color and title. Both were from a book, also named *The Blue Castle*, and the whole tacky eyesore was as much a member of the family as I was. I adored every inch of it, but the neighborhood had gentrified around us, and three, four letters arrived a month offering to buy it so that it could be knocked down and replaced with a McMansion. An act akin to murder.

I took a quick shower, adding product to my roots to give my brown hair lift. I picked through my wardrobe and settled on a moss green V-neck sweater that made me look preppier than I really was. I did my eyes and brows, even adding a touch of gloss to my lips.

When I finally went downstairs, the family room TV was blaring a conservative talk show. Blue Castle rules said Gramps had to have it off by three p.m. on weekdays. Weekends were set for liberal TV only, Ant's and his husband, Nicholas's, preference. Afternoons/evenings were neutral for Dad and me. Not that I ever watched the TV, but having rules about these things kept us from killing each other.

Gramps was asleep in his recliner, so I turned down the TV's volume before heading to the kitchen for food. I'd just made it when our doorbell did its five-note chime.

My heart thumped a jiggy rhythm way more out of tune than our bell. *Sheesh*, they were even faster than expected.

I pressed my head against the fridge in a sudden fit of anxiety and repeated, "I'm just a girl who found a dead seadragon" three times. "Wish me luck," I murmured to the house. I could almost feel it patting me reassuringly on the back in reply.

I sent a quick text to Dad and Ant, telling them someone was at the door and that I'd be out to the production shed after I got rid of them. Dad and Ant would totally understand that as a "Don't interrupt" message. Rude of me, but facing whoever was outside would be easier without my crazy family around. They'd be able to tell at a single glance something was up. The lip gloss was a dead giveaway.

When I opened the front door, three magic-handlers were waiting for me, my first prospective buyers. They were obviously magic-handlers because they were also the most unbelievably drop-dead gorgeous beings I'd ever seen.

"Sasha Clems?" a stately, older Hispanic woman asked in a lightly accented voice.

"That's me." I automatically gave her my best pleasing-the-rich-people smile. Knee-jerk response that came with living where we did. With that, my jiggy nervousness disappeared, just like always once I was in action.

"Please allow me to introduce myself. I'm Diamella Valenzuela Jara, and I'd like a moment of your time." She handed me a business card.

Based on the woman's practical black pant suit and even more practical black pumps, I'd have guessed her an accountant or something. Her extreme beauty and the massive string of emeralds around her neck said otherwise. She also had a steely, I'm-in-charge look in her eye that implied expectations.

I disliked her on sight, and not just because members of the Clems family didn't trust people that weren't us.

The second handler was dressed more old-Europe-floral-rustic-chic. Her blonde hair looked professionally coiffed, and she wore a tad too much makeup as if trying to hide that she was no longer in her 40s. Or 50s. Or 60s. She was still gorgeous for the retiree-set.

She stood close to and slightly behind Mrs. Valenzuela, looking nervously at her rather than me.

I didn't like her either.

The third handler was the youngest by far, and I recognized him. I'd had his poster on the ceiling of my room during my less-than-fully-developed-tween-brain years. What for all the love of his overly devoted fan club was Aristotle Montague-Smith-Montague doing here?

He stood a full head taller than his companions, with dark hair that curled elegantly to the side, large, wide-set eyes, often described as "mysteries of the night" in memes, and defined cheekbones over skin so smooth my hand twitched wanting to touch.

Bad idea.

Embarrassingly bad. Particularly bad at this exact moment. I shoved my hand behind my back so I wouldn't be tempted.

Aristotle was only two years older than me and I'd been *such* a fan. Magic-handlers weren't usually teen idols, or any kind of idol for that matter. They worked hard to keep to themselves. Based on the fact that the books and vids and posters of Aristotle were stolen candids and "unauthorized," he hadn't sought to become one either, but his life story was so unique that everyone knew it and he was just so darned cute. Selling him the Semis had genuine appeal. I grinned in his direction, glad I'd cleaned up.

Aristotle didn't meet my gaze. He stood as far from the other two as possible, his attention on the twenty-five-foot flagpole in front of The Blue Castle, what Gramps called our "heritage" flag. It was white with a red cross and a defiant upheld hand in the center.

"An Ulster flag?" Aristotle Montague-Smith-Montague asked in his very upper-crust British accent. He sounded both disapproving and condescending as if he thought me too stupid to understand the meaning of Gramps's flag.

Right.

He might be treacle tart for the eyes, but apparently he was also a total snob without a sense of humor. I widened my smile. "You don't like 1970s Irish politics?"

Aristotle turned to look at me slowly as if he were avoiding the final moment where he had to make eye contact. "Not particularly."

"I'm still hoping '*Our day will come.*'" I raised my fist and said it teasingly so that he'd know I wasn't personally obsessed with a united Ireland. (Gramps was.)

Mrs. Valenzuela gave a sharp shake of her head Aristotle's direction. Then she turned the intensity of her gaze on me. "You should invite us in."

"Sure." I stepped back, still watching Aristotle, who had hunched his shoulders. He looked as if he'd prefer to be anywhere but the doorstep of a rundown ranch house.

Mrs. Valenzuela led the way into The Blue Castle. The older woman followed on her heels like an anxious child. Aristotle hung back several paces and then hurried past me in a rush.

Seriously?

I glanced down at the business card. It had Mrs. Valenzuela's name in beveled gold letters and two addresses: one in San Francisco, the other in Santiago, Chile. It was well known that the Chilean magic-handlers were the tops in the world and currently headed the Magic-Handlers Alliance. The Chileans were also the ones who'd purchased the last seadragon Semis. They'd come to power in the magic-handling world not long after. Or so it was said.

The four of us stepped into The Blue Castle's kitschy, yellow-with-white-daisies, wallpapered living room. It was dated but warm and inviting and always smelled like melting wax, even though we never lit candles. Mrs. Valenzuela and the older woman sat on a daisy sofa that matched the wallpaper. Aristotle stopped against the wall and glanced around at Gram's decorative clutter, everything from silk roses to crocheted afghans to Russian nesting dolls, and lots of it. His expression was that of someone deciding if he was going to put his Italian leather loafers onto a stepping stone covered in dog poop or a surrounding tar pit.

Aristotle Montague-Smith-Montague was a disappointment. I bet he'd never even held a job in his entire life. (A Clems family surefire way to determine character.)

I leaned against the door molding and watched for any signs that I'd read him wrong. Also, staring at him was no punishment.

He turned to look at one of Grams's favorite *The Blue Castle* (the book, not the house itself) quotes done as a cross-stitch on the wall. "*Almost all the evil in the world has its origin in the fact that someone is afraid of something,*" he read.

Man, wasn't his accent gorgeous?

His tone was superior and condescending, even if the quote itself was oddly un-uplifting for a household decoration. Grams had had a funny sense of humor.

Change of mind: No way did I want to sell the Semis to Aristotle. I sent him a full-on pander-to-the-wealthy smile. "I could make you one if you like." I nodded at the cross-stitch.

"Both of you, take a seat," Mrs. Valenzuela said in less request and more militaristic order. Aristotle glanced at the single daisy-print loveseat we'd have to share, folded his arms across his chest, and stayed against the wall.

What a snood. (Snob + rude. Ant's favorite insult for obnoxious rich people. Someday when I was rich, I was going to be a moral, kind, thoughtful rich person, and stay employed.)

With a shake of my head to make my hair float flashily down my back, I sauntered over to the loveseat. My cheeks ached from holding my smile in place, but I refused to show that his attitude was getting to me.

"So you got my report on the seadragon?" I asked Mrs. Valenzuela. "I can't tell you how amazing it was. So big. And . . . and . . . purple." I was going for helpful and clueless, although I might have layered it on a bit thick.

"Yes, the seadragon," Mrs. Valenzuela replied almost too quickly. "Tell us everything you saw. In detail."

Which I took to mean she wanted to know about the Semis but didn't want to ask. Before I could begin my tale, she gave a darting look to first Aristotle and then the older woman, who shifted uncomfortably in her seat, crossing and then uncrossing her arms.

What was that all about?

Obvious answer? If I were them and I had magic-spells available, what I'd want in place was a spell to detect lying.

The older woman kept her attention solidly on Mrs. Valenzuela. She tucked her upper lip between her teeth, looking worried. Aristotle stared at Gramps's flag out the window with a blank expression on his face. He didn't seem to have much of a personality.

I'd better assume there was a lying spell in place already and tell my story doing no actual lying. Conveniently, I had plenty of practice as avoiding honesty was a Clems family talent. "I went to the beach to go running. I run there twice a week, Tuesdays and Fridays, weather allowing. On Sundays, I run our neighborhood to avoid all the tourists. Mondays and Thursdays, I switch between a couple of local parks, the Wharf's rec trail, and Carmel. Carmel-by-the-Sea that is, but only pretentious people actually call it that. Saturdays and Wednesdays are my days off."

I proceeded with my story exactly as I'd recreated it in excruciatingly tedious detail. I'd parked three spaces to the right of the trailhead to the beach. I'd been careful when walking the boardwalk through the dunes as there were several sections where the wood was rotted and collapsing. I'd checked the tides the night before, and low tide had been at 4:28 a.m., so there was plenty of beach exposed for running.

The magic-handlers remained silent. Was I overdoing it?

I threw in some questions to break things up. Was it important to know what songs I'd selected for running? Did the variety of birds on the beach make a difference because I was pretty sure they were seagulls and loons, but I could run through some other possibilities if it would be helpful.

I got minimal replies.

I kept going, fighting off an anxiety that they weren't buying my re-created account even though I hadn't told a single untruth.

Mrs. Valenzuela stared at me like I was a squirrel to her hawk.

The older woman went back and forth between glancing at me and staring worriedly at Mrs. Valenzuela. Aristotle slid out a glossy black phone and typed into it. How bad-mannered was that? (I had a moment of serious cell envy anyway.)

I finished my tale and then looked to Mrs. Valenzuela, keeping myself all wide-eyed and squirrel-like. "Did I miss anything?"

"You were very thorough," she replied evenly, as if holding tight-rein on the fact that I annoyed her. "Is there anything you might have accidentally left out?"

A dangerous question. "Accidentally? No."

"Intentionally?"

Excellent comeback, and I had to admire her focus. And smarts. She'd caught my evasion. Unfortunately.

I frowned, as if confused. "Like what?"

Silence. I furrowed my brows and glanced at the older woman. She looked down at her lap.

Nope. Not one of them deserved the Semis. I wanted someone thoughtful and conscientious to have it. Someone the seadragon would approve of. Someone I liked.

Since Mrs. Valenzuela wasn't going to admit why she was really here, and I needed a distraction, I turned my attention to Aristotle. "So you're not really British, right? I mean, that's what I've read about you anyway. You're adopted." He didn't look native British, more Greek or Turkish or something like that. His exact ethnicity was a hotly debated internet topic. Along with whether debating his ethnicity was fair-game because of his fame and wealth or if it crossed a line regardless. I normally wouldn't have touched it as a conversational topic, but offending him worked in my favor. Fingers crossed.

He shifted to look out the window as if I hadn't spoken.

Even though my words deserved such a snub, I flushed.

"Let's not get distracted," Mrs. Valenzuela cut in sharply. "You didn't say if you touched the seadragon. Did you?"

I turned slowly back in her direction. It was another difficult question to evade, and I struggled to come up with an answer that would work. I wasn't left with much and the longer I waited, the more suspicious I came off. Time to tell the truth.

I locked my hands together as if suddenly nervous. "Well . . . I'd hoped you wouldn't ask that because . . . well . . ." Long pause and then I spoke in a rush. "I tried to pull free one scale so I could take it. I mean, I know it's wrong. Totally wrong. And I'm really sorry. It's just that I need money for college and well—"

Mrs. Valenzuela leaned abruptly forward, a "Gotcha" expression on her face. "You didn't tell us that before."

"I'm so, so sorry." Then I explained it all in detail, including the embarrassing moment of falling on my butt because the scale had been attached too well and that, in the end, I hadn't been strong enough to pull one free. "Do you think it's important? Cause I'd really rather not have anybody else know."

Mrs. Valenzuela looked to the older woman, who gave a very French-style nervous shrug.

Interesting. And telling. Guaranteed the older woman was the lie detector.

Mrs. Valenzuela pursed her lips again, but this time she seemed more disappointed than expectant. "Are you certain there's nothing else?"

Total trap question. "I'm so sorry I haven't been of more help. I could take you out to the beach where I found it if you like. I have my own car—"

"That won't be necessary," she snapped back.

Phew. She believed me. I felt it in my gut, and the house creaked as the walls settled better onto the foundation. It agreed.

I turned my attention back to Aristotle. Irritating him seemed my best chance at getting them out the door. "You in town long?"

He glanced up from his phone, brows knit together, attention darting across the room to avoid me. I batted my eyes at him in a so, so, so obvious way anyway. "We could maybe grab lunch."

Mrs. Valenzuela stood up. "I believe we have everything we—"

The front door slammed open, and my brother-in-law, Nicholas, burst into the room, all six-foot-tall, wild hair, furious Mexican of him. "I had to find out on Facebook?" he shouted in full-on salty mode.

The older woman and I both jumped to our feet.

Seriously, though? I'd been so close to getting them gone. Also, Nicholas was the calmest, sweetest, coolest guy in our family. I'd never heard him raise his voice before, not ever. Whatever he was doing, he was totally faking it. Which meant Ant and Dad were involved. I'd *told* them not to interrupt. (Clemses never listened to each other. Just a fact of life.)

"I figured Ant would keep you informed," I said, putting a nice sheepish touch to my voice and heading over to Aristotle, just to annoy him more. This time, it wasn't even strategic. He just deserved it for being such a snood. "Nicholas, let me introduce you to Aristotle Montague-Smith-Montague. You know, *that* Aristotle."

Just as expected, Aristotle bit his lip in dismay and backed over to the front window, which had daisy curtains to match the wallpaper and furniture.

Nicholas ignored him and zigzagged his pointer fingers at Mrs. Valenzuela. "This isn't happening. My client," he pointed at me, "won't be speaking to anyone without representation. Especially not the three of you. You may all go."

Nicely played.

"We aren't lawyers," Mrs. Valenzuela said sharply, "and I'm not—"

"*Mira, señora,* I'm a lawyer. Attorney-at-Law, State Bar of California, specializing in Criminal Law and Malpractice, and I am saying you need to leave."

The older woman coughed in an overly loud, obvious kinda way. Mrs. Valenzuela glanced in her direction and then back at Nicholas, her eyes narrowing.

So that was how magical lie-detecting worked. Nicholas wasn't an attorney. He was a paralegal working in migrant farm worker protections. On the side, he volunteered at Legal Aid for the Unhoused.

"I believe we've finished here anyway." Mrs. Valenzuela turned back to me. "The only remaining matter is the footage you recorded. You'll need to hand over your mobile."

"Absolutely not." Nicholas pushed in between the two of us.

I shook my head. "My dad needs the views. He gets to post it first."

"Already completed," Aristotle said quietly, holding up his phone.

Wow, Dad and Ant had been fast. "Well, then, it needs to stay exclusive." I eyed first Aristotle and then Mrs. Valenzuela as if it had suddenly occurred to me they might try to do an influencer grab.

Mrs. Valenzuela took a long, frustrated breath. When she spoke, her tone was overly conciliatory. "I promise not to release anything on your mobile to the public."

"It'd be a betrayal of my dad's dream to even take the chance." I went all wide-eyed-squirrel again. "But even more, I can't afford a replacement phone."

"We'll replace it for you," Mrs. Valenzuela said quickly. "Whatever you desire, including a lifetime cellular plan."

I grinned as if I loved that idea. (Which I did!) "Really?"

"Actually, not really," Nicholas added as if on cue. "If this is a negotiation, then my client and I need to confer in private. We'll let you know our terms."

I sent him a grateful look, which I happened to notice Aristotle catching. He looked straight at me for once. A cute little furrow appeared between his dark brows, and he tilted his head to the side, considering me. As if I'd done something out of character that'd caught his attention.

Crap. (Along with a dozen stronger expletives that Clems family rules barred me from saying even in my head.)

Nothing to do but keep going. I stepped over to Aristotle. He backed up against Gram's curio cabinet. A curl of hair fell onto his forehead. I itched to brush it back into place, just to see what he felt like. He must have read this in my expression because he physically recoiled and swallowed hard, his Adam's apple bobbing.

His appalled expression should've been a good thing. I'd *intended* to offend him. Only my neck, my face, even my eyes, flushed warm with a totally unfair humiliation. Stupid rich boys. I balled my fists and kept going. "Now about our lunch date . . ."

Chapter Four

"Nicky, you're brilliant," Ant sang out the moment the magic-handlers left, and he, Dad, Gramps, and our dog, Barkley, charged out from the back of the house.

"Had to protect our little girl," Nicholas replied, patting me on the head.

I snorted. No one ever protected me around here. As if in agreement, Barkley sat his large rump on my foot. He was a Labernard (Labrador x Saint Bernard) and had a particularly large rump. I scratched the itchy spot behind his right ear, feeling more rattled by the whole magic-handler visit than I wanted my family to see.

"You should've talked louder," Gramps said. "I couldn't hear a thing."

"Put your hearing aids in," the other four of us said in unison and then exchanged knowing looks. We were such a cliché.

The front window creaked as if in agreement.

There was also a staged feel to our conversation. As if we were all performing. Which we were since we were dealing with magic-handlers and who-knew-what spells they'd left behind. Performing was the reasonable thing to do.

"You should see how many shares the video has received, sweetheart," Dad said, chucking me on the shoulder. He was nearly as tall as Nicholas with a movie-star smile and twinkly blue eyes that he regularly used to get himself out of trouble. Ant was shorter, ten years older than me, less manipulative and more dependable than Dad, a compulsive activist, and into swimming. We had different moms.

Ant slung an arm around my shoulders. "We're so proud of you. You couldn't have done a better job with that video of the dead seadragon."

"I know," I said, forcing a nod of agreement I didn't really feel. Barkley whined and rubbed against my hand for more attention. I patted his head.

Aristotle had seen through me. I'd screwed up.

I *hated* screwing up.

I couldn't talk about it. Even apart from any spells listening in on us, Clemses weren't the kinda people who discussed failures.

"Another fifty thousand subscribers, here we come," Dad continued, launching into his favorite topic. "I'll be able to pitch agents. Then hook-and-reel some big-name sponsors. This could be it."

Yup, Dad was on a roll. Good for him. Sort of. There were plenty of life moments I wished he would get a normal nine-to-five, pay our bills on time, and act more like everyone else's dad. Also, even Ant was concerned that the bell curve of online channels was heading to polar south.

Ant hugged me even tighter, the man-stubble of his jaw scratchy against my skin. "I've got a short of the seadragon ready to post. You're about to be famous."

"For like half an hour," I said dourly, which was both an automatic response to their enthusiasm and me still stewing about Aristotle. I hated that there wasn't anything I could do about the situation. No going backward. No fixing whatever Aristotle might think he knew about me. I had to wait it out. We had a Clems-ism about that: *Sometimes life required a crockpot over a wok.*

Crockpots always made food too mushy for me.

***

Next Goal: Continue to be as *normal Sasha* as possible while waiting for the hype to swell and die, so that I could figure out what to do next.

In my efforts to be *normal Sasha*, I complained to Dad and Ant for the duration of my interview for Dad's channel. Then I didn't call in sick to my Job #2 at the movie theater but did give my boss a heads up I might attract some looky-loos. She insisted I come in. Ticket sales had been down lately.

Once there, I spent the first half-hour telling my story to my two favorite work friends, Marisol and Ty, while restocking concessions. I didn't tell them the truth, of course, but they loved my recreated version.

I used my story to make a deal with them, deals being the foundation of all important Clems family social interactions. If Marisol and Ty helped me hide from any magic-handlers or reporters or anyone else that showed up looking for me, I'd engage in conversation with one person of their choice, meaning a magic-handler, so that they could video and post it online.

I got instant agreement. Marisol and I traded nametags. Ty took over the cash register so I could keep my back to the guests as I filled drinks.

Sure enough, an hour later, two tall, overly muscled Nordic gods walked through the ticket entrance, one wearing an honest-to-dog snow coat with the Swedish flag on the back. They stared at a poster for a zombie romance movie. I ducked behind the counter to watch them in the back mirror. I hated them immediately. They both had a cocky swagger and walked with their heads tilted back as if to be above the little people of the world. "Please not them," I said to Marisol.

"But—"

"Please?"

She subtly shot a few photos of them anyway.

Not long after they'd disappeared, Ty spied a Japanese woman in a sheath dress, pink high heels, and enough ropes of pearls around her neck to tie off a cruiseship. A group of skater boys drooled as she sashayed past.

"I like *her*," I said.

Ty didn't, especially after watching the ticket manager approach her stiff-as-a-royal-butler in his effort to please. She handed him a used coffee cup and walked away. Snood move on her part.

Next was a Middle Eastern couple. Him the picture of sophistication and casual CEO-like wealth. Her in a sapphire hijab with a face so gorgeous I thought I heard the back mirror crack as it overflowed with beauty.

"Them," I said with a defeated sigh.

Both Marisol and Ty nodded.

The moment I walked over, I knew the joke was on Marisol and Ty. Magic-handler beauty was distinct, and gorgeous as they were, up close this couple didn't have it. I chatted with them anyway. Turned out they were neurosurgeons from Texas on a Carmel getaway.

Marisol and Ty fulfilled their part of the deal since the couple would look like magic-handlers regardless.

I returned home that night with nothing catastrophic having happened, which then left me feeling an impending doom that it soon would.

I would've liked to have discussed this with someone, but since I couldn't, I double-checked that our mail had been collected and that Gramps hadn't left either the stove or his car on.

I loved on Barkley for a bit, filling his bowl and plumping his favorite pillow. Once he was settled, I transferred the original and faked videos of the seadragon to a thumb drive and set my phone to download as much as it could hold of a twelve-hour documentary on the National Park System to make sure the original was one hundred percent gone just in case my phone got hacked or stolen. Should've thought of this hours ago.

From there, I checked my social media apps. I had ten thousand new friend requests and a hundred times that in comments on my feeds. Guaranteed every single person would disappear once the hype was over. People sucked.

According to our local news channel, the entire coastline had been shut down. Drone owners reported that anyone attempting to enter the airspace met an invisible perimeter, magical in nature.

Ugh. If the handlers would do that to a public beach, they for sure would've done something to The Blue Castle.

And me. Double ugh.

Other than my tweenage crush on Aristotle, I'd never cared all that much about the magical world in the same way I didn't care what had killed off the dinosaurs or how the internet actually worked. Until this moment, it hadn't been worth expending the brain space. I finally fell asleep wondering if that was maybe a mistake on my part.

I didn't have dog duty with Mrs. Lee the next morning but woke early anyway to go running since I'd skipped the day before. I was out the door by 5:45 a.m. for a five-mile loop around our neighborhood. Almost immediately, I noticed something odd. Flashes in the still-dark sky, like shots of a bunsen burner sitting sideways.

Dragons. Flyers. Or what're commonly called truedragons.

I didn't let myself stop running but kept an eye on them. The flashes weren't large, so the truedragons wouldn't be either, but truedragons doing flyovers of our town wasn't just unusual but unheard of. Magical-creatures avoided people. Nor were they trainable or domesticable.

Also, maybe it was my imagination, but the truedragons seemed to circle the vicinity of the high school.

I cut my run in half and went home, the something-going-wrong feeling on my heels.

I had Job #3 that morning. It was an easy one: trash collection and general cleanup at Dennis the Menace Park.

Dennis the Menace wasn't a garden-variety park but an over-the-top, super-star, voted Monterey-Bay's-best-park-for-the-last-sixty-years running park filled with multiple play structures, a rock-climbing wall, a skatepark, man-made mountains with slides, a lake, tunnels, a rope bridge, and a full-sized 1924 steam engine. Until a few years ago, kids could climb all over the steam engine, but too many kept breaking their arms and the umbrella parents had it fenced off.

Umbrella parents being my Dad's words for parents who during rainy weather blocked up my elementary school's drop-off zone in order to get out of their cars and escort their kids with an umbrella the twenty feet to the school entrance. I'd always had to run for it, downpour or not.

So stupid. I loved that train and sometimes, when no one was around, I'd climb the fence to sit on the top and chat with it. I couldn't do that today as the park was already full of people. I started my round of changing out the garbage liners instead.

No one too good-looking showed up during my shift, but I felt weirdly watched and kept scanning the sky for more truedragons.

Back at the movie theater that evening, no magic-handlers showed up. Instead, the student bodies of the local high schools came by in search of magic-handlers. Our boss was seriously happy. My feeling of being watched increased.

That night, I laid in bed with Barkley and went over all the reasons this craziness was totally worth it. Because it was. My family's lives would change completely once I'd sold the Semis. I'd help Ant, Nicholas, and my dad. We'd become a normal family rather than one constantly on the edge of collapse. (I'd found another ninety-day late notice from the mortgage company posted on the fridge. There went my college savings account. Again.)

It was all so, so close. Well, sort of close. I mean, I still had no idea how to find the right buyer for the Semis. Details, details.

I was jolted out of my thoughts by a white piece of paper floating gently and unnaturally from the ceiling to land on my stomach. Barkley nosed it and went back to sleep.

What the . . . ?

I sat up and glanced around. Nothing moved and the room was silent. I picked up the paper. It was a short note written in the worst handwriting I'd ever seen. It read (I think):

Do the ethical thing before they come after you.
N 45.007438, W 54.745720

~Bob (Robert Minh Quan)

Chapter Five

Job #4 was waitressing at a café in the touristy part of Monterey (a.k.a. Cannery Row). I hadn't worked there long enough to get the coveted weekend shifts. I still did decent tips on weekday lunches when the weather was nice, and it was nice three days after I'd found the Semis. Yes, I counted time that way. Can I really be blamed? I'd count the other way if possible—how long until I could make a move?

I arrived at work tired and freaked out by the note and made a deal with my server-friend Javi to let me assist in the kitchen in trade for fifty percent of my tips for the next month. (I tried for ten days, but he bargained hard, and I was too wound up to fight for it.)

Not going to lie, that note spooked me, and it didn't even make sense. What was the ethical thing? Who were *they*? Who was *Bob*? Why did any of these unknown people think I had the Semis? Because even though the note didn't say so, that had to be what it was about. Also, getting money and helping my family *was* the ethical thing here.

To make things worse, the note had crumbled into magical nothingness before I could do more than recognize the presence of the GPS coordinates. Thanks, Bob.

"Hey, Sasha," Javi said, as he collected the tray for Table Two. "You're going to have to handle Table Seven. And yes, I'll let you keep their tip. They're refusing to order anything or vacate until you come out."

"Reporters?"

"Uh. No. Magic-handlers. Hope you don't mind if I sneak a few photos."

Great. I slipped over to the doorway to look.

Mrs. Valenzuela and the nameless European lie detector were sitting side-by-side in a booth by the side window. Across from them was Aristotle.

A heady sense of relief rose like soda bubbles from the depths of my being. Here was the doom I'd been waiting for. Phew.

"I found a dead seadragon," I murmured to myself several times. "I've told everyone I can think of all about it." I took a deep breath, straightened my apron, grabbed an order pad, and went out to face the upcoming catastrophe.

Mrs. Valenzuela and the older woman caught sight of me right away. Aristotle didn't. He'd pushed aside his paper placemat and napkin-wrapped utensils in favor of a black laptop. He typed on it rather frantically, his brows knit together and the cutest pout on his perfect lips. This guy even did hyper-focused well. (Still hated him.)

"What can I get you?" I asked him while ignoring the others, which would likely piss off the lot of them but fit the Sasha persona I'd fed them before.

"Please sit down," Mrs. Valenzuela said, her tone even more curt than last time. She wore her massive emeralds again, this time with a maroon pantsuit.

"Do you have Chardonnay?" the older woman asked in a nervous French accent.

Chardonnay? Really? Here? "How about a glass of water?"

She nodded her acceptance as if bestowing an anxious gift on me.

"And you, Mr. Montague-Smith-Montague?" I asked. "Can I get you anything?"

He glanced up from pounding away on his laptop to glare at me. I froze under the sheer weight of his piercing, gorgeous gaze. "Not unless you know something of the Bulgarian-Serbian wars of the thirteenth century."

"Uh. Yeah. Definitely."

There was a long pause and then Mrs. Valenzuela glanced at the older woman, who suddenly jerked upright and muttered something under her breath. I couldn't make out the words, although it didn't seem English. She tapped her index fingers together and relaxed.

An eerie chill dripped down my spine as if Javi (or Ant) had slipped an ice chip down the back of my shirt. I'd never seen a magic-handler cast a spell before, but that had to be what she'd done. Freaky. But also kinda disappointing. In the movies, spellcasting usually involved an oversized leather book and much yelling and stomping around.

Either way, I'd better go back to not lying. "Three waters, then. I'll even make it on the house." I took a step backward with a glance at Aristotle. "And a bottle of Xanax," I murmured softly to myself.

Aristotle shot from his seat, outrage written in the hard line of his mouth and furrow between his brows. Apparently, I hadn't murmured softly enough.

"Sit down, Ari," Mrs. Valenzuela said.

He ignored her and followed me. I gave a nod toward the tourist family at Table Two, a hint to Aristotle to keep his cool. Based on the way he swung around to place himself between me and the kitchen, he didn't catch my meaning. "I have a paper due in two hours. It's finals week. I am not messing up my GPA because you choose to be difficult." He grabbed me by the elbow, none too gentle. "Would you please cooperate?"

I started to pull a jiujitsu move Dad had taught me for such moments but then hesitated as I didn't want a scene, either. Instead, I did what I hoped would still bug Aristotle the most. I stepped into his touch, letting loose my inner-tween-fangirl once again. It wasn't hard to do. He smelled like new-car leather and wood polish and that same curl as last time had fallen forward over his forehead.

I batted my eyes at him. "And here I thought I'd made my willingness to cooperate . . . " I strung out the word in all its suggestive glory but then had a brain freeze under the sheer beauty of his penetrating, mysterious gaze and the sudden realization that Aristotle Montague-Smith-Montague and I were *touching*. His hand. My elbow. A connection had been made. Oh. My. Dog. (Not that I had much sensory experience in my elbow, but still.)

Whatever witty quip I should've offered next sank and drowned.

I was such an idiot. He was still a cad.

Aristotle towed me back to the table. The father of the tourist family stood up as if to come save me. I smiled reassuringly at him and went with Aristotle without fighting.

"Was that entirely necessary?" Mrs. Valenzuela asked in precisely spaced words.

"Yes," both Aristotle and I said in unison. Him grouchily. Me less so. I jerked my elbow free. Nice as it was, his touch made me too jello-brained.

Mrs. Valenzuela gave us both a school-principal-vs.-disobedient-student stare. "Sit. Both of you. Miss Clems, your attorney wanted an offer. Thus, we have an offer. A generous one."

I went wide-eyed, eager, possibly overdoing it. But talking about money? Oh, yeah.

Aristotle returned to his laptop, fingers flying before he was fully seated. I grabbed a chair from the table behind me. Rather than sit facing forward, I straddled it like a horse, turning the chair back into a barrier between them and me. "I've answered your questions," I said. "My Dad has posted the video. What else is there I could possibly have?"

"The Semis," she said.

Whoa. Direct much? "The what?" I wrinkled my brow, as if in confusion. My pretend lack of understanding was way over-the-top, but I was edgy. He and all his negative energy were making me so.

"The Semis," she said again. "The creature's raw magic. We're willing to make you a very generous offer for it."

"You think I have it?" I let a pleased look cross my face as if totally flattered. "That would be so cool."

Mrs. Valenzuela didn't soften. She wasn't buying it. Crap. She kept going. "Five million. In dollars or Euros or S&P 500 stocks. Your choice."

Double whoa. "What would I do with stock?"

"Ten million," Mrs. Valenzuela said.

"One hundred million," Aristotle said without looking up. "Can we just get this over with? I need to go."

"That's a lot of money." Enough that the air in my lungs evaporated faster than I could draw in more.

One hundred million dollars.

Just like that.

It was one thing to imagine unimaginable quantities of money. It was another to have it right there, out loud, in front of me, dollar signs and zeros, doing a line dance for my benefit.

Was my dislike of these people really all that important?

Only my family had another saying, one that we repeated over and over again because it was so integral to what made a Clems a Clems. It went like this:

The first time you go into a new bakery, look over your choices carefully and then select the least fancy item in the display case. Pick a plain-jane brownie or muffin over a cupcake buried in frosting and bedazzled in fondant and sprinkles. The more work the baker puts into beautifying an item, the less he's expecting it to sell on taste alone.

Or in other words, never trust the highly decorated or anything intentionally too good to be true.

I turned again to Aristotle because I needed to slow things down, give myself a moment to think, and bugging him was becoming a habit. "You're like nineteen, right? So, college? Where do you go to school?"

"Twenty and Stanford," he replied without looking up. "History major with a minor in societal ethics. Accept the deal so I can finish my paper."

"Wow." I inflected a Stanford-ranking volume of awe into my voice. "That's a really . . ." I was about to say "useless thing to major in" but decided that since he's the one that raised the dollar amount to the nine-digit level, I should be more generous. ". . . impressive choice," I finished. "And Stanford. I doubt I'd be allowed to step out of the parking lot there."

I was going to major in Business Management. Very practical. Provided I went to college at all. (And let's be honest, Ari's choice of major had everything to do with him never-ever-ever actually needing to be employed.)

"Agreed," he replied, none too kindly.

I narrowed my eyes. He'd apparently missed my generosity.

I was tempted by the offer. Really, really tempted. It was more money than I could imagine, would save my family and The Blue Castle, solve all problems, and give me a normal life. It'd all just be done.

And yet . . .

Mrs. Valenzuela pinned me with her steely, expectant gaze. "Ari's suggested amount isn't unthinkable. Will you accept it?"

The people in front of me, and more especially their offer, were a cupcake slathered in pink buttercream topped by an edible treasure box of jewels and gold.

Therefore, the cake would taste like cardboard.

"Say yes," Aristotle, no . . . Ari, muttered. (If Mrs. Valenzuela got to call him that, then so did I.)

I pursed my lips. "I mean, who doesn't want that much money? Maybe I could buy Stanford. Or at least one of those super-special redwood trees that grow there." Snide, I know, but I just couldn't help it. Also, UC Santa

Cruz had redwood trees, too, just saying. "But then what happens when I don't have this Semis thing to hand over?"

Mrs. Valenzuela leaned in my direction, her face turning red with intensity. "You *do* have it. There isn't any other possibility. And I *will* take it from you. It's only a matter of whether you get something out of it as part of the deal."

I sat back, gripping the chair and putting more distance between her and me. "Umm . . . excellent scare tactics." And effective.

I should totally give in.

Everything would be so much easier if I gave in.

I wouldn't have to struggle if I just gave in.

And yet . . .

"Maybe I don't have what you want."

The French woman coughed, loud and obvious.

Crap.

No.

I must not have phrased my words vaguely enough to get by her lie-detection spell. Which wasn't my fault. I'd stuck a "maybe" in there. That would've worked on Ant.

Only this wasn't Ant, and there wasn't anyone else to blame. I'd screwed up. Again.

Crap. Crap. Crap. "Okay, let's deal."

Before Mrs. Valenzuela could respond, the door to the diner burst open and my dad stomped in. He wore a gray jumpsuit from his Job #1, a luxury-car-only oil and lube shop. His furious red face contrasted beautifully against it as he pointed a quivering finger at the magic-handlers. "You . . . you . . . criminals . . ." The words rattled out of his chest, barely coherent. They also contained a faint whiff of irony that likely only I caught. He's the one who'd done prison time for embezzlement (twice). Also, his performance was unoriginal. Nicholas had used an angry entrance to end my last interview with these people.

I was still over-the-moon, yes-I'll-mow-the-lawn, handle-garbage-day, and clean-Gramps's-bathroom grateful. "What's wrong?" I asked in a worried tone to match his fury.

He could barely get the words out. "They . . . ransacked . . . The Blue Castle."

The French woman didn't cough.

I sat straight, all playacting coming to an abrupt halt.

Ari looked up from his laptop. "What's The Blue Castle?"

I ignored his ignorance and kept my attention on Dad. "Is Gramps okay? Barkley?"

"Terrified," Dad shouted. "They tied Gramps up and locked them both in the pantry."

"Please calm down, Mr. Clems," Mrs. Valenzuela said in a much calmer voice than she'd used on me. "Have a seat and let's discuss this rationally. We've just made a very generous offer to your daughter. I'm sure she'd appreciate your counsel in giving her acceptance."

Dad snarled at her. "I don't know who you think you people are—"

"Magic-handlers," I spat out the word in as ugly a tone as Nicholas had used back at our house. Apparently, we really were on repeat.

I felt Dad's anger to the tips of my toes. The Blue Castle was sacred. It was ours and they'd violated it. I turned to glare at Ari. "So much for minoring in ethics. What would your professors think of taking an elderly man and an arthritic dog hostage like that? Did you really think it would motivate me to *trust* you?"

"I wasn't part—" he started, but Dad cut him off.

"You're not to come near my daughter, our house, or anyone else in our family ever again. Do you hear me?" Dad stepped back to make room for me to stand. "Go get your purse."

"Wallet, Dad. I don't carry a purse." But I knew what he meant and went to tell Javi that I had to desert him. Also, the family at Table Two had their phones out and pointed in our direction. Great.

When I returned from the back, the three magic-handlers were all watching me. Ari's hands were poised over his laptop but unmoving. "The offer won't stand for long," Mrs. Valenzuela called out. "Don't be foolish, Sasha. There are more dangerous elements out there than us."

Another vague threat, *really*?

I paused, suddenly remembering the floating white note. "Give me a second, Dad. I've got a question for them." I went back over to the table, stepping close enough to Ari that the Table Two family wouldn't be able to overhear. "Who is Bob and what does he want?"

"Bob?" He looked baffled.

"Robert Minh Quan," I corrected.

"No one of importance," Mrs. Valenzuela snapped out so quickly I'd barely finished saying the name.

The French woman coughed yet again.

Chapter Six

"Gramps is really okay?" I asked as we sped away from the café in Wellington, Dad's 1968 Chevy Camaro. Dad only *sped* places.

"He's so okay that he wasn't the one who called me. He was too busy contacting news stations. Ant rang me up." Dad said it with a chuckle that held a full tank of genuine anger underneath. Also, he came to a complete halt at a stop sign. He usually viewed stop signs as suggestions only. "How much did they offer you?"

I met his look, Clems gaze to Clems gaze. I saw fury, yes. But there was something else even deeper—knowing.

He knew I had the Semis.

I'd thought he might since neither he nor any other member of the family had brought it up. His look was total confirmation. "One hundred mil," I whispered.

He nodded and then hit the gas so gently I didn't have to brace myself. Right.

It hung there in the car between us, the truth of that much money and what it would mean.

I said nothing else. If I were a magic-handler, I'd have bugged our cars as it was well known that people were chatty and let their guard down when driving. Dad went silent as well, which I took to mean he realized the same.

Dad drummed his fingers on the case of keys he kept taped to the center console, an unusual mannerism for him. The keys were part of his Job #2. He maintained fancy cars for the hoity-toity of Carmel, keeping their vehicles running and polished and ready on the off-chance one of the owners decided to do more than go out and pet their prizes. Also gave him easy access to exotic car parts for his channel, if he was careful.

He drummed his fingers all the way to the freeway on-ramp. He was trying to tell me something.

The thing about my Dad was that he was a risk taker, someone who saw GO FOR IT printed in greenlight letters on everything and everyone around him. It's how he'd ended up in jail (twice), impregnated both Ant's mother and mine (Vegas trips), and racked up so much debt I'd been on my own financially since birth.

But with all of his failures, he also had a habit of being brilliantly, fantastically right. And so charming that no one ever said no to him, including me.

"I called Grandma George in case anyone shows up at her place," he said. Grandma George was Grams's best friend since childhood and thus family if not biologically related. "You call your mother yet?"

"I thought it better if I didn't."

"You should call her sooner rather than later." He went back to silently drumming his fingers.

Huh. My Dad usually pretended my mother didn't exist. But the mention of Grandma George . . . Dad had a key to her garage in the box he was drumming his fingers on. He maintained her car, too, even though it was just an aging Toyota nicknamed Dr. Trent and the DMV had taken her license away last year for bad eyesight.

Then it hit me.

Holy Not-a-Dog.

Dad was suggesting I steal a set of keys from his stash, borrow a client's car, and run to my mom who was currently living in Panama. And by suggesting it, Dad thought I should hold out on Mrs. Valenzuela. Either he thought she wasn't trustworthy or he thought I could get more money. Likely both.

***

We found Gramps on the front lawn giving an interview to a local TV reporter. Ant's Prius was parked on the street, along with several black vans that looked like law enforcement.

We listened while Gramps energetically told of being asleep in his lounger right until the moment his attackers threw a hood over his head.

He'd managed to arrange himself and the reporter so that his cherished heritage flag fluttered in the background.

When he moved on to the story of his love of Grams, the book *The Blue Castle*, and the history of our house, Dad motioned for me to follow him inside.

Ransacked wasn't a strong enough word for what we found. Total demolition with a flair for disaster fit a lot better. If there was an item that hadn't been upended, emptied, or probed, I couldn't see it. The floral sofas were upside-down, the wall art had been removed, the curio cabinet and any other object with a door had been emptied. Even the Russian nesting dolls had been opened, one-by-one.

The kitchen was just as bad. There were food and dishes everywhere. The tang of Gramps's garlic salmon sauce permeated the air.

My heart hammered angrily in my chest. Seriously? Would I really have hidden the Semis in a container of shredded lettuce? It was way too large for one thing.

For the first time in my entire life, Dad dropped an F-bomb. He didn't even apologize. Fit the moment perfectly.

Worst of all, the house didn't creak nor windows rattle nor lights flicker. The house itself had gone into hiding.

I banged my fist on the side of a Formica cabinet. What kind of horrible people did something like this to people like us?

"John Foster Clems?" The voice was male and Darth Vader-deep. A black man in a uniform stepped over a frozen steak to join us in the kitchen. He was Dad's age, built like a big rig, and had an I'm-in-charge-here posture that was not unlike Mrs. Valenzuela's. He extended a hand, face serious. "Agent Thomas. Emmanuel Thomas. You must be Sasha and John Foster. I'm with the Bureau of Investigations, Magical Division. We arrived quick as we could."

Dad shifted seamlessly into his good-ole-boy persona, slouching a tad, tilting his head casually to the side. He even scratched his ear as if he didn't hear well. Law enforcers were not one of our family's favorite types of people.

I left, heading up to my room. Like the rest of the house, it'd been tossed from one end to the other. My mattress was against the wall, my clothing was everywhere except in the closet, and my laptop was gone. Oddly, the ransackers had left my cash stash tidily piled on the windowsill, even the pennies. I did a quick count. Still $532.07. Apparently, the ransackers were so rich my money meant nothing to them. (So lucky!)

I'd kept both my phone and the thumb drive on me, so those were safe. But still . . .

Even with the destruction and my fury, I didn't want to make a run for it as Dad had silently suggested. I wasn't feeling a run vibe in my gut, not when it was us versus the magic-handlers. Not when The Blue Castle had taken a hit. I wanted a bit of retribution in blood. (As a rule, I believed deeply in nonviolence to solve problems but it felt good to be pissed.)

I righted my mattress and put the cash back in the teddy bear it had come from, doing so way more aggressively than either item deserved.

Ant showed up a few minutes later, Barkley on his heels. "Production shed's been gutted." He took off his glasses to rub at his eyes. He wore a damp "Swim Monterey" T-shirt, meaning he'd come from the pool.

Barkley threw himself at me in a slobbering mess of stressed dog. I crouched to hug him. Ant went down on his knees too. "Everything's been taken," he continued, choking on the words. "The server, the cameras, the backups, all of it. I can't believe this. The bad guys aren't supposed to win."

"Oh, Ant." I put one arm around him and drew him into Barkley's and my circle. My anger slipped, and I fought back tears.

"I mean, I had my laptop with me and everything from the shed is backed up online. But it's like PETA just failed to save a whale or the Rainforest Foundation lost a deforestation lawsuit."

I hugged him tight, fighting off an incoming pity party. "It *will* be okay. We'll make it okay." And the price of the Semis had just doubled. Dad's and Ant's dreams were worth every bit of the difference. The Blue Castle's soul was priceless. How double dare they.

Ant half-released me to wipe at his eyes. "Anyway," he said, pulling himself together. "There's an Agent Silva downstairs who wants to interview you. He kept trying to get me to call him by his first name, but like that's going to happen with Gramps around. I like having meals to eat."

I laughed a little. So did Ant, which broke the tension. Family legend said Grams would take a broom to anyone who took the Good Lord's name in vain, dropped a profanity, or failed to use properly respectful titles. Gramps just refused to cook for us.

"You're holding up great, kid," Ant said and pushed back to his feet, offering me a hand. "*Keep whipping those eggs.*" It was another Clems family saying that had to do with Gramps forcing the rest of us to help him make meringue. Ant said it with a tilt of his lips, almost a smile.

Ant also knew I had the Semis.

***

Once the Bureau of Investigations, Magical Division (BIMD—worst governmental acronym ever) finished interviewing everyone and had a long argument with Dad about crime-scene processing and whether or not we could stay in the house, we started righting The Blue Castle. (Dad won the argument. Yes, he was that good.)

Gramps burst into tears when he saw the destruction of his bedroom, the room he'd shared with Grams their entire marriage. He spent the rest of the day with the beloved cross-stitch of the words Gram had first used to tell him she loved him pressed to his chest. Other than that, we kept our emotions to ourselves.

I eventually called my mom since my dad had suggested it. Unsurprisingly, she didn't answer.

Then I did a google search for Robert Minh Quan. The top hit was a guy selling educational videos for kindergarteners. Not likely the right person. I gave up, grabbed my comforter, and collapsed onto my bare mattress. Barkley joined me, and together we fell asleep.

I dreamed of Ari, a past-due reward for a terrible day. He was just so pretty to look at, especially when I didn't have to worry about his evil, I'm-better-than-you attitude.

We were at Dennis the Menace Park and sat side-by-side on the top of a bridge shaped like a half-sun, our feet dangling above a slide that ran underneath. In real life, this isn't possible because of closely placed metal bars. That bridge was *high*. It's a miracle the umbrella parents hadn't had it torn down already.

"Hey," Dream Me said to Dream Ari.

"Hey." Dream Ari made even the single word sound lyrically high-class and beautiful. Like him.

There've been many studies on magic-handler appearances. Researchers said their looks were based on the perfection of a specific symmetry. They were all uniquely gorgeous, but they were also all uniquely the same.

Ari wasn't like that, and that's what made him so delicious. He was less formulaic, a rounder-faced Timothée Chalamet or super-handsome Harry Potter. He had something appealingly cute about him that was as much about non-perfection as it was about perfection, something non-magical because he hadn't been born a magic-handler.

He'd been found as a four-year-old in an Egyptian hospital. Where he'd been dumped by his bio family after he'd swallowed a Semis and ended up in a coma. Normally swallowing a Semis meant a long, painful death, but Ari hadn't died.

The Egyptian government had loudly declared that he wasn't one of them and that they didn't want him. Conveniently, the magic-handling families did want him, and he'd ended up being adopted by a baron in England.

"Did you get your paper done?" Dream Me asked Dream Ari, just to hear him speak again.

He looked at me as if I'd grown horns or something.

Maybe I had. I reached up to feel. No horns.

I swung my legs back and forth in the air, enjoying the open space below us. I usually got vertigo when I climbed the Sun Bridge.

"I finished," he finally said. "Barely. I have two finals tomorrow, though. Could I ask you not to do anything that might interrupt them?"

"I've zero desire to mess with your schedule. No interruptions here at all, and it's great that you're so smart. I didn't know that about you. I always saw you as more of a Britain's Next Sex Symbol than a Smart Kid."

He looked away as if my compliment had offended him. Fair enough, it hadn't really been a compliment. Even in dreamland, I enjoyed antagonizing him.

I kept talking. "It's not my fault you're having to write papers in diners and cram for finals. I had nothing to do with it. You can blame your own people for that. Also, why are you following me about? I get Mrs. Valenzuela. She's the apex predator of magic-handlers or whatever. And the French woman has a spell that can detect lies. But why bring you? What do you do for the Alliance, magically speaking?"

He just looked at me. No expression. No reaction. Steady and gorgeously dark eyes. Mysteries of the Night, indeed.

Only then did I realize that I'd just arrived way late at a super obvious party. The fun and games were done, the cops had arrived to send everyone home, and there I stood with an empty plastic cup in my hand, entirely alone and feeling stupid. "This isn't a dream, is it?"

I *hated* feeling stupid. Hated, hated, hated it. It was *way* worse than screwing up, especially when produced by a rich boy (shades of Zachary Stults, *The Faithless Schmuck*, and our make-out sessions in the drama prop room gone wrong).

"This *is* a dream," he replied carefully. "Your dream. I added myself into it and made it more substantial."

"Substantial." I did a quick wardrobe check: running shorts and an oversized "Women love Irish Boys" T-shirt that I'd stolen from Dad.

Now that I was noticing clothing, Ari's became baggy pajama pants and a matching collared shirt, buttoned to the neck. Gramps had pajamas just like them only his were stained. Ari's had an expensive sheen and a scrolly monogrammed MSM on the pocket.

"So this is what you do," I said flatly. I didn't like this. Not at all. "You have a spell to violate someone's dreamscape. Why are you doing it to me?"

"To learn what you know of Robert Minh Quan."

"Okaaay." That was unexpected. Like I'd tell him anything even if I had something to tell. Nor did I believe him. Boys, especially rich ones, lied. Ari knew I had the Semis. That was his actual goal. (Yes, I realized my biases against the rich were hypocritical when my life goal was to become rich.)

"Sorry?" he asked, tilting his head to one side. "Are you agreeing to share information? I'm unclear."

"Try sarcasm."

"I did. It tasted like chicken."

"I—" What I'd been planning to say stumbled on my tongue and did a face-plant. I looked over at him. He met my gaze all deadpan.

But . . . what . . . ?

"Was that humor?"

"I don't believe so, no." He blinked, just once.

I looked at him even harder. "I didn't know you had it in you."

"Yes," he replied, all bland British stoicism. "I'm aware of your good opinion of me."

"Cute." More humor. I didn't like this either, especially as his gorgeous eyes twinkled with a sudden light. Something about our conversation amused him.

Our relationship worked much better with me in charge. (Yikes, no. It was *not* a relationship. Torture session was more on point. Waterboarding.)

He didn't get to take over by being witty. Time to put him back in his place. "Humor aside, let's deal. I'll tell you what I know of Bob if you'll tell me what you know of Bob."

"I don't believe—"

"I'm not done," I said, raising my voice. "I also want something as a sign of your good intentions. You'll understand, I'm sure, that I don't particularly trust your kind of people." I waved my hand up and down in his direction. "So before we even get to Bob, I want to know what other plans the magic-handlers have for me and my family."

He flinched at that.

Got him. I'd thought I would. "I already know you all are behind what happened to my house. You don't have to pretend otherwise."

"No, you're wrong. I wasn't involved and based on the volume of calls Mrs. Valenzuela made immediately after your departure, she wasn't either."

I narrowed my eyes. If he was lying, I couldn't tell. "But your people *are* planning something."

"I don't have people."

I waved my hand in his direction a second time. "Your Alliance. Mrs. Valenzuela and such."

He said nothing.

"Clearly, they are planning something."

"I'm not part of their plans." His voice dropped, and he rubbed the bridge of his nose as if tired. "I have no knowledge of what they'll do. I only thought—" He jerked sideways as if some invisible hand had grabbed him by the shoulder. "Bloody hell—" Then he was gone. Like poof.

My pulse did a zero-to-sixty. "Ari?" Something was wrong. Something *bad.* Not bad-dream bad, but something in real life. My hand on the Sun

Bridge shook. "Ari?" I tried again, more high-pitched screech than words. I loathed everything about him, but I didn't want him hurt.

Then in another poof, I wasn't sitting on the Sun Bridge any longer. I was back in my bed, Barkley snoring at my side, my heart drumming at the back of my throat. What had just happened?

Something floated down from the ceiling, barely visible in the dark. It landed on my face, and I brushed it aside in a panic.

White paper.

I shifted to keep from waking Barkley and held it up to the light reflecting from Gramps's flagpole.

Same bad handwriting.

You've maybe twenty-four hours before they figure out you hid the Semis at the school. 45.007438 N, 54.745720 W. Run.

Chapter Seven

No way was I running.

I wouldn't be scared out of my own home, not even if Bob's note left me freaked-out and shaking the rest of the night. While it was *possible* Bob was trying to help me, more likely he was attempting to con me for his own purposes just like Mrs. Valenzuela and Ari. The golden rule of Clems-isms was *Don't trust anyone.*

I wouldn't.

Also, Clemses didn't run.

Nor would I follow the GPS coordinates Bob had sent me. Completely apart from the fact that the paper had crumbled again the moment I'd finished reading it and I had no idea where he wanted me to go, it was all too convenient.

I wouldn't run.

I would sneak out of town with the Semis using a well-considered plan. Or sort of well-considered. It was three a.m. by the time I worked through my panic at the significance of the note and my worry over Ari's disappearance to decide on a plan. (Who freaking worried about a magic-handler?!)

What I'd do once away from home, I'd worry about later. For the moment, the goal had to be leaving in such a way that I had several hours drivetime before anyone noticed.

Step One (of *sneaking* away unnoticed): Pack for the part.

When I left The Blue Castle the next morning, I wore running pants, an oversized hoodie I'd stolen from Nicholas, and a Laguna Seca Raceway ballcap. I had with me all my important forms of ID, my phone, the backup thumb drive, and my cash. The thought of using the cash killed me, but I didn't dare take my debit card or anything else traceable. Besides, if this worked out, $532.07 would be as important to my financial situation as a sneeze in the ocean. (Yes, I wrote a check from my college account for the late mortgage payment before leaving.)

Step Two: Snag a set of keys.

Dad drove me from The Blue Castle to the café on Cannery Row to collect Gladys. We stopped for coffee on the way. While he went into the She Sells Shack, I riffled through his key box, choosing a set that belonged to a client who spent most of his time on the East Coast. When Dad returned with the coffee, he gave me a knowing look but said nothing.

He gave me another look when he dropped me off. "You be careful today. Lots of crazies out and about."

"Don't I know it." I gave him a thumbs-up, and he grinned back. He totally knew I was running. (Correction: not running, *sneaking* out of town.)

Step Three: Mrs. Lee.

I knew the moment I pulled up to her 1920s Spanish mansion that I was in trouble. She was one of those ultra-thin, older ladies who looked like she might blow away if one breathed too hard. Not frail, though, just slight and sharp. She stood under the bougainvillea at the top of the mansion's front steps, her hands on her hips and a dour expression on her narrow face. "Punctuality is only behind cleanliness when it comes to godliness."

Shoot. Three minutes late. This was going to take a while.

I forced my gaze down to my feet, trying to portray an abject apology that I didn't feel. Silence was always my best bet with her. She was weirdly hard to lie to, probably because she just didn't care what I said or thought.

"You think God was late to the Creation?" she continued in her pointed, brittle voice.

I focused on not fidgeting and let her wear herself out.

It took a while. A long while. So long that I had a near-compulsive need to check the time on my phone.

When she finally finished berating me, I suggested I rectify my errors by taking the dogs to the Carmel Mission for their walk in an effort to absolve my sins through religious osmosis. I mean, I didn't actually say it like that. Another Clems-ism was *Bake the performance, Don't burn it,* but going to the Mission was part of my plan anyway.

"If you're going to Mission Park," she said without looking at me, "use the stroller. I don't want Charlotte tired. You always walk too fast. And check Emily for snarls before bringing her home as the groomer was just here yesterday. Anne will want to stay on-leash the entire way. She has energy this morning. You never walk her long enough."

"Yes, Mrs. Lee." I made a courteous nod with no simmering resentment at being told the same freaking thing every time I took her dogs out. I had bigger problems.

Once Mrs. Lee finished sermonizing, I gathered up fifty pounds of dog paraphernalia and headed to Gladys. Mrs. Lee supervised me with her hands still on her hips and a scowl on her face. "No need to rush so," she complained.

Actually, there was.

I collected the dogs one-by-one and with exaggerated care ruffled each little be-ribboned head and checked that each hand-knit sweater was on straight as I placed them into Gladys. The dogs were Yorkshire Terriers, tiny little things with perky ears and tails that looked like smaller versions of Toto. It was hard not to adore the Brontë Sisters. (My nickname for the dogs, not Mrs. Lee's. I'd never decided if their names were intentional or not.)

The Brontës liked me, too, but they adored Mrs. Lee. Nothing made them and her happier than returning home when we were done with our morning walk. Since the dogs were so small and not really in need of much exercise, I'd always figured that moment was the true point of my employment.

Which, when it came right down to it, was kinda sweet.

Step Four (of not running): Drop the Brontës off somewhere safe. What could be safer than a 250-year-old church filled with elderly Catholics?

I drove fast enough to hurry but not so fast some local snood would take photos of Gladys for the benefit of the Carmel Police Dept. I figured that once I arrived at the Mission, I'd pretend that I'd found the dogs running loose and hand them over to a kindly priest or parishioner. The dogs were all microchipped. They'd be home by lunch.

Except that when I arrived, the Mission was all locked up. Signage said Closed on Tuesdays.

Dog Damned, now what?

A lack-of-sleep headache chose that moment to knock its arrival on the inside of my skull. One of the dogs yapped impatiently from the back seat.

"Thank you. That helps." I pulled around the corner from the Mission and parked behind a yard maintenance truck, cracking the window to let in a briny morning breeze. I leaned my head against the steering wheel, too tired for a major complication this early in the plan.

I couldn't return the dogs to Mrs. Lee. I needed to leave the car here, walking distance from Dad's client, and do so in a way that no one would notice it for a few hours. Plus, I needed to leave now, not later in the day when there'd be more people around the high school.

I could let the dogs loose in the walking trails across the street. The paths were popular, the surrounding mini-villas belonging to a mix of rich hipsters and retirees. The Brontës would be found, eventually.

Only what if a coyote or fox or mountain lion got them first? I couldn't risk that.

Okay. Change of plans. The Brontës would have to come with me. I'd leave them somewhere safe later on. Best I could do.

Decision more-or-less made, I unloaded the stroller and packed up the dogs and their stuff.

The stroller wasn't made for rough terrain. It bounced and jostled over the dirt path, and all three dogs yapped steadily in complaint. I hushed them best I could, but for such tiny things, they were as loud and opinionated as their owner.

My headache beat harder.

Second change of plan. I needed to ditch the stroller and the bulk of the dog stuff.

Somewhere from the depths of my throbbing head, I got another idea. A fun one too. I could stage my own kidnapping. Hopefully, the magic-handlers would get blamed.

The park was coastal woodland with scrubby trees, wild grasses, and lots of sage. There were side paths and small clearings at regular intervals, and I pushed the stroller into one not visible from the main path. I scattered doggie blankets, water bowls, treats, and the four laminated copies of emergency instructions around the clearing. I scuffed up the ground, left some of my hair on a bush, and even spit a few times to deposit DNA. No idea if that worked or not, but it seemed smart in the moment.

I put the Brontë's on their leashes, laid the stroller on its side, and jumped up and down on the frame, making it cave in. Then with a grimace of pain, I forced myself to smash my phone against a tree, leaving screen shards everywhere. A nice, telling touch. Then I removed the battery, chucked it into the trees, and put the remains of the phone back in my pocket to be discarded elsewhere.

Once done, I stuffed all three dogs in the front pocket of my hoodie and power-walked the rest of the park. Twenty minutes later, the Brontës and I "borrowed" a canary-yellow Mercedes from the secondary garage of Dad's client and drove off.

Step Five: Car theft. Done.

Step Six: The high school.

Ten seconds behind the wheel and my headache eased up. Also, I *sped* just like my dad, and in this car, none of the locals were likely to care.

Even the Brontës liked the car. Annie Pup, the youngest and most energetic of them, exhausted herself sniffing every crevice of the leather upholstery and then curled up in my lap. "Annie Pup's going on an adventure," I sang out to her, feeling loopy. "Charlotte and Emily are coming along too."

Truth? I didn't hate having them along. Company was a good thing.

I parked behind the She Sells Shack and packed the Brontës in my hoodie pocket again. Nothing attracted helpful bystanders faster than dogs left in a locked car, even a high-end one.

Entering the school and the Drama Room went well. I found the Semis where I'd left it, shimmering with its inner light of purple and blue. Pretty, but ugh, I still had zero desire to touch it. I hunted the stacks of boxes and props for gloves. Considering the drama department's penchant for princess musicals, there had to be some here somewhere.

I couldn't find any.

But Emily found something even better.

Emily was the diva of the Brontës, both in personality and looks. While the other two were short, curly-haired yorkies, Emily was long-haired. Her fur parted down her back in a perfect line and fell in a smooth waterfall on each side to skim the ground like a formal robe.

Emily sat her rump on a tasseled pillow, her head cocked and ears perked as if daring me to make her move. Directly behind the little diva were three large plastic bins marked ProLearn Reality Simulators.

"No way. That's too perfect."

Emily bobbed her muzzle as if accepting a compliment meant for her. I patted her little be-ribboned head, more than willing to give her credit for the find.

Ten years ago, the teacher of the life sciences class had talked the school administration into purchasing fake pregnancy bellies. And not just ones made of stuffing. These had air bladders and electronics and expanded slowly, making the experience as real as possible. (My high school may have had some teen pregnancy problems in the past.)

Only, the girls in the class had refused to wear them unless the boys had to do it too. The teacher was convinced by their arguments and made two weeks of fake pregnancy mandatory for everyone.

The umbrella parents had picketed. The project had been scrapped. The bellies had gone into storage. Storage turned out to be the drama department.

I grabbed one of the fake bellies from the box and disassembled it, removing the bladder and electronics so that it was just a neoprene shell. The Semis fit perfectly inside and the whole thing strapped easily under my hoodie like a backward backpack. I examined myself in a mirror. Yup. Pregnant. (Truth: Looking pregnant grossed me out, but I forced myself not to think about it.)

Pretty clever, if I did say so myself. Between the Semis and the dogs riding in the hoodie pocket, I looked ginormous. If lumpy.

This was going to work.

Except when I slipped out of the building, a cop car was parked alongside the Mercedes at the She Sells Shack.

"Crap," I whispered. I slipped behind an oak tree to spy out the scene. "What else? What freaking else?" My pregnant belly went suddenly, overtly heavy. (It wasn't. I could barely feel the Semis at all.)

I needed that Mercedes.

The cop car was a black and white cruiser, so city police, not Sheriff, CHP, or BIMD. A cop stood in front of the Mercedes, examining it.

In any other situation, I would've tried to brazen the whole thing out. Expensive cars were par-for-course around here. Literally, The Pebble Beach Golf Course hosted one of the largest, fanciest car shows in the country. The cop could be just admiring it.

I kept watching. The dogs squirmed with an occasional leg or nose poking out of the pocket. I tucked their various parts back in and hushed them.

The cop circled the car. She looked in the driver's window, then bent her head to talk into a gadget on her shoulder. Charlotte, who was bossy and difficult at the best of times, wiggled her head out, bit my hand, and leaped for freedom.

I did the most awkward dive forward in my life, the Semis belly crushing the air out of my lungs, but I caught Charlotte, barely. She yapped wildly as I shoved her back into the hoodie pocket.

The cop turned to look at us. I sauntered as casually as possible in the other direction, jutting my belly forward.

All three dogs yapped. My head pounded.

I kept walking without looking back.

I made it to the next street corner without the sound of sirens. Phew. Now what?

"I love dogs. I love dogs. I love dogs," I muttered to remind myself. (It was true. I did.)

Charlotte poked her head out again. This time I was ready, so she didn't try to escape but gnawed on the edge of the pocket instead. Lovely.

I needed a place to leave them and another car.

I was only a mile from The Blue Castle but going there was out of the question. So were any of my friends' houses or our neighbors. No Clems would be that foolish.

I was suddenly reminded of driving home from the café last night, Dad drumming his fingers, and who specifically he'd brought into the conversation.

I got another idea.

***

Grandma George's real name was Georgiana Elizabeth Blythe, which she loathed and wouldn't answer to. She and her "roommate," Grandma Fee, short for Fiona, had been my primary caretakers after Mom left and while Dad was in jail. Yes, "roommate" is a euphemism, not that either of them would admit it. Generational thing.

In fact, our most repeated family story was the day Ant staged an intervention for Grandma George and Grandma Fee. This was right after same-sex marriage became legal in California for the first time. I'd been young and don't remember it, but Ant called the entire family together and tried to force Grandma George and Grandma Fee to admit they were a couple. He went on and on and on, but neither of them gave him squat. *Squat* being Grandma George's word.

Instead, they'd used every single possible, obnoxious euphemism in existence for "couple" in denying it. Gramps made a handwritten list and gave it to Grandma George on her birthday. It's still hanging in her kitchen.

Ant got so frustrated he'd screamed that it was people like them that made it hard for the younger generation to come out. Then he picked up Grandma Fee's ashtray and heaved it through the front window.

A neighbor was driving down the street, saw the window shatter, and thought someone was attacking the two old lesbians. The neighbor called the police, who showed up in force. Grandma George let them handcuff Ant and drag him outside before explaining what had happened.

Ant never lived it down. We'd used the story to test any new boy he brought home. If they looked horrified, shocked, or offended, it was a solid *no* from the family.

The best part happened three years ago when Grandma Fee died. In order to settle Grandma Fee's estate, Grandma George was forced to admit that they'd been legally married the first week it had become possible, a good two months prior to Ant's intervention.

Go, gay grandmas.

Grandma George lived seven miles inland in an area that'd nearly been taken out by wildfires three times in my lifetime. So rolling hills, scrub oaks, and lots of brush.

I'd run out there a couple of times in getting ready for races. With the hills, it was a great workout. With the dogs and pregnancy, I couldn't run it. I could walk it, though. Totally doable. Also doable would be borrowing her car.

I couldn't leave the dogs with her as they would be a dead giveaway that I'd been there, but otherwise, this could work.

And really . . . did I want to leave the dogs so soon? Much better to keep them and bring them back when I returned in a day or two. Who wants to travel all alone?

The pocket the Brontës rode in bounced against the belly as I walked, jostling them around. They quickly tired of this. Annie Pup wiggled. Charlotte tried to bite me and then chew her way to freedom. Emily whined. "I love you guys, but you're not making this easy on me," I lectured. "The sooner we get to Grandma George's, the sooner you can come out."

They kept fussing.

After the first hour of walking, Annie whimper-yapped in her I-need-to-pee voice, and I had no choice but to free them for a bit. All three ran straight for a street puddle, which would've horrified Mrs. Lee, who was firm about them only drinking bottled spring water. Hopefully, they'd just been thirsty and would now take naps.

When I put them back in the hoodie pocket, the Brontës' protesting got worse. I swapped their positions back and forth as I walked. I cooed and petted and even pleaded. Maybe keeping them just to not have to be alone wasn't actually worth it . . . ?

Emily whined her discomfort. Charlotte chewed the edge of the pocket so badly it tore. Annie peed right down the front of the belly. I stopped for pee breaks every twenty minutes after that, but the damage was done.

The going was slow. Mrs. Lee would've reported the dogs missing by now. Search teams were likely showing up at her house, my house, the Mission. BIMD would find out. Maybe the freeway was even being watched.

Three and a half hours after leaving the She Sells Shack, we arrived at Grandma George's house. Averaged out as a thirty-minute mile. Pathetic.

Also, Grandma George sat in a plastic chair in front of her wide-open garage waiting for us. Her white hair was perfectly coifed, and she wore a pressed jogging suit in lavender. "We thought you'd be here hours ago."

"I—"

"Not a word. If anyone asks, I need to be able to say I haven't *heard* from you."

Excellent logic. But she'd known I was coming? Had Dad been trying to tell me to steal *her* car?

Actually, in hindsight that seemed kinda obvious.

Grandma George gave a ladylike snort. "Close your mouth. The smell of those dogs is going to attract flies." She pushed herself up from the chair, balancing on her walker. "Come here. I have something for you."

I went over, lips sealed.

Grandma George rummaged through the basket under the seat of her walker. "You didn't think I'd be left out of this, did you? Here, take this." She shoved a manilla envelope and the keys to Dr. Trent at me. (Dr. Trent: 1998 Toyota Corolla sedan, low mileage.)

"The envelope contains Visa gift cards and a cellphone from Nicholas," she continued. "Plus one more thing. Hopefully, you won't need it, but better to be safe than sorry." She held up a small gun, a ladies' gun, elegant with etched flowers on the silver barrel and a pearly white handle. Grandma George pointed it at me.

Gratitude swelled in my chest. I teared up and parted my lips to thank her, tell her to thank my family. She put a withered, bent finger against her lips reminding me to keep silent.

But this . . . the gun was special. Meaningful. She kept it in a velvet-lined display case on a shelf in her living room. It'd belonged to Grandma Fee.

Grandma George pulled the trigger and a small yellow flame popped out the front. She reached forward, and with a surprisingly strong grip for someone her age, tugged me in to kiss my forehead.

"Ant and your dad are headed to San Luis Obispo in the hopes of drawing pursuers down the coast. Take a different route. The pregnancy is brilliant by the way. You're just like your Grams. Just like the heroine in her book. No 'colorless nonentities' in this family. But child, don't you dare get caught."

Chapter Eight

Total Funds: $3540.07
Cash: $540.07
(I found an extra $8.00 in a pair of Ant's jeans while cleaning up.)
Gift Cards: $3000.00

Should be more than enough to last a good month, if frugal.

Someone-not-a-Clems might think it odd that my family would encourage me to do this.

My mom would think we were all crazy. She'd freaked when a week after I got my driver's license, my dad had handed me the keys to Gladys, given me a map, and told me to drive to Arizona where she was busy counting rattlesnakes. Dad had said he was tired of her annoyingly emotional emails begging to let me visit. In truth, he'd just wanted a daughter hardy enough to make her own way in the world.

Mom was currently in Panama counting dwarf sloths. Some people are perpetual students. My mom is a perpetual research assistant.

I didn't want to go to Panama. My relationship with Mom was fine, but nothing with her was ever easy. She was so absent-minded that when she was focused on something that interested her, she tended to forget the rest of the world existed, including little things like buying food or paying the water bill or that her ex-husband had put her daughter in a car, given her a map, and sent her off to visit.

I'd arrived at her research headquarters and then sat in a way-too-hot trailer for three lonely days waiting for her to remember I was coming.

Also, driving to Mom would require using my passport to cross the borders of multiple countries, a surefire way to be noticed.

I drove east out of a long-standing habit of avoiding LA traffic to the south and Bay Area traffic to the north. The Brontës curled up on the passenger seat in a lump of fur and tails. The lighter-gun went into the driver's door pocket. The Semis sat in its pregnancy get-up on the floor. The phone, which turned out to be Courtesy of the Monterey Bay Homeless Coalition per the sticker on the back, rested on the seat beside me.

Very smart of Nicholas as he was endlessly complaining about his homeless clients losing everything they borrowed, so no one would miss the phone. However, when I tried to use it to google a map, it didn't have cell service. Disappointing, but fair enough.

When this was over, I was going to buy myself the most expensive, most top-of-the line phone in existence. Whatever that was.

I'd expected to have a brilliant plan on what to do next by this point. Other than avoiding my mother and traffic, I had zero ideas, and the lack of sleep made it hard to think.

An hour into our drive, Charlotte disappeared into the back. Moments later, we were treated to the sour ammonia odor of more dog pee.

Crap. (It was only a matter of time before that happened too.)

We needed supplies, especially carpet cleaner and puppy pads. Food also. I hadn't had anything to eat since my early morning decaf, as my stomach grumbled to remind me.

I felt weird about stopping, though. Maybe this was me being paranoid, but moving felt safer, as if any spell cast in my direction wouldn't work on the go. (No idea if that was a real thing or not.)

An hour later, we hit California's Central Valley and the aptly named town of Los Banos. Three years of high school Spanish told me the name translated to "the toilets." Which after Emily also took a visit to the back seat was about how the car smelled.

We had to stop.

I spotted a Buysco Superstore, and even though it meant putting on the Semis and the urine-drenched hoodie, the Brontës and I went in. I power-walked the shopping, checking over my shoulder every half an aisle. Maybe it was our smell, but no one seemed interested in me and the Brontës stayed hidden. I kept the number of purchases at twenty-three so that I could use the under-fifteen-items self-checkout, and we hurried out.

I cleaned the Brontës' makeshift toilet spot with a cleanser so strong I had to crack the windows to breathe. Then I dumped the remains of my old cellphone, the hoodie, and a small mountain of used paper towels in the Buysco dumpster. Phew. Done. Without any magic-handler sightings.

When I returned to the car, Charlotte, of all dogs, wanted to curl up in my lap, and Emily gave a dainty lick on my hand. Annie Pup looked at me droopy-eyed and head-down from the passenger seat. Gratitude for the work I'd gone to for them?

Unlikely, but I'd take it anyway.

I scratched under their collars and cooed out how much I loved them and ate the grossest veggie and cheese sandwich I'd ever tasted while we drove away. The dog food I'd purchased may have been a better choice.

We headed north up the Central Valley for no reason other than avoiding LA. I stuck to backroads, traveling through alfalfa fields and almond orchards. Nothing around to attract magic-handlers unless they were specifically looking for me. I regretted eating and not just because the sandwich had tasted so terrible. Tired and hungry kept me focused and awake. Tired and full, I drooped, eyes first.

The fourth time I drifted Dr. Trent into the rumble strip, I knew I had to stop.

I pulled into an orchard where I could park unseen and leaned my seat back, listening to the rustle of the leaves on the trees through the cracked windows. The Brontës climbed on top of me, rumps wiggling, noses snuffling against my shirt, Annie Pup nearly on my face. All very comforting. I closed my eyes. "Love you guys, but please don't pee again until I've napped."

When I woke not long enough later to yappy barks, the Brontës had deserted me and were scrambling around the front dash. How they'd gotten up there, I had no idea, but their tails were wagging madly and they were pushing around each other so excitedly that I put a hand up to keep Annie Pup from sliding off. "What's up, Sisters?" I asked, my voice scratchy from my too-short nap. Dr. Trent was still the only vehicle around. No magic-handlers.

Then I saw it.

An insect on the outside of the windshield. It was twice the size of a bumblebee, and instead of fuzz, its black and yellow stripes were shiny, almost metallic. It also had a wickedly large, thorn-like stinger coming off its butt. A bee-dragon.

A creepy-crawly feeling of being watched tiptoed up the back of my neck. As if the bee-dragon itself were studying me. It spread its wings and lifted off.

"Roll up the windows!" I screamed.

The Brontës went wild.

The windows were all hand-cranked. No way could I get all four up fast enough to stop the bee-dragon. Instead, I hit the ignition, threw Dr. Trent into drive, and slammed on the gas. The Brontës slid off the dash as we jerked forward. I caught them one-by-one while frantically looking for any sign the bee-dragon had joined us and trying to get up to speed as fast as possible.

No bee-dragon in the car that I could tell.

"What just happened here?"

Annie Pup and Charlotte's ruffs were up. Emily's hair was too long to have a ruff, but she made up for it by flagging her tail and jerking her head back and forth on high alert.

Seriously, though. Magic creatures were super rare. One shouldn't have just shown up like that. Had the magic-handlers sent it?

I didn't think so. Common knowledge said that magic creatures weren't trainable and couldn't be domesticated, not even by handlers. A magical-creature kept in captivity died, their Semis turning to dust.

The Semis must be attracting them then. One more reason to dislike it.

An hour later, we hit the outskirts of Los Banos again. I'd been so freaked that I'd managed to turn us entirely around. More lost time. Less distance from home. And I was still tired. Bah.

Not wanting to either stop or return to the territory of the bee and its many hive friends, I kept south. We hit I-5, whose only purpose was to go to LA, which I still didn't want to do.

I turned onto I-5 anyway and drove for another forty-five minutes, then got off and took another backroad east toward Highway 99, and then north again. Basically, the Brontës and I spent our afternoon driving in a giant rectangle. Total waste of time and gas. But also a confusing trail if anyone followed me . . .

Another hour later, I pulled off at a truck stop for a toilet for myself. When I returned to the car, Charlotte was growling with her lip raised and Annie Pup was gnawing on a white piece of paper. I tugged it away from her with an irrational sense of relief.

Good job so far. Stay off the main highways and away from major cities. Both will be watched. I'll help you as I can. N 45.007438, W 54.745720
~ Bob

***

Things that went wrong over the next few hours:
- The note from Bob crumbled into magical dust and disappeared before I could memorize anything other than the first two digits of the GPS coordinates: Forty-Five.

- Annie Pup got carsick and her vomit was so foul I had to pull over immediately. Luckily, I'd bought plenty of carpet cleaner.

- While stopped to dump the vomit, paper towels, and more used puppy pads into a trash can at a fast food place, I used the wi-fi to do a quick google of myself. My disappearance had made the news but without any mention of the kidnapping at the Mission. Totally disappointing considering the effort I'd put into staging it.

Things that went relatively right:
- There was no mention online of the dogs or my sudden pregnancy or any sightings of me anywhere near where I'd actually been. There were lots of sightings of me in oddball places. I'd never even been to New Mexico before. (Perhaps I should head there?)

- Forty-five degrees north was near Portland, which was only an eleven-hour drive. Not that I was heading to Portland, no way.

- When I once again became too tired to drive, we stopped for the night in one of those sprawling towns made of people with really long commutes to the Bay Area. I played fetch with the dogs to wear them out and then used a gas station wi-fi to finally google the last time a seadragon had died.

It was an interesting story although not nearly as dramatic as the movie. The year was 1994. The place: Rose Harbor, Gwaii Haanas Island National Park, British Columbia, Canada. The finder had been an unnamed marine biologist. The Semis and the biologist had disappeared for several days only to show up in Vancouver where the Semis had gone on to sell by private treaty to the Chileans. (Private treaty meaning the price was so high no one wanted to admit just how high. I had to google this too.)

- Vancouver wasn't too far from Portland. (Not that I was going to Portland.)

Things that went incredibly right:
- While researching the last Semis and Canada, I had one of those crazy why-not, could-be, the-stars-sometimes-aligned thoughts. The kind I'd been waiting to strike all day in terms of a destination. This wasn't about that, but rather Bob.

I googled Robert Minh Quan and Canada. Up came a series of papers written by a PhD student in the 1990s about a North Pacific sea lion species on the verge of extinction. Then I found an obituary of a thirty-something Asian man with a grim expression. Robert Minh Quan had died in a boating accident in a Western Canadian fjord in 1994. A fjord that just happened to be sneezing distance from . . . Rose Harbor, Gwaii Haanas Island National Park.

Bingo. (Woohoo! Hurray! Aren't I brilliant on occasion?!)
Robert Minh Quah *had* to be the biologist who'd found the last Semis. A biologist who was also clearly a magic-handler. I still wasn't going to Portland.

***

As exhausted as I was, I had a hard time falling asleep. Part of this was the uncomfortable shape of Dr. Trent's seat. Part was Charlotte's snoring. Mostly though, I couldn't stop thinking about Bob. Magic-handlers supposedly had the best PR agents out there and stuff on the internet wasn't always true. (Case in point: Bob's death.)

Plus, if it'd been a magic-handler that had found the previous Semis, why would he have sold it to the Chileans? Why not just turn it into a spellbook, stash it in a fourth-dimensional library, and become super powerful himself?

It didn't add up. Maybe the entire article had been a plant. Maybe Bob worked with Mrs. Valenzuela, and his job was to lure me away from my home and family so she could grab me. Or maybe exhaustion made me even more paranoid than usual.

When I finally slept, I dreamed of Ari. We were at Dennis the Menace Park again, but rather than the top of the Sun Bridge, I stood on the bottom of the slide beneath it. Ari paced the sand in front of me with his hands in his pockets, his perfect lips pressed together, and his eyes narrowed.

I jumped down, relieved to see him. "Are you okay? I worried about you."

He shook his head, pissy in a stiff-upper-lip kinda way. "Why have you run? I told you not to make this harder. Do you not ever listen?"

That he was angry rather than injured or anything like that brightened my mood. "I call double negative. So yes, I always listen to no one. Also, I didn't run." And then, since he was likely reporting back to Mrs. Valenzuela, "I've been kidnapped."

Hi grimaced. "No, you have not."

Then suddenly I woke up back in the car, something hitting me on the forehead, something like a small fluffy dog tail. "Not now, Annie. I was having a good dream." I went to push her away but was hit on the arm. I blinked my eyes open just in time for two more somethings to land on my face.

I could just make out the SaveMart Store lot where we'd parked. The Brontës were curled up with the fake belly on the floor. Charlotte had even managed to get the Velcro undone and climb halfway inside, which I took to mean it was warm. I reached down to pull them away but was interrupted by an abrupt hail of more white papers dropping like an indoor snowstorm. In seconds, the dash, the dogs, the passenger seat, and I were all covered.

"Sheesh. Pushy much?" I picked up the nearest, angling it to catch the light.

They know where you are. They know where you are. They know where you are. They know where you are. They know where you are. They know where you are.

Chapter Nine

Total Spent: $221.04
Total Funds Remaining: $3319.03
Cash: $540.07
Gift Cards: $2778.96

I ran. (Drove. Raced. *Sped.*)

My heart heaved against the inside of my ribcage, and I gulped down air as if sprinting the opening of a race. Which I totally knew better than to do.

I slammed through the parking lot, squealing the tires as I took the corner to join a string of early-morning commuters. No magic-handlers so far. Maybe Bob was wrong.

Breathe.

Slow down.

Relax. (Right.)

"Don't drive too fast," I said to the Brontës. "Don't draw any attention. *Bake the performance, don't burn it.*"

No one answered.

We hit the intersection before the freeway overpass just as it changed from green to yellow. I came to a totally inconspicuous, abnormal-for-me stop.

Breathe more.

I needed to pick a direction. Right or left? North or south on the freeway?

North would be toward Portland. "I'm not going to Portland."

One of the Brontës yapped at me from the floor as if in disagreement, but knowing a couple of facts about Bob didn't equate to trusting him.

The light was still red and I was still obeying traffic laws when a line of luxury cars turned off the freeway from the south. A Porsche, several Teslas, a Jaguar, a Rolls-Royce, all driving by me on the opposite side of the road. I ducked automatically and then straightened because Dr. Trent was too old to be driverless.

But Dung-of-a-Great-Dane, there were *twelve* of them.

I gripped the steering wheel so hard my knuckles cracked. Come on light, turn green. Come on. Come on. Annie Pup climbed into my lap and put her front paws on my chest to lick at my chin as if trying to be reassuring. I kissed her nose and then nudged her down so that she couldn't be seen.

Bob had been right. They'd known where I was.

Or had been.

I still didn't trust him. I'd go south.

The light remained red, but the cross-traffic dried up. I considered running it. My foot inched across the brake pedal, ready to release.

I watched the cars in my side mirror as they turned into the SaveMart parking lot. Annie Pup rubbed the side of her head against my arm. Emily hopped up on the passenger seat and shook her long mane of fur as if to make sure the rest of us all noticed her displeasure. Charlotte bit her ear.

"Please don't fight right now. Our lives are in danger." Or at least a whole ton of money. "Turn green. Turn green. Turn green."

This had to be the longest freaking red light in the state of California. And that was saying a lot. My foot continued to creep until only the edge of my sole pressed the brake.

Emily, with her nose in the air, jumped to the backseat. The other two followed.

Don't do anything impatient. Don't get noticed.

The smell of sour ammonia wafted through the car again.

Gross. Hopefully, they'd used the pads I'd laid out.

The light finally turned, and it was like a NASCAR announcer yelled "boogity, boogity, boogity" into my ear. I slammed the gas, hit the blinker, and cut across three lanes of traffic to head south. Dr. Trent's wheels squealed yet again. "Shouldn't be doing this," I said out loud. "I *know* better than to do this."

Twenty uninterrupted, no-one-chased-me miles later, I finally took a normal breath. "Thank you, Bob. I mean, maybe. This does not mean I trust you." Even if Bob had been the single magic-handler to offer help without demanding anything in return.

Which was a dumb reason to trust him. There were too many uncertainties where Bob, the random note dude, was concerned. And yet . . .

My gut, the most Clems part of a very-Clems-me, gave a commanding gurgle. As if trying to get my attention.

I took several deep swigs from a water bottle and ate a Powerbar.

The feeling didn't go away. My very-Clems-gut thought I should head Bob's way.

I didn't trust him, but I did trust my gut. Charlotte climbed into the back and based on the smell, took a dump.

***

Since I was already headed in that direction, I decided to stay south, cut around the bottom of the Sierras, over to Las Vegas where I wouldn't drop in on Nicholas's awesome parents, and *then* head north to Oregon. Also, taking a circuitous route would hopefully throw off the magic-handlers.

Decision made, I relaxed a bit more.

Several hours later, we stopped at a small-town truck stop outside of Bakersfield, the kind that held a mini grocery, three fast-food restaurants, a carwash, and showers. I'd been to this place several times before on Dad's Craigslist-car-part-hunting-vacations, so I knew it was big enough for me to be able to do some decent shopping. Also, gas stations were one of the few places where it was unremarkable to leave dogs alone in a car.

I filled up Dr. Trent and then parked at the side of the main entrance. The dogs could stay put. But the Semis . . .

I'd pretty much ignored it since dumping it on the floor yesterday, which did not feel respectful toward the seadragon. At the same time, it still grossed me out.

I didn't want to put it back on, but leaving it with only the Brontës as guards seemed stupid. With my face pinched in distaste, I velcroed up the belly and then put the harness under my new, pee-less hoodie.

I collected our necessities and was halfway down the snack aisle when my pregnancy get-up slipped. As in suddenly dropped a good foot down the front of my body. The left shoulder strap had come entirely undone. Shoot. I'd apparently done a crappy job of strapping it on.

I grabbed at the belly, trying to keep it in place. A lady in a boat hat and grandma shorts paused to smile at me. "I carried low too," she said. "Don't worry, misery now means an easier delivery later."

"Thanks," I said all fake-cheerful while filing her advice in my really-didn't-want-to-know drawer.

The moment the woman turned away, I slid my arm inside of the hoodie and fixed the loose strap. "Stupid belly," I murmured to it. "Are you trying to make me drop you?"

The Semis didn't answer. (Thank Dog. Cause that was the last thing I needed.)

I grabbed a bag of veggie chips and some dried fruit. I considered buying some beef jerky which would fill me up, but I'd been an on-again-off-again vegetarian for a while and all other things considered, the meat products were way overpriced.

The shoulder strap started to come loose again right as I stepped up to the cash register. Conveniently, the clerk's slack-jawed, slow-speech, squinted-eye appearance screamed stoned. Also, he failed to charge the lady in front of me for her six-pack of beer. I couldn't let a money-saving opportunity like him slip by.

"You busy later?" he asked, eyeing me slowly up and down.

Wow, he must really be out of it. With the pregnancy, the hoodie, my hair under a hat, and forty-eight hours without showering, I had to be looking pretty bad.

"I'm not into weed," I replied politely. He'd accidentally bagged both a toothbrush and water bottle without scanning them, so I felt obligated to be polite. "But, thanks."

He nodded. Seemed likely he got this answer a lot. I ran a gift card through the machine. The stoned clerk stared past me with a glazed, half-frozen look on his face. "God of the Freaks of Nature, I will gratefully die now."

"Um, okay, let's do that after you hand me my receipt?" I turned to see what he was staring at. I half expected a semi-load of dope or something. That wasn't it, and I froze myself.

She had dark skin with thick black hair that fell in floaty curls to her waist, princess style. She wore a miniskirt in pink leather, a cream fuzzy sweater that showed off her perfect boob-to-waist-to-hip ra-tio, a matching pink fuzzy headband, and golden sandals that laced up to her knees. It should've been a horrible mix of styles, but she couldn't have been more beautiful.

"Crap, crap, crap." This couldn't be happening. Not again so soon. I'd already had a near-miss today. And why hadn't Bob warned me?

Well . . . he *had* told me the major freeways would be watched and to avoid them, which I hadn't done.

I turned back to the stoned clerk in the hopes that the magic-han-dler hadn't noticed me. If I stayed facing away from her, maybe, just maybe, she'd wander off into the store and I could duck out unnoticed. "Wanna walk me outside?" I murmured to the clerk. "We could use the employees' exit."

"Sure," he replied a little too excitedly for comfort, but he'd be easy to ditch.

Someone tapped my shoulder. "Sasha?"

Quadruple Crap.

I hefted my shopping bags to wallop her and bolt. Only in doing so, the belly slipped and I had to lurch to catch it, releasing the bags.

"That is you, isn't it?" the magic-handler asked. She had an accent. Lots of strong vowels and funny inflections. Southern Hemisphere English. "Bob sent me."

It was the single thing she could've said to halt me. "You know Bob?" I didn't turn to face her but force-relaxed my posture, faking calm while I adjusted my hand under the belly as if cradling my unborn child.

The stoned clerk cleared his throat. "Does this mean you aren't offering me sex for pot?"

Neither of us looked in his direction.

The magic-handler came up beside me. "I wouldn't say 'know' Bob exactly. He's not one that someone *knows*, right, mate? But I'm here because of him. I'm here to offer assistance."

Huh. Bob *had* promised to help.

Not that I was foolish enough to just believe her. (Or him.)

What she *was* doing was attracting attention. The clerk had re-turned to staring at her like he wanted to fall to the ground in full-on genuflection. (So fickle.)

Several other customers halted to watch us. No cells had been pulled yet. I needed to get out of there before they did. "Let's go reminisce about Bob outside."

"Sure thing."

I grabbed my receipt, balanced my bags against the belly to keep it in place, and headed out.

The girl even walked beautifully, like a model on a runway. Long legs swinging her hips in such a smooth, even cadence that a guy heading the other direction tripped on a crack in the sidewalk while staring. Why were magic-handlers so allergic to subtlety?

I didn't take her to Dr. Trent. Instead, I walked around the corner of the mini-mart and positioned us next to the commercial dumpster where I'd dropped the morning's fouled puppy pads. Once there, I relaxed my grip on the belly, letting it slide down to my knees.

"You can trust me, Sasha," she said, all friendly-like. "I'm supposed to go with you. To help."

I arranged my face in a stern-and-unrelenting-Dad look, from the few occasions he'd tried and failed to parent me, and put out my free hand. "ID."

She looked at me as if she didn't know what I was talking about.

I rolled my eyes. "Give me your identification documents, passport, whatever."

"Right." She grinned as if this were a lark and then opened a purse at her hip to pull out a wallet with one of those high-end repeating labels all over it. I put down my bags and snatched it from her hand. I did it less to be rude and more because she was taking forever, and I'd been away from the Brontës for too long.

Inside I found a wad of US cash, several credit cards, and an Australian driver's license with a photo of the girl in front of me and the name of Jedda Lynn Jacobs of Point Piper, New South Wales, Australia. I took the cash and pocketed it just to see what she would do.

Which was nothing.

Meant nothing also, considering just how rich she probably was.

"Purse," I said.

She handed it over more reluctantly.

I found an Australian passport with her photo and a cellphone.

Of course, she had a phone. Who didn't? But a phone . . .

She could call Mrs. Valenzuela with a phone.

But Bob *had* said that he'd help. (Not that I believed Bob.)

I looked her over. Her outfit was so skintight there wasn't much chance of hiding anything on her person. She could've hidden something in her hair, which was so full-body, curly-perfect that I twinged with jealousy. Mine endlessly went flat and thus spent most of its time in a ponytail.

I didn't trust her, but she could be a source of information. I could also ditch her later if needed. She looked too much like a princess to put up a fight. I took her purse, passport, phone, and wallet and chucked them all into the dumpster.

She screeched. "You did not just do that."

"Did." Felt great about it too. I slouched my shoulders in the exact way my Dad did when going for an uncaring-casual look. It would've been perfect if I hadn't had to lift the belly back into position at the same time. "I'm going to my car now. If you wanna come with me, you can. Get in the passenger side. If you try to retrieve your stuff first, I'll be gone by the time you're done."

***

Of course she followed me to Dr. Trent.

"I love doggos," Jedda said upon sliding into the passenger seat. The Brontës went straight to her, noses sniffing, paws exploring, tails wagging happily.

They weren't supposed to like her.

I wouldn't. No way. "Talk," I said, once we were heading south again. "How did Bob contact you?" Seemed a good idea to check her honesty index.

"The usual way," she replied. "You do have the Semis inside that prego belly, don't you? Cleverly done, girl."

No way would I be distracted by compliments or the fact that there was something charming about Jedda Jacobs. However, driving with the loose belly on was in itself distracting. It wanted to lean forward against the steering wheel. "So Bob contacted you with a funky message that randomly showed up on your phone? Is that right?"

"Phone?" She gave me a quizzical look. "Yeah, no. He knows better than to trust a phone. He uses a messaging spell."

Points to Jedda for knowing that.

Jedda shifted sideways and crossed her legs as if she were on a settee in a French manor rather than in a late-model sedan. Charlotte and Annie Pup returned to the back seat, but Emily stayed with Jedda as if claiming the new addition for herself. "Oh, I get it," Jedda said. "You're testing me, right? Have a fair go. I'm an open book."

"Why did Bob pick you?"

"He didn't—"

I quick-glared her direction. The belly flopped forward again. "You said—"

"I know, I know, calm down. There wasn't heaps of time for explanations is all, so I condensed. Bob contacted my grandmother. She put me on a plane to find you."

"Your Australian grandmother?"

"Aboriginal Australian, the distinction is important."

Aboriginal. Fair enough. I shifted the belly so that it sat on my left side against the door. "Australia was the closest help Bob could find?"

"Obviously." She paused dramatically as if waiting for me to acknowledge just how obvious this was.

Emily rubbed her head against Jedda's fuzzy sweater, and Jedda stroked her waterfall of fur. If dogs could purr, Emily would be doing so. Fine. More points to Jedda for Emily's good opinion.

On the other hand, Jedda had made no effort to include Charlotte and Annie Pup. Total loss of points for picking a favorite Brontë. (I hadn't meant to tally whether or not Jedda was someone I didn't inherently hate, but I totally was.)

When I didn't respond, Jedda continued. "How much do you actually know about the Alliance and magic?"

"The basics." Total lie.

"You know about Australia being neutral? Us and the Congolese. The Congolese hoard magic rather than use it, and Australia stayed out of the Alliance because we have plenty of our own spellbooks thanks to Australia's 'Great Slaughter.'" She used air quotes as she said it, flashing gumball pink fingernails. "Because of the 'Great Slaughter,' we also have a national prohibition on killing magical-creatures that we actually abide by. If Bob wanted someone outside the Alliance to help you, Australia was his only choice."

Five points. Not only did everything she'd said make sense, I'd just learned several new facts about magic-handlers.

The Semis was now shoved uncomfortably under my armpit. I saw no easy way to fix this. Loss of two points since with Jedda here I wasn't going to be able to take it off. This put her at positive three.

Time for another test.

I told Jedda about the luxury cars showing up that morning and my getting away just in time without mentioning Bob's warning notes. "How did they find me? I left my phone at home."

"No idea. It's unlikely they'd trace you through a phone, though. A government agency might do it that way but not handlers."

"I've always heard that the magic-handlers have the cell system rigged."

"That's just what they'd like you to think, but it's not true. Handlers are notoriously paranoid about technology. It's a nut they can't crack with spells, so they don't rely on it."

Ten points for extremely useful information. But at the same time . . .

"This last week would've been much easier if I'd known that."

Jedda laughed, deep and rich to match her accent. "Gotta love a girl who knows how to use sarcasm."

"That wasn't sarcasm."

"Right, mate. The thing is, a lot of the tales about magic-handlers aren't true."

"Ri-i-ight?" Twenty points if she was being honest, but I found myself skeptical. "So magic-handlers can't tell the future?"

"Not a chance. Not that there haven't been those that tried, but never successfully."

"Make the earth's rotation stop?"

"Obviously not. Magic-handling world got a good laugh out of that movie, though."

Nice for them. "How about controlling the stock market?"

"A hundred years ago, absolutely. Today? No way, too much impregnable technology."

I felt forced to give her the twenty points just because I now knew more about the limitations of magic-handlers than the vast majority of planetary inhabitants. I wanted to know more. Her current points balance was positive thirty-three, but I wasn't done yet.

"What about the spellbooks themselves? You do take a Semis, turn it into a book, and lock it up in a fourth-dimensional library, right?"

"Sort of. It's complicated and most spellbooks are actually scrolls. Spells prefer their words not be separated by page turns."

"Spells have opinions?" I hoped I didn't sound as incredulous as I felt.

"Like, yeah. You really don't know anything about anything, do you?" Jedda's tone was totally condescending. Her snoodishness made me grumble a bit in irritation. How exactly would I know any of this?

Negative twenty-two points. Thank goodness. Her point scale was getting too high.

I waited until we were headed up the Tehachapi Pass to ask the most important question of all. "How do I avoid a spell to find me?"

"Yeah, no. It wouldn't be a finding spell. They rarely work. It'd be something else."

"Like what?"

"No idea."

Negative eleven for not providing an answer. Back to zero. "What kind of spell did you use to find me?"

"I didn't. I didn't think I *would* find you." She said it with a laugh. "My grandmother called and said Bob told her that you were heading south near Bakersfield and to keep an eye out for a white Toyota. I was on the receiving end of whatever spell Bob is using."

"Then Bob must have a finding spell."

"I already told you, finding spells don't work. He's using something else. No idea what it is, so don't bother asking. He's a known recluse. No one's seen or heard from him in thirty years."

"Other than your grandmother."

"She mentored him when he was a teenager."

Made sense. Plus, Jedda was kinda awesome. Fifty points.

Chapter Ten

Total Fund Remaining: $3777.71
Cash: $1140.07
(Including $600.00 cash snagged from Jedda. Nice!)
Gift Cards: $2637.64

Jedda was a talker. So was I. Apart from the whole magic thing and the whole money thing and the whole excess beauty thing, we had a lot in common and the conversation never stopped.

And, okay, maybe I had a bad habit of getting too attached too easily to houses and cars and animals and people I shouldn't. But I liked her. I even liked staring at her beauty, if not quite so much as I did Ari's.

She'd graduated last year in Communications from a university in Melbourne, loved fashion and shopping and her extended indigenous family. More than anything she wanted a serious boyfriend, but she scared off normal boys and the magic-handling boys in Oceania were more interested in her grandmother's spellbooks than her.

Boys could be lousy. We both agreed.

She also had an extremely useful spell. So useful, I agreed she could cast it, watching her carefully as she silently moved her lips, just like the old European woman had done back in the café. Gave me unpleasant chills.

"Done," she said. "Now anyone driving slower than you within a kilometer's radius will automatically move out of your way."

"My Dad would pay good money for that spell." While the casting of the spell still grossed me out, I was totally fine with the results of the magic.

Even though I liked her, I didn't trust her. I left her and the Brontës in a motel room for the night in Provo, Utah. I figured if anything went wrong,

I'd be free to take off and trusted that Jedda was a good enough person to return the Brontës to Mrs. Lee. Yes, I told Jedda that if she contacted other magic-handlers, she'd never see me again. She'd rolled her eyes.

After leaving and stopping to shower at another truck stop, I made a quick shopping trip to prepare for a cold night as there was snow crowning the nearby mountains. And err . . . truedragons. Which wasn't inherently about the Semis. Truedragons liked both mountains and cold. Unlike me.

I bought less showy clothing for Jedda, more stuff for the Brontës, a thermal sleeping bag, and a flathead screwdriver. I hid Dr. Trent in a tree-lined parking lot behind a church and snuck around the surrounding neighborhood to steal a Utah license plate. I swapped out Dr. Trent's license, set the alarm on the phone for an hour and a half, climbed into the sleeping bag, reclined the car seat, and crashed.

When the alarm went off, I drove to another church ten miles away while still zipped in the sleeping bag. Rinse and repeat two more times.

On my fifth nearly identical church and sleep cycle, Ari appeared. Finally.

We sat side-by-side again at the park, this time at the top of parallel slides embedded into a fake rock hillside. Ari wore his old man pajamas again. He looked amazing.

"Are you alright?" I asked. "You keep disappearing. It makes me worry."

"You need not have *worried*." He said it all crisp and starchy and British.

"*Sheesh*, I'm not a monster. Give me some credit. The first time on the bridge, you freaked out and then disappeared. I thought someone had come for you. Then you were being all salty last night and everything faded to black. Clearly, something is going on."

Dream Ari squinted as if trying to puzzle me out.

Doggone it, his eyes were just so deep and dark and gorgeous. "What, is the sun in your face?" I asked to break the moment.

"I don't believe there is a sun in your dream," he replied, all literal-like.

I sighed. "Will you just tell me what happened?"

"The first night, someone woke me. We can only communicate this way if I also am asleep. Last night, you were too restless. I couldn't keep the spell in place, and then it wasn't me who woke, but you."

Good point actually. Bob's notes had ruined things (sort of). "Who woke you the first time?"

"That's not a topic of which I can speak."

"So Mrs. Valenzuela woke you."

"No. I believe she is staying at her Atherton house."

"Where are you staying?"

"My school apartment."

I wrinkled my nose at him. This conversation was going nowhere. He was being so literal. Annoyingly literal.

Hold up. *Intentionally* literal? Was he doing it on purpose? He totally was. "You. Are. So. Annoying."

"Look," he started, going all British-offended.

I stared hard at him, pretty sure his reaction wasn't real either.

"I'm not being coy. If they ask specifics of our conversation, I can't lie. We should stick to neutral topics."

"Who's them? Actually, I can answer that myself." Meaning Mrs. Valenzuela's goonies. Regardless of my worrying about him and starting to see through him, Aristotle Montague-Smith-Montague wasn't my friend.

"How did your finals go?" I asked while I considered the best way to introduce what I really wanted to talk about.

"Fine. My last one is tomorrow. We don't need to speak on topics quite that neutral."

"Perfect. Name the three magic-families that aren't part of the Alliance."

He raised his brows at me in question, but I just smiled.

"There are only two. The first is in central Africa, most usually associated with the Democratic Republic of the Congo. The second is in Australia."

"Is it true that magic-handlers have spells on the entire cellphone system?"

He gave me another puzzled look. "No."

I wrinkled my nose. I happened to know it made me look cute and brought out my dimples. Grams's book had a saying about how a girl with dimples always got her own way. "Why not?"

"Spellcasting on technology is problematic. Phone-tapping must be done the old-fashioned way and magic-handlers are so closely watched by BIMD that they can't get away with it." He said it kinda lecturing-ly, in a way that came off as paternalistic as if I were a dense student lucky enough to get his help.

Gah! He could be so irritating. Possibly still on purpose.

Jedda had said the same thing, though. Yes, I was testing her. Or maybe I was testing him. That they'd both passed was a relief for some reason.

Only I shouldn't want to feel relieved. Why was I so horrible at disliking people once I got to know them? "Why are you doing this? What do you want?"

"The Semis."

"Well, that's direct."

"I believe in being so. Have you read William Penn?"

"I haven't." I'd never heard of William Penn. Ari was baiting me. Time to change the subject. "I bet you've never held a job in your life."

He just stared at me. Bingo. I'd been right about him.

"I'll make a deal with you," I said with a smirk.

He lifted his chin in interest.

"Not for the Semis."

He looked down his nose.

"Tell me how to avoid the magic-handlers that are chasing me, and I'll let you make *an offer* for the Semis. Note that I'm not agreeing to accept the offer, but I'll let you pitch me." Just so I could have the joy of turning him down.

"My offer will not be as good as Mrs. Valenzuela's."

"You made her offer for her."

"Correct, but it wasn't my funds. I don't have that level of funds."

"Don't you?" I glanced at his monogrammed pajamas.

"I didn't say I don't have money. I just don't have that level."

I pushed myself off the top of the slide and whooshed downward. Once back on my feet, I turned to look up at him. "Fine. Just tell me how to avoid the magic-handlers. That's the part of this bargain I really care about. Can you talk about that without getting into trouble?"

Between one blink of an eye and another, he was next to me, standing close, so close that I stared up at the crease where his very defined lower lip ended. He had soft-looking lips.

"The answer depends on what spells they are employing."

I gave myself a shake and took several steps backward, trying not to think of his lips and instead focus on my question. That took a beat longer than I would've liked. "What spells are they employing?"

"Not a finding spell. Those never work."

Which also was what Jedda had said. "You're not as helpful as I'd like."

"My deepest apologies," he said, an ironic tone to his voice. "I shall be more helpful once I've completed my final tomorrow and gotten a full night's sleep."

"Whatever." The park's garden maze was to our right. I started in that direction. "What kind of spellbook did Mrs. Valenzuela create with the last seadragon Semis?"

He touched his neck.

"What?"

"Her emeralds. She wears them to remind everyone that she has a spellbook that turns ordinary stones into jewels. A good lot of the magic-handling world thought the Valenzuela family's choice a waste of a Semis, but with the changing economy and more limited opportunities for magic-handlers, it worked out financially for them."

Interesting. "Will you get in trouble for telling me all this? For telling me how to avoid magic-handlers?"

"It would be highly suspicious if you didn't bring up the topic at some point. Also, I haven't actually told you anything outside of common knowledge."

"But you could."

He followed on my heels as I wound my way through the green hedges of the maze. He was a good height to do so. That'd always been a thing for me. Not just that I liked tall boys, but that I liked them just so. He didn't loom, but I was entirely aware he was there. I also liked that he wasn't bothered by being the follower rather than the leader. That was important, too, and made it seem as if his lecturing, paternalistic crap had really been just that: crap. "Who should I trust?" I asked, to be provocative.

"No one."

Excellent answer. "Not even you?"

We finished the maze and stopped at the metal outlook tower in the center. He studied it with an expression of deep concentration. "I revise my previous answer," he said as if making a decision. "You should trust me."

Which I took to mean I should not.

It was getting harder and harder to hate him, though. He wasn't what I'd originally thought. He was more of a deliberate, witty-at-times, somewhat nerdy, frustrating *guy*. If he'd been at my high school, he'd have been the kid who spent his lunches studying in the library to have an edge come AP test time. Studious, reliable, boring. (If unemployed.)

I'd always respected those kids.

I climbed the lookout tower so that I was above him and launched into the Gay Grandma story in all its brilliant glory. Ant's determination to pin them down. The grandmas' avoidance. The euphemisms.

Ari listened but didn't laugh at any of the good parts. Surprise, surprise. He probably thought we were all crazy. (Which we were.)

I kept on, layering the humor on thick as I told him of the ashtray through the window and the mob of cops showing up. I sat down so my feet dangled over the edge of the platform and ended my tale with Grandma George producing the marriage certificate when Grandma Fee died.

Ari still didn't respond, which left me feeling put-out. He could at least fake-enjoy my performance.

"Why are you telling me all of this?" He looked up at me with a crooked tilt to his head and furrowed brows.

"To see how you react so I can judge you."

"So a test."

"Yup."

He considered. "Well, your Grandma George sounds astute and very much in control of her own life in a situation that must've made it difficult for her to do so. By *situation*, I mean being in a relationship with someone of her same sex in a time period where she would've been treated harshly for it. She also seems protective of Grandma Fee. I find that endearing and perhaps enviable. Grandma George is to be applauded for creating and sustaining a life she wanted regardless of the pressures to conform either from her earlier years or from your brother."

Huh?

It was a good answer. (And probably would've earned him a high grade as an essay question.)

"Have I given you enough feedback from which to judge me?" There was a touch of snark to his voice.

"Crap. You're not supposed to pass. I can't just be forced to like you."

"You needn't *like* me. We wouldn't want to shatter your well-considered delusions of who I am." He placed his hand on the support bar of the tower and stared steadily up at me as if offended.

It was a total act. I could totally tell.

"With that," he continued, his voice slowing and evening out. He may even have smiled just the tiniest bit. "I do appreciate your sharing something so deeply personal with me. People rarely do."

***

When I woke the next time, a white note sat on top of the sleeping bag.

N 45.007438, W 54.745720
~*Bob*

I grabbed the notepad and pen I'd left sitting on the dashboard for this moment. With chilled fingers, I jotted down the N 45 and W 54 before the note disintegrated.

"Progress," I announced to the back of the latest church. Then I drove to the nearest gas station, bought a very large decaf coffee, and used the wi-fi to google the coordinates.

I got an entirely blue screen. Not helpful.

When I scrolled out, the blue turned out to be the Atlantic Ocean off the coast of Eastern Canada.

Eastern.

Canada?

Seriously?!

Bob wanted me to drive all the way to Eastern Canada?

Oh. My. Dog. I was *not* driving to Eastern Canada. For one thing, I'd end up spending every dime of my money. For another, it was just too far and I didn't trust him.

My gut gave a gurgle. Who was I kidding? Not myself. Apparently, I was driving to Eastern Canada.

Chapter Eleven

Total Spent: $841.87
Total Funds Remaining: $3298.20
Cash: $1125.07
Gift Cards: $2173.13

Having Jedda along is costing me, but I'm doing an excellent job of making frugal spending choices.

"Okay, talk in an American accent," I said to Jedda the next morning. She'd already done British and it'd been hilarious. We sat across from each other at a strip-mall diner in a desert town named Salina. Salina meant salty, if my high school Spanish served me right.

I was not feeling salty. I was enjoying myself. And I was enjoying her. I couldn't help it. She was a great travel companion. She'd even cast another whispered spell to keep our food perpetually hot so we could eat and chat and not hurry. Nice.

Nor had Jedda complained when I'd shown up at her hotel room, handed her a bag with no-label jeans, a T-shirt with a dancing cat on it, a boring beige coat, and a wide-brimmed sunbonnet, and told her to throw her designer clothes in the trash. She'd even insisted on cleaning up after the dogs before we left so that the maid service didn't have to do it.

Impressive. This was the kind of rich person I was going to be.

"I am an American citizen," she said, sounding like a country western singer being smushed by a rolling pin so that the twang stretched out. "I'm damn proud of it and my arsenal of weapons of amassed destruction."

She raised a fist into the air while pretending to burst into emotion-ridden tears.

I started laughing so hard a sting of orange juice came out of my nose. A table full of old guys wearing matching uniforms of flannel shirts, Carhart jackets, and dirty Wranglers turned to glare at us. "Hush," I said to Jedda as attracting attention was the last thing we needed. Also, my Gramps would totally have been sitting with the Carhart clan. "It's not okay to offend the regular guy. Can't you do magic-handlers? Or rich people?"

"I am the President of the United States," Jedda said, slaughtering just as badly the distinctive Bostonian accent of President Bernatella. "Obviously."

"Better." We grinned at each other over the vinyl diner table and our plates of food.

I glanced through the window to where the Brontës were waiting for us in Dr. Trent just outside. A minivan backed in across the way. It had a huge vinyl advert for an essential oils company on the window in pink ombre.

"Tell me about Aristotle," Jedda said while taking a bite of food. She'd ordered a French toast sandwich with fritters and brown sugar oatmeal on the side. This girl could eat.

I'd had a terrible time deciding what to order as this wasn't exactly a vegetarian mecca. Not that I was a vegetarian. I should be. I kept meaning to be. Places like this where the smell of crispy sausage permeated everything made me fail. I'd ordered a turkey bacon omelet, hoping it was ethically sourced.

"I've always wanted to meet Aristotle," Jedda continued. "Everyone says he's a total *Tall Poppy*."

"*Tall Poppy*? Love it." Even if I had no idea what it meant, it fit him perfectly.

I glanced around to make sure no one could hear us. I totally wanted to talk about him, of course. "He's just what you'd expect. All stiff and proper British. He seemed way more interested in studying for his final exams than in the Semis."

"That makes sense," she said. "I mean, he already has his own raw magic as it is."

"As in the Semis he swallowed?"

"The two Semis," she replied, taking a bite of her oatmeal.

"Two?" I halted in lifting a forkful of omelet to my mouth. That wasn't on his wikipage.

"It's why everyone thinks he lived. I mean, that's why Mrs. Valenzuela and her ilk think he lived. My grandmother doesn't have any better theories."

"Didn't a bunch of kids die after their parents fed them Semis trying to follow his example?"

"Not just kiddos, although it's a prime example of why the Alliance keeps so quiet about all things magic. People do these ridiculous things, and then they blame us when it goes wrong."

"No magic-handlers tried it?"

She gave me a look as if I'd just said something astute, and then leaned forward, lowering her voice. "This isn't for certain, mind you, but it's rumored that the Alliance did take on non-magical volunteers and gave them two Semis just like Ari, and they also died. If that's true, and it sounds like something the Alliance would do, then Ari really is super-special himself."

"You make the Alliance of magic-handlers sound pretty horrible," I said.

"Me and my people would be the first to agree with you."

Yet another thing in which we had perfect accord.

***

"Are you going to stop for petrol soon?" Jedda asked hours later. "I need to use the loo."

"By that you mean bathroom, right?" I was teasing. Everyone knew what a loo was.

"The toilet," she clarified. She gave me a toss of her floaty hair as if she knew very well what I was doing. Earlier, I'd caught her running her fingers through her hair while doing a silent mumble thing, so pretty sure she used magic to keep it looking so perfect. Lucky. Her hair was pretty amazing.

We were somewhere in Colorado, although without a map or GPS, I had little sense for where. Pretty country, though. We'd spent a good chunk of the day driving through skyscraper mountains, tree-littered valleys, and even seen what we thought might be an elk. Jedda had said moose. I'd said large deer. Jedda cast a recognition-spell that said woolly mammoth. We settled on elk.

It was late afternoon, and the landscape had flattened to plains that if filmed for a movie would have vast herds of roaming buffalo. The passing towns seemed right out of the 1950s, and Jedda kept using words like "quaint" to describe them. We were having fun and making most excellent progress eastward too.

I found her a *petrol station* with a *loo* and we grabbed *sangas* from the sandwich place next door. The *bloke* who sold them to us said there was a park with a reservoir just east if we wanted to picnic. He also suggested he join us while staring wide-eyed at Jedda and ignoring me.

Which totally didn't offend me. Not at all. No way. Not that the same thing didn't happen everywhere I went with her. He'd probably just noticed my pregnancy and wanted to be respectful. That was it.

We drove to the reservoir.

"This is a park?" Jedda asked after we'd followed a barren dirt road to where it dead-ended at flat, brown water. "What do people do out here?"

Only a few twiggy trees bordered the edge of the water. "No idea. Fish, maybe?"

We walked over to a beat-up picnic bench. I played fetch with the Brontës while Jedda laid out our food. "You want me to warm your *sango* for you?" she asked.

"Sure."

She did the silent murmur thing again and immediately the air was filled with the scent of melting cheese and warmed bread. Yum. She used magic so casually that I was getting used to the idea.

I wanted to bring the conversation back to Ari again but couldn't figure out how. I *had* managed to slip in several times that Bob lived in Florida.

Emily dropped the fetch ball at Jedda's feet. The other two were over by the tree with their noses to the ground. Apparently, there'd been doggos here before. Jedda reached to pick Emily up, but Emily changed her mind and dashed back to the other two, pushing between them and launching into a series of excited yaps.

I stood to go investigate, just in case it was a snake or scorpion or something like that. (Did Colorado have scorpions? No idea.)

It wasn't a snake or scorpion. I wasn't exactly sure what it was. It was fist-sized with four legs sticking out from a scaly, pearly pinkish-brown shell that was more striped than tortoise-like. It had a pointed snout with whiskers and a long snakey tail. It moved in a slow creepy-crawly way my direction.

"Kill it," Jedda screamed.

I jumped. So did the Brontës. We also all backed up. The thing kept plodding along my direction. This was likely not intentional on its part as I stood opposite it in relation to the dogs. "What is it?" It didn't appear dangerous. It plodded kinda slow.

"It's a *Chaetophractus draco*," Jedda said. "Keep the doggos back." She shoved past me and then shoved the Brontës away with her foot, even Emily who yipped at the rebuff. "They're related to the South American armadillo. I'd heard they'd made their way this far north, but I never expected to see one."

She snatched up a large rock with a pointy edge, and I was one beat too late in understanding that she'd been serious in her first exclamation. I lunged but not fast enough to keep Jedda from kicking the poor creature over with her foot and then mercilessly smashing its soft belly.

The magic-armadillo-thing screeched, high-pitched like the proverbial nails on a chalkboard.

"Oh. My. Dog." I shoved Jedda sideways, but it was too late. She pushed me away and took several more strikes with the rock. My sprouts decided they wanted to be vomited back up and I shoved my fist to my mouth to keep them in place. The Brontës fled to Dr. Trent.

"Nailed it," Jedda cheered and then dropped down to hunt through the poor dead creature's innards with her bare hands.

This wasn't just gross, it was immoral. "You said Australians didn't kill magical-creatures." I near shouted the words.

"We don't kill our own. Everyone kills the Americans'. You've got more variety than anyone else. Frankly, it seems fair payback considering how much of the world's resources your nation hogs."

Normally, she'd have me on the resources truth but not right now. Especially when she'd made such a big deal about Australians not killing. Not needing to kill. She'd specifically said they didn't have to because they had so much magic of their own.

Had it all been a lie to gain my trust?

"Found it!" She squealed with excitement from her spot in the dirt. "Want to see the Semis before I send it to my family's library?"

"Absolutely not."

She held up her dusty hand anyway, and while maybe I should've been too horrified and disgusted to give in, I looked.

It was tiny, just a splinter of pinky-orange-brown light against her palm. "So much power in something so small," Jedda said, then began silently moving her lips once again. She clapped her free hand over the tiny Semis in her palm, and there was a sudden, small puff of pearly pink smoke from between her fingers. "Done. See. Easy." She opened her hands. They were empty and entirely clean.

I tensed from my feet to my torso to my face. This kind of spellcasting, I didn't like. "You turned it into a spellbook?"

"Yeah, no. A full transformation would take way too long. I bound it to me and sent it to my family's library for later. I can't tell you what a find this is. *Chaetophractus* make for the most amazing defensive spells. That alone will have made this trip worth it."

Yup, she'd lied about needing more magic.

***

We drove for another hour in a heavy and awkward silence. The Brontës hid in the back seat, even Emily.

It was like Dad and Gramps always said: *People who talk, lie.* (Including them.)

I'd add that people (Australians), who came off as the perfect friend, are putting on a performance. The safer road (relationship) was to just not believe anyone. Ever.

Also, I had one more test for her. If she didn't pass it, I'd ditch her. I didn't think she'd pass.

I turned south at the next deserted-looking crossroad.

"Where're we going?" Jedda asked.

"Florida."

"No, I know that. I mean, are we stopping for some reason?"

"I need a loo." Truth: A good lot of road-tripping was based around the timing of this particular need.

"Look," she said. "Obviously, you're mad. But do you have a right to be? Magical-creatures eat each other. They have to in order to survive.

Non-magical-creatures eat each other too. You ate sausage for breakfast this morning."

"Turkey sausage."

"Right mate, and is a turkey any less dead when you eat it than when I take a Semis? I gave it a swifter, kinder death than a truedragon would have."

She had a point. Maybe I was a hypocrite. I didn't care.

"You've got to understand what this means to me," she continued. "You of all people. You stole the largest Semis discovered in my lifetime. It's not like you did it to donate to a children's shelter or force world peace. You just want to sell it and make money."

I kept driving.

"Let me ask you a question." I turned down an overgrown path heading toward a bunching of trees.

Jedda gave me a quick, nervous glance. "Have a go."

"What specifically did Bob say? How was his message to your grand-mother worded?"

"Well, I didn't see it," she said, but she twitched. I might not have caught it if I hadn't been watching for it. (While watching the road, too, of course.)

"What did your grandmother tell you it said?"

She licked her lips. "That Bob thought you weren't getting a fair play. That he wanted to guide you on the path he himself followed, but that he couldn't do so directly since the Alliance was after you and he's terrified of them. He thought that having a neutral magic-handler along would help you make it to Florida. More than anything he wants to help. He cares about you. So do I."

"Liar." None of that sounded like the Bob of my notes, and Bob wasn't in Florida. I slammed on the brakes. Then I reached down into the door pocket, drew out Grandma Fee's butane lighter and pointed it at Jedda. "Get out. And . . . err . . . take your jacket with you. It's windy."

Chapter Twelve

Total Spent: $1001.31
Total Funds Remaining: $3138.76
Cash: $1075.07
(Paid cash for lunch and dinner as cash tips are better for servers.)
Gift Cards: $2063.69

Don't trust the Australians. They are wolves in kangaroo clothing.
~ Bob

"Now he tells me."

It was pitch dark. I'd just pulled Dr. Trent between two big rigs at a truck stop because I couldn't drive a mile more. It'd been nineteen hours since I woke up in Utah, and I'd taken to drilling my fingernails into my palms just to keep myself awake. The Brontës were curled up on the floor around the Semis again, making small doggie snores. After the chat with Jedda about spellbooks having opinions, I'd taken it out of the belly thinking a bit of fresh air might be good for it. That I could tell, it didn't care.

What was worse, Jedda knew about Dr. Trent. I was going to have to find a new mode of travel, which sucked. But as Gramps liked to say, *Burnt soup was never going to be edible.*

I threw a blanket over the dogs and Semis, slithered into the thermal sleeping bag, and crashed.

Only to find myself back at Dennis the Menace Park.

Ari and I stood next to each other on the rope bridge this time. It had a jiggly feel to it that I hated even in the Dreamscape. I grabbed the handrail and hung on tight.

"Hey." Each corner of Ari's lips lifted a tad, not enough to be a smile but enough to hint that he might consider smiling. He wore a red Stanford hoodie and jeans. He looked good in jeans. And in red.

"You dressed down for me," I noted, not even trying to hide that I was glad to see him.

"You seemed to disapprove of my pajamas." He stressed the last word all British. Py-jaarr-maaas.

I rolled my eyes just because. Pestering him was totally soothing.

"What?" He stood straight not even touching the rope handrail. He probably had perfect balance or something.

I clutched the rope a bit harder. "I thought I disapproved of everything about you."

The corners of his lips twitched higher. "Yes, but I think you're coming around."

I narrowed my eyes at him all suspicious-like, but I was playacting and making it obvious. Another word for it might even be . . . flirting . . . ?

I wasn't flirting. Only an idiot would real-flirt as compared to annoyance-flirt with a guy like him.

Either way, it felt good.

I'd better stop.

"Why is it that you disliked me from the first?" he asked. "Because you did, back at your house and the café. What did I ever do to you?"

"You existed . . . ?" A lousy, rude answer, and I only said it in a knee-jerk fashion because I was still busy admiring him *and* hating myself for it. I decided to explain as another test, one that hopefully he'd fail in order to remind me of all the reasons I should not be flirting with him. "My grandmother, Valerie Jane Sterling, grew up in a family like yours."

"British?"

"Rich." I said it like the slur it was.

He said nothing in response.

"She lived in upstate New York. Big house, controlling parents, lots of expectations on what she could and couldn't do, could and couldn't think, and who she could and couldn't marry."

"Ah," he said as if he understood something.

"She had a best friend, and they spent all their younger years plotting to run away. They had this book, you see. The heroine's name was Valancy Stirling, almost the same as my Grams's name Valerie Sterling. Valancy was a rich girl whose family was burying her alive, metaphorically speaking, until one day she stood up and walked out on them to create a new life for herself, make her own friends, and even meet someone who she loved."

"*The Blue Castle.*"

"How do you know that?"

"Your quote on the wall intrigued me. I looked it up. The author is L.M. Montgomery who is famous for her *Anne of Green Gables* stories. I can't claim the privilege of having read either that book or her *Blue Castle* book, but I'll make a point of doing so if it pleases you."

"It wouldn't. Don't expend yourself."

"Expending was not on my agenda." He made a quiet sound deep in his throat that almost, but not quite, sounded like a laugh.

"Are you mocking me?"

"Never."

He totally was. He watched me, clearly enjoying that I didn't like it. "I take it that your grandmother was inspired by *The Blue Castle* book to run away."

I suddenly didn't want to tell him the rest. It was too personal, a doorway into me that I wanted the address of kept private. At the same time, it had all happened sixty-five years ago and wasn't directly about me. I spoke slowly. "Grams's family was going to force her to marry a horrible older man. She took courage from the book and refused. Then she and her best friend, Grandma George, took off together."

"That explains the connection. Regarding the car you stole, that is. Georgiana was your grandmother's co-conspirator. The two of them relocated to California, took up residence in your small town. Your grandmother married your grandfather and passed on to her descendants a general sense of suspicion when it comes to those of higher means."

"It's not just the wealth." I hesitated and took a breath, trying to put it into just the right words, because it was also why I'd never, ever trust him. "It's using wealth to control everything, to act superior even when someone actually isn't, never having to work to earn your place, always being the most decorated cupcake."

"Cupcake? That makes no sense." He studied me, really looking, as if searching for pieces of Grams in me. Or maybe pieces of the old New York lineage.

I couldn't help it. I squirmed, making the bridge wiggle and forcing myself to grip the rope even harder. I was supposed to look at him, make him feel uncomfortable. Not the other way around.

"Let's talk about your hang-ups for a while. You were abandoned and then adopted, right? That must've left you pretty damaged." It was a rude, horrible thing to say, and my entire family would've looked at me aghast. Just then, I didn't care.

Ari cocked his head. When he spoke he was all calm and cool, as if his history didn't bother him at all. "I was lucky. Lord and Lady Montague-Smith-Montague did their best by me. If I have hang-ups to complain about, they are of my own doing and my own fault, not theirs or anyone else's. Did I pass the test?" He asked the last in a quieter voice.

"What test?"

"That's what you do, don't you? You endlessly test people so that you can write them off as not worthy of you."

"I do not do that." I totally did that. We both knew it. "New question," I said abruptly. "Is there any chance that magical-creatures are stalking me?"

***

His short answer was yes, but it wasn't me, it was the Semis. (Surprise, surprise.)

His longer answer was to question me about every magical-creature I'd run into so far: the seadragon, the various truedragons, the bee, and the creature Jedda killed. Yes, I told him about Jedda. Didn't seem to be any reason not to.

"The seadragon wasn't you," he said when I was done. "It was me."

"You?" I scoffed. "You weren't there."

"I was. In Monterey, that was. I was given a room at one of the hotels that overhang the bay and ordered to stay in place. At the time, I was focused on not missing my finals and losing an entire quarter's worth of work, so I didn't realize the reason. Not that it would've mattered if I had known, Mrs. Valenzuela would've forced me regardless. But the seadragon was coming for me."

There was so much to unpack that I almost didn't know where to start. No, actually I did. "Why was the seadragon coming for you?"

"Because raw magic is attracted to raw magic, and magical-creatures really like me," he said as if I were stupid.

Yeah, no way did he get to do that. I gave him a hard shove, putting my weight into it, and then held tight to the rope railing when the bridge swayed under my feet. "Why would I know something like that about magic? Why would I know magical things are attracted to you?"

"I thought you knew my story?" He said it curiously as if he *wanted* me to know his story.

"You were a normal kid. Ate a minnow-dragon or two. There was a coma. You became a magic-handler. Lots of completely idiotic, brainless, teenage girls lacking any and all common sense go gaga."

He nodded as if he agreed. Then he leaned forward, putting his hand on the rope railing next to mine. My skin warmed just by his proximity, and I resisted an urge to slide my hand over until we touched. The bridge dipped forward, making me fight to stay on my feet and destroying the urge.

"That's the thing, though," he said as if unaware of the change in balance. "I'm not really a magic-handler. Or at least I'm not a magic-handler in the same way as those of the Alliance. I lack the gene. They checked."

"Clearly, you can do spells."

"It's believed that people like me, those who ingested magic and survived, were the progenitors of the magic-handling families. Likely animals converted the same way too. There's no actual proof that magic changes DNA, but Professor—"

"Back on topic," I said as he was getting sidetracked and I wasn't all that interested in magical genetics. Seemed he liked to lecture in general, though, not just when being intentionally annoying.

"I'm not a magic-handler in the traditional sense. I'm more of a magical-creature myself."

I looked him up and down. He looked human enough. He didn't have any odd protuberances or an opalescent color scheme.

He nodded again, crinkling his eyes as if he'd caught my thought and appreciated it. "I wasn't changed physically. I am who I was born, but I carry raw magic within me in a way no one else does. Thus I attract magic creatures because I'm part of their ecosystem. For some reason, my being human draws them quite strongly. No one knows why, but it's something I have to watch out for."

I made a humming of consideration. "So the seadragon was hunting you?"

"No. Seadragons don't hunt land creatures. The seadragon was dying. But the magic itself doesn't die, and the magic has its own will. It would've pushed the seadragon toward the nearest, best chance of a connection to another creature. That would've been me."

"You make the Semis sound alive."

"It's not. Just magical."

I let go of the rope railing with one hand to rub at my forehead. None of this made any sense. But what else was new? "Okay, so you were in Monterey because . . . let me guess . . . Mrs. Valenzuela . . . wanted to attract the seadragon to collect its Semis once it died. If she knew it was dying, then she must've been the one who shot it with the harpoon."

"Maybe, but—" He snapped shut his mouth and straightened abruptly, causing the bridge to give a strong shake. "It was harpooned?"

"Didn't you go see it?"

"No. I wasn't invited. A fact I never considered on its own before. I was preoccupied."

"With your finals."

"Yes. Tell me of the harpoon."

Man, it was nice to know something he didn't. I told him what I'd seen, even explaining that I'd videoed it. Perhaps that was trusting him a bit further than I should've, but at this point, I didn't see any benefit to keeping the secret.

His lips turned down as I spoke. He ran a hand through his hair and then played with the strings of his hoodie, all very restless and agitated for him. Apparently, he really hadn't known.

"Listen," he said. "This is extremely bad."

"Especially for the seadragon." Although if someone had to be the bad guy in this, I was glad it wasn't him.

He nodded while looking out into the distance, toward where the ocean would be in real life. "I need you to do something. It's going to seem strange, but just trust me, alright?"

Yeah, right. "I don't trust people."

"Don't trust me, but do it anyway."

"Tell me what it is."

"Stop sleeping at night. Not even a nap. They're going to make me continue contacting you, and I need some time to research what you've told me before chasing after you again. I can't find you if you aren't sleeping."

"Don't sleep?" I wasn't doing a good job of sleeping anyway. "What?" His words finally sank in. But what?

He slowed down, speaking as if I were an infant, totally talking down to me. "When I'm in your dream, I know where your sleeping form is located geographically. I can mark it on a mental map. That's why Mrs. Valenzuela has me casting the spell. When I wake, or when one of her people wakes me forcefully, I have to tell her where you are."

"You . . ." Blood pounded in my forehead and my tongue was caught between Grams's rules on profanity and an extremely nasty word I wanted to call him. Grams won. "Donkey butt."

Two people were going to con me in one day?

Seriously?

I mean, I'd figured he was reporting our conversations back to Mrs. Valenzuela, but still.

Maybe it was the compounding aspect of the betrayal, but this hurt even worse than Jedda. He should've told me. "Where am I right now?"

"Gas station parking lot on Highway 70 just outside of Limon, Colorado."

I jerked sideways to run from him but the bridge wobbled, so I did an awkward dance backward while trying to cling to the rope railing. He grabbed my wrist which both steadied me and held me in place. "Haven't you heard what I said? It only works if we are both asleep. Don't sleep at night when I'm sleeping. Or keep yourself moving, like in a car. That's the other way to stop me from joining your dreams. Sasha, you can trust me on this."

"Screw you," I said and forced myself to wake up.

Chapter Thirteen

Screw you. Not the strongest insult out there, but the only other person I'd ever said those words to was the infamously slimy, *faithless schmuck,* Zachary Stults.

Man, had I fallen hard for Zach. He'd been a year ahead of me in school, the only underclassman on the varsity soccer team at Carmel High, and the son of a congressman and investment banker. US versions of royalty.

Needless to say, we didn't meet at my high school, and although it took me a while to figure this out, he avoided introducing me to anyone at his. Total snood move.

We'd met on the beach after I'd gotten bored at Ant's and Nicholas's pre-wedding, force-the-families-together shindig at Lover's Point. I happened to notice a guy walking the edge of the surf, and there'd been something so stop-and-stare amazing about him that I'd just had to go introduce myself.

I was in insta-love at a hundred paces, and he saw me for the recently shucked oyster I was.

Zach was so amazingly good-looking and charming, and he told me this whole sob story about his life difficulties. I fell so, so, so hard.

Hard enough to help him sneak out of his house when his parents confiscated his car. Hard enough to make us each duplicate keys so he and I could have our own secret spot at the high school. Hard enough to take up shoplifting when his parents refused to buy him the high-end sportswear all the other Carmel Soccer kids were wearing and that if he didn't have would end his sports career. (How could I possibly have believed this!?)

Truth, though, the one time I met his parents, they were every bit as awful as he'd endlessly described. We'd met in the back office of the store that sold the sportswear under the unhappy eye of the store manager who'd caught the two of us stealing. Yes, his parents had paid the bill. No, they hadn't bothered to ask my name.

Embarrassingly, that wasn't the end of Zach and I. The end was him not returning my calls for two weeks and then me showing up at the high school prop room and finding him entwined with some girl in a Carmel High cheer outfit.

I'd gone home and spent two days crying. Ant had noticed, forced the entire story out of me, nicknamed Zach, *The Faithless Schmuck*, and pointed out that this was why it was better to go through life jaded until I met someone decent, someone dependable, someone not gilded-over-rot, someone I could trust.

Screw you, Aristotle.

***

Since I couldn't sleep, I bought caffeine pills and drove west. I hadn't felt chased since picking up Jedda in Bakersfield, but I did now. They were out there, no doubt coming, and once again I didn't know what to do next.

I arrived in Denver and randomly picked a freeway exit and a motel that looked rundown enough that it wouldn't cost too much. The room itself was beyond crappy, but I was able to take a shower. Even with the caffeine, continued driving was out of the question.

"The wi-fi's decent," I said to Annie Pup while doing a side bend to keep my body moving and my brain awake. The Brontës didn't seem to care about the room but watched me with judgmental eyes as if totally aware of just how much I'd screwed up. "Guaranteed no magic-handler would be caught dead here." Unless, of course, they came looking for me. Which was bound to happen eventually. (Caffeine made me both wired and maudlin. Hence my habit of generally avoiding it.)

I needed a plan, an idea. Nothing came.

The Brontës fussed. Charlotte sniped at Emily's tail and Annie darted at Charlotte as if trying to stop her. I threw a pillow at the lot of them and then immediately felt terrible about it. "Sorry. Everything will be better when I have a plan. Not having a plan sucks. *They* are going to find us." I plopped down next to the Brontës and the Semis. Charlotte immediately bit me on the ankle. "Keep it up. If I fall asleep, we're all doomed."

I turned on the ancient TV. Nothing but infomercials. I forced myself into some fast-paced yoga flows, so fast they bordered on jumping jacks.

"I could buy a used car off Craigslist," I said to the Brontës who'd settled down around the Semis. "Only, even a junker will take every penny we've got." I paced from one side of the room to the other. "Hitchhiking is also out. Do people even do that in real life?"

Annie Pup cracked an eye at me as if trying to be supportive and then closed it again.

I did ten real jumping jacks and then twenty burpees before plopping down in the room's vinyl chair to research public transportation options with my cell. Turned out the Greyhound bus system didn't allow dogs. How ironic.

Charlotte gave me a baleful stare as if she'd read my mind about the bus. "I know," I said. "People suck."

Amtrak did take dogs, and a train left Denver the next night, but there were two problems. First, only one dog per passenger. Second, dogs were only allowed on journeys of less than seven hours. From Denver, that left us in the middle-of-nowhere Nebraska, which distance-wise wasn't really all that far. I hadn't realized how slow trains were.

Also, Amtrak only ran three times a week. If I tried to make my way east, one small Amtrak trip at a time, it would take weeks. I'd run out of money long before the Canadian border.

I rubbed at my eyes, discouragement a lead dog leash around my neck. Why hadn't I left Jedda standing next to that garbage bin in Bakersfield? Why hadn't I just assumed Ari lied about the purpose of the Dream-scapes? This all would've been so much easier if neither of them had been involved.

I did a few more burpees, feeling put-out and well . . . lonely. Traitor she might be, but having Jedda along had been nice.

It was late enough (early enough?) that the TV switched over to the Denver morning news. One of those awful, overly happy news guys with too big of a smile and an annoyingly upbeat voice began to talk.

Next to him on the screen was a giant photo of me. Oh, ugh.

I crouched before the TV to listen.

"Morning update on Sasha Clems and the stolen Semis. I know our viewers are following this as closely as I am. The search continues with no recent sightings." The picture changed to a studio photo of all three Brontës sitting together in a pink basket surrounded by daisies. "But with three dogs wagging along and a reward for the return of the most valuable Semis in history, how hard could this be?"

I abruptly turned off the TV before I had to listen to more. I was going to fail. It crept over me like the slow oozing of motor oil across a newly painted garage floor. Which had happened once. Right after Dad had rather abruptly decided to remodel The Blue Castle's garage. I'd tripped over a used canister while sneaking into the house at two a.m. Huge mess.

No.

I couldn't fail.

When I'd made that mess in the garage, I'd woken Ant who'd helped me clean and repaint. Dad had never known.

I needed a new idea. I needed Ant.

***

I couldn't just call Ant, so I did something sneaky, something that no one but he or I would think of.

I used some of my gift card funds to open an email account with one of those guaranteed-anonymous-and-untraceable email hosts under the name Christine Stickles. Then I went to Ant's ancient, totally embarrassing, 2007 coming-out-tweenage-boy blog and had Christine Stickles post a comment offering to boost the blog's web traffic. Christine Stickles was my least favorite character from *The Blue Castle*, and posting on Ant's ancient blog was my favorite way to pester him when he was busy. He got a notification *every single time.*

Then I waited, feeling antsy. Hopefully, Ant was swimming this morning and thus up early. He'd been a high-diver in school and still went to the pool four mornings a week.

An hour later, Christine Stickles's email received an invitation from a Reverend Stalling of the Anglican Church to donate to an upcoming fundraiser.

My eyes welled with tears.

Ant would help me. Ant always helped me. And yes, every bit of his response was also from *The Blue Castle*. Reverend Stalling was Ant's least favorite character.

The Brontës were asleep so I went to the bathroom and shut the door before clicking the donation link. I got a rainbow screen with a single question: *Who's the daddy?* So Ant. So easy.

I typed in *"The Faithless Schmuck."* It's what Grams had nicknamed her least favorite character in *The Blue Castle*, a guy who'd taken advantage of the sweetest, most innocent character, gotten her pregnant, and then ditched her. No, Ant hadn't been terribly original in nicknaming Zachary Stultz.

A fuzzy, low-quality video popped up on my phone of Ant's face, nerdy handsome with a stubble-beard, wire glasses, brown hair parted tidily to the left. I started to tear up again and forced it back by sheer will. (Ant had a high-end phone with a superb camera. I took the current low-quality to mean he was using some other phone, one not traceable to him.)

"I'm-so-glad-to-see-you." I spat the words so fast they all strung together. "Dr. Trent's been made. Photos of the dogs and I are everywhere. I need help to get out of Colorado."

"Whoa. Slow down, Sis."

I took a deep, shaky breath and sat on the cracked counter of the motel's bathroom. Lack of sleep was making me loopy. "Are we safe to talk?"

Ant's face bobbed around on the screen as if he was walking. He also appeared to be outdoors. "We're fine to talk. But, *sheesh*, tell me you're okay first. Yesterday's news had you dead in like fifteen different ways."

Fair point that I probably should've addressed first. I gave a jittery laugh. "I'm fine. It's all going fine."

"Liar."

"That too." I didn't want to worry him or the rest of the family, though. "Really. I'm good. But the magic-handlers are close. I need to ditch Dr. Trent and get out of Colorado, preferably in an eastern direction." Then I paused. "Are you guys okay? Dad hasn't done anything crazy since I left?" I should've asked this first as well.

A building loomed up in the background of Ant's screen. The outside of the poolhouse. He cleared his throat. "Dad's fine. The press and BIMD are underfoot. Gramps is loving it. Dad's livid but keeping his cool. Barkley has fleas."

Oh, no. He was allergic to them. "Did someone call the vet? The medication from the vet is the only stuff that works, even if it's expensive."

"As I'd ever just let an animal suffer, and yes, Nicky called the vet."

Phew. "You're really all okay then?"

"Fine. Worried about you. Now back up and tell me everything. Because none of us have any idea what you are trying to do or where you are going."

Oh. Probably true. I told him the whole of it, every step of my journey, including Jedda and Ari's betrayals and all my problems with traveling with the dogs.

"Why Bob?" he asked when I'd finished. Ant must've stopped walking as the building behind him stopped moving.

"I don't trust him," I said quickly.

He pushed up his wire-rim glasses on his nose and gave me a raised eyebrow look.

"He's come through for me," I said defensively, "but I don't trust him."

"He wants something. What has he promised you?"

"Nothing. He's just been helpful." Which both sounded and tasted bad as it left my mouth. The best con men always helped at first.

Bob didn't have that feel, though. His notes weren't flattering. He seemed more angry than friendly. My gut said that Bob was a paranoid magic-handler who didn't like or trust me and could be somewhat relied upon *because* of that. (So very Clems.)

"Just be careful," Ant said. "He's probably not what you think."

"Who is?"

Ant snorted. Then sighed. "Where are you exactly?"

"Denver."

I got a view of tree branches and a blue sky. He'd started walking again. "Ant?"

The up-close of his face returned. "I know a sort-of influencer in Lincoln. If we can get you there, I can convince him to drive you to Chicago. Even if he doesn't keep his mouth shut about you, no one will believe him. He's a nutter."

I straightened with interest. This had possibilities. Nutters I knew how to deal with. I googled the distance between Denver and Lincoln while

Ant kept talking. "He's not dangerous or anything. I met him in person at a Poverty Reduction International conference last year, and you could take him in a fight. The only thing is that I'll have to offer him something in return."

"Like what?" I asked, my focus on a map on my phone. Lincoln was too far to take Amtrak from Denver, but if I drove east to a town called Fort Morgan, I could get to Lincoln without triggering the dog-time-allowance-rule. Plus, it'd be easier to sneak in three-dogs-pretending-to-be-one at a smaller train station. If the dogs and I costumed up, it was totally doable. I grinned at myself in the bathroom mirror, which also was a grin at Ant on the phone.

He frowned back. "Kills me to say this because it's a loss for Dad and I, but if you offered him an exclusive interview of everything that has happened so far, he'd drive you anywhere you want."

Chapter Fourteen

Total spent after shopping spree: $1454.79
Total Funds Remaining: $2685.28
Cash: $1050.04
Gift Cards: $1635.24

The Clemses had another saying: *Make the table's centerpiece so extravagant no one notices the plastic forks.*

When the Brontës and I arrived in Fort Morgan, Colorado the next evening, we were no longer Sasha Beth Clems and three yorkies. Instead, I was a redheaded girl with freckles, heavy eye makeup, and henna tattoos wearing a red maternity miniskirt. The Brontës had horribly uneven buzz cuts that I'd covered with little blue sweaters and were riding in a single small carrier with a massive "It's a Chihuahua Thing" sticker on the outside. Our disguises were most excellent.

"Goodbye, Dr. Trent," I said with an awkward pat on the car's hood as I hefted the Brontës' carrier. "Thank you for getting us this far. Hopefully, you get home quick. Tell Grandma George the gun came in useful." I'd left the lighter-gun in the glovebox. Any kind of weapon, even fake, seemed a bad idea on public transportation.

The Fort Morgan station was one lone building, like something out of an old Western movie. Several people stood under floodlights near the tracks. I eyed them to make sure none were overly attractive. They weren't, so I stepped to the side of the building, into the shadows, to wait.

I put the dog carrier down and grabbed my phone to get the e-ticket ready and set a countdown timer for 180 seconds, the amount of time the internet said Amtrak trains stopped for boarding.

The Brontës fussed in their carrier, squirming and pushing their little black nose through the air holes. Someone gave a long stream of yaps.

I had a plan for this and crouched down, which wasn't easy to do with the belly and short skirt. (While miniskirts weren't really my thing, I could totally pull it off. Runner's legs and all.)

"Shhh . . . work with me here. Just be quiet for like ten minutes. Please? Pretty please? No one can know there are three of you." I shoved a handful of doggie treats through the air holes.

The ground quivered and the air rumbled with the sound of the approaching train. This had better work. My stomach churned with the sheer volume of potential disasters ahead of us. I dumped half the doggie treats into the carrier.

The moment the train came to a screeching, groaning halt, I started the phone's timer and picked up the carrier. Plan was to wait until the last twenty seconds so the conductor couldn't do a close inspection of the carrier.

The train door slid open and a woman in a blue uniform stepped down. She had a ticket reader in her hand and a grouchy expression on her face. Not reassuring.

One-hundred-sixty seconds. Emily yapped excitedly.

"Go eat your doggie treats."

The conductor scanned the other passengers' tickets and let them board. She seemed an efficient, no-nonsense type.

One-hundred-two seconds.

Once everyone was onboard, the conductor glanced around and then turned as if to leave. Early.

No.

I jumped forward. "I'm here. Don't leave without me."

"Hello, mate."

The words came from a dark corner to my left. I near leaped out of my skin.

Jedda stepped forward. Like me, she wore a costume—baggy jeans, a Colorado Rockies baseball jersey, and a safari-like green hat. None of which hid her overwhelming beauty.

I panicked. Then I got angry. This was not happening. *This* was not what was supposed to go wrong. Not her. Not now.

"I ditched you." (Eighty-five seconds and counting.)

"Dirty thing, that," she said, conversationally. "I had to walk four hours to find a bloke to lend me a mobile. Do you know how much of Colorado is just open fields?"

"You boarding?" the conductor called, sounding pissy.

"Yes," I yelled back.

Jedda grabbed me by the arm, but I ripped free and bulldozed past her, dog carrier first. Even if she followed me aboard, I was better off on that train than here, alone, with her.

"Sasha Clems," she said, sounding deeply Australian and deeply disgusted, "you're being a flaming idiot."

I kept marching toward the conductor. "From the moment we met, you lied to me. I'm guessing you're still lying. All this friendliness is fake. You can cut it."

Jedda grabbed me a second time, right as I arrived at the open door of the train. "Give us a moment," she said sweetly to the conductor. Then she turned back to me. "I barely lied. I really do like you. I'm here to help."

"Trains wait for no one," the conductor announced as if reciting a well-known adage.

I tried to hold up my phone for the conductor to scan but Jedda jerked my arm backward nearly making me drop it. (Thirty-five seconds and counting.)

The train's horn hooted. Jedda and I both jumped. I wrenched free of her. The conductor scanned the e-ticket and then nodded me impatiently forward without glancing at the dog carrier. "You got a ticket?" she asked Jedda.

"No," Jedda replied. Hope rose in my throat that this might all work out after all. "But," Jedda continued, "I'll buy one online from my seat."

My hope died. "Please, don't let her," I begged the conductor. "She's stalking me."

The conductor started to reply, but one of the Brontës took that moment to begin wildly yapping. Emily. An excited, I-love-you-bark aimed at Jedda. Shoot. A second Brontë joined her. Charlotte. Not now.

The conductor snapped her arm up, blocking me from climbing onto the train. "How many dogs you have in there?"

"I . . ." Then it hit me. The perfect answer. "It's my service dog, and her puppy who is in training."

The conductor leaned over to look in the air vents. I prayed that in the low light all she saw was the blue of their outfits and not that the Brontës were wearing mini turtlenecks with embroidered collars rather than service vests. And, err . . . wished I'd thought of the service dog angle earlier. I totally would've bought fake jackets. (Yes, I realized it was morally wrong to impersonate a service dog. No, at that exact moment, I didn't care. Once I'd sold the Semis, I'd make a donation to a service dog foundation to make up for it.)

The conductor peered harder. "I don't think Chihuahuas are usually—"

"I have anxiety," I said, speaking even faster. "About trains. And going too fast. And other people. And stalkers. Makes me vomit in public places."

The alarm on my countdown timer went off.

"She's lying," Jedda said with a scoff. "She's the least anxious person on the planet."

Little did she know.

The horn on the train sounded again as if the engineer was trying to hurry us along.

"Fine," the conductor said.

It took me several racing heartbeats to realize she spoke to me and not Jedda. I nearly sagged with relief. Then I jumped on the train. Jedda tried to follow, but the conductor put her arm out again. "No stalkers allowed."

Emily was so worked up from seeing Jedda that I spent the first hour fighting to keep her quiet while also sending apologetic looks to everyone around us and worrying about Jedda.

There were three ways Jedda could've found me: through Ant somehow, through the gift card purchase of my e-ticket somehow, or through a spell on Dr. Trent somehow. Well, perhaps there was a fourth: a spell on me somehow.

My bet was on Dr. Trent. (And, err . . . hope.)

Nor were we safe now. If I were Jedda, I'd race out of Fort Morgan as fast as possible to beat the train to its next stop.

When we made that stop, I peered anxiously out the window at the passengers waiting to board. No sign of her. Phew. One more stop before Lincoln.

Right as the train lurched forward again, I heard the sudden trickling of a very small dog emptying a very full bladder onto a pee pad. The sour odor of it hit me long before the sound stopped.

Now this was the kind of problem I could handle.

I lugged the carrier of dogs into a claustrophobically small loo. The moment I opened the carrier door, the dogs rushed out, straight for the toilet. I slammed the lid down just in time. Gross.

I quickly swapped out the dirtied pee pad, watered the dogs from my own water bottle, and played a miniature game of fetch to wear them out. When we exited the bathroom, the dogs back in their carrier, a tall guy with bushy sideburns stood just outside. "All yours," I said.

"Five hundred to go back in."

Sheesh. "I'm *not* riding in the bathroom. The dogs aren't that noisy and I cleaned up the smell right away." (Okay, Emily was pretty noisy.)

The guy cocked his head and scrunched up his face, super-confused. "I meant with me?"

Long pause as it dawned on me what he meant. "Oh, gross. Gross, gross. No. Just no. Eww. This is *worse* than toilet water. I'm pregnant. Have some respect, dude."

"I—"

"Conductor," I yelled loudly and determinedly, "I've got another stalker." As if to assist, all three dogs broke out in yaps.

The guy turned bright red and ducked in the other direction.

Apparently, there was a downside to my outfit. Really, though, when it came down to it, and if I forced myself to look past the gross-gross-eww factor, the dollar amount could be seen as a form of flattery. Even more, he hadn't recognized me.

I hurried back to my seat, keeping an eye out for anyone else who might take my appearance the wrong way. (There were no Clems-isms for this situation.)

The Brontës squirmed and circled in their carrier, little tails thumping the sides and each other. Back at our seat, I did a quick scan to make sure none of my fellow passengers were paying attention and then pulled

Emily out to sit on my lap as she seemed to be the instigator. That worked until I fell asleep and woke to the feel of the train slowing and no Emily.

Great.

A quick glance out the window showed a large, well-lit train station. Maybe a dozen people were waiting to board although none were Jedda, thank goodness. I went to hunt Emily.

I spotted her almost immediately, curled up in the lap of a dead-asleep woman. Emily looked me right in the eye, her muzzle cocked and the tip of her tongue lolling out between her teeth.

"Emily, come," I whispered.

She dove for the floor. Her host didn't stir.

"Ummm," a voice called from the front of the train car. "Is someone missing a dog?"

Sheesh, Emily was fast.

Twenty minutes later, the conductor, two other passengers, and I cornered her in the baggage storage nook. The very unhappy conductor followed us back to our seats. "Amtrak Services Standards Manual Section 4-14, *Pets must remain inside carrier at all times. Pets are not permitted on seats. Pet must be odorless and harmless, not disruptive, and require no attention during travel.*"

"I'm so sorry," I said for the ten thousandth time. "We'll get off at the next stop." Which was conveniently Lincoln, Nebraska.

The conductor glared, but there wasn't much else she could do. Not so Emily. When I shoved her back into the carrier, she dribbled pee all over my hand and then yapped for ten minutes straight.

Chapter Fifteen

I left the Amtrak train certain of two things. First, public transportation wasn't going to work with the dogs. Second, I either had to get my hands on another vehicle or find a safe place to leave the Brontës. In other words, my next step was to talk Ant's friend into loaning me his car.

After a quick check to make sure neither Jedda nor anyone else beautiful was hanging around, I headed to the station's restroom. I sent a quick message to Ant's server letting him know that my trip had been uneventful. Haha. Then I toned down my makeup and moved the Semis from the pregnancy belly to my duffel. No need to give my disguise away, and removing the belly allowed me to pull down my miniskirt some.

Once done, I headed out to the street to meet Ant's friend.

A twelve-year-old-ish boy with brown hair and acne leaned against a streetlight, looking eagerly in my direction. He wore a T-shirt that read "Obnoxious!" in upside-down letters and held the torn top of a pizza box with the name "Christine Stickles" written in thick black ink.

"You've got to be kidding me." I walked over. "Please tell me you're old enough to drive."

The boy turned bright red. That I could see this in the hazy, yellow, four a.m. lighting seemed a bad sign. Only Ant would end up friends with an anti-establishment, activist, online influencer *whom he'd even met in person* without bothering to make note of the person's entirely inappropriate age. Seriously, Ant?

The kid shoved his hand forward. "Matthew Cronkowski at your service, *My Dearest Lady*. Call me Cronk. Everyone important does."

I looked at his hand without taking it. "Where's your car?"

Cronk turned his offered handshake into an awkward reach-for-the-sky stretch. "Fritzie's on his way."

"Fritzie? Didn't Ant swear you to secrecy?"

"Relax, *My Love*. Fritzie's my producer. We need him for the interview. Besides, Fritzie's got his license already and his parents are out of town. We borrowed his mom's minivan."

I groaned. I couldn't help it. Ant was so, so, so dead.

Plus, there went my hope of a loaner.

Cronk frowned back at me. "It's a high-end vehicle. Leather interior. Bose sound system. Heated seats. You'll like it. If you can put up with the stench of capitalism, that is."

I groaned again right as a maroon minivan pulled up next to us and an Asian version of Cronk got out. His T-shirt had a picture of a German Shepherd with a bone hanging from its mouth and read, "If you can't find this humerus, I don't want to be your friend."

"Ryan Sugimoto," he said with a head nod that he wasn't old enough to pull off. "Wus' up?"

"Call him Fritzie, *Lady Love*," Cronk added, opening the sliding door of the minivan for me.

"Call me anything but *Lady Love*." I climbed in only for lack of other options.

The interior of the minivan had been rigged with wires and what appeared to be six webcams evenly spaced around the ceiling. "Excuse you, didn't Ant say no video or photos? It's audio or nothing. Remove the cameras or I'm done here." (Liar.)

Fritzie looked down his nose at me. "Duh. The cameras face outward. You didn't actually think we'd travel without a security setup, did you?"

I glanced at the cameras again. They were indeed turned to face the windows. My mistake. "Just being careful."

"Of course *Our Lovely Lady* is careful," Cronk said and slammed the side door closed.

"Don't call me that either," I yelled back loud enough to make sure he heard.

He got in the passenger seat. "How about *Dearest Ducky*?"

Gag. Now he was being intentionally irritating, which for some reason eased *my* irritation. "How about just Christine?"

"Boring," Fritzie deadpanned, taking the driver's seat.

They were starting to grow on me.

I let the dogs out to explore and leaned back to get comfortable. It was still dark outside, I bled exhaustion, and the minivan's seat heaters were on. I needed sleep.

"So, *Christine . . .*" Cronk used special emphasis on the name and then shined his cell light right into my eyes. "You ready to start the interview?"

I tried to swat the phone away, but he pulled it to safety before I could connect. "It's my bedtime."

"No way. Antony promised we could have as much of an interview as we wanted, and I want the full drive to Chicago."

Yet another thing to murder Ant over. "I'll give you one hour. Then I need to sleep. Like really, really need to sleep. Your interview will be worthless if I get to Chicago and promptly get caught because I'm too tired to think straight."

"Seven hours of interview," Cronk said. "The drive will take eight so you'll still have time for a nap at the end."

"Two hours," I replied back. "I need to full-on crash, not nap."

"Seven-hour interview," Fritzie said from the driver's seat, "And I'll use my mom's credit card to buy you twenty-four hours at a Hilton."

"Won't your mom notice?" Not that someone else paying wasn't appealing. Plus, with borrowing the car not an option, I'd need some time to figure out what to do next.

Fritzie made a rolling, shaking motion with his head, a clear sign of disdain. "It's just a credit card charge. It goes to her office, and as long as it's a Hilton, no one will question it."

"She's a total *cappie*," Cronk said.

"She's embarrassing," Fritzie agreed. "But easy to steal from. You'll take the deal?"

I rubbed at my forehead, pretending to consider. "Seven hours is a *lot* of talking. I'll give you three."

"Six-and-a-half," Fritzie said, "I'll put our gas on my mom's credit card, too, so you won't have to reimburse us."

Nice. Also, Fritzie had clearly figured out my weakness.

I was still too me to give in. "Six hours, but I get to sleep first. Your mom pays for the hotel room, fuel, two meals along the way, and whatever dog food they sell at gas stations."

The boys glanced at each other.

"Sold," Cronk yelled, making a fist bump to the sky.

Yeah, they were kinda great.

***

After my sleep but prior to starting the interview, I insisted that Cronk and I get the Hilton taken care of. We found a business-traveler-type place that would be unremarkable to his mom's accountant and was in walking distance of Chicago's commuter train system. Only problem, it didn't allow dogs. I had an idea on that, though.

The interview itself wasn't nearly as bad as it could've been. No, I didn't tell Cronk and Fritzie the full truth. I left out Ari and the Dreamscape along with any details that might get my various family members in trouble. Yes, Cronk and Fritzie tried to dig extras out of me, but I was a better liar than they were interviewers.

The boys were quite Clems-like really, hard to dislike in that sense. Plus, Cronk was acing Calculus at a local community college on top of his high school classes, and he'd donated a third of his ad revenue to a charity that helped people prepare for a zombie invasion. (And other more realistic emergencies too.)

Fritzie had a golden doodle, three cats, and a pair of life-bonded African Gray parrots and was aiming to be his class valedictorian and the CEO of the ASPCA someday. Impressive!

"So, guys," I said a full eight hours later. The words scratched against my worn-out throat, but our destination Hilton was only a couple miles away. There was one more thing of utmost, if also deeply upsetting, importance we needed to discuss. "I might be able to do you one better than just the audio interview."

Cronk swiveled around in his seat to peer eagerly at me. "You change your mind about photos?"

"Not that. Too risky. However, you'll like this. It'll solve the problem of anyone thinking the recording of me is fake."

Fritzie jerked straight in the driver's seat. "I. Did. Not. Use AI for the Antifa interview. The guy who started that rumor is a troll."

I patted Fritzie on the shoulder reassuringly. "I wasn't thinking that. More that you guys getting proof and me making traveling on public transportation easier might be a twofer."

The boys gave each other a look. Cronk wet his lips, a cannily interested look in his eye. "What did you have in mind?"

I spotted a giant Hilton sign. "How about you return the dogs to their owner for me? No one could deny the interview was real if you had them." I kept my tone light, but something sick settled in my belly. Betrayal.

"Hell, yeah," Cronk said and did a fist punch toward the roof of the minivan again.

"I love dogs," Fritzie said, which I already knew and had given me the idea. "Plus," he continued, "we could film them, right? The dogs will be our storyline for the series. We make them the protagonists. It wouldn't even be hard to pull off since you talk about them so much. And then, best series finale ever, we livestream their reunion with their owner."

"That would be amazing," I said, faking excitement. Mrs. Lee was bound to be dramatic either way.

"I could—" Cronk started.

"Duck," Fritzie screamed.

Cronk hit the floorboards in a trained-military-personnel, I've-prac-ticed-this-before maneuver.

I stayed in place. Other than Fritzie's yelling, nothing had happened, and there were no waddling poultry present. "What's going on?"

Then I saw it. A stretch limo parked under the Hilton's front portico. A group of five overdressed people stood next to it. One of them had dark skin, shiny princess curls, and wore white platform go-go boots and a pink, fluffy tulle skirt. (Of course, it was Jedda. Of course, she looked great in the outfit.)

Adrenaline flooded my body, and I dove sideways. My seatbelt locked and caught me halfway. The Brontës jerked awake and Charlotte yapped in complaint.

"*Glowies?*" Cronk yelled from his spot on the floor.

"Magic-handlers." I unlocked my seatbelt and dropped down as low as I could get, pulling the dogs off their seat to join me. My hands shook. "Just keep driving. And don't do anything too obvious. We don't want to attract their attention."

"Duh," Fritzie said, enjoying himself.

We drove several miles and stopped behind an apartment complex. "Let's see what the cameras picked up," Fritzie said.

"I told you cameras were a good idea," Cronk said as Fritzie pulled out a silver laptop.

"The cameras were my idea." Fritzie brought up a picture of the Hilton on the laptop screen. It showed exactly what I'd seen before—limo, five magic-handlers, one of them Jedda.

"That's the hottest girl I've ever seen," Cronk said all awestruck.

"Trust me, she's a nightmare."

"Keep talking," Fritzie said, nudging me with this elbow. "I want an entire episode out of this. The tension in your voice is amazing." Annie crawled into his lap and licked him on the chin approvingly. Blech.

I sighed and did as he'd asked. "Only a magic-handler would have the audacity to wear haute couture to a kidnapping sting. Jedda Jacobs is no friend of mine." I paused. "Even if the dogs like her." (I wasn't against helping Cronk and Fritzie with the plot of their series if I could.)

Cronk gave me a thumbs-up. "I don't know that it's a sting, though. They weren't trying to hide."

Fritzie shrugged and scratched Annie's belly. "We could do a second drive-by to see what they're up to. Maybe cruise the parking lot. More footage for the series as well." He said the last with a lingering tone.

"Yeah, no." I wasn't that helpful. "More importantly, how did they find us?" It couldn't have been Dr. Trent this time. Nor my borrowed cell-phone. I'd removed the battery back in Nebraska, just to be safe.

"It wasn't us," Cronk said. "We haven't told a soul."

"I know that." Even apart from the fact that I liked them, they'd get more publicity with me still on the run.

"It's likely to be a tracker," Fritzie said.

"Maybe they're working with the Feds," Cronk suggested.

"Magic-handlers hate all things governmental." I picked up Charlotte and put her next to Emily who circled unhappily in my lap. She seemed worried. (Or I felt worried, one or the other.) "It could be a spell."

Cronk and Fritzie glanced at each other. "Or," Cronk said, shaking his head, "they got the minivan's license plate off the security camera at the train station. Once they had Fritzie's mom's name, they hacked her credit card and found the Hilton reservation."

"That's what I would've done if I had their resources," Fritzie agreed. "Totally straightforward."

A spell seemed much more straightforward.

The thought of a spell also made me feel like grabbing the dogs and curling up on the floor again. How did I fight a spell?

The only person I knew who had even a hope of answering that for me was Ari.

Yeah, not going there.

Besides, I didn't know for sure that it was a spell. It totally could've been the cameras/minivan/credit card scenario. I *wanted* it to be the cameras/minivan/credit card.

"Now what?" Fritzie asked.

"I don't know." I really didn't.

"Shopping," Cronk said. "You need a better disguise before we drop you off. Fritzie, *my man*, drive north until we hit a mall. Sasha, *my love*, you'd better take another nap. Things may get crazy when we're no longer here to protect you, and I want you well-rested."

"Works for me." Sometimes it was nice to have someone else take charge.

***

I did sleep. Surprisingly. One would've thought I'd be too worried about Jedda and the other magic-handlers to do so or too suspicious of what Cronk and Fritzie would dream up if not watched or too distraught at knowing I had no choice but to leave the dogs (which I was), but I was also just that tired.

I only woke when Cronk made a loud armpit fart right in my face. I backhanded him across the chest as an automatic reflex, barely missing Annie who he held in his arms. "Shoot, sorry." (This wasn't a new reflex. Ant had always found it funny to startle me out of sleep too.)

Cronk smirked. "No worries."

"Where are we?" I pushed Cronk backward out of my space and sat upright. We were in the parking lot of a shopping mall. Both boys stood together in the open door of the minivan, looking pleased with themselves. Fritzie held Charlotte and Emily.

"We have it all figured out," Cronk said. "Shopping first. Then you have a 2.7-mile bus ride to the Metra commuter line." He held up a printed-out train map highlighted with yellow zigzags.

I pushed my way out of the minivan, forcing them to back up even more. "Where did you get the map from?"

Fritzie cuddled the dogs closer to his chest as if worried I might take them from him. "My mom keeps a port-a-printer under the passenger seat."

"Convenient."

"Entitled," Cronk said and shoved the paper into my hands so I had to take it. Then he gave me a second one. "The Metra train will take you to downtown Chicago. From there you grab a bus," he handed me another paper, "to Union Station. However, the distance is also walkable." He handed me a fourth paper. "Amtrak leaves from Union Station, so once there you can go to pretty much anywhere on the planet."

"Or the country at least," Fritzie said.

Cronk handed me a sheaf of papers that appeared to be a list of Amtrak routes and boarding times. "Well done, right?" He gave me a pleased look. Almost too pleased. Victoriously pleased even.

Suspiciously pleased.

I narrowed my eyes at first Cronk, then Fritzie. Emily squirmed trying to get Fritzie to loosen his grip.

Then it hit me.

I handed the stack of papers back. "Holy Huskydoodle, you set me up."

Cronk shook his head back and forth. "No. We didn't. We wouldn't do that."

I rolled my eyes. "Not with the magic-handlers. I didn't mean that. Duh. For the dogs. You liked my idea of letting you take the Brontës. So you set things up so that I had no choice but to leave them."

Both boys looked suddenly anywhere but at me. Fritzie took another step backward with Emily and Charlotte.

Nailed it. And again, so Clems-like. I pointed a finger at Cronk. "Caught you."

"It was your idea," he said. "You're the one who suggested we use the dogs in the series."

"No, I didn't."

"Yes, you did." He raised his voice, sounding even more sure of himself.

"No, I didn't."

"Yes, you did."

"No. I didn't. I suggested that—" I stopped. He was trying to distract me. Successfully even.

The thing was, though . . .

When it came down to it, dropping me in who-knows-where-sub-urbia and making me take a slow route to downtown Chicago worked in my favor. No way would Jedda or any other magic-handler anticipate it. Nor would they expect me to have Amtrak as my goal considering that I'd just gotten off of it that morning.

Which gave me another idea on how to lose the magic-handlers if they were indeed following the cameras/minivan/credit card scenario. "I'll make you a deal. You take the dogs and drive north. Use your mom's credit card to buy gas and more dog food along the way so that the magic-handlers follow you rather than me. In exchange, I'll not only let you take the dogs, but I'll let you film a brief, bad-ly-lit-to-hide-my-hair-color video of me saying goodbye to them. You can use it for the opening sequence of the series. It's likely to be a hugely emotional and gripping moment."

Cronk perked up. "And maybe if the magic-handlers chase after us, we'll get more footage of that hot girl!"

Gag. "Yeah, maybe that too."

"Duh," Fritzie said, turning Emily away from me and into his chest.

***

I walked into the mall with puffy eyes, a runny nose, and two red welts on my neck that if they'd been farther apart would've made me look like I'd tangled with a vampire instead of a small dog. Goodbyes were hard. Charlotte was resentful, and I didn't handle guilt well.

It was still the right thing to do.

I found a maternity store with a discount section to console myself and an hour later left the mall having changed into the first of my three new outfits: Blue/green camouflage leggings, matching ballcap, and a white tee that read "Brought to you courtesy of a US Soldier." I'd also bought a pair of oversized sunglasses, and in a brilliant move that I wished I'd thought of earlier, a cheapo, chin-length "celebrity" wig in curly black.

I decided to walk rather than take the bus to save money. I found the train station right where Cronk had marked on the map, and since I was headed into downtown Chicago, I used the train's wi-fi to google directions to Pelaratti's Pizza. It'd been showcased on Gramps's favorite foodie show a couple of months ago and had looked amazing. Total financial splurge, but I'd always found pizza to be emotionally consoling. (I hadn't been able to force myself to eat any of the gas station crap offered by Cronk and Fritzie.)

Even apart from guilt over abandoning the dogs, I hated being so alone. I was fine alone when running or something like that but otherwise really, really liked having other people around. Grandma George had once said that it was probably because I'd spent so much of my childhood alone during the rough years after my mom left and while my dad was incarcerated. Being entirely on my own left me feeling unanchored, adrift.

I found Pelaratti's on the street-floor of a rundown building with a metal fire escape stairwell coming down the front. Too cool. The foodie had said this place could get crazy busy in the evenings, with lines down the street, but it was early and seemed quiet now.

I went in. The inside was all aging neon signs, red leather booths, and the most unbelievable smell of rising yeast, tomatoes, and cheese. A waitress in a checkered apron and matching kerchief greeted me.

"I'll take one of everything."

"Yeah, sure. Whatever." She gave me a been-here-before, side-eye look.

"You get that a lot?"

"And aren't you original."

I followed her to a booth and took a seat. More than enough space for me and three dogs. If I'd had three dogs that was, which I didn't. I swallowed past a thick lump in my throat. Fritzie had better remember to put on their coats when the sun went down.

I ordered a super veggie, super deep-dish pizza.

"You know that's meant to feed four, right?" the waitress said.

We'd be four if the Brontës were here. "I'll take a doggie bag."

She sniffed and left. I pulled out the Amtrak map and used the wi-fi to google leave times. The news on that wasn't good. The closest I could get to Eastern Canada was Boston. The next direct train to Boston didn't leave until Monday evening. It was Saturday.

There was a train to North Carolina that left Sunday late night and a train to Missouri that left Sunday dinnertime, but neither was the right direction. "Stupid magic-handlers," I muttered. "Why are you making this so hard?"

"You say something?" The waitress reappeared with what had to be the most gorgeous-looking pizza I'd ever seen balanced on a tray. The edge was crusty and just a tad crumbled. The tomatoes steamed and the whole thing was so thick that I just knew it would be bursting with all the mushrooms, olives, spinach, peppers, and broccoli promised on the menu.

"Uh, nothing," I said to the waitress, wholly focused on my meal.

She sighed dramatically. "Anything else?"

"I'm good."

She left. I grabbed the fork and knife to dig in. The smells exploded as I cut, the crust flaking. I raised a forkful to my mouth.

A black stretch limo pulled up outside the front window.

My frontal lobe throbbed. "Seriously?"

Then again, Gramps's foodie had said this place was known for attracting CEOs, megastars, and influencers. A limo didn't have to mean a magic-handler. I kept one hand on my belongings and lifted the fork a second time.

The limo door cracked open and a white go-go boot slipped out followed by brown legs and pink tulle.

The throbbing spread to the rest of my brain. "Again?"

I shoved out of the booth, grabbing the entire pizza at the last moment since an unattended full meal was a dead giveaway someone had just fled. I needed to buy myself as much time as possible.

Literally, buy.

I found the waitress in the kitchen. "You can't be back here," she said.

"Fifty-dollar tip if you'll let me out the back door unseen." Hopefully, there was a back door. "Please?"

"I—What?" the waitress's face scrunched in confusion.

I grabbed a wad of cash I'd stuffed into the front of my duffel and handed it to her along with the pizza. A cook came from around the corner. The backdoor must be there somewhere. (Hopefully.)

"Hey, what's going—" he started.

I pushed past him. "Paparazzi out front. Please help me. I'm B-list trying to get on a reality show. My agent will kill me if anyone finds out I'm pregnant. You have to help."

"Again?" the cook muttered and showed me out the back. Hopefully, I hadn't tipped the waitress too much.

Chapter Sixteen

Total Spent: $2168.99
Total Funds Remaining: $1971.08
Cash: $690.00
(I gave the waitress $340.00 and must have dropped my coins on the floor in doing so. Sigh.)
Gift Cards: $1281.08

Jedda had put a spell on me.

Had to be. Nothing else fit.

I rushed-walked out the back of the restaurant in the opposite direction of the limo. From there, I turned toward the overly tall buildings of downtown Chicago while scanning every person and vehicle. I saw nothing suspicious and no one followed me. At least Jedda wasn't hard to lose.

But at this rate, it was just a matter of time before she caught me. Nor would Ant be of assistance this time around. Which left me one option. An option I hated, didn't want to think about, refused to consider.

No way was I contacting Ari to ask him how to beat Jedda's spell. He wasn't on my side. He was a toad, a wretch, a snood. He was also likely to tell me what I wanted to know. He'd been forthcoming so far and it wouldn't be hard to Dreamscape with him and then immediately leave wherever I was so that I'd be long gone before Mrs. Valenzuela showed up.

No.

I mean, yes. I had zero other options.

No. The Brontës would agree if they were here. I pictured Charlotte snarling at him and Emily turning her back. (Annie would immediately forgive him.)

Yes. Contacting Ari was the practical thing to do.

"No," I said aloud as I walked.

***

I fell into Dreamscape-land immediately. My sleeping self rested on a bunk bed in a hostel that I'd stumbled upon and decided would suit my purposes. In other words, it was cheap. The moment I had what I needed from Ari, I was out of there.

My dream self sat cross-legged on the front deck of Dennis the Menace Park's boat-shaped jungle gym.

Ari stood in front of me on the sand, his arms crossed over his chest, his eyes narrowed. "I thought I told you—"

I waved my hand at him, cutting him off. "Yeah, yeah. No time for lecturing. I've already been found, which is what I need to talk to you about. And don't worry, I'm still pissed at you. But I need something and I'm reasonably sure you'll tell me the truth, so I'm holding my pissiness aside for the moment."

He frowned, opened his mouth as if to say something, then closed it. When he finally spoke, his voice had lost its irritation. "I liked your hair better before."

I'd removed the wig, so he meant the red which I hadn't had time to wash out. Snood of him to point it out. I stood up so that our heights weren't so unequal. His attention went straight to my swollen-looking abdomen. Crap. Apparently, a dream version of the Semis had come along. "No comments. None. Zip. Nada. We clear?"

He did a little half-quirk of his lips, and my heart went wild in response.

"I don't have much time, so listen up. Jedda Jacobs can track me somehow. She found me back in California. She found me in Colorado and twice in Illinois. She isn't visiting me in dreams, so she isn't using the same method as you. Do you know how she's doing it?"

Ari straightened in interest. "Did she touch you?"

"Touch me? Probably. Does that matter?"

"Most magic-spells require the handler to have physical contact with the subject before being cast."

"She didn't touch me prior to Bakersfield. She claimed Bob told her where to go, but she's lying. Although he's tracking me somehow too."

"So it could or could not require physical contact then." Ari pursed his lips looking thoughtful, like someone who enjoyed pondering a difficult problem in the way super-smart people did. "Robert Quan is a bit of an enigma," he finally said. "I've been unable to learn much about him, and I'm an exceptionally good researcher. The thing about finding or tracking spells, though, is that they aren't terribly useful. They almost always seek to create a straight line between the handler and the subject, which with the earth being spherical is problematic over distances; the spell wants to go through the earth rather than curve around it. Then the second problem is that unless you create a spellbook specific to the person you are trying to find, the spell gets easily confused and tends to lead the handler to the most famous person with a similar name."

"So Sasha Obama?"

"Sasha Baron Cohen would be more likely. Spells like matching initials."

I snort-laughed, imagining what a bunch of magic-handlers showing up on either doorstep would look like. "Enough distracting me. Somehow Jedda is doing it anyway. As are you."

"That's not how my spell works, though, and mine is unique." He seemed to think about it. "The Australians' most powerful spellbook was created to convince the European settlers to leave." His voice took on some momentum. "The original spell wasn't successful, but it backfired into an exceptionally good Intentions Spell. My best guess would be that Jedda's using that. If I'm right, the spell wouldn't manifest your current location but rather your intentions for the future. The stronger your intentions, the easier it is for her to know where you'll be. Or at least that's my guess. And, of course, the spell would be more effective if you were a descendant of the original settlers."

"I'm not." The rest fit, though. I'd spent so much time planning and preparing to get myself and the dogs to Fort Morgan, where Jedda had shown up. Then, Cronk and I had discussed at length our choice of Hiltons, and I'd specifically picked the pizza place because of the foodie. My stopping in Bakersfield had been more of a whim, though, so maybe she'd told the truth about finding me there accidentally.

My good mood evaporated. How was I supposed to travel without planning my route? "To hide from her, I have to not think about where I want to go?"

"It would be even better if you just didn't know."

***

Step One of Brilliant Plan for Leaving Chicago and Beating Jedda's Spell: After leaving the hostel, I found a hotel down the street that I hadn't known existed before showing up on its front entry. (Downside, I had to drop $175 (plus tax) for a room.)

Step Two: I spent the night planning out in exact detail how to take Amtrak south to Missouri. I studied a map. I looked at photos and watched YouTube videos of the Chicago Amtrak Station. I booked a ticket for the following evening. (Turns out tomorrow was Easter Sunday, which I had totally forgotten about but explained the lack of departing trains.)

Step Three: Come morning, I changed into my next maternity outfit, a *Little House* get-up (prairie dress, straw hat). I stole a hotel pillow to stuff under the dress, making me look less pregnant and more like I'd gained a few pounds. I wrapped a stolen hotel blanket around my shoulders, put the wig on at an intentionally crooked angle, and headed out the door prepared to impersonate the destitute. I figured that if anyone looked my direction, I'd talk to myself and gesture toward the sky. Nicholas would be royally offended at this, but it was a great disguise. I made a mental promise to donate to the Chicago Homeless Shelter once I'd cashed in on the Semis to make up for it.

Step Four: I walked to the Amtrak Station, weirdly pausing every once in a while to glance around for the Brontës. I thought I heard Charlotte bark and Emily whine and my belly felt oddly light without them squirming around in a pocket. Several times I even spoke to them, and I kept worrying that they would get cold. I attempted to wipe out these thoughts by picturing my destination in as much detail as possible.

Step Five: I arrived across the street from the Greyhound Bus Station, which happened to be not far from the Amtrak Station. At near the same moment, a black, tinted-window towncar pulled to a stop in front of the entrance.

No.

Shoot.

Not again. (Apparently my clever plan wasn't all that clever after all.)

Panic seized me, brain and body. The building behind me was a storage facility with no doorways or pillars or anything to duck behind. No parked cars either. If I was about to get caught, at least Thank the Dog the Brontës were safe with Cronk and Fritzie.

I did the only thing I could. I headed to a trashcan chained up to a lightpole and pretended to root through it. It reeked of human barf.

I wanted to barf, and only somewhat because of the smell.

The passenger door of the towncar swung open. Rather than Jedda, two extremely handsome men in dark suits and with shiny gelled hair climbed out. One of them said something back to the driver that I was too far away to hear clearly but possibly was in Russian. Neither glanced in my direction. See? Nicholas was right. No one ever looked at the unhoused.

I might have a chance after all.

Both men headed toward the terminal. The glass door slid open and a stunningly gorgeous Indian woman exited. She wore a dark pantsuit with a vibrantly purple scarf around her shoulders. The three of them began what appeared to be a rather heated conversation, possibly in Italian. Still, no one looked in my direction.

Behind the woman, just inside the glass doors stood one more magic-handler. Male. Tall. Dark hair.

Red hoodie with a Redwood Tree on the front.

I panic-froze a second time. Our eyes met. I couldn't make out his expression, but no doubt it'd be knowing. Possibly even triumphant.

Traitor.

Ari was going to rat me out. I had mere seconds to come up with a way to stop him. I needed a lightning-flash brilliant idea. A plan. Something.

I got nothing.

He just stood there.

The glass doors slid closed, hiding Ari away. The two men returned to their towncar, and the woman took up residence just outside, her arms across her chest, one foot tapping as if impatiently waiting for the others to leave her territory.

Ari watched me through the glass. His gaze cut through the barriers and my costume. But he didn't come out.

Huh?

I slouch-walked to the next trashcan down the street as casually as possible.

I mean, I was grateful Ari hadn't turned me in. Really, really grateful. Sort of grateful. This did not mean I forgave him for holding out about the Dreamscape. Especially as it made no sense. I couldn't see how it benefited him to let me walk away with the Semis.

Also, where was Jedda? She'd shown up every other time I'd had a near-miss.

Did this mean it wasn't her spell nor Ari's spell that had found me this time but some other spell? Some unknown spell? Why hadn't Ari warned me about that?

Duh. Because he wasn't actually on my side regardless of what current circumstances looked like.

Agh!!!

I had no idea what to do next.

No.

Idea.

Which had the obvious advantage of not giving Jedda a way to track me.

I kept walking, checking trashcans, until I was a full block away. Then a second block. I took breaks in doorways and watched my surroundings while trying to appear like I wasn't. No one followed me, but rather than feeling better, fear gathered in my stomach. I had no way out of Chicago.

The buildings above me grew taller and swankier and a few more early morning walkers appeared, all heading in the same direction. I followed in an effort to blend. The buildings stopped abruptly at what appeared to be a city park along the edge of a body of water. One of the Great Lakes? My sense of Geography ended with the Rockies even when I was thinking clearly.

The street between me and the park was filled with cars and people and activity, again all heading in the same direction. Some kinda gathering. Considering the date, my guess was an Easter egg hunt. I straightened my wig-hat-combo and dropped the blanket in a doorway to look less homeless. (Which didn't count as littering as a real homeless person would find it, right?)

A bus disgorged a load of men and women dressed in colorful nylon shorts, wicking shirts with name-brand labels, and running shoes.

This wasn't an egg hunt.

It was a Race Day. (Or likely both.)

A slow smile spread over my face. A Race Day I could handle. Plus, it gave me an idea. Why not just run my way out of Chicago? Or even better, buy a bike? I could point myself east and pedal without any specific goal for Jedda to latch on to. (Or south then east because massive-body-of-water.)

There were downsides, starting with where I could buy a bike on Easter Sunday. Finances were an issue, too, as I'd have to pay retail.

In the meantime, I decided to change my outfit as my prairie-get-up wasn't either race-day or supportive-family attire. I went in search of a port-a-potty. Which sent me into a totally inappropriate fit of stress-giggling when I imagined Jedda's spell telling her that I was deeply in search of a loo.

The park itself was a typical huge multi-use place: lawns for sports, shade trees, tidily manicured borders and walkways. I found the port-a-potties and changed into my third outfit: jeggings (so grade-school), a fitted white pregnancy tee, and a blousy, drapey floral kimono thing. I ditched the wig and pillow and put the straw hat and sunglasses back on. Since no respectable eighteen-year-old would dress this way, I should look thirty at least.

From there, I meandered through the crowd as if searching for friends. Every time I got jostled or anyone glanced my way, I jumped a foot. A mom with a stroller and three kids complimented my hat, and I nearly bolted.

I was busy fake-cheering at the finish line when out of nowhere someone wrapped their arms around my waist, warm breath hitting the back of my neck. A very smooth, very male voice whispered into my ear. "Hey, there you are."

I screeched and jerked free, spinning to face the voice. "Whoa, excuse you, what the hell?" (Sorry, Grams.)

The guy jumped back just as fast. He was a total stranger, although a clichéd one with sun-bleached hair, sun-kissed skin, and sunny-day

Ray-Bans. "I'm so sorry. I thought you were my wife. She has a similar flower shirt and is wearing a hat."

I settled back down as several people were looking our direction. Was there something too attractive about this guy? I couldn't see his eyes behind his glasses, but he had an excellent jawline and immaculately tousled hair.

On the other hand, he wore a faded T-shirt, flip-flops, and khaki shorts so threadbare they had strings hanging from the legs. Not exactly magic-handler attire. I might be becoming a little paranoid.

Sue me.

"I'm really sorry," he said, backing away with his hands up as if both trying to prove his harmlessness and concerned I might be slightly unhinged. (Which wasn't that far off.)

Either way, the race was ending so it was time for me to leave in search of a big-box store that sold bikes. I let the guy go first so that I could head the opposite direction.

I'd walked the length of one of the grassy fields, when Mrs. Valenzuela stepped out from behind a bush, her emeralds gleaming at her neck. On her heels were the two Nordic gods that'd come by the movie theater and the Indian woman from the bus station.

No.

Not her. Not now. This could not be happening. (That phrase was becoming way too common in my life. Also, I hadn't yet recovered from my last scare.)

Adrenaline hit me like that first burst of water at a carwash. I bolted back the way I'd come, the Semis slamming against my middle with each step. I ignored it, pushing myself to top speed, glad I wore my running shoes.

I made it maybe fifty strides when three more magic-handlers came around a corner in front of me. The French lie-detector woman, an Asian man that looked like he might practice Sumo in his free time, and one of the Russians.

#@$%*! (That was the incoherent tangle of exclamations that both went through my head and managed to stay clean enough not to offend Grams.)

The car wash of adrenaline turned into Niagara Falls. I turned inland, cutting across the grass in the direction of the high-rises. Back to the street. Back the way I'd entered the park. Back somewhere other than here. As fast as I could run. The Semis slamming my torso with each step.

The closer I got to the street, the more people I had to dodge my way through. "You alright?" someone called out.

"Call 911," I yelled back, shoving my way around a large group.

"Race is over," an annoyed person hollered.

"Sore loser much?" a third person said.

A girl in rainbow tights pointed a phone in my direction. Great.

I made it to the street but there was too much traffic to cross. My breath heaved in my chest from not warming up. My hands clenched. I couldn't keep my feet still as I waited for the light to change. I bounced back and forth, flexing my knees and heels. So close, so close. If I could make it across the street, I had a chance.

A black van slammed to a stop directly in front of me. Before I could do more than note it, the side door flew open and two BIMD agents rushed out. Agent Thomas and Agent Silva, who'd both been at The Blue Castle after it'd been ransacked. They were dressed as if on SWAT maneuvers.

"Sasha," an accented female voice called to me from behind. Mrs. Valenzuela. She didn't even sound winded. (Magic? Had to be if I was winded.)

The two Nordics were coming at me from my right and left. I had maybe ten seconds to figure a way out.

"Five hundred," Mrs. Valenzuela said, "To end this right now." I heard the zeros of the millions clear as day.

Chapter Seventeen

I didn't trust government bureaucracies or agencies or whatever other names they had. My dad didn't and Gramps didn't and Ant didn't. Nicholas did, but only because he believed that societal problems couldn't be solved without societal interventions. Dad and Gramps always responded to him by pointing out that "government help" sounded good in political ads, but when it came down to it, government agencies' *real* priorities rarely assisted the regular guy (or girl).

I trusted Mrs. Valenzuela's priorities even less. Her offer wasn't tempting. I doubted it was real. More likely, she just wanted to slow me down, trap me without creating a scene, and steal the Semis.

I ran straight for Agent Thomas, who opened his huge arms and caught me as if I was a long-lost child. This wasn't comfortable as he had gadgets across his chest, on his shoulder, and around his waist. "Can you get me out of here?" I begged.

"Happy to help," he said, in his deep, resonating Darth Vader voice.

He hustled me into the van. Agent Silva followed. Agent Silva had been the guy to interview me back in The Blue Castle. He had a sharp military haircut and big smile. If he'd been employed elsewhere, I might have thought him friendly.

"Check her," Agent Thomas ordered as someone I couldn't see slammed the door shut. The van jerked forward, and I caught myself on a side railing to keep from falling. There was a screen barrier between us and the driver and no other windows. The whole place had the feeling of being stuck in a low-lit box.

Agent Silva moved my direction. "I'm really sorry about this," he said with an apologetic smirk that showed very white teeth. Then he patted me down.

I objected.

It didn't stop him.

But the weirdest thing happened.

Agent Silva didn't touch my belly, like, not at all. Since I hadn't previously been heavily pregnant, it was an odd omission.

Maybe he was wary of the Semis too?

"Nothing." Agent Silva stepped back against the far wall of the van.

"Sit," Agent Thomas barked in his Vader voice, and I did, sliding to the floor. Agent Thomas and Agent Silva both sat across from me, also on the floor. (One would've expected that BIMD could afford vans with seats.)

Agent Thomas put a cell to his ear and glanced at me. "Yeah, we hooked *Catfish.*"

Catfish? Was that the best they could come up with as a codename for me? "Actually," I pointed out, "*Catfish* swam right to you, no hook involved." Not the smartest thing to say, but my veins were a soup of blood, leftover adrenaline, and offended dignity.

Agent Thomas ignored me and continued his phone conversation. "Warn the upstairs that *Catfish* is going to make the news. Cells galore." He shot a glare in my direction as if it were my fault that everyone over the age of eight owned a phone. "No, she doesn't have *The Egg.* Our best guess is she handed it off to someone before we caught her or she hid it in the park. I've got guys searching."

I stared at him. Huh? Was he blind?

He gave me another look. "She ran from the handlers, so unlikely she gave it to them. Check to see if she has any family in the area."

The conversation went on like this for several minutes while I sat there confused. Finally, Agent Thomas put the phone down with a hard glare in my direction. "It'll go easier for you if you tell us where you hid it."

Agent Silva dropped a hand on my ankle as if trying to be comforting. He'd be the good cop to Agent Thomas's bad cop, of course. When he spoke, his voice softened, all kind and compassionate. "I know you're scared. I can't imagine what this last week has been like. We're here to protect you, Sasha. You and *The Egg*"

"*The Egg,*" I repeated back to give myself time to think. They didn't actually believe I was pregnant, did they?

I placed a hand on the hump of my fake belly to see what they'd do. When neither reacted, I tapped it several times. Still nothing. "Can I borrow your phone to call my dad?" My phone, along with my money, was tucked in the belly with the Semis, the belly that they seemed totally unaware of.

"We'll cut you a deal," Agent Thomas growled. "No prison time, no fine, no nothing, and a call to your dad, if you'll just tell us where it is."

They really, truly couldn't see it.

Which meant…?

Which meant the blond guy at the park must've done something. Spelled it.

Ugh. A massive family of oversized ants with sucker-feet metaphorically climbed from the back of my heels up my legs and my spine to my neck. I shuddered, and Agent Silva patted me on the ankle again and offered me a bottled water. I took it just to give my hands something to do other than curl.

Once again, I missed the dogs something fierce. I missed Annie licking my face, Emily expecting to be worshiped, Charlotte getting nippy when she'd had enough. Okay, maybe not the last. But I missed the comfort of them.

"Sasha?" Agent Silva asked, all concerned again. "Where's the Semis?"

When all else fails, blame the butler. "Jedda stole it."

They gave each other a look.

"Jedda . . . ?" Agent Silva said with a fake-puzzled tone to his voice as if he didn't recognize the name. Yeah, right.

"Jedda Jacobs," I said, going along with Agent Silva's fake ignorance. "She's Australian and a magic-handler. I picked her up in Bakersfield because she offered to help me, and then I left her in Colorado when her story stopped adding up, but she found me here. She must have a finding spell."

"Finding spells don't work," Agent Thomas ground out as if he were annoyed by that.

"That's what she said. Everyone keeps finding me anyway. Jedda was waiting for me at the Greyhound terminal. There were other magic-handlers there too. Two Eastern European guys and an Indian woman. Perhaps more, I don't know. I ran and then tried to blend in at the park, but she found me again. She did something. Another spell, I think. I didn't even notice it happen other than she touched me on the arm in a crowd of people. I took off running. It wasn't until I started seeing magic-handlers popping up everywhere that I realized my bowling-ball bag holding the Semis had disappeared."

"But if you no longer had the Semis," Agent Silva asked, "why did you run?"

"Duh. There were magic-handlers chasing me."

***

They drove me to a hotel where two more black vans were parked outside. I was hustled through a sidedoor by BIMD agents, up an elevator, and deposited into a hotel room. It was all very secure with zero opportunity to sneak away.

"Can I borrow someone's cell?" I asked. The room had no phone and I didn't dare take off the belly to free my own. Not without knowing how the Invisibility Spell worked or what would end it.

"Later." Agent Thomas sat me in a chair at a table and returned to speaking into his phone. "I don't care that it's Easter, brunch time, or the middle of someone's Sunday services, I need *The Team* online. And someone had better notify the Undersecretary—" He stopped abruptly and glanced my way. I was, of course, listening with total interest. "Contact the *Top Dog* and get us a plane to DC." Another pause. "Don't you tell me that. BIMD absolutely has the authority to call up a C-37."

Agent Silva cleared his throat, gave a meaningful look at Agent Thomas and then the door. "Perhaps it'd be better to take this outside?"

Agent Thomas glared at both of us, grunted and headed to the door, phone still to his ear. "There's got to be *someone* who's nonreligious."

"Sorry about that," Agent Silva said once we were alone.

I wasn't displeased. Any delay seemed a good thing, and I'd have a better chance of talking my way into borrowing a phone with just one of them here.

"Are you going to feed me?" (Truth: Dinner last night had been a vending machine raid. Breakfast had been a bagel from the hotel that had cost $7.99 without cream cheese. My food angle wasn't just about softening him up. I was starving.)

Agent Silva made a long-suffering sigh. "I'll call room service." He pulled a cell from his back pocket. Bingo.

Not long after, the hotel door opened and another BIMD agent brought in a rolling cart. Before the door slammed shut, I got a quick view of Agent Thomas pacing back and forth in the hallway.

Agent Silva stepped outside for a moment while the other agent set up three platters on the room's table and ushered me into the sole seat. Agent Silva returned before I'd even had time to lift the covers. He took a seat on the edge of the bed opposite me, leaning forward and clasping his hands between his knees, very friendly-like. "Looks like our travel is going to be delayed. We'll all be staying here tonight. Then in the morning we'll move you to DC until *The Egg* shows up. For your own safety."

I gave him a wide-eyed, innocent look. "Agent Thomas can't commandeer us a plane today?"

"Best not to bring that up in front of him." Agent Silva gave me a wry smirk as if he and I were on the same team against the ornery Agent Thomas. That worked too.

"Can I use your phone to call my dad now?" I put a bit of wobble in my voice.

"Agent Thomas called your dad."

Doubtful. "But I haven't."

"Yes, well . . ." Agent Silva didn't squirm. Guys like him just didn't, but he tilted away from me as if uncomfortable. As if he knew very well I should be allowed access to a phone.

I rubbed at my eyes, let my lower lip drop, and glanced down at the dishes in front of me in a forlorn way. "Thank you for the meal. I haven't eaten since yesterday morning."

"Anything you need."

I sniffed loudly. "Don't you have kids? Wouldn't you want them to call you if they were in trouble?"

"Twin boys. Thirteen years old. I'm on your side here, Sasha." He gave me a look that may have been pained. Hopefully, it was pained.

Even more perfect. I turned to the food not wanting to lay on my emotional manipulations too thick. My choices were meatballs and pasta, something dripping in a green sauce that looked Mexican, and a pretty standard all-American meatloaf dinner. "Why does BIMD want the Semis?" I asked. "Wouldn't you just have to sell it to the magic-handlers?"

He gave a chuckle. "BIMD's funding is bad right now, but not that bad."

I glanced up through my lashes as if I appreciated his attempt at humor and then turned my attention back to the food. The meatballs were a no. The Mexican dish was a possibility, although guaranteed it had chicken or pork or something inside, and I still felt called out by Jedda's vegetarian-hypocrisy comments. The potatoes on the meatloaf plate looked hand-mashed. It wasn't like I had to eat the meat.

"Are you trying to establish a price tag?" Agent Silva asked. "We heard Diamella's offer."

"A price tag?" That was unexpected. Nor did I want him seeing me as mercenary. I cleared my throat. "I care about the Semis itself. It's a national treasure, something that belongs to all of us. It should go to someone ethical." I tugged the plate with the potatoes closer to me.

"Smart girl."

"Yes," I agreed, collecting a napkin and placing it on my lap with one corner folded carefully away from me. "The magic-handlers are awful. I'd much rather anyone other than them have it. Especially Jedda Jacobs." I kept my voice entirely innocent, but hopefully not too innocent. Then I used my fork to create a line of empty space between the meat and everything else on the plate. The green beans had a crispy, fresh look to them. Yum.

Agent Silva abruptly stood and paced the short distance to the door and back as if agitated, an interesting change. I took a bite of potatoes to buy time before my next attack. They melted on my tongue, a mouthful of starchy, salty, pillowy goodness. My eyes went wide in enjoyment. (But it wasn't deep-dish pizza. I was still disappointed not to have sampled that.)

Agent Silva made several circuits of the room and then stopped just past my table. When he spoke, his voice was intense and lowered. "I'm going to tell you something I shouldn't. I'm hoping it will help you see BIMD as your friend."

Yeah, right. I widened my eyes as if totally pulled in. "I'll listen."

"We've got a team of scientists that are working on other usages for a Semis. Amazing usages that benefit humanity at large. We're having a hard time convincing the upper echelons it's possible, but we're close to a breakthrough. Wouldn't it be rewarding if your Semis were to power the electrical grid of the entire Eastern Seaboard? Houses, businesses, cars? The whole shebang? And not just for a few months, but decades, maybe even centuries. If you want to do the ethical thing, then telling us where you hid it is the ethical thing. BIMD wants *The Egg* in order to benefit everyone."

"That's incredible." And it was. Like really. If we could power the world with magic, we'd solve climate change and put a dent in poverty. Ant would love this.

Only Ant would also point out that it sounded almost *too* amazing. I took another bite of potatoes. Agent Silva watched me expectantly.

"Why do you call it *The Egg*?" I asked to change the subject. "It's worse than *Catfish* as a code name."

"Code name? No. It *is* an egg. Or half of one, as it needs a second half to reproduce and fertilization doesn't create just one offspring but thousands. Of course, that will never happen with yours since it's the last."

What?

I put my fork down and shot my gaze to his, utterly taken aback. I did it so fast that I caught the quickest look of satisfaction on his face as if he'd wanted to shock me and knew he'd succeeded. As if in doing so, he'd won something.

"I witnessed the extinguishing of an entire species?" The words were so horrible, I had a hard time getting them out.

"Didn't the magic-handlers tell you?" Agent Silva's expression returned to the deeply concerned, chummy face I was accustomed to.

Holy Corgi Crap. This was bad. Awful. A million times worse than failing to stop Jedda from killing the sparkly armadillo. "The very last one? You're sure? How do you know that?"

"Magic-handlers," he replied. "We track the handlers. They track the larger magical-creatures, waiting for them to die to take their Semis. The seadragons are, I mean were, the largest of all."

I pictured the seadragon's final moments. How it had been so beautiful and in so much pain. "You're a thousand percent sure it was the last one?" I didn't want it to be true.

Agent Silva smiled at me. With everything he'd told me, his expression seemed obscene. He took a seat across the table and leaned back in his chair. "That's why everyone wants yours. There won't *ever* be another this big. Sasha, how about I go make some calls up the food chain? Skip Agent Thomas and the BIMD hierarchy. I bet I can get you more than five hundred million. Then you'll not only get filthy rich but can rest assured that your Semis will benefit humankind."

Chapter Eighteen

Total Spent: $2437.49

(No changes, although guaranteed that hotel would eventually charge me for the stolen pillow and blanket.)
Total Funds Remaining: $1702.58
Cash: $690.00
Gift Cards: $1012.58

Perhaps my financial situation wasn't my most pressing concern, but staying on top of it made me feel more in control.

For the first time, I felt a genuine sense of sympathy for the Semis. Like it was an abandoned orphan who had no chance of ever finding a family.

Then it occurred to me that I was carrying around dragon sperm as a pregnancy and got grossed out.

Or at least sort of. Next to that was this huge sense of responsibility. As if by witnessing the death of the last seadragon and taking the Semis, I was now responsible for the entirety of the species. I'd listened to too many of Ant's rants on the horrors of extinction not to feel truly and deeply struck.

The moment Agent Silva left, I returned to the table and ate every meatball, half the Mexican dish, and sampled the meatloaf. Then I crashed on the hotel bed.

I wanted to discuss this with someone, anyone, but preferably Ant. I wished the Brontës were here. I didn't like being alone.

Knowing what the Semis was, even though it would never reproduce, I couldn't sell it to someone like Mrs. Valenzuela.

BIMD's power-grid option seemed a good idea on the surface, but there were flags flying big and red around Agent Silva's story. For one thing, Agent Silva had been playing me as much as I'd been playing him. But also, him bypassing BIMD suggested that he worked for some other organization or person. Maybe it was the FBI or CIA or Congress. Maybe it was someone worse.

I ran a hand over my gut, which gurgled in complaint rather than support. Meant nothing since downing all the meat had left me with an upset stomach.

"Come on, Bob," I said to the room in general. "I could use a white note right now."

Nothing.

Eventually Agents Thomas and Silva returned, and I spent the rest of the day in front of a laptop being interviewed by *The Team* from DC. They were better interviewers than Cronk and Fritzie. I was still a better liar.

I went to bed that night prepared to discuss this with Ari, and if nothing else, demand an answer as to why he hadn't turned me in. I woke the next morning having dreamed about Barkley's fleas. Agent Silva stood over me, shaking my shoulder. A female BIMD agent came in behind him, maneuvering another food cart through the door.

Agent Silva whispered near my ear. "$1.3 billion. Final offer. Cash, offshore funds, or treasury bonds. Think it over."

It took a long moment for what he'd said to sink in. Then I was suddenly awake, entirely awake, with pictures dancing around my head of massive yachts, mansions perched on ocean cliffs, me at UC Santa Cruz, then grad school, then a PhD paid-for-in-full. I opened my mouth to enthusiastically tell him I'd take it.

Then I shut it. No way would I be that stupid.

✦✦✦

The best chefs aren't afraid of a simple recipe.

The thought popped unbidden into my head as I picked through my breakfast, avoiding the sausage but eating the eggs, hashbrowns, and fruit bowl. I *would* do better as a vegetarian.

Here was a simple recipe: $1.3 billion was so much money that I couldn't even count the zeros. Just like Mrs. Valenzuela's offer, it was too much, too soon, too good to be real. Agent Silva was a liar.

I was not giving the Semis to him. I was going to Bob. Bob was the only person who so far hadn't tried to swindle me and had brought up ethics.

Once I'd finished eating, Agent Silva and another agent hustled me out of the room. "Can I call my dad now?"

"Later," the female agent said as we walked down the hall.

"You haven't even read me my Rights yet. I want a lawyer. And my dad."

Agent Thomas waited for us at the elevators. "Could you shut up?" He pushed me through the open doors.

Not hardly. When we exited into the lobby, a group of tourists stood at the front desk with their luggage. I waved at them. "Hey, I'm the missing girl from California. Could you call my dad? John Foster Clems. Tell him—"

Agent Thomas slapped a hand over my mouth, turning me in an about face with the same motion. I tried to bite him in a total Charlotte move. He released me just in time.

"Everything okay?" one of the tourists called out.

"Call John Foster Clems," I hollered loud as I could. Agent Thomas made a lunge to cover my mouth again, but I was ready and ducked under his arm. "Tell him Sasha's being taken to Washington DC to be tortured. I need help."

I caught a glimpse of someone holding up a cellphone as Agent Thomas hauled me the opposite direction. "You can inconvenience me," he said, "but you are going with us."

"Sasha . . ." Agent Silva said in a kind, concerned voice.

I rolled my eyes at his tone. That ship had sailed, hit an iceberg, and sunk.

Seemed likely my dad would get the message, though. Good. He'd make a huge stink, which couldn't but help.

Agent Thomas gave me a push in the small of my back to get me going, putting his phone to his mouth with his other hand. "Pick up Plan B."

We'd made it around the corner and down a hall when one of the exterior hotel doors blew open in an eerily unnatural way as if hit by a sudden hurricane wind. There was no one nearby to have caused it and no wind. My entourage halted, and Agent Thomas shoved me behind him as if expecting an assault.

We all stood frozen for a long moment. Nothing else happened. "Could it be . . . ?" Agent Silva asked.

Agent Thomas shook his head. "No."

"Magic-handlers?" Being rescued hadn't occurred to me, but if I was being rescued by them, then it was a frying-pan-to-furnace situation.

Agent Silva grabbed Agent Thomas by the arm. "We should at least—"

"No," Agent Thomas said again.

"—try the new device."

Just as unexpectedly as the door had blown open, the blond guy from yesterday appeared just past Agent Silva. One moment the space was empty, the next he stood there. Poof.

I jumped. My agents continued to argue as if they were unaware of him. I took that to mean they were.

The blond guy was younger than I'd thought back in the park, early twenties. He wore roughed-up khaki shorts again and a gray T-shirt that fit him oh-so-well. His blond hair was shaggy, and he had that mix of chiseled features and rounded baby face that made his whole look scream low-on-cash surfer.

He put a finger to his lips while smirking at me. Without his Ray-Bans, his eyes were a brilliant periwinkle blue. He began moving his lips silently, spellcasting.

I didn't trust this or him. Seemed likely he just wanted to steal the Semis.

Agent Thomas yelled about protocols. The female agent held up what looked like a black stapler and waved it in the direction of the still open door.

There was a sudden pressure in the air, not a wind or anything like that but rather what it would feel like if there had been a wind, a feeling on the skin without the movement. It wasn't coming from the stapler but the blond guy's spell. I didn't know how I knew that, but I did.

He crooked his finger at me in a come-hither motion. I took this to mean I also was now invisible. Ugh, but okay. I headed the opposite direction, stepping carefully around Agent Thomas, who didn't notice.

I stayed as quiet as possible while slipping into the maze of corridors that made up the hotel's conference rooms.

The blond guy came after me, of course he did. I started running the moment I was far enough from BIMD to do so unheard. "Hold up," he called out in the same overly smooth voice he'd used at the park. "I'm trying to help you."

Weren't they all?

"Who are you?" I demanded, slowing my pace when the corridor I followed ended at a T, and I needed to pick a direction.

"Chadd Deaver," he said, coming up behind me. "Double D, in the Chadd. Not double D, as in either of our bra sizes."

I turned right, him still on my heels. "That doesn't even remotely make sense. Also, way to start a conversation with an insult."

It tripped me up, though. Magic-handlers didn't say things like that. Ari wouldn't have for sure. There was something different about Chad-Double-D and his warm, syrupy voice. Also, my bra size was a solid B, which was just fine, thank-you-very-much.

"I didn't mean to insult you." He tried to touch my shoulder, but I ducked away remembering Ari's warning about spells and physical touch. Two spells on me were already two too many. "To prove myself," he continued. "I'm supposed to bring up your grandmother. Your grandmother who isn't really your grandmother and who had a secret wedding certificate and an ashtray thrown through her front window. I'm Ari's boarding school roommate and he's on his way to collect you."

"Now he shows up?"

***

Chad-d and I rushed through the hotel's catering quarters to an exterior exit. He left me at a loading dock with a "Wait here and tell Ari not to mess this up" comment and then left to go distract BIMD. Moments later, a dark gray BMW coup pulled into the parking lot. It was low-slung with tinted windows and a shiny coat of paint, the kind of car that should've gone from sixty to a dead stop with a swerve, squeal, and smoke coming out the back. It didn't. It approached slowly. As if the driver feared scaring me off. I nicknamed it Baby Shark.

The tinted window rolled down and Ari peered out. He wore aviator sunglasses and a crisp white button-down shirt, open at a starched collar. Who our age dressed like that? "Get in."

I giggled. Maybe it was Chadd's influence, maybe the sudden freedom from BIMD, maybe seeing Ari again, but giddiness bubbled through me as if I'd sucked down a bag of carbonation. (Was that even possible?)

I hummed the Baby Shark theme song as I climbed in. "I have an *entire list* of questions," I said before I'd even settled into the leather seat. That was all I got out. A riot of yapping erupted from the back.

"You have the Brontës?" He'd locked them in a carrier big enough for a bullmastiff. Next to them sat three shopping bags overflowing with puppy supplies. "I'm so happy to see you," I squealed to them, not Ari.

"You call them the Brontës?" he asked, sounding all upper-class frigidity, like how he'd been when we'd first met. "Don't let them out."

"Drive on, *Jeeves*," I commanded over my shoulder as I opened the carrier.

"Buckle your belt first."

"We're in a parking lot." I threw open the cage and scooped up Annie Pup, smushing her little face into my neck, and then reached for the other two. Ari had gotten their haircuts fixed. They now looked like short-legged versions of Chinese Crested. (Sort of.)

"Well done." I grabbed a half-full bottle of water sitting in a cup holder.

"That's the dogs' water," Ari said, with a real and proper British horror.

I swigged it back. "I don't mind sharing." This was fun. (Whatever this was.)

Ari shuddered and drove us through the parking lot as if he was a centenarian. He looked both ways twice before turning out of the hotel's lot, and we would've made more speed if the Brontës got out and pushed. Baby Shark was capable of so much more. And shouldn't we be hurrying?

A quick glance around showed no signs of limos, towncars, or vans of any color. "Okay, back to my questions." I took another swig of water. "I've even added one more. Why didn't you Dreamscape me last night to tell me you were going to rescue me? And if your friend can make me invisible, why didn't he do it yesterday rather than let me get chased by Mrs. Valenzuela and caught by BIMD? And why do you have the Brontës?"

Ari stopped for a yellow light that flickered red for the barest second and then . . . turned back to green . . . ? I glanced over to catch his lips silently moving. Nice one. We proceeded forward.

"My sincerest apologies that I couldn't help yesterday." If possible, he sounded even more stiff. And wooden. And distracted, really. That's what it was. Not stiffness at all but as if only a portion of his attention was on me. Interesting, and kinda offensive. "I arrived in Chicago at the last minute," he said. "Chaddwick's spell—"

"Chaddwick?"

"I understand it's a family name."

I snickered. "He didn't tell me what Chadd was short for." I fluttered the back of my hand at Ari. "Back to my questions. You were saying about the spell?"

He shot a quick, worried glance at the dashboard clock. "Chadd's spell couldn't have helped you yesterday. There were too many handlers present and thus likely a number of counter spells already in place. We were lucky it worked on the Semis. The reason I didn't join your Dreamscape was because Mrs. Valenzuela specifically told me not to do so. We already knew where you were and there are rumors that BIMD is working on a device to recognize spellcasting. Mrs. Valenzuela didn't want to give them anything to practice on. Since Chadd had already spelled your belly and it hadn't set anything off that I could tell, he and I decided it was safe to ignore Mrs. Valenzuela and sneak you out anyway."

"Ah, the stapler thingy. Good news for you. Pretty sure BIMD's device doesn't work."

"Very good news." There wasn't a whiff of sarcasm in his voice. "As for the dogs . . ."

Charlotte chose that moment to make a flying leap from my arms toward Ari. He caught her one-handed and gave her back without looking away from the road. The motion was so automatic, he'd clearly had practice fending her off.

"You don't like dogs." (Huge strike against him.)

"I don't believe in distracted driving."

"Right." I couldn't help it. I snickered. Then I downed the last of the water.

"I took the dogs because your friends in Nebraska—"

"Cronk and Fritzie?" I said it all ditzy cheerful just to get a rise out of him.

"Yes, them." He put Baby Shark's blinker on even though the next turn was a good quarter mile ahead.

I did another check of our surroundings. Still no one following, chasing, or otherwise aware of us. Something bothered him, though. Or better said, something bothered him *and* he was a terrible driver.

Ari continued. "They told everyone that the reason you stole the dogs was because one of them accidentally ate the Semis and you had to wait until the *proper moment* to retrieve it." He put so much emphasis on *proper moment* that I snort-laughed. The way he'd said it, though. Was that how richies referenced using the loo?

"Cronk and Fritzie are brilliant."

"If you say so. They also said you were going to donate the Semis to the Norwegian government in order to help the spread of socialism across the globe."

I laughed harder. "Does anyone believe them?"

"No." Ari finally made a right turn into the empty lot of a car stereo store. The nearby buildings were all faded and un-updated, and we were the only car in the area worth more than a couple grand. "I don't know that we should stop this particular car in this particular place."

Ari nodded. When he spoke, he sped up as if attempting to get all of my questions answered as fast as possible. "While it was clear that Matthew and Ryan were lying regarding Norway and the Semis having been swallowed, there were handlers who thought it possible the Semis had shrunk itself and the suggested dog event occurred. They lobbied for a veterinarian dissection to look for biological changes. I thought it a good idea to make the dogs quietly disappear." He gave a glance at the dash clock again and then down at Charlotte who had her chin and paws on the center console and peered his way with ears perked and a sappy expression on her little face.

Huh. She's the last one I would've expected that from.

"Thank you for saving them," I said. "And I mean that. Well done."

He cut the engine and glanced at the dash clock again. "It was nothing."

"And thank you for saving me. I mean that too." I said it quickly. Gratitude officially expressed, I also quickly changed the subject. "So what's going on here? You seem kinda tense."

He opened his car door. "Can you drive a manual transmission?"

"Have you met my dad?"

He came around to my side of Baby Shark. "You drive. Get on the motorway and keep going for twenty minutes. After twenty minutes, and

I need you to time it well, pull off again and park. Turn off the engine and just sit there. The car can't move until I verbally tell you it's time. Do you understand?" He didn't wait for me to answer but ducked to climb into my seat, forcing me to wiggle myself over the center console.

"What are you going to be doing?" Charlotte tried to make a leap his direction. I held on to her, barely.

"Having a nap. Don't wake me up."

Ah. Got it. "You're going to Dreamscape someone. Who?"

He didn't answer.

I adjusted Baby Shark's mirrors, sneaking glances at him, hugely curious.

Charlotte tried to climb into Ari's lap, but he pushed her away. Gently. For someone who didn't like animals, he was careful with her.

He closed his eyes and mouthed words too low for me to hear. It was distracting in a gross-me-out-kinda-way but also in a now-I-can-stare-unabashed-at-Ari-way. Was it weird that I found him more attractive in person than in the Dreamscape?

Actually, pretty sure I'd previously thought him better looking while dreaming than when I'd initially met him in person. So maybe his attraction was just increasing?

"Drive, Sasha," he murmured when I just sat there.

Fine.

I put Baby Shark into gear, humming her song as I did so, and slammed us into reverse with all the power and squeal of tires the car was capable of.

Ari's eyes jerked open. "For feck's sake."

I hit the accelerator hard and swung us out on the main road, thoroughly enjoying myself. Zero to eighty in six seconds. "Go to sleep."

"Slow down first." His voice rang high.

I sighed with fake disappointment but obeyed. (Didn't want to scare the Brontës.)

Twenty minutes later, we stopped in a tidy neighborhood of 1960s brick bungalows lined with shade trees. Ari was out cold.

Charlotte cocked her head and put a testing paw on his lap. When he didn't respond, she crept over and settled against his chest.

Was it wrong that I was mildly jealous? "He's just going to reject you," I whispered to her in warning. Then again, it was Charlotte, and she was no wimp.

She nestled against him and closed her eyes. *Sheesh.*

With nothing better to do, I eased off my seatbelt and swiveled around to see what all he'd packed for the Brontës. The answer was everything he *could*—toys and food and bowls and treats and jackets and leashes and blankets and hairbows in seven colors and tons of puppy pads. Nicely done, Ari. Charlotte blinked an eye open and twitched her nose in agreement.

Since Ari hadn't roused, I decided to slip outside with the dogs for a potty break and a game of fetch. I eased up on the door handle, trying to keep the telltale click as soft as possible. Only there was no click. Nothing happened.

Shoot. The doors must lock automatically and the unlock button would be noisy. Well, nothing to it. I hit the button.

Nothing happened again.

I hit it several more times. Then I reached over Ari and tried his door. It also didn't open or unlock. Charlotte curled her lip at me.

I tried the windows, all four of them. I tried the trunk release. Still nothing.

Freaking magic-handler. He'd spelled me into the car.

CHAPTER NINETEEN

"You freaking spelled me into the car!" I put ten-waiting-minutes of pent-up anger in my voice. Yes, I'd followed instructions and left him alone until he'd opened his eyes.

Ari gazed at me from his prone position with utter confusion, like someone who'd been deeply asleep and had woken to a furious girl yelling at him. "What's wrong?" He sat up, bringing Charlotte with him like a football crooked in his arm.

Annie and Emily were curled against the Semis in my lap. They'd both taken my side and glared at Ari with their tails lowered. "Every time I think I can trust you, you do something like this."

"I'm reasonably certain you don't trust me." He quirked a corner of his lip at me, all of his earlier stiffness and tension disappearing. Apparently his Dreamscaping had been successful.

"And I shouldn't. Why are you helping me? Why?"

"Perhaps it's because I genuinely like you, Sasha Beth Clems." The other side of his lips went up into a genuine smile. The first one he'd ever given me. His eyes lit and his cheeks dimpled.

My mouth went dry.

Charlotte let out a low growl, objecting to my reaction.

I swallowed hard and then made a rude noise halfway between a Pssfftt and a snort. "You don't like me. I'm horrible to you. You just want the Semis."

"One out of three right, anyway." He swiveled around to put Charlotte in the dog carrier. She tried to squirm free, but he was the stronger and won. Once she was secure, Ari grabbed a fresh water bottle and downed the whole thing. Charlotte yowled in annoyance.

"I want you to trust me," he continued. "Truly trust me, so that when I tell you something, you believe me. When I make you a promise, you know I'll keep it. When you are ready to hand over the Semis, you'll *want* to give it to me. Not Mrs. Valenzuela, but me."

I stared at him. Which led to a moment of admiring his magnetic eyes and smooth, touchable skin. A curl of hair had fallen over his forehead, and I wanted to fix it so badly it was like my fingers were tipped in magnets with him being iron. Charlotte yowled again, a long, drawn-out objection.

But trust? Real trust? Yeah, right. No way. Never going to happen. I wasn't that stupid. Annie Pup began violently whapping me with her tail.

Ari smiled again, pleased with himself, as if somehow, for some reason, he'd already accomplished the first step in his evil plan. "Sasha, start the car."

I didn't. "I don't trust people."

"Then it's time you learn. I have eight days before classes start, and I'm dedicating them to you."

"I don't think so."

"My wards will keep the other magic-handlers from finding you, and if you let me determine our direction rather than doing it yourself, Jedda Jacob's spell won't be able to track you."

All of which was super useful. I grimaced in annoyance. "You're backing me into a corner of options that may work."

"Of course, they'll work. I don't lie. Ask me anything."

"Who did you contact in the Dreamscape?"

His smile thinned.

Perfect. Charlotte yowled yet again, calling out to him as if her little puppy heart was bursting. The other two dogs joined in.

"My family." He said it slowly, each word dragged involuntarily after the last. "Who live on the far side of the globe where it's currently the middle of the night. There may be repercussions for my helping you. They deserved to be warned."

Made sense. But he didn't look at me when he said it.

Let the lying begin. (Or . . . err . . . continue.)

***

I spent the next couple of hours forcing Ari to talk about himself. He hated it in a very rich-people-don't-show-off-way. So fun for me.

We covered his growing up in England, which included a castle, private tutors, servants, and all the other clichés of the wealthy. His adoptive parents were old, like Gramps old, and he called them Lord and Lady rather than Dad and Mom. Weird.

I made him talk about his teenage years, boarding school, and Chadd, which he didn't mind as much. From reading between the lines, it was clear Ari had not been part of the popular crowd. Chadd had been the poorest kid at the school. They'd bonded through a lack of better options.

I dragged out of him the details of his life at Stanford. He lived in a townhouse with three roommates. None of his roommates were magic-handlers, but none were particularly intimidated by him either, Stanford being Stanford. Also, he studied a lot. Like 24/7 including vacations, holidays, and meals. Taking time off to help me was entirely out of character. And thus that much more suspicious.

All of this made me way more knowledgeable about Ari than his fan club who endlessly linked him to starlets that it turned out he didn't know. He only showed himself to the world when forced to by the Alliance and hated publicity. Ari was, he admitted, an introvert who watched rugby on TV when not doing homework. (Also, I'd been right. He'd never once held any sort of employment. Sigh.)

"You need a job and better hobbies."

We'd switched seats once we were out of the suburbs, him driving, me holding all three dogs. His driving still sucked. We'd been trailing a big rig for a good ten minutes now. He either needed to pass it already or distract me from reaching over, grabbing the steering wheel, and forcing him to do so.

"I have a hobby. I write spells. I'm quite good."

Not the distraction I was looking for.

I wrinkled my nose and shook my head. "I meant something like tennis or online poker, not killing animals. That's immoral." It did give me an idea, though. "Give me a list. Every single spell you can perform."

"What?" He choked out the words, horrified.

Love it. I fake-smirked at him. "Giving up already on your I'll-tell-you-anything-you-want-Sasha pledge?"

"No," he replied quickly. "I'll answer. It's just that asking a magic-handler what spells they have is akin to asking one's net assets. It just isn't done."

"It's rude," I added fake-helpfully. "I'm rude, but remember, you like me. So, no excuses."

"You're not rude." He quick glanced my direction, almost shy about it.

"I'm totally rude."

"No. You're outspoken and suspicious—"

"Suspicious?" Pretty accurate, actually.

"Suspicious," he repeated and did a half-smile as if settling into the idea. "Also aggressive and garrulous, even if your word choices are sometimes less than—"

"Hey, are you calling me low-class?"

"Definitely not." He put on Baby Shark's blinker to pass the big rig. "Besides, class distinctions are a terrible way to judge character."

"Nice one. My brother would love that."

"I'm sure." He laid on the gas.

"Finally," I murmured so low he wouldn't hear me. Didn't want to distract his driving.

Baby Shark surged forward and around the truck, then pulled back over and slowed down. I had to force myself not to scream.

"Just to be clear," Ari continued once we were cruising again at a lowly 72 MPH, "I don't view you in a negative sense, barring your tendencies with salts and wounds, both mine and yours. You have a great strength of character, in determination and tenacity, but also in responsibility. You've been careful that no one, not even the Brontës, is hurt by your actions. You're also clever and thoughtful and have a deep loyalty to your family. To quote my namesake, *We are what we repeatedly do.*" He gave another quick, half-shy look my way.

"Well now, that's just . . ." I'd been about to say ridiculous, but a small warmth of pleasure crept up my neck and choked the words. On the other hand . . . "As my Gramps likes to say, *Flattering words are the surface bubbles on a very flat glass of champagne.*"

"Also," Ari continued as if I hadn't spoken, "You're blindingly pretty."

Chapter Twenty

Spells Ari listed out for me after I changed the subject because his compliments (fake or real) made me uncomfortable in a way I didn't like (or perhaps liked too much):

- The Dreamscape Spell, his masterpiece.

- Locking Spell. (As I'd discovered.)

- Standard Warding Spells, various. These stopped spying, gave physical defenses, warned when other magic-handlers got too close, etc. (Useful.)

- Several hundred small practical spells that he explained in detail to the point that I got bored. Things like the Red-light spell, heating water in a teacup, making his cellphone theft-proof, and keeping the bathroom tidy. (The last being directly related to Chadd.)

- Another long-but-more-interesting list of what Ari called "Erroneous Spells." These included a spell for healing that worked but left the body part fluorescent green for several years afterward, a spell meant to remove stains from clothing but removed the clothing instead and Ari had never figured out where they go or how to get them back. And one that was supposed to make a vivid sunset but instead brought clouds that rained blood.

He also explained that most Semis *harvested* by handlers were too small to produce anything more than a single spell. Which was one more reason the big ones were so valuable. They became spellbooks containing a whole slew of spells although the spells had to be similar in nature and/or interconnected. His Dreamscape Spell was one of these. Took thirteen different spells to get us both to Dennis the Menace Park.

"Gonna be honest," I said once he'd exhausted himself. "The more I hear about magic-handling, the more disappointed I am. Your spells seem more like toys than say nuclear weapons."

"You *want* me to have a nuclear weapon spell?" He said it all amused-like and looked pointedly at my belly where all three dogs were curled up asleep against the bump of the Semis.

"Of course not."

"Thought not."

"But I expected it."

"Typical." Now he sounded all disgusted and superior, but it was totally fake.

"I'm so rubbing off on you."

"Probably." He gave me a small smile.

"And you're enjoying it."

"That too."

Emily woke up and stretched her head back in a giant doggie yawn, bumping into Charlotte who jumped to her feet as if looking for a threat. Ari reached over and petted Charlotte's shaved back to calm her down. It was an absent-minded thing on his part. Charlotte arched against the touch in doggie ecstasy. Lucky dog.

Ari put the blinker on, something he appeared to be anal about.

"Are we stopping?" I asked.

"For petrol."

We weren't even below the quarter-tank mark. "Worrywart much?"

"*By failing to prepare, you are preparing to fail.* Benjamin Franklin." He moved us over to the slow lane. "Now, back to the topic at hand. Non-magic-handlers assume that creating spells is easy. Like writing a term paper or something."

"Term papers are easy?"

"For some of us." More pleased superiority, also fake. I was so rubbing off on him. "Consider cooking instead. Creating a spellbook is like at-tempting to create a cake when the ingredients keep insisting they are crumpets. The big ones are like creating a hundred-course, formal meal with a dozen chefs each insisting they are in charge."

"You're making me hungry."

"I'll buy you food, although not from the petrol station." He pulled us off the freeway. "Or think about it as a lawyer writing a legal contract where the pen and paper keep adding in clauses and commas wherever *they* believe it's needed."

I considered that for a moment. "So what you're saying is that your Gone-Wrong Spells all had typos?"

"That's one way to look at it." He took a laughing breath, making his chest expand. He had a nice chest, solid and broad. "Just to be clear," he continued. "My Erroneous Spells were early attempts and part of the learning process. I haven't had a spellbook backfire in years."

"I didn't mean to imply you weren't skilled."

"Yes, you did."

"Okay, I probably did. I can't help it."

"I know. But if you're rubbing off on me, then I must find a way to rub off on you as well."

We bypassed several gas stations and drove a mile or so until Ari found one that was entirely empty, rather rundown, and thirty-five-cents-a-gallon-cheaper than the others. Likely he was more interested in the emptiness than the price, but well done anyway.

Once stopped in front of a pump, he craned around to scope out the station. "Can I borrow your hat?"

"Huh?"

"Your hat. To obscure my face."

I handed it to him. This Ari seemed a different person than the boy in the poster above my tweenage bed or even the snood who'd first come to The Blue Castle. This boy I couldn't help but like. (Dang, one wouldn't expect a wide-brimmed straw hat to go with his young-attorney outfit, but he looked amazing.)

"Much obliged." He peered around a second time. I did the same. Still no one about, magic-handler or not.

Charlotte and I glued ourselves to the window to watch him. Emily had gone back to sleep and Annie Pup had never woken up. A tiny, brilliantly colored blue bird landed on the top of his pump and watched him too. Yeah, he was that good-looking.

A VW Bug pulled up kitty-corner to us, and Ari turned his back to it, going into hiding mode. He turned even further when a twenty-something brunette wearing a clichéd jeanshorts-westernhat-cowboyboots outfit got out. She noticed Ari immediately. Of course she did. "Hey, there," she called over.

Sheesh, was she blind to the fact that Charlotte and I were sitting in Baby Shark also ogling him? Not that I wanted to be noticed, but being overlooked was the worst.

Ari went all stiff, as if he were one of those toys with a string holding all his parts together and the string had suddenly snapped taunt.

The girl tried again. "Can you help me with my pump?"

I gagged. "Worst pickup line ever."

Ari hunched as if under attack. It was a weird reaction. I started to open my door so the girl would know he had company and leave him alone, but before I could, she shrugged and turned away to run her credit card. Close one.

Another car pulled up behind us, and I craned around to make sure it wasn't a luxury vehicle. Nope. It was a beater four-by-four driven by an older guy with a two-foot-long beard and protruding gut. He checked out the girl and ignored Ari.

"See," I whispered, just loud enough for Ari and the dogs to hear. "Not everyone adores you."

"Not helping," he mumbled back, still all hunched and stiff. One would think he'd be more accustomed to fame after all these years, but he clearly wasn't. I made a mental note to pester him about it.

His pump clicked finished. He put it away and then looked at the girl, gauging the distance between her, him, and Baby Shark's driver's door. She caught his look. "OMG. Are you—"

"No," he screeched and fled around the back of Baby Shark without collecting his receipt. The bird, which on second look wasn't a bird at all but a tiny truedragon, flung itself at Ari's head, snatching at the hat as if trying to remove it. Apparently magical-creatures really were attracted to him.

Ari batted at the miniature dragon and crashed into the beard-guy who was using a window scrubber on his headlamps.

Charlotte launched herself barking at the window. The other two dogs startled awake and also barked in alarm. The moment Ari slid into Baby Shark, Charlotte bolted over the top of Annie and Emily to leap into his arms. He gathered her into his chest, breathing heavily as if he'd run halfway down panic-attack-road. Charlotte licked his face.

I sighed. "Downside of traveling with Aristotle Montague-Smith-Montague."

Chapter Twenty-One

Total Spent: $2587.49
(The hotel charged $150.00 to my gift cards for the pillow and blanket.
Are you freaking kidding me????!!!!)
Total Funds Remaining: $1552.58
Cash: $690.00
Gift Cards: $862.58

On better news, Ari didn't let me reimburse him for fuel, even when I
half-heartedly tried to insist.

I bid my time asking about Ari's reaction to fame. He was so freaked out that it seemed a kindness to let him lecture me about the magic-handler world instead. (A freaked-out Ari was an even-slower-driver-Ari, believe it or not.)

This time he covered money, my favorite topic. Turns out that magic-handler wealth wasn't due to gaming the stock market or secretly controlling the governments of half the world's small countries, but generational. This was because most strong spellbooks had been created prior to the Industrial Revolution and were pretty much useless in modern life. The magic-handlers had been forced to become exceptionally good investors. I found the whole thing both fascinating and appalling. Also, Ari used his spell to change every red light immediately back to green. If my Dad could do that, he would never again need brakes.

We stopped at a drive-thru deli in the late afternoon somewhere in Ohio. I was being careful to not look at any road signs to keep Jedda from knowing where we were headed, but once off the highway, I figured it was safe. Ari bought us two matching sangos—whole wheat bread, loads of veggies, light on the mayo, cheese, and no meat. Turns out Ari was just as food-conscious as I was and a longtime vegetarian.

Luckily the deli worker was straight and male.

From there, we headed over to a park. Shades of Jedda, but it made sense with the Brontës.

Ari parked Baby Shark under a stand of leafy shade trees so large and dense there was no hint of sun. The trees ended at a large pond, its surface rippled by a breeze and two quacking ducks. I exited the car, stretched, and took a breath of earthy, fresh air. "I like it here."

Annie and Emily beelined to the edge of the pond closest to the ducks. Charlotte followed at Ari's heels which he didn't object to. She was totally growing on him.

We took our lunch to a picnic table. Ari deep-cleaned the surface with no less than ten disinfecting wipes while muttering a spell. So thoughtful. Charlotte got bored staring at him and wandered off to join the others in duck-stalking.

"Next question you have no choice but to answer," I said once we were seated across from each other and the food unwrapped. "Tell me about the spell that makes magic-handlers all so attractive."

He shot me a horrified glance. "Can't we talk more about money?"

I nudged him with my foot under the table. "The Beauty Spell makes you uncomfortable?" I hadn't expected him to get freaked out so fast.

He bit into his sanga and chewed slowly before meeting my gaze. "I never had it cast on me."

"Common knowledge." I waved a hand at him. "Tell me more."

He put his sanga down and folded his arms across his chest, looking over at the dogs as if he'd much prefer to join them than talk to me. "If I must."

"You must. You promised."

He sighed. "It's from the Semis of a Blue *Morphinae draco*. Every family has a spellbook based on *Morphinae* in the same way every family has a spellbook of personal wards. The spell is cast on a child during infancy in order to influence bone structure and such. I was too old." He said the last so properly he sounded like a stodgy, seventy-year-old butler. Or as if he were admitting something hugely embarrassing. "I don't regret that," he continued. "It's important to just be yourself."

"Easy to say when you naturally look like you do."

He pressed his lips together in a firm, if unhappy, line.

Interesting. I nudged his leg a second time. "Gorgeous people are usually more . . . I don't know . . . vain about it? You never seem lacking in confidence with anything else."

He closed his eyes.

Time to home in on what I wanted to know. "Girls noticing you totally freaks you out."

A pinkish color seeped up the front of his neck. It contrasted nicely against his white collar.

Then it hit me. Suddenly and all at once. As if everything I'd pestered Ari about had ping-ponged off him and back at me. Bam. I understood his problem. It was so obvious.

"Mother of a Malinois, you don't think you're good-looking."

Ari turned positively crimson.

"Because you don't have the Beauty Spell like all the other magic-handlers. You're insecure." I didn't even try to hide my surprise.

Charlotte ran full-speed in our direction, racing to the rescue. Ari scooped her up.

"Are you blind to mirrors . . . ? Were you born with an over-inflated sense of modesty . . . ? You have girls falling all over you, like all the time. What more proof of your beauty do you need?"

"None of those people know me, okay?" He sounded strained to the point of cracking. Charlotte whuffled against his chest, and he stroked the top of her head like she was an anti-anxiety therapy dog. "Can we not talk of this any longer? Please?"

I stared at him.

He wanted people to like him. Not his appearance. Him. And he seemed genuinely vulnerable about it.

My traitorous heart thumped, thumped, thumped against my ribs. Ari with a vulnerable spot was more attractive than everything else about him.

He was making me really start to like him.

As a boy.

A hot boy.

A vulnerable hot boy.

Which was so, so wrong. Also, I was going to have to get him a disguise. He was just too stare-able.

****

"I've another question," I said once we'd finished our sangas and green teas in a silence filled with embarrassment on his side and self-lectures on why-I-shouldn't-soften-toward-Ari on mine. I didn't actually have a question, but we needed to break the awkwardness, so I found one. "Why haven't you just taken the Semis from me? Or why didn't Chadd at the hotel? Or any of the others? Jedda didn't even try."

The sun was going down and the temperature dropping. Charlotte was still in his lap and she watched me with her head just above the table, the look in her eyes protective. "Once the Semis bonded to you," he said, "stealing it would damage the magic."

Wait, what? It was my turn to go all tense and unhappy. "Bonded? What does that mean and how come no one told me before?" Meaning him.

Ari piled the remains of our lunches onto his paper plate, being tidy about it. When he spoke, he sounded better, almost as if me taking a turn being distressed cheered him up. "There's a saying by Confucius that magic-handlers like to quote—"

"Skip that. Tell me about the bond. And how to get rid of it."

He now took a turn nudging me with his leg and let the corners of his mouth crinkle up into another one of his small smiles, very definitely feeling better. "*Where the wind blows, the grass bends.* That's the saying regarding raw magic. And barring the fact that most handlers miss the point of the quote, the idea is correct. Raw magic moves that which exists around it, including people, as it becomes habituated to them. It moves them in the ways it thinks they need moving or that the person themself want to move. That's the bond. You don't want to be rid of it."

"Yeah, I do."

Something bright landed on his arm. A firefly maybe. It twinkled like a miniature jewel. "There's a good chance it guided Chadd and me in freeing you. Likely it pushed me to reunite you with the dogs. It's definitely the reason it's been so easy for you to evade the handlers."

"Easy?" He was right about the dogs, though. I'd missed them so much and Ari rescuing them hadn't benefited him in any way.

Still . . . the idea of the Semis pushing me around, squashing me, like a blade of grass . . . My stomach churned under the pregnancy belly. If I upchucked here, I was totally aiming for Ari's loafers. "You're making me feel sick."

He studied my face, his lips still turned up, and raised a hand as if he was going to touch me but then dropped it back down. "If someone was to take the Semis from you forcibly, causing you distress or pain in the process, the Semis would know and be tainted. Any spells created from it would be janked-up in dangerous, deadly ways. That's why Jedda didn't just take it from you. Or Mrs. Valenzuela or the others. You have to give it away willingly."

I sent him an incredulous look. "But if that's true, then I needn't have run. I could've stayed home and auctioned the thing off because no magic-handler could touch it without my permission."

Another firefly landed on his shoulder and he glanced over, noticed it, winced, and shook his arm to displace it. It didn't budge. I looked down to find a posse of them wandering my belly. I'd never heard that fireflies had a magical variety, but it fit. Then I remembered Jedda and the armadillo thingy. "You're not going to go on a killing spree here or anything, are you?" I raised a protective hand between him and my belly of fireflies.

"Their magic is too small to be worth collecting." His smile disappeared.

I removed the firefly from his shoulder, just to be safe, and put it on my belly with its friends.

"Running was correct." A touch of sweat beaded on his forehead, and he kept his attention on my face in a way that would've been more flattering if it hadn't been clear he was avoiding looking at the fireflies. "Less ethical handlers will steal magic over having no magic. Happened to the Montague-Smith-Montagues once." A firefly flittered between us and he took a deep breath as if steadying himself. "Even the more honorable handlers might consider stealing the Semis just to keep it out of the hands of a rival like Mrs. Valenzuela. And no one wants BIMD to get it. Yes, you did the right thing by running."

"Good to know." Then I had another thought, one I didn't like even more than the rest. "Could the Semis be causing you to . . . you know . . . like me . . . more than you might have otherwise? So that you'll, you know, help me?"

A firefly landed on the top of his head, which I decided not to tell him. He pressed his lips together and got a small furl in his brow as if he hadn't considered the idea of the Semis influencing him before.

Something deep inside me quivered. I didn't want him to utter a sigh of relief or happily exclaim, "So that's why!"

When he finally spoke, his words were thoughtful. "I didn't like you at first. That changed during our visits in what you call the Dreamscape. The Semis has no influence there. I believe that the changes in how I view you are genuine."

Phew.

And then *Sheesh*, I really shouldn't be caring about how he felt about me.

Also, he hadn't said the Semis wasn't manipulating *me* into liking *him*. Against my better judgment and overall dislike of the Semis, that thought had some serious appeal. On the other hand, the Semis must be sexist if it thought the best way to help me was to make me drool over a guy in the hopes of what . . . ? He'd be charmed into wanting to be my protector? Ugh.

Still, I'd take it. As Gramps had once said, *Never look a good scapegoat in the mouth.*

"Can we go back to the car now?" he asked urgently. "I really don't like insects."

Chapter Twenty-Two

"This hoodie, black jeans, Converse on your feet, we get your ears pierced, and a beanie to smush down your hair. You'll look like a skater." I held up various articles of clothing for Ari to inspect. At my insistence, we'd staked out a high-end clothing store at an outdoor mall right before closing. Both store employees were male. Great selection. Ari hated everything I chose, but I'd already put together a couple of fun outfits for both of us. Someday, when I had my money from the Semis, I was going to buy an entire new wardrobe from a place like this.

"No piercings," Ari said, our gazes meeting. I sighed in disappointment even though the piercing had been to get him to agree to the rest. He'd already boohooed an Asian boy-band look and a football jersey/mullet-wig/cowboy hat. The last being in honor of gas-station-girl.

Truth: Ari looked amazing in everything I tried on him. I kept noticing little things I hadn't before. Like his ears. I'd always liked ears. No one else even thought of them or noticed them, but a quality guy had a quality ear. "If you won't get your ears pierced, could I at least cut your hair?"

Ari's eyes went wide in mock horror. "I've seen your work, remember."

"Hey, the Brontës looked great."

"Great being a euphemism for absurd."

"Not punny." Oldest joke in the world, but he smiled anyway, a quirk of his lips as if he . . . you know . . . was entertained by me.

I smiled back, also entertained, and appreciated how perfectly his nose fit the rest of his face.

Someone giggled over to our right. Three girls watched us from the entrance to the store's changing rooms. Shoot, I'd meant to watch for problematic customers.

Ari pivoted to a rack of clothing and grabbed a pair of stodgy navy slacks as if it were a shield. "Ignore them," he whispered.

"Does that ever work?"

"No."

More giggling. The girls headed our way.

I got an idea. A fun one, possibly stupid and risky as well, but it was so dumb that it might work. "Can you fake an American accent?"

"No."

"Give it a try. Jedda could, and it was hilarious. Pretend to be your friend Chad-d and play along."

I didn't give him a chance to think further. Ari was best when just pushed. "Hiya, girls," I said with an obnoxious Texas accent. I turned to speak over my shoulder so that my belly was hid behind a rack of clothing. I was back in my *Little House* get-up with my hair in braids and my face full of mock freckles. Pretty excellent disguise in my opinion, but not one that matched Ari's lawyer look. "Can I help y'all?"

Even more giggles. No recognition of me on their faces. Excellent. "We were wondering," the tallest of the three said, "if that is . . . Aristotle with you?" It started off as a statement but ended with a question.

I thrust my belly into view. "This here guy? Naw. Don't I wish. This here is my babydaddy, Doug."

The girl who'd spoken gave her friends a quick, horrified look.

"Are y'all talking about me?" Ari said in a voice so deep it sounded like it came from his knees. I wasn't sure what it *was*, an attempt at Southern or something, but it was dead-on non-British.

"Well done," I murmured.

"Oh, we're so sorry," the second girl said, not sounding sorry at all.

The third girl rolled her eyes. "He isn't dating anyone right now anyway, and he certainly didn't get some haggie girl pregnant."

"Haggie?" My grin faded. That cut. I wasn't *that* bad.

"Whatever," the second one said. "She's way too hideous for Aristotle."

Yeah, that cut even more. Not that it mattered. Who cared what a bunch of tweenies thought. Not me. I was way beyond caring. Totally beyond. I'd barely even heard them in the first place.

"It's another look-a-like," the first girl said, sounding deeply disappointed.

"Heya, girls," I said, still in my twang, "you know who looks like a hag and—"

Ari jerked on my arm and spun me around, like he was Fred Astaire pulling me into a dance, into his arms.

"What are you—" I managed to get out while grabbing his shirt for balance. He took my face into both of his hands, tilted my chin back like something out of a movie starring Ginger Rogers, and touched his lips to mine.

My belly got in the way.

I was still entirely swept off my feet. I wrapped my arms around his neck, forgot about the girls, the store, my annoying pregnancy, and our need to keep a low profile. I kissed him back. I kissed him like I'd spent all afternoon thinking about kissing him. (Which I had, deep down inside.)

Something hit the floor with a thump. A pair of sandals I wanted to try on just because they were cute and I knew he'd pay for them. I must've dropped them.

Okay, here's a truth when it came to kissing.

I didn't click with all guys. Not even guys I liked, guys who were hot, guys who seemed like they should be perfect for me. Zach, *The Faithless Schmuck*, had set a standard hard for any other guy to match.

Ari blew Zach off the beach, out of the water, and across the pond to Japan.

We clicked. Two magnets coming together. It even sounded like there was a physical noise when it happened. "Like the glory of Greece," I whispered when I pulled back to breathe.

"Sorry?" The word was more soft breath than sound.

I peeked a look at the three girls. They still watched us. One of them had her phone out, but it was limp in her hand.

For the moment.

I should probably be concerned about that. There was a lot here I should be concerned about. I shook my head, trying to remember what those things were. His kiss had been that good.

"Don't let them bother you," he murmured against my ear, making me shiver. "*No one can make you feel inferior without your consent.*"

I laughed and buried my face in his starched shirt. He smelled like dryer sheets, the good kind, and fresh air. "Eleanor Roosevelt? Now?"

At least I knew that one.

"Seemed appropriate." He released me but ran his fingers across my cheek in doing so. "Should we purchase those sandals you dropped? It might be better if we exited posthaste."

"What sandals?" I brushed the lock of hair from his forehead, the strands silky against my fingers. He gave a soft, deep chuckle that made me think about kissing him all over again.

***

We were quiet on our way out. Ari insisted on carrying our purchases in a very gentlemanly way. For once I didn't pester him with questions. I just . . . well . . . now that the kiss was over, I should be making jokes, teasing him, lightening the mood, flirting even, but I couldn't.

A twisty, uncomfortable ache sprouted in my middle. The further we moved from the moment, the more I felt unbalanced, uprooted, uncertain.

Ari shuffled the packages in his arms and dug around in his pocket for his key fob. I picked up our pace, wanting to rid myself of the achiness by hugging the Brontës.

"What did you say to me in the store?" Ari asked, sounding both curious and cautious.

"About cutting your hair?"

"About Greece," he clarified.

"Oh, that," I said quickly. "It's nothing." Only it wasn't nothing, it was the seed of the ache.

I'd quoted Grams's book at him. The line she'd used to first tell Gramps that she loved him. The line she'd turned into a cross-stitch that hung over his bed. Ari didn't get to know about that.

"I've heard it before, but I can't—" Ari halted dead and turned to me. The glow from the nearest parking light reflected something deep and intense in his eyes. Something urgent. He dropped the shopping bags to the asphalt. "Run."

"What?"

"Run!" He shoved me on the shoulder and then craned back to stare at the night sky. I stayed in place and did the same.

Nothing up there but stars. Then I heard a noise. A distant shu-shu-shu. "What is that?"

"Dragon," he said urgently while shoving me forward a second time.

"Dragon!" I leaped over the pile of shopping bags as if they were the last gate in a hurdle race. I'd seen this movie. The people usually died.

The sound of the shu-shu-shu shortened and condensed as if the wingbeats were getting faster, nearer.

"Hurry!" Ari yelled, grabbing my hand as we raced toward Baby Shark. A shadow, large and serpentine and right above our head, circled and banked. Long, twisty neck. Mustard, opalescent scales. Torso the size of three BIMD vans parked end-to-end.

Ari and I stumbled to a stop.

Its leathery wings tilted backward, slowing as it gazed at us from yellow, malevolent eyes. Its whip-like tail hung so low it nearly dragged on the ground, and it flared its front claws as it came at us, each one a curved knife the size of my arm.

Death wouldn't be pretty.

Ari let go of my hand, and I crumpled to the ground, covering my head with my arms as best I could. An Italian loafer took up guard to my right. Then another to my left.

I peered up from under my arm. Ari stood over the top of me, his hands in the air, a look of concentration on his face, his lips moving. If he spoke aloud, I couldn't hear it over the nearing, drumming beat of shu-shu-shu.

Wind whipped my hair into my eyes and beat a foul odor of rotten eggs up my nose. The dragon's snaky head hauled back cobra-like.

I screamed.

Ari snapped his fingers, all fierce and sharp. The silvery claws passed inches over his head.

The dragon roared as it lifted away, a mixture of train engine, trumpet, and dying cow. Several car alarms went off. I had to cough to breathe, the air was so thick with sulfur.

"It's coming back," Ari said, pulling me to my feet. "We can't outrun it."

I shook so hard, my teeth clattered. "We're going to die. We're going to die. We're going to die."

"We are not going to die," Ari said, his voice intense and overly loud. He hauled me to my feet and spun me behind his back all Fred Astaire again.

I clutched his shirt, still quaking, and buried my face between his shoulder blades. The shu-shu-shu grew louder a second time. "We're so going to die."

"Fine, we're going to die." He raised both arms over his head again, the muscles of his shoulders rearranging under my hands. I pressed against him, closing my eyes.

Ari whispered something soft and sibilant and not in English. He began to tremor, his murmured words spreading outward under his skin, speeding up, intensifying, until his entire body vibrated, like a single, sustained note from a really loud bass guitar.

I peeked open my eyes to see the dragon's scales gleaming in the streetlight as it dropped down, its eyes laser-focused on us. I tried to scream again, but the sound solidified in my throat blocked by the taste of sulfur.

Ari turned to face the dragon. I shifted with him. "I always wanted to die rich," I managed to mumble.

Ari's vibrating went nuclear. He snapped his fingers so violently the movement jolted down his arms, through his torso, and into me. The magic burst forward, pushing us backward in rebound.

The dragon slammed to a halt midair, its wings shooting wide and its head flinging up and back to balance. It dropped to the ground with a crash that rocked the pavement and set off more car alarms.

Apparently, we weren't going to die after all.

"Stay here while I take care of it." Ari's voice was deep and growly. He tremored and relaxed, then tremored again, as if his magic were resetting, rebuilding. He stalked forward, raising his arms, all fierce and determined.

Reminded me of . . .

Well . . .

The intensity of the dragon as it came after us.

The dragon lay sprawled on its belly, its tail and wings smashing several cars, its eyes open but hazy and stunned. I flashed back to the seadragon on the beach, its massive eye blinking at me and then the horror of watching it die. I pictured the poor little armadillo thing and its screech when Jedda had smashed it with a rock. I felt the weight of the Semis strapped to my middle and the knowledge that I was the seadragon's protector. "Don't you murder it," I screamed, launching myself at Ari.

He continued forward.

I grabbed his arm in the hopes of breaking whatever spell he was preparing. "No way are you taking its Semis. No way is another magical-creature ending up dead."

"I'm not—" Ari began, trying to pull free.

I held tight. "Lie later. We're leaving." I tugged him backward toward Baby Shark.

"Sasha, magical-creatures this size have legal protections. I would never—"

"Not now."

His hand still vibrated in mine, his magic keyed up.

The dragon didn't seem inclined to come after us, so I detoured to our shopping bags and shoved them into Ari's arms. That way, he couldn't do the whole snapping routine without me knowing it was coming. Ari sighed loudly as if he thought I was being foolish.

I glared at him.

We made it to Baby Shark, but before climbing in, I looked back at the dragon to make sure it didn't have an obvious broken wing or anything. No way was I leaving it vulnerable to the next magic-handler who showed up.

The good news: The dragon was shaking its head back and forth like a stunned dog and had raised its wings off the nearby cars.

The bad news: The three girls from the store were huddled together under the building's portico with their cell phones out.

Chapter Twenty-Three

"I wasn't going to hurt it," Ari insisted after downing three bottles of water. Charlotte planted her paws on his chest and frantically licked his neck.

"Liar." Fury burned so hot under my skin that even my hair felt on fire. My fingers locked hard around Baby Shark's steering wheel. (Yes, I was driving. We needed away. Fast.)

He pushed Charlotte down to stop her licking. "The larger dragons are endangered. Besides, only a fool harvests a Semis in public."

I pressed harder on the accelerator. We were on a two-lane road, dead-straight, lots of trees, no traffic to get in my way. "So if you were somewhere deserted, you'd have pulled a sword and killed it?"

"I don't own a sword. I planned to cast my Dragon Disorientation Spell. It buys me time to get away."

"This happens often enough to have a special spell?" My voice rose with every word.

"Sasha, why are you so upset?"

"I'm not upset." Baby Shark hit 105 mph.

"Please. Slow down."

I pressed harder on the accelerator. The speedometer topped out at 160. We had a way to go. "You totally lied after swearing you'd be honest."

"No, I didn't. Sasha—" He latched onto the door grip with one hand. The other clasped Charlotte as if she was about to be sent flying.

"You never told me about your Dragon Disorientation Spell nor your Knock-the-Dragon-From-the-Sky Spell."

"I told you I had wards." He glanced at the speedometer. "A speeding ticket is a terrible idea. Sasha . . ."

"Stop saying my name. You're being a *Tall Poppy*."

"No idea what that means."

Neither did I. It's what Jedda had called him and seemed especially insulting. I took my foot off the gas pedal, though. He was right about the ticket, dang it.

He half-raised his hand as if to touch me but then returned it to Charlotte. "Did it ever occur to you that the reason you assume everyone around you is lying is because you yourself lie so much?"

"No, I don't."

He gave me a raised-brow look.

"Okay, fine, I lie. I have to. But don't put this on me. I'm not the one who wanted to kill—"

"I wasn't—" He abruptly cut off and pinched the bridge of his nose as if fighting a headache or the beginnings of a case of frustration. He reached for his phone. "It's late and we're both tired. I'm going to book a hotel for the night."

"Fine. Get two rooms." I glowered at the front windshield. "The dogs stay with me."

***

The moment the Brontës and I were alone, I ripped off the fake belly and shoved it in a dresser drawer. Then I took a hot shower where I beat myself up emotionally while blaming Ari, the Semis, the dragon, and Mrs. Valenzuela. (No idea why her specifically, but it felt right.)

It didn't help that without a raging argument to distract myself, it was impossible to avoid what was really going on. The thing that I hadn't been willing to tell Ari, wouldn't tell Ari, would fight/argue/distract to avoid telling Ari, but was true nonetheless.

He'd spooked me.

Badly. Worse than the Stephen King movie Gramps had made me watch with the freaked-out clown that had given me nightmares for weeks.

Ari had gotten past my defenses, my sarcasm, my ability to keep-him-in-his-place. He'd reached inside and exposed my silent, secret, neediness-of-a-thousand-colors-and-complex-knots that normally stayed hidden in my atriums and ventricles and aorta. (I'd taken Anatomy my junior year.)

Not even Zachary Stults had done that, hadn't even come close.

I barely knew Ari.

It wasn't just that he'd protected me from the dragon. It definitely wasn't just the attraction.

It was Ari's hand touching mine, the way he'd cradled my head, looked in my eyes, the sound of his voice when he whispered his stupid quotes. And before that, the way we'd talked and joked and teased, the stories he'd told, the way he'd let Charlotte win him over. That he didn't eat meat. That he paid for things. That he embarrassed so easily. That he was so dependable.

It wasn't just the attraction.

It was . . .

It was terrifying.

It was also part of the game. I *knew* that. I knew what he wanted.

I was supposed to be the one taking advantage. I was the game master. I was supposed to *use* him. Not . . .

Not . . .

See? The situation was so bad, I couldn't even bring myself to define what exactly it was I was supposed to not do.

I was an idiot. Complete and total. Failure of all failures. Once he had what he wanted, he'd desert me, and it would be my own stupid fault.

I wanted to cry. I wanted to hit him with a baseball bat or at least a rotting banana. I needed my brother. He'd talk sense into me. Just like he had with Zach, *The Faithless Schmuck*.

I threw myself onto the bed. For once, the Brontës didn't climb all over me but curled up in a lump on the far side. I used the cell to contact Ant's server, but he didn't answer so I left him a rambling voicemail listing out all the reasons I knew Ari was wrong for me.

It was like Ant's and Gramps's discussion prior to the last presidential election. Ant had spent months trying to impress on Dad, Nicholas, and me all the ways that then Senator Bernatella had proved herself to be worthy of the highest office. Gramps's response had been that her desire to be president superseded all Ant's arguments.

Ari was the same. He wanted the Semis. He was too good to be true. End of story. (He'd never even held a freaking job in his entire life!!!)

I googled "Aristotle Montague-Smith-Montague" and "dragon."

Took two clicks to find those horrible girls' video. There he was—his arms in the air, stalking toward the downed dragon, all intensity and purpose and superhero-like hotness. He looked like someone about to make the kill of a lifetime.

Only Ari was not an idiot.

As he'd pointed out, there was no way to murder something that large and not get noticed. As much as I hated admitting it, he'd told the truth about not intending to harm it. Which did not mean I believed anything else he'd said.

Weird thing, though, there were no good shots of me in the video. At first, I was behind Ari's back and then there were these odd flashes of bad street lighting that kept hitting at just the right moments to hide me. It was hard to tell Ari even had a partner.

I checked the video's description. Also no mention of me.

Luck? Or perhaps the Semis?

Maybe I'd better start being nicer to it.

I collapsed on the bed to watch the video several more times. When I finally fell asleep, the Semis, the Brontës, and I were all curled up together. I went straight to Dennis the Menace Park.

This time we were side-by-side on the swing set. Ari sat still, his feet on the ground, studying me. I swung gently back and forth while wearing my new T-shirt but no pants. I stopped the swing and jerked my T-shirt down to cover as much of my thighs as possible. "You could've warned me," I near shouted. "Do we have to do this?"

"I thought it might be easier." His voice was so neutral it was clear he was trying not to antagonize me.

"Easier for whom?"

"It's your dream."

"If that were true, I'd have pants on."

He carefully didn't look at my legs. He kept his head turned to study my face instead, which was worse. I couldn't make eye contact and stared at the backside of a fake cement hill across the way. A circular tunnel ran through the middle, just large enough for a five-year-old to walk through without scraping their head. I should crawl inside in the hopes Ari's dislike of germs would keep him out. (In real life, the tunnel reeked of pee.)

"We kissed," Ari said evenly, "and fought off a dragon. For unknown reasons, you're angry and picking fights. We've gone backward in terms of trust."

Trust. It was always about trust with him. "I hated kissing you."

Ari smiled, a knowing smile, a smug smile. "No, you didn't."

A vise snapped taunt around my chest. My heart stopped beating for lack of space. I sputtered. Like really sputtered. I needed to say something, put him off, deny it. Nothing came out but wheezy air and spit. (Not in his direction. I didn't actually spit on him, Thank Dog).

"I—No—You—" I managed. I was not this girl. This needy, flustered, sputtering girl. I refused to be this girl.

Ari put a hand on the chain of my swing and peered at me. "So your anger is about the kiss?"

"No."

"You sure?"

Time to go on the attack. I cleared my throat, smiled, and stretched out my bare legs, going all Sasha-on-flirt-alert. "We didn't kiss." I tapped my index finger on the back of his hand. His eyes followed the motion. "You kissed me. And it was pretty good. I mean, you were pretty good. Unexpectedly so. As stuffy as you are, I thought your kissing would be a little more . . . I don't know . . ." I trailed off, batting my eyes in a way that was so over-the-top it should send him spiraling into his own personal hell of anxiety.

He turned to look straight at me, steady-like. His lips quirked as if he knew what I was doing and enjoyed the performance. Crap.

My innards curled into a ball of jelly. "Look," I spoke bluntly, quickly. "Sometimes two people are drawn to each other. Like magnets. That doesn't mean it's a good thing or a right thing, it just means they happen to be two magnets sitting on the same countertop with nothing else stronger to attract them. We kissed. It's done and over. Now we're two magnets that are happier on that fridge holding last semester's grades and a reminder to smog the car. Unless you want me to ditch you, right here, right now, just take off running with the Semis and not come back, you're going to drop this."

Ari furrowed his brow, watching me. "Should I have asked permission first?"

I turned my swing to face his, kicked him in the shin, and forced myself awake.

A white note settled on my face. "Excellent timing, Bob. And by the way, what's up with contacting me only when you are of no utter use?"

I turned on the light to read the note anyway.

The youngling Brit? Really? That's who you choose to align with next? Ask the Brit what he and the Alliance plan to do with the Semis. See if he tells the truth.

~Bob

Chapter Twenty-Four

The Problem: Ari wasn't going to drop the whole kiss thing.

My Preferred Solution to the Problem: Give Ari's fan club the name of our hotel and his room number. When they arrived, use the distraction to steal Baby Shark's keys and Ari's credit card so that the Brontës and I could go it alone.

Obstacle to Preferred Solution: Jedda and her stupid spell that I had no way to evade other than Ari.

What Shouldn't Be a Problem But Was: Bob saw Ari as a liar. This should leave me feeling validated, only the reverse happened. I questioned why I was trusting Bob if I didn't trust Ari. (Because I was trusting Bob way more than I should. As much as I'd like to deny that, it was true.)

All along, it'd been a gut thing with Bob, but my gut was tethered to my needy, short-sighted heart that wanted Ari to not be conning me, to be as honorable and rock-steady as he seemed. Clearly my gut had issues.

I was close to giving in on Ari. The neediness swelled every time I thought of him, pictured him, remembered our kiss. I wanted to give in.

No.

He was manipulating me. I *knew* that. Shades of Zachary Stults.

I couldn't give in regardless of what my gut (and heart) wanted to do. I had to try harder, be more difficult. I left Ant three more rambling messages about Bob and Ari and all my problems.

When Ari and I left the hotel at five-thirty a.m. the next morning, I was bleary with exhaustion from avoiding another Dreamscape and thus sleep. I should immediately have started a fight but was just too tired.

Didn't help that he looked amazing, thanks to me. He wore a faded jean jacket with a high collar, a knit hat, and a pair of wrap-around glasses. He'd also followed my instructions to not shave. Which made his famous face less obvious but the resulting shadow turned his lips into targets to torture me.

I wore an outfit worthy of Jedda. Skintight maternity jeans, polka dot tank, a teeny, fuzzy shrug in bright pink with a matching beret, and my new sandals. So. Not. Me. Ari gave me an appreciative look anyway, darn him.

I climbed into Baby Shark and closed my eyes.

When I woke hours later, the sky had lightened into drizzling gray clouds that matched my mood and we were pulling into a four-story parking garage. The place had the feel of . . . "An airport? We're getting on a plane? To where? And won't that give us away? Planes require IDs and X-ray machines."

Ari rolled down the window to take the entry ticket. "We aren't getting on a plane, just swapping for a rental car as the girls at the store captured my BMW on their video."

Good point, although it would've been a better one if I'd thought of it. Ari gave me an assessing look as we drove through the garage. "About last night . . ."

That hadn't taken long.

I sent him an intentionally flat, keep-your-distance look. "What we need here are boundaries."

"If you think I kissed you to convince you to give me the Semis, you're wrong." He said it with a quick, curious glance to gauge my reaction as he pulled Baby Shark into a parking spot.

"Boundaries," I said louder.

"Just putting a truth on the table."

I continued as if he hadn't spoken. "You don't get to cast spells without asking my permission, especially the Dreamscape Spell. You also don't get to kiss me. We're going to pretend that never happened and it will never, ever happen again. Got it? If you even mention the kiss, I'll steal your phone and give your phone number to the head of the Aristotle Montague-Smith-Montague fan club."

He turned to study me for a moment, being thoughtful about it rather than the horrified I'd hoped for. "Sasha . . ."

"And stop saying my name like that. I don't want to hear a word more." I folded my arms and faced the blank wall of the garage to avoid staring at that darned curl of hair that had once again fallen over his forehead. (A totally unfair advantage on his part.)

"Got it," he said mildly. "No more words." He exited Baby Shark and began collecting our stuff. "But just to continue the conversation, if you think I kissed you in an ineffective attempt to dig out your master plan, that's wrong too."

"I hate you."

"I noticed." His lips curled at the edges as if trying to repress mirth. The Ari I'd first met never would've found this entertaining. Ari was channeling *me*.

I exited the car, giving Baby Shark a gentle pat to say goodbye. I'd gotten attached. Once I had my money, I'd offer to buy her from Ari.

Signage said we were at Dulles Airport, Washington DC. I hadn't realized we'd come so far. In my head, we were still in the Midwest.

We arranged the dog carrier with one of us on each end and piled as much of our stuff on top as possible. Ari kept glancing at me as we walked through the terminal. Since we could've used one, there wasn't a single luggage cart around, although Ari murmured a spell to make our load lighter.

"If you think I kissed you to dissuade those girls from hitting on me, that's also wrong."

There were too many people around to respond as I would've preferred so I glared at him. He sent me a raised-brow, curious look in reply.

I believed him, though. He hadn't used me to fend off those girls. Ari wouldn't do something like that.

We made it to the shuttle and wrestled the dogs and our bags on board. It was early enough that the shuttle was empty other than us. Ari settled into a seat for two, scooting over so that I could join him.

I wanted to. I *really* wanted to. I intentionally sat across the aisle.

He tilted his head, watching me again. "If you think—"

Enough of that. "Bob contacted me."

Ari turned fully my direction, eyebrows raised, interest captured. (Well done, Sasha.)

"When? And how?"

"Floating note. Last night. He knows I'm with you and doesn't approve. He told me to ask what your people want to do with the Semis and implied you'd lie about it, which I was already assuming."

"Of course you were." He nodded understandingly. Too understandingly.

"You going to answer?"

A family of five, luckily with no teenage girls, joined us on the shuttle, ending our privacy. Ari and I remained silent until we stopped at car rental. Then we reverse-engineered the whole dog carrier, bags, us routine until we were under a portico outside. "Wait here," Ari said, "while I collect the keys."

I folded my arms over the top of my belly and rocked back on my heels not liking being left behind. "If the desk clerk is female and under sixty, walk away and pick a different agency."

A grin inched its way across his face, crinkling his eyes and making his dark pupils twinkle. "Yes, *Luv*."

"Ewww. Don't *say* things like that."

He shook his head and chuckled softly.

Little flutters of imaginary butterfly wings tickled my stomach at the sound. He was just so charming and—

No.

He did not get to do this to me. I glared at his back as he walked into the rental agency.

When he returned, he'd set aside the humor and had his serious-Ari face on, which was somehow worse. Meant he was planning something.

Neither of us spoke until the dogs and our stuff were safely ensconced in a creamy blond Chevy Malibu, which I'd have immediately christened Malibu Barbie if it wasn't too on-the-nose.

"Sasha, I've been thinking," Ari began once we were in and buckled. He'd glanced over to check. "Enough with the games. It's important that we understand each other clearly, directly. The reason I kissed you—"

I burst loudly into the *Barbie Girl* song. I sang so loud all three dogs howled and Ari winced. I *do not* have a pleasant singing voice.

That I knew the lyrics to *Barbie Girl* was Ant's fault. He'd taught it to me when I was five in a misguided attempt to dissuade me from the crass commercialism of the toy industry. The song is also rather suggestive, so I made a point of singing it to the front windshield rather than Ari. "You didn't answer Bob's question," I said the moment I finished.

"Sasha . . ."

"You want me to sing it again?"

He sighed and gave me an arched, shrewd, entirely disappointed look. As if I'd failed somehow.

Nope. He didn't get to do that either. I wasn't being weak. Cutting off Ari was smart.

Ari put the Barbie Mobile in reverse. (How could I now not with the name?)

"You haven't asked where we're going," I said, to break a silence that felt way too loaded.

"With the end of dry earth in an eastward direction and your telling Jedda your final destination was Florida, I figured north."

Very insightful. I considered bursting into song again. Maybe that one about letting the dogs out?

We exited the airport into more drizzling rain and onto a freeway wide enough for a heavy commute. I made a point to not look at any signage to not tip off Jedda. *North* and *Eastern Canada* were hopefully vague enough to keep her at a distance.

"It comes down to computers and technology," Ari said abruptly.

"What does?"

"Bob's question. That's what you want me to talk about, right?"

"Right." Bob's question seemed a nice, safe, totally meaningless subject. Or at least better than all the things I *didn't* want to talk about.

"Technology is the next frontier in magic-handling as both technology and spells function on the basis of language, or languages." He went deep into his lecture mode, telling me about needing to write spells in computer languages in order to affect technology, and how difficult that was and the skill level needed and the challenges of stray keystrokes that randomly appeared in code if one wasn't on top of them. He seemed to know a lot about it. Since I knew nothing, it was his most boring lecture yet.

Intentional on his part? His way of unloading the tension between us?

Probably.

He droned on for a good fifteen minutes as we passed through rain and suburbs. I freed the dogs, humming to myself as I did so just because. They piled onto my lap, Charlotte with her head cocked in Ari's direction enjoying the sound of his voice.

I leaned my seat back, settling in for a long haul. Ari shot me a side-glance. "You could at least pretend to listen."

"Why would you say that? I'm totally listening."

He made a harrumphing sound not usually found coming from people under sixty. "The language issues make both creating a spellbook and casting it in say C or Python or JavaScript a million-times more complex than say a spell in Ancient Sumerian which I can at least learn to speak. That was an example only by the way. I don't speak any form of Sumerian."

"Good to know." Then what he'd said struck me. I dragged the seat to straight, jerking myself upright and forcing the Brontës to rearrange themselves. "Wait. What did you just say?"

"I don't speak Sumerian. I do have some Ancient Phoenician but just phonetically and only because of a spell inscribed on a burial—"

"What did you say about JavaScript?"

Charlotte sat up on her haunches, ears perked, tail thumping my belly, waiting for Ari's answer. The other two headed for the back seat.

"It's why your Semis is so important. Only an extremely powerful Semis is capable of being shaped into the volume and architecture of spells needed to form a functioning software system. It's a huge undertaking."

Charlotte whacked me several more times with her tail. I barely felt it. "A software system that does what exactly?"

"Whatever I want."

Every emotion I'd passed through in the last twenty-four hours, the good, the bad, the embarrassed, the spooked, all of it disappeared into a black hole of horror.

Such a relief.

So very right.

This was how I was supposed to view Ari. None of the neediness of before. I narrowed my eyes at him. "Are you trying to tell me in a round-about, overly detailed way that you and Mrs. Valenzuela and the others all want the seadragon's Semis in order to take over the internet?"

He jerked as if surprised by my vehemence. "It's not that simple—"

"You totally do, don't you?" My voice rose to a high pitch. The heebie-jeebies that usually crawled under my skin in these moments decided to do a spin-dance in my stomach. "If you controlled the internet, you'd control everything and everyone. All the things ordinary people already think you're doing, but it turns out you aren't yet. How much worse can the planet get?"

"You're taking this all wrong." Ari darted a defensive look my direction, which made Charlotte growl at me.

"You could hack our bank accounts and steal everyone's money, take over the federal government, the CIA, the FBI, BIMD. You'd control the news, social media, online conversations even, and in ways worse than is already being done. Nothing would be safe. The only way for us normal people to fight back would be to give up technology and return to the Dark Ages."

"That's not—"

"Even then you'd still win because all the Medieval spellbooks would be useful again. And this is why you killed that poor, innocent seadragon?"

He flinched. "I told you, I didn't kill the seadragon. I'd never do that. Neither did Mrs. Valenzuela's people. I had a friend check and Mrs. Valenzuela didn't know until the day before that it was in trouble. Someone else shot it. I wasn't able to discover more before needing to intervene for you and the dogs, but you have to believe me when I say that it wasn't me."

"Whatever. Some other magic-handler killed it to take over the world."

"I don't want to take over the world." Frustration tinged his words. I was totally getting to him. Charlotte grabbed for the edge of my shrug, worrying it back and forth.

"Liar."

"I'm not—" Ari splayed his fingers wide against the steering-wheel. His jaw tensed, and a muscle under his ear twitched. He drew in a deep breath, held it for a long moment, and then let it out in a slow, audible stream, struggling to remain calm.

Good.

He pulled off the main freeway onto an expressway. "There's a reason I'm majoring in history and minoring in societal ethics, and not just because anything technology-related would have every other magic-handler at my throat."

"You know a lot about computers, though? Enough to make a spellbook in code?"

"You're asking all the wrong questions." His voice rose to fill the car.

Charlotte tugged backward on my shrug and I had to catch her to keep her from falling off my lap. "You totally *are* capable."

His cheeks flushed pink. "Fine. I've been taking online courses in Computer Science under an assumed name since I was fourteen. I already have a Bachelor's and am working on my Master's." He paused again and then added in a less frustrated voice, "School is easy for me as long as I stay focused and stick to a strict time schedule. But I'm not trying to take over the world."

Yeah, right. And what a relief. No part of me, not my gut nor my heart, nor even my neediness felt any sort of softness for him now. "If I gave the Semis to BIMD instead of a power-hungry magic-handler intent on world domination, what would they do with it?"

Ari pressed his lips together and took several sharp breaths through his nose as if working hard not to lose his temper. When he spoke, his voice was uneven and high and the muscle in his jaw ticked again. "Rumors say BIMD has been experimenting with using magic as an alternative energy source."

I didn't try to hide my glee at that. "Wouldn't you agree that for someone like me, an alternative energy source sounds pretty great?"

"Only if it's true. Another rumor has them creating the world's most destructive weapon."

Crap. Good point. "If I sold the Semis to Bob, would he also use it to take over the world?"

"I told you, I don't want to—" Ari paused and ran a hand through his hair, trying to regroup.

How much further would I have to push him to make him crack? Because that could be fun too.

"I have no idea what Mr. Quan plans," Ari said, still fighting to stay calm. "But it seems likely."

Bummer. I paused to check in with my gut, which pointed out that Bob had brought up ethics from the very beginning, unlike Ari who hadn't until push-came-to-shove. And the more Bob had contacted me, the more Clems-like he seemed. My Gramps got grouchy like him. Ant and I used snark like it was toilet paper. My dad pretty regularly disappeared when he was needed. Yup. Ari and Bob were nothing alike, and Bob was sure to have something better to pitch me.

Charlotte gave a snarly lurch on the edge of my shrug causing a ripping sound. I kept my attention on Ari. "What happens to the internet if you create a spell-software that's a dud? That seems like a real risk based on your history of typos and spells-gone-bad and—"

The tic in his jaw went wild. His hands clenched The Barbie Mobile's steering wheel so hard the dashboard shook from the pressure. "Would you just stop," he shouted. (Yay, me!) "I already told you I haven't had a spell go wrong in years. I've told you I'm exceptionally good at what I do. I'm careful. I'm ethical. I'm not trying to harm anyone. I'm not the enemy here."

"That's what all evil enemies say."

Ari slammed a fist against the steering wheel. The dogs and I all jumped, Charlotte releasing my torn clothing. Ari muttered something under his breath, and I tensed in case I'd pushed him so far that he'd spellcast against me. Instead, he dropped one of the foulest profanities ever created.

Maybe I'd gone too far?

Nah. This was me winning, proving he wasn't nearly as virtuous as he claimed. "Language, language."

He muttered a few more things that if I ever said around Gramps would leave me cooking my own meals for life.

"Here's another thought," I said cheerfully. "What if you create a spellbook to master the internet and it gets stolen and the spells janked-up? What happens to the common people when you or one of your fellow magic-handlers in the Alliance screw up that way?"

"I loathe the Alliance." He spat. "I loathe the vast majority of magic-handlers, people like Mrs. Valenzuela who manipulate the rest of us. How can you not see that? If I broke the cyberspace language barrier using the strongest Semis in existence, I would put in safeguards, build spells to keep others out. I *want* the world to be safe."

"But—"

"No." He shook his head, violently. "Stop with the buts and the arguing and the attacks. You have been intentionally thinking the worst of me since we first met. You want to be that type of person, that's fine. But no more lying about why you're doing it, what you're avoiding. Because I know what's going on. Here's a truth that you don't get to dodge."

The lump in my throat came back. I broke out into song anyway. "*Who Let—*"

"Quiet," he shouted, silencing me. "I'd been thinking about kissing you long before I did it. You apparently haven't noticed, but I can't stop staring at you. Or talking to you. And when you get too close to me, I can't think straight." He paused to take a sharp breath, still furious, still over-a-cliff. "There you were in the store, goofing around, treating me like a dress-up doll, making us both laugh. Those girls ruined it and hurt your feelings, and you were looking at me with distress in your eyes. I kissed you because I wanted you to know how wrong they were, because I had an excuse to do it, because I wanted to protect you. Furthermore, you know this."

The lump in my throat slid down to my belly.

"You're just scared," he finished with a snarl.

He was right. Every last bit of it. And with that, I tumbled head-over-neediness in love with Aristotle Montague-Smith-Montague.

I opened my mouth to belt out another song, lost all ability to remember lyrics, and went with the next best thing. "I need to pee."

Chapter Twenty-Five

"Can you hold it?" Ari asked in a voice banked of emotion as if having declared himself he no longer needed to be upset. "I'd like out of the suburbs before stopping."

"I can hold it." I didn't need to pee. I needed to freak out without a witness.

A leaden silence settled between us. Was he freaking out too? Horrified by what he'd admitted? Working up a way to deny everything? (My preferred choice for awkward declarations.)

The countryside turned into barns hunched between rolling fields and canopies of trees. The sun broke through the clouds making the world glitter with sparkly light and fresh spring dew. We even passed a horse-drawn buggy driven by a young Amish couple. For once, Ari's tendency to drive too slow was the right thing to do.

I'd *fallen* for Ari.

Which experience said would leave me a floor mat or borax-slime or unbaked bread dough or something else found on a dirty floor embedded with crumbs, dog hair, and shoe-dirt.

Of course I was scared. This was Zachary Schultz, *The Faithless Schmuck*, all over again but worse. I seriously needed to pee. (Again, not really.)

Eventually we stopped at a combination gas station and pizza restaurant in a barely-big-enough-to-exist Pennsylvania town. The moment The Barbie Mobile halted, I ran for the ladies' room.

I threw shut the door, hit the deadbolt, and shoved my hands to my eyes, prepared to be knocked flat by the stupidity of it all. (And terror.)

Nothing happened.

I banged my fist against the wall and dug my fingers into my palms. Still nothing.

That was weird.

I replayed Ari's declaration in my head, the passion and anger and look in his eyes. Instead of panic or helplessness, something soft and sweet flowed under my skin, coating my ribs like stove-warmed maple syrup. It must've taken a lot of actual *liking* to get him that upset.

Liking of me.

I banged my fist against the wall again. Then I pulled out my cell and called Ant on his super-secret communications server. Ant would put a stop to me going all mushy.

Ant didn't answer, surprise, surprise. However, there was a voice-mail. A reedy, older voice repeated my name multiple times as if I'd answered her call. *Sasha? Sasha?*

"Grandma George?" (Apparently, we were both bad at this.)

Sasha? Ant made me keep this horrible little phone because he's being watched, but it hates me. I heard your messages about trusting. Child, there are some topics where your Dad and Gramps and Ant are ovens left puffing out heat without anything in need of baking. When it comes to trust, there are Good People out there too. You just have to be open to finding them.

A giggle bubbled up my throat. I pictured Grandma George pointing a bony finger at Dad and Gramps and telling them to turn down the temperature.

Or pointing at me.

The giggle died.

I gave a huff and went back outside. Ari and the Brontës waited by a street sign offering bargain prices on single-slice pizza and cigarettes. The dogs had their noses to the dirt. Ari held a plastic baggie open in front of him. Something small and brown lifted from the ground and floated itself inside.

Magic poop collection. Nice. And good for him for overcoming his aversion to germs to be an ethical animal caretaker. Zachary never would've done that. And was it really that bad that Ari'd never been employed? He worked really hard at everything he applied himself to. That should count for something.

Ari looked over, caught me watching him, and smiled.

Thump, thump, thump. There went my heart again. I pressed my palm to my chest. The rhythm of it beat against my fingers.

Ari was dependable, honorable, steadfast, a *Good Person.* "Maybe this doesn't have to be so hard," I murmured.

The truth of it settled like the last piece of a puzzle in its own, unique slot. A perfect fit. "I trust Ari." The words were barely loud enough to be considered sound.

My gut gave a gurgle of agreement.

Maybe this *was* just that easy.

Ari waved at me and started my direction, all three dogs on his heels.

Ari, I believe you. The words beat to the same rhythm as my heart. I cleared my throat to call out to him, to tell him.

A half owl, half dying-car-starter screech pierced the air, and a Doberman-sized truedragon dropped from a tree. Its coppery wings snapped wide and then beat hard, arrowing straight for Ari.

Ari's eyes went wide. He scooped up the dogs and bolted for The Barbie Mobile.

Zach wouldn't have thought to protect them.

The dragon darted after him.

Ari made it to the car and shoved the dogs inside. Then he raised his hands over his head in spellcasting mode.

"Don't you kill it," I screamed, racing in his direction. Even as the words left my mouth, I knew he never would.

***

Ari, I believe you.

The truedragon chased The Barbie Mobile out of the parking lot with more shrieks. I shoved my hands against my ears. All three dogs howled back at it.

"Sorry about that," Ari said with a sheepish glance my direction. "I knew it was there, but the small ones usually stalk rather than attack."

"No worries." *Ari, I . . . I* couldn't just blurt it out. I needed to be casual, ease into it. What was casual? Talk about the truedragon? The Brontës? My fake need to pee? Nothing seemed right.

Ari held up his phone, checking the GPS. (While driving even!)

The Brontës climbed en masse onto my lap, Charlotte taking up residence closest to Ari. Each dog now had a lavender bow on their little doggie foreheads. Ari again.

I loved on the Brontës for a moment before deciding that if casual conversation wasn't possible, I'd awkwardly blurt out the words after all.

"Ari, I . . ."

"Magic-handler ahead."

". . . believe you."

Ari jerked The Barbie Mobile across the lane-line onto a side road, pitching us all sideways. I grabbed the Brontës with one arm and the door with the other.

"Good." He sounded unnaturally calm, but he also lead-footed the accelerator. Yet another way I'd rubbed off on him. "Since this is the second batch I've sensed today."

"I meant . . ." I trailed off as his words sank in. "Second batch of magic-handlers?" I turned toward the window, my throat going tight and alarm coursing under my skin, but saw nothing worse than more rolling farm fields, grazing horses, and eroding asphalt. (Pennsylvania backroads were pretty crappy, although not as bad as California's.) "Are we being chased?"

"I don't think so. I picked up on three magic-handlers at Dulles, none of which—"

"Wait? Three? All the way back at the airport?" I swiveled to stare behind us in more alarm. A rusted Jeep followed a couple hundred feet back, but that was it. "Why didn't you tell me before?"

"You told me not to talk."

"You ignored me. How close are they?"

Ari did his silent-lips move. At the same time, the car jounced through a rough spot of road, and I steadied the dogs. Ari shook his head. "Can't tell anymore. My range is about five miles, which is excellent, just in case you were wondering. Most magic-handlers can sense one mile if they're lucky. Either way, they aren't chasing us."

"So, you'll know about other magic-handlers before they know about us, right?" This was not the type of trust I'd prepared myself for.

"Right." He bobbed his head. "I mean, hopefully. There are other strong magic-handlers out there, of course. And physics gets involved since we're moving, which can cause a warping of the magic, but—"

I took a sharp breath. "We're so going to get chased."

"Even if another handler senses me, they won't know who I am unless they can see me."

"But they're looking for us. That's why they're here."

Emily gave a low, nervous whine.

"Well, yes. After the dragon video—" He swerved suddenly. "Did you see the size of that pothole?"

Pothole. But no magic-handlers. I monitored the odometer and after ten miles (then twenty, then thirty) of no more warnings from Ari, I relaxed enough to return to my previous goal. I cleared my throat.

Charlotte squirmed, her butt wiggling so hard she knocked Annie Pup half off my lap. I rearranged them only for Charlotte to climb her front paws up my chest, lift her lip, and expose a needle-like canine, daring me to provoke her into sinking it into my chin. *Sheesh*, Charlotte's jealousy was getting a bit out of control. As if to underline this, the other two dogs growled at me in solidarity.

Couldn't really blame them for liking Ari so much since, ya know, I did too. I decided to wait a bit longer, just to keep the peace.

Several hours later, we passed a signpost inviting us to "Experience, Explore, and Enjoy New York."

Grams and Grandma George's home state. Was that a good or bad omen? That the condition of the road got even worse wasn't hopeful.

The Brontës headed to the backseat where Ari'd laid out three little doggie bowls and more poop pads. The moment they were distracted, I turned to Ari once again. "Ari, I—"

Bang.

The sound was so loud, so abrupt, Ari and I both ducked as if the windshield had imploded. (It hadn't.)

"What just—" Ari started, then cut off as he fought the steering wheel to keep the car steady. I listened for the familiar flap-flap-flap of loose rubber repeatedly hitting the road. Yup. "Flat tire. Pull over. I can fix it."

It took me seven minutes and twenty-nine seconds to change out the exploded tire. Far from the family record, but not bad considering Ari insisted on helping me retrieve the spare and then had trouble finding it. Once done, he used a spell to remove every speck of rust and dirt from my hands.

The moment we piled back into The Barbie Mobile, Charlotte took up her former spot on my lap giving me another raised lip.

This was getting kinda weird. Suspiciously weird. Maybe it was just a coincidence, but it felt like the universe was out to stop me from talking to Ari . . . ?

"Owner's manual says to keep under 45 mph on the spare," Ari said, glancing at his phone before starting the engine.

"Owner's manuals lie," I replied to test my theory.

Charlotte growled but nothing else bad happened. Huh.

We proceeded at 41 mph. I tried again. "We could buy a new tire."

"Takes too long. We're already behind schedule."

"What schedule?" Still nothing bad happened. My theory must be wrong.

Over the next two excruciatingly slow hours, Ari sensed five other magic-handlers and I fell asleep. Between my lack the night before and today's emotional Ferris wheel, I had to. I woke hours later when Ari cut The Barbie Mobile's engine.

We'd stopped in a rental lot of vehicles covered in colorful graphics meant to announce to every other driver within half-mile visibility that they too could Rent-this-Camper. Apparently, The Barbie Mobile was going to be a short-term relationship.

We both got out of the car, leaving the dogs inside. No magic-handlers nearby, nothing to pop a tire, hopefully no dragons. Only movement was one of the larger RV's backing up while making a slow beep-beep-beep of warning.

It was way past time for me to try again.

Ari paused to stretch, arms raised high, back curved, big yawn. His yawn sent me yawning too. I finished and turned to him. "Wait up, There's something I need to tell—"

Crack. Then the sound of breaking glass coming from the backing RV. Ari and I spun that direction. The side window had shattered where a tree limb had fallen through it.

The door to the rental office flew open and no less than ten people flooded out. "Get back in the car," Ari said. "Before someone recognizes you."

I did. But also . . . Seriously?

Maybe it wasn't me speaking that was the problem. Maybe it was specifically me wanting to tell Ari I believed him.

Which was weird. And by weird, I meant magical-in-nature-weird.

A shiver of grossed-out started at the base of my spine and spread.

Ari wasn't behind it, though. He had no reason to spell me into not telling him. Nor Jedda, nor Chadd, the only other two magic-handlers I'd been near since home.

Which left some unknown person and spell.

Or . . .

I remembered suddenly what Ari had said about the Semis bending the people and the world around it to assist its bonded person. I didn't feel particularly bonded to the thing, but I had spent a full twenty-four hours going over and over in my head why it was a bad idea to get attached to Ari. And not just in my head, either. I'd told my brother about it out loud. And the Brontës. If the Semis had been paying attention, it must've noticed.

I gave the top of my belly a sharp pat. "Yeah, listen up Semis-thingy. I'm doing my best by you, but if you keep screwing with me, I'll drown you in the nearest sewage facility. Got it?" All a total lie, and the way things were going the Semis likely could tell that too.

I'd just have to time things better.

The RV that Ari rented was the smallest of the possible options. It held an over-cab bed, built-in table with bench seats that turned into a second bed, closet, kitchen, and toilet/shower combination. (I literally had to stand over the toilet if I also wanted to stand under the shower.)

The Brontës loved it, running in excited circles and investigating every crack and corner. Ari took disinfecting wipes to all the flat surfaces. I kept my mouth shut to avoid the engine from blowing up or anything.

It needed a name.

"We'll stop for supplies next," Ari said, once he was satisfied the germs had been wiped out. (Haha.) "But let's travel another couple hours first. There are magic-handlers east, south, and west of us."

"Meaning we're going to get chased." And even more, making it a bad moment to risk the Semis creating more havoc.

"We aren't being chased," Ari continued.

"Yet," I muttered.

An hour or so after dark, Ari pulled us into a RV park next to a man-made river that turned out to be the Erie Canal. Go figure, I hadn't realized that was a real thing that still existed.

"All should be good for the night," he said after parking in a numbered spot and tugging a screen across the front windshield. "No one around. My wards will wake me if that changes."

I nodded my understanding.

Ari cooked. I cleaned, then played fetch with the Brontës. Once they were worn down, I converted the table and benches into a bed for us.

Ari came out of the toilet/shower combo wearing his monogrammed old-man pajamas. I fluffed my new pillow to keep myself from going all loopy in admiring him. Ari started to slide behind me in the narrow aisle, but totally unplanned, unpremeditated, no time for the Semis to stop me, I grabbed his arm and swung around. *"Ari,IBelieveYou."* It came out mono-syllable fast.

Ari put a finger to my lips and smiled softly. "I know that already."

He knew? All of my efforts had been for nothing?

Well, shoot.

I looked at him, really looked for the first time since this morning. His shoulders sagged, his face was gray, his eyes had bags, and the corners of his lips turned down as if there was nothing left to hold them up. He was exhausted.

He'd gotten as little sleep as I the night before and that was after having fought off the dragon. Then he'd spent all day driving and sighting magic-handlers. The warmed-maple-syrup feeling returned, starting at the place where his finger rested against my lips and spreading to my fluttering heart. "You are so irritatingly noble," I whispered.

"I'm sorry I yelled at you," he said, tugging at my lower lip with his finger, then stroking downward to my chin. "But I meant every word I said."

I warmed even more. "I believe you."

He looked at my lips and raised his brows in question. I stood up on my toes, leaning into him, the most natural movement of my life. His lips touched mine, brushed them really, barely a touch. It had none of the intensity of his first kiss, less Olympic-quality-jack-knife-off-the-high-board-for-the-gold-medal and more . . .

Tender.

I kissed him back, aiming for a reverse-twist-into-a-swan-dive but at the last-minute switching to tender too.

Chapter Twenty-Six

Seems safe to stop worrying about my finances for the moment and track something else instead.

Tally of kisses between Ari and me prior to our next day's drive:

- Number one at 5:25 a.m.: Rose-petal-soft wake-up kiss instigated by Ari. I slept through it, although he insisted it happened.

- Number two at 5:35 a.m.: I ambushed him over the RV's mini-sink after we both finished brushing our teeth. This one counted for two. It was that good. (And minty!)

- Number four at 5:49 a.m.: Alarm on Ari's phone went off, which I used as an excuse to snag the phone and ransom it back for a kiss. Surprise, surprise, he agreed with no fussing.

- Number five to five hundred starting at 6:25 a.m.: Ari tugged me over to a picnic bench to make out while not watching the sun rise. At this point, I stopped counting due to volume and frequency. Tallying kisses was not one of my better plans.

"So," I said some hours later while putting the remains of our lunch salads in the RV's mini-fridge. We were either in Vermont or New Hampshire. (Never could tell the two apart and intentionally hadn't been paying attention.)

"So," he replied back all happy-like. He'd just returned from levitating a dog poop over to a trashcan. (I was really liking that spell!)

"So." I traced the side of his neck with my finger. His skin was both solid and soft. And silky and warm. And delectable. Pretty much everything I and every tween girl on the planet had always imagined it to be. (I was *touching* Aristotle Montague-Smith-Montague! Repeatedly! Could life get better?!)

I stepped away to avoid getting distracted. Yes, I knew I was being an idiot by going full-steam down this path. Yes, I was that into him, all-in even. Yes, my gut was all-in too. "Before we head off in Redfern—"

"Redfern?"

"Name of our RV. There's a fern on the side and Dr. Redfern is a character in my Grams's book, *The Blue Castle*." I lunged to the left in an attempt to beat him to the driver's seat. Couldn't resist.

Ari caught me around the waist, swinging me over to the passenger seat. "Redfern it is. However, you aren't on Redfern's lease and can't drive." He leaned in as if to kiss me but when I relaxed in his arms, he dropped me backward onto the passenger seat. When he took the driver's seat himself, the corners of his lips quirked up. The Ari I'd first met would *never* have done something like this.

I grinned back but also snatched his phone again. (The first thing I was going to do after trading the Semis for money was buy myself a phone like his. Yes, I was starting to think, dream, picture the money again. Canada was close!)

"You can't blackmail me into letting you drive."

"I'm not." I grabbed his hand and touched his thumb to the phone's screen. Charlotte made a halfhearted growl.

Ever since I'd lectured the Semis, we'd had no more disasters. I took this to mean the Semis had gotten the message. Charlotte too. Her previous objections had settled into grumbles. I swiped open his phone. (Seriously, I needed one of these.) "I'm giving you a gift."

He raised his eyebrows.

I typed in what I remembered of the GPS coordinates I'd captured ages ago and then tossed the phone to him before I could see what popped up on the screen. "I'm gifting you the extremely vague and somewhat odd GPS coordinates to find Bob. Then if I ditch you, which I'm not planning on doing but who knows, you'll be able to find me again."

Ari stared at the phone. "Greenland? Can we even drive there?"

"Uh no. Not Greenland." I glanced over and sure enough his phone showed white for glaciers. "Typo. Try 45 North and 54 West. Don't tell me where we're going."

He frowned, concentrating on the phone. "Won't Jedda be waiting for us either way, since you know the coordinates?"

"Wait for it. Bob's smart." Which in hindsight, might be why his instructions were vague and odd. Gotta love the guy.

Ari's frown deepened. He messed with his phone, probably scrolling to find the nearest landmass. I scooped up Charlotte and scratched her behind the ears to resist looking over his shoulder. When Ari said nothing, I got impatient. "Bob must want me to drive in a certain direction. Then he'll either intercept me or send better instructions. Since I won't know the when-where-how until it happens, there isn't anything for Jedda to pick up on other than ocean."

Ari put his phone down, still frowning. He placed his hand on the ignition but didn't start the engine. "Why are you putting so much hope in this stranger rather than me?"

"I'm not." Okay, I totally was.

Ari gave me a stony, sideways glance. "*Trust a man and he will be true to you; treat him greatly, and he will show himself great.* Ralph Waldo Emerson, adjusted to fit the context."

"How about, *We don't know where we're going, but isn't it fun to go?* Barney Snaith from *The Blue Castle*." I touched him on the arm to try to bring back our mutual flirtiness. Barney was Valancy Stirling's love interest in *The Blue Castle*. A non-conformist, naturalist who married the dying heroine to save her from having to spend her final days with her evil family.

Ari started the engine, still looking stony. "I read your *Blue Castle* book," he said after pulling us back onto another highway banked in trees. "It wasn't what I expected."

"You hated it."

"I didn't hate it."

"You totally did." Which should've been fine. No one not-a-Clems understood our obsession with *The Blue Castle*.

"Have you considered what an oddity it is that your grandmother's history lines up with the book? So much so that it seems too much a coincidence." He spoke carefully.

I sighed. Why, oh why, couldn't we stick to flirting?

"Grams found *The Blue Castle* when she was a kid. The heroine's name was Valancy Stirling. Grams's name was Valerie Sterling, so it was like Grams found herself in the book. She copied it, minus the dying-of-heart-disease aspect, which was a red herring anyway. Grams created a new life in the same way Valancy Stirling did. She married her own Barney Snaith, and they lived happily-ever-after in their own Blue Castle. No coincidences." (And really, once I had the money, the first thing I would do was pay off Grams's house's mortgage in homage to her. Then I'd buy a phone.)

"But—"

"No buts." He didn't get to disagree. Then I had a different thought. "Wait. This isn't about *The Blue Castle*, is it?"

Ari shifted uncomfortably in his seat. It was so unlike him that Charlotte and Annie lifted their heads to stare. "You know nothing about him," Ari finally muttered.

"Who?"

"Mr. Quan."

"You mean Bob?" He was still stuck on that? "Yes, I do." I tossed a ball to the back of Redfern, sending the dogs chasing after it. Then I reached over to kiss the side of Ari's jaw, driving distraction or not.

For the briefest moment, he fanned his eyes closed. Very brief. It was a miracle he hadn't shoved me away. We were, after all, moving down the road at the revolutionary speed of 53 MPH.

I returned to my seat and rested my socked feet on the dash, trying to force a sense of communal comfort. Charlotte brought the ball back, so I tossed it again. "Once we find Bob, he'll pitch me, and what he says will be so good, so ethical, that even you'll agree he's a better choice than your plan for world dominion."

"I'm not—"

"Correction, your plan for world protection, with only minor amounts of dominion involved."

He snorted, humored. A move in the right direction. "What if you're wrong?"

"I'm not." I could totally be wrong but would return to paying my own expenses before admitting it.

"Even if he's a modern-day Emmanuel Kant, your plan benefits you but not me."

Whoever Emmanuel Kant was.

I slid my feet to the floor and swiveled to face him. "You didn't think I'd hand over the Semis just because you're an excellent kisser, did you?"

Ari gave me a sharp look that I couldn't interpret. "I thought . . ." He shook his head as if throwing out the rest of what he'd planned to say and starting over. "I want both. I want the Semis and you."

Which would have been totally hot, except that he'd put me second and the Semis first. "I'm not giving it to you."

He lowered his voice. "*Even if I knew that tomorrow the world would go to pieces, I would still plant my apple tree. Martin Luther.*"

"What does that even mean?"

"It means I have five and a half more days until my classes start to change your mind."

***

We stopped at a gas station in Maine several hours later. Ari kissed me extensively before leaving to use the men's room. Felt kinda competitive, as if he had something to prove. (We'd agreed to not use Redfern's loo to avoid having to figure out how to empty it.)

Several dragonfly-shaped insects buzzed at his head as he dashed for the store. Some kinda magical-insect most likely. "Poor Ari." Not. He deserved it for ruining the easiness between us.

The moment he was gone, all three Brontës bolted to the back of Redfern, yapping. I went to investigate and found a white piece of paper floating gently down from the ceiling. I caught it before the dogs could shred it.

Stop messing around. You're in danger. Half the world's magic-handlers are headed to New England. Did the Brit even tell you the truth?
~Bob

"Yeah, actually. He did." Take that, *Bob.* I may also have been feeling competitive with something to prove.

When Ari returned, I didn't tell him about the note. Instead, I kissed him as if he'd been gone for months instead of minutes. He turned pink and lost all ability to breathe. So did I. My kiss totally outdid his, just saying.

"I gave Chadd access to my corner of the Montague-Smith-Montague library," Ari said as we returned to driving. "In exchange for helping you. I thought you should know how committed I am." He said it as if making a point.

"I . . ." I paused, searching for something I'd sacrificed that was better than his. I came up blank and went for the next best thing. "I didn't ditch you in any of the thirteen opportunities I've had since Chicago."

He tapped his fingers on the steering wheel as if thinking. "I've put together a foolproof plan to get you across the Canadian border without needing to hand over your passport or get IDed."

"I managed to elude Jedda, not once, not twice, but three times across three states." Pause. "What foolproof plan?"

"I traded Chadd my library for him flying out. We're on our way to collect him now."

The dominos he'd lined up all fell in careful order inside my head. "He'll use his Invisibility Spell to get me across the border." A good plan, dang it. Pretty sure Ari'd just won round two of whatever it was we were doing here.

On the other hand, the timing of Ari's announcement seemed rather convenient. "Why didn't you tell me before?"

"Jedda's spell."

Another good point. He was on a roll. Unfair.

"One caveat, though." Ari cleared his throat, as if uncomfortable. "It would be better if Chadd didn't know about us."

Whoa. Shades of Zachary, *The Faithless Schmuck*, who'd made sure I never met any of his friends. "Explain."

"Chadd is a charismatic . . ." Ari paused as if searching for just the right word. ". . . arsehole."

"Language, language. Isn't he your friend?"

"He is. But he's definitely a . . . you know what I mean. He's also the only handler I trust not to call Mrs. Valenzuela. And that's only because he wants my library."

Something was off in his voice. It was subtle, but I knew him too well to miss it. I turned to study him. Was he gripping the steering wheel a tad too tight? Were his shoulders contracted, hunched a bit even? Was he uncomfortable but working hard to hide it from me?

That would be a yes to all three.

I bit at the corner of my lip. Maybe I shouldn't be all-in after all.

Then again, in the past, when he'd been uncomfortable like this, there'd been fan-girls involved.

Oh. Got it. Phew. "It's not me specifically that's the problem. Chadd will humiliate you for liking someone."

Ari ducked his head.

Nailed it. No hidden agenda, just his usual insecurities. I patted him on the leg, pleased. "Don't you worry. I got this. I'll protect you and control all urges to jump you at the same time. Chadd will never know." (Round three to Sasha.)

He didn't look relieved.

We met Chadd in a small Maine town that, not kidding, was named Carmel. It couldn't have been more unlike the Carmel-by-the-Sea of home, though. This Carmel was inland and all about white, clapboard farmhouses and American flags rather than Spanish villas and bougainvillea.

Chadd waited for us at a bus stop, an oversized backpack at his feet. With his threadbare khaki shorts, T-shirt, and shaggy blond hair, he looked just as I remembered him—an overly gorgeous, totally stereotypical, surfer. He waved energetically in our direction.

The moment Redfern stopped, I jumped out to greet him.

"Hey there," Chadd said with a huge, golden retriever smirk.

"Hey there back at you." I opened Redferns's side door so he could toss in his backpack. He did and then lifted me off the ground in a double-barrel hug.

Which gave me a fantastic idea.

The best way to hide my attachment to Ari was to hit on Chadd. Which wouldn't even be hard because he was delicious, too, if not quite so delicious as Ari.

"Great disguise," he said with a nod to my belly. Then he pushed past me to Redfern's passenger-side door and yelled, "Shotgun."

"Cheater." But well played.

I climbed into the back and came around to sit on the floor between the two boys. All three dogs went for Chadd's shoes with tails wagging and ears perked. Annie Pup latched onto his shoelaces. Chadd didn't notice but gave me a pat on the head as if I were a pet. I slapped his arm, and he smirked as if he'd done it just to get me to react. Yeah, Chadd was . . . that word Ari had called him. I could work with that.

"Dude, you're in so much trouble," he said to Ari.

Ari glanced up from his phone and nodded with a quick, apologetic look to me. Then he gave a shake of his head to Chadd that I couldn't interpret. It was a tense shake.

Weird. And suspicious.

Or not. (I seriously needed to stop second-guessing Ari.)

"Until that dragon attack video," Chadd said, still speaking to Ari but dropping a hand on my shoulder. "There were, no kidding, wagers on whether you were helping the NoMa girl or had kidnapped her."

"NoMa?" I interrupted.

"Non-magic-handling," Ari explained with a second apologetic glance in my direction as he pulled Redfern back onto the road.

I lifted Chadd's hand off my shoulder and placed it on his knee, letting my fingers linger. "Can we all agree that it's gross to call me a NoMa?"

"We agree," Ari said quickly. "Chadd, use your manners."

"Oh, sorry, Sasha," Chadd said with a flirty smile. "I'll try to remember, but it's been nuts. Even before the video of the dragon attack, the whole handler world turned upside-down looking for you guys. Two days ago, a Brazilian and a Nigerian nearly battled it out at the airport in DC. Yesterday the Italians caused a bunch of Pennsylvanians to panic and evacuate their town. Last night, some girl who looks like Sasha was taken captive for several hours in Rochester. The moment the first kidnapper released her, a second picked her up, just because. It's like a mini-war-games out there with zero sightings of you and handlers casting egos and spells in all directions. BIMD has agents everywhere and lawyers are showing up in droves."

"Didn't we get Redfern somewhere near Rochester?" I asked Ari, my voice rising. Chadd's stories appeared to follow the path we'd driven.

"Yes, but don't worry about it. We aren't being chased."

"Worrying? Who's worrying?" I forced myself to think about all the money I'd be making soon and then turned to gaze adoringly at Chadd. "There are lawyers that go after magic-handlers?"

"It's an entire subgenre of law," Ari cut in. "Spells used against other spells tend to warp and go awry with unintended consequences. It's kept quiet to avoid false accusations, but most nations allow for property recompense in situations where there's collateral damage. In the US—"

Chadd cut him off. "Boring, dude."

Ari winced.

"Dude, rude." I pointed a finger at Chadd. He didn't get to talk to Ari that way. I also hauled Annie Pup away from Chadd's shoelace before she chewed through it. Charlotte climbed across my feet to lean against Ari's leg. Emily joined her. None of them wagged their tails.

"A few of the gossips contacted me," Chadd continued. "A couple of mafia-type East Europeans too. I blew them all off."

"Anyone touch you?" Ari asked.

"Not an idiot, dude."

"Neither is Ari," I snapped back, my flirtiness stumbling.

Chadd put his hands up all playful-like. "Never said that. Have you seen this guy's grades?"

He'd implied it, which I didn't say out loud. Instead, I batted my eyes at him and then ogled his biceps. "I'm sure yours are just as good."

Chadd looked me over, his lips quirking. I met the look with an innocent smile. "Have you run into any Australians?" I asked to change the subject yet again.

"None. Why Australians?"

"Jedda Jacobs," Ari answered. "She's got an Intentions Spell on Sasha."

Chadd shuddered. "The Australians are the worst. Almost as bad as the Brits."

"Rude again." I kept my tone upbeat, barely.

"Feisty and protective again," Chadd said with a laugh.

"Leave her alone." Ari placed his hand on my shoulder, much as Chadd had done earlier. Tingles raised along my collarbone and I shivered.

Chadd's eyes went wide. He looked first to Ari, then to me, then back to Ari. Crap. A toothy smirk spread across Chadd's face. "Dude. So that's how you did it. I wondered."

Ari went rigid. "No!"

"Ari didn't do anything," I burst out. "I'm using him to get to Bob, not the other way around. Plus, I'm seeing a guy back home. Javi. I'd never mess up my relationship with Javi by getting involved with someone who will inevitably leave me." An excellent lie.

And it was a lie. Of course it was. I had no fears of Ari leaving me. No way. He'd never do that. I forced even more vehemence into my voice. "There's nothing, absolutely nothing, nada, never, nothing-burger, going on between Ari and I. Don't even go there. You're barking up a tree containing the wrong freaked-out cat."

Chadd stared at me, mouth dropped half open.

Ari removed his hand, slowly.

I winced. I'd protested waaaayyy too much.

Chadd snickered and patted me on the head a second time. "If that's what you want everyone to believe, I won't nay-say. But when Ari's charm wears off, you should give the Semis to me."

Chapter Twenty-Seven

The Canadian border crossing ended up being straightforward.

Except that Ari sensed six other magic-handlers nearby. Chadd only sensed one, but his magical-range was much smaller than Ari's. I spotted a black van that may or may not have been BIMD.

Ari was calm throughout, and thus, so was I. (Mostly.)

Chadd's Invisibility Spell worked perfectly. Ari cast a Privacy Spell to create a bubble of silence around the dogs and me, and we made it into Canada without incident.

Canada looked pretty much just like Maine except that the street signs and road advertisements were now in French. The landscape was endless Christmas-type trees mixed with maples. California was going to seem like a sucked-out, desiccated desert after all of this green. Way to make my homeland look bad. But also, once I had the money, I should buy a vacation home somewhere with lots of trees and maybe a lake.

Ari drove. I sat on a stool Ari'd purchased for me after Chadd and I had rock-paper-scissored for the passenger seat and he'd won. Charlotte and Annie Pup were at my feet, Emily in my lap. Since Chadd was snoring, I leaned my head against Ari's side.

Next step was dropping Chadd off. Ari was properly vague on the details but after several hours of driving, I started seeing more houses, and the highway headed onto a smaller, gray version of the Golden Gate Bridge. In the distance, the tops of buildings pushed up above the trees. Definitely not San Francisco but a good sign that we'd be rid of Chadd soon. (And that much closer to Bob!)

"Sasha?" Ari asked, in that steady, reassuring tone he did so well. "Quebec City was never a place you specifically planned to visit, was it?"

"No. Why?"

"Oh, shit, dude," Chadd bellowed, jerking both awake and halfway out of his seat at the same time.

"Language," both Ari and I said in unison. The dogs all jumped to their feet.

Chadd pivoted to the window. "There are four magic-handlers somewhere nearby."

"That keeps happening," I pointed out. "Ari says not to worry. They aren't chasing us."

"I sense seven," Ari said evenly. "No eleven. No thirteen—"

"Wait. Are you saying we *are* being chased?" I punched him on the arm. "I knew it. All this time—"

"We're not necessarily being chased," Ari said, quickly.

"Six more coming from the direction of the city," Chadd said. "All headed to the opposite side of the bridge." He paused, then added as if trying to be super clear, "Same place we're headed."

We drove onto the bridge. No choice. No exits.

"Nineteen for me," Ari said.

"We. Are. Totally. Being. Chased."

"Probably," Ari said, still sounding way too calm.

My heart raced from zero to panicked so fast that I felt it in my eardrums. I slid the dogs onto the floor to peer out the front window. "I didn't give us away. I haven't looked at a map since Nebraska, and I know nothing about Canada." There wasn't anything suspicious in front of us other than the rest of the bridge.

"You didn't pre-purchase a ticket home, did you?" Ari asked Chadd. "Or do anything else traceable?"

"Of course not. Besides, you said I'd be flying out of Boston. And, dude, we've got a Lamborghini to our right with a handler driving."

"I know that," Ari replied.

"Can we lose them?" I asked.

"In Redfern?" Ari asked incredulously. "Twenty-two."

"Please, please stop counting," I begged.

"A limo just settled in behind the Lamborghini," Chadd said, his voice high. "Four handlers inside."

Jedda was usually found in limos.

"We run for it," I said. "I drive. Fast as we can go. Attract the Canadian police. Let them rescue us."

Ari shook his head. "We're almost out of petrol. I planned to stop outside the airport."

I glanced at the dial. It was down to the empty mark. "Now you decide to be a risk taker?"

"What are we going to do?" Chadd asked.

I looked at Ari. So did Chadd. So did Charlotte, who circled anxiously at my feet. Ari pressed his lips into a line. His brow furrowed. Redfern went weirdly silent.

Then Ari released one hand from Redfern's steering wheel, grabbed his phone, and tossed it to Chadd. "Guide me. Find us a shopping mall or some other place full of people. If we have to have a confrontation, we need it to be as public as possible."

Chadd went to work. I picked up Charlotte. Annie Pup poked her nose out from where she'd hidden under Ari's seat.

"You're going to fight them off?" I asked.

"Fifty-four magic-handlers? I'm not that good."

"Fifty-four?" A tremor ran down my back.

"Plus BIMD," Chadd added, not glancing up from the phone. "Pretty sure their vans are on our tail as well."

"How can BIMD even be in Canada?" I asked.

Neither one answered.

We exited the bridge to find a line of luxury vehicles racing toward us on a side road, including several Teslas, a Mercedes, a Bentley, and a Range Rover. "It's like the Car Week parade at Pebble Beach."

"A parade throwing spells at us," Chadd added.

"My wards are holding," Ari replied. "No one will cast anything so strong it would cause a scene in front of witnesses."

The line of magic-handlers slowed, pulling in behind us as we passed.

"They aren't going to stop us?" I asked.

"They'll wait for privacy. Chadd, do you have a public place for me?"

"How about a Buysco parking lot? That's sure to be full of people and cameras."

"How far?" Ari asked.

"Three exits."

Ari nodded and glanced at me. "Sasha, I know you aren't ready. I know you don't want this. That it isn't what you planned. But it's either me or one of them. You have three exits to decide what you want to do with the Semis."

A cement block of not-in-this-lifetime refusal solidified in my bones. "No." I stood, holding onto Ari's shoulder to balance. My pregnant belly brushed against his arm.

Absolutely not.

I hadn't made it to Bob yet. I wasn't ready.

Ari squeezed my hand. It didn't make me feel better. In fact . . .

He had to know he was my best option at this exact moment. He'd know I knew it too. I slid my hand off of his shoulder and onto the back of the seat. "Did you set me up?"

Ari recoiled as if I'd slapped him. His brows drew together and his eyes narrowed with outrage. "How can you ask that?"

"How can I not?" But I believed him. He wasn't a good enough liar to fake that level of offended. I stepped to the back, away from the boys. "Bob?" I whispered so low that neither of them could hear. "Help?"

Nothing happened.

I stepped even farther back and pressed my hand to my belly. "Okay, Semis. Your turn. Pop all their tires or cause a bomb to go off. You got this."

I peeked out the side window and spotted the limo. No signs of sudden destruction.

What next?

Stall.

I returned to my stool as we exited the highway. "Stay straight for half a mile," Chadd said. "Turn right past a gas station. Then a left and there'll be the backside of a Buysco."

"Blow up the gas station," I whispered to the Semis. "Or bring an earthquake to cause a fifty-foot crevice between us and everyone else."

We made it to the perfectly intact, no-disaster-struck gas station. I spotted the distinctive blue edging of a Buysco warehouse roof to our left. "Turn right," I ordered.

"Not right. Left," Chadd insisted. A moment later, we pulled into the back loading area and followed the building around to the front.

When we arrived, the parking lot was empty. There wasn't a soul around, and the store's glass doors were covered in large orange posters in French.

"Out of business?" Ari said, incredulously.

"How can it be out of business?" Chadd repeated. "Google didn't tell me."

This was good. We'd have to find a new location. Hopefully, on the far side of town or, even better, the next town over. (Redfern's gas tank permitting. Maybe the Semis could help that way?)

An engine revved somewhere behind us and then tires squealed. A Lamborghini screeched to a halt in front of us, forcing Ari to brake. A limo slid to a jolting stop next to it, and then a Range Rover swung a U to take the other side. One moment the lot was empty, the next we were surrounded. Even worse, more vehicles and several lines of black vans filled the exits, cutting us off.

This was bad. "Thanks for nothing." I glared at my belly.

"Two hundred thirty-eight," Ari said, his hands still over-gripping the steering wheel. "Not counting BIMD."

"Who shouldn't even be in Canada," I added, but I also got an idea. I whipped around to face Chadd, my belly hitting him in the head. "Make me invisible. Like in Chicago. Then you and Ari keep the handlers and BIMD busy while I sneak away with the Semis."

"That will only work on BIMD," Ari said, cutting Redfern's engine. "Sasha, you have to make a choice."

"Something else then." I paused waiting for an idea. Come on, come on. I was not giving up.

A classic blue Jaguar pulled in behind the limo. It was immediately joined by an Aston Martin and one of those really tiny British cars. More vehicles followed, circling us and parking.

Ari stood, extracted Annie Pup from under his seat, and collected Charlotte. "Come to the back where we can't be seen."

I did. So did Chadd. I ended up standing between the two of them. Chadd touched me on the arm. "I can't invisible you from handlers, but I can invisible the Semis like I did in Chicago. I can also invisible myself, but only for a few minutes. Five at the max before I wear out. The handler's wards will still tell them I'm there, but with the volume of people present, I should be able to sneak away. Then you find me later. Your plan but with a twist."

Could work.

Also meant trusting Chadd. I didn't like Chadd. I turned to Ari to see what he thought.

The walls and floor around us suddenly shook as if struck by an earthquake. Chadd's hand on my arm held me steady or I'd have fallen sideways. A loud voice outside yelled something unintelligible, possibly in Hindu.

Ari murmured under his breath. The shaking stopped. He turned to me, the dogs still clutched in his arms. "Chadd's plan is too risky. Give the Semis to me. I can send it to my family's library."

"You'd give it back after?"

"I—" he started.

The ceiling above us screeched as if pried at by a massive can opener. All three of us ducked. "Hold on," Ari shouted over the noise. He put the dogs down, raised his hands, and did his murmuring thing again. The screeching immediately died.

"Ari won't give the Semis back to you," Chadd said, tightening his hand on my arm. "He can't. A library is the first step in the transformation process and that can't be undone. But I'm not capable of turning a Semis of this size into a spellbook. Didn't Ari tell you? My family's the poorest and the weakest of the magic-handlers. I'd *have* to give it back to you."

I looked again at Ari. "Is Chadd telling the truth?"

"Regarding his family and his magic? Yes. He couldn't send your Semis to a library. But neither will five minutes of invisibility get him far."

All three dogs sat on their rumps in a line, watching us with ears perked. Tiny canine judges.

"Please, Sasha," Ari said softly. "You know me. You can trust me."

No.

Only yes. I did trust him. Ari was solid.

Charlotte leaned in Ari's direction. She agreed.

Someone banged on Redfern's window. I turned to see a piece of paper held flush to the glass. *Sasha Clems, Japan would like to speak with you.*

Outside, someone hollered through a bullhorn. "Sasha? This is Agent Silva. We've got your back. Come out slowly and we'll protect you. And the Semis."

A totally inappropriate giggle escaped my mouth. Stupid response. I was in serious trouble here. But, *sheesh.*

Chadd squeezed my arm a second time. "Sasha, Ari's manipulating you."

"No, I'm not," Ari snapped back.

Agent Silva continued to yell on the bullhorn in the background. The note plastered to the window was replaced with a second one. *Japan will double BIMD's offer.* Several inches over, scrawling red writing appeared on the window itself. *China will triple Japan.*

"Ari tries to be manipulative," I replied, fighting another giggle, unable to help myself, "but he doesn't have the knack for it."

"Bet he didn't tell you about his Attraction Spell," Chadd continued. "The one that makes girls think about him constantly and obsess over his entirely mediocre looks."

"He doesn't have an Attraction Spell." I looked at Ari. "You don't have an Attraction Spell. You would've told me when you listed out your spells."

The color in Ari's utterly gorgeous and entirely kissable face seeped downward. He opened his mouth but then hesitated before finally speaking. "I can explain."

I froze. What?

I went cold, then hot, then cold again.

"He was twelve," Chadd said. "He had this thing for a Costa Rican magic-handler but she wanted nothing to do with him."

Ari pressed his eyes shut. Someone knocked on the window. Another note appeared, but I didn't bother to read it.

"Ari being Ari," Chadd continued, "he solved the problem by collecting the Semis of an *Olora draco. Olora dracos* are known for spells about romance but also have unreliable magic, which is why no one in the last two hundred years other than him has been stupid enough to turn one into a spellbook."

"I didn't know," Ari mumbled. He peeked open his eyes to glance at me. "I wouldn't have done it otherwise. I was a child."

"You used a Romance Spell on me." I said it flatly.

"I didn't." Ari shook his head.

"He didn't," Chadd agreed, smirking. "He accidentally used it on every female on the planet under the age of twenty-five."

Ari gave a shudder of abject humiliation.

Chadd nodded, clearly enjoying himself. "It's the biggest joke of the handler world this generation."

My breath heaved hot and angry out of my chest, rattling my ears and eyes on its way out. This could not be happening. "All those girls stalking you. All the photos and fan sites and utter devotion . . ." It was so, so obvious now that I knew. Of course it was a spell.

A lock of dark hair fell onto Ari's forehead. I was struck by an overwhelming urge to lean into him, brush it back, touch him, soothe myself.

My skin crawled in revulsion, and I jerked to face the other direction. Someone had written a phone number and about twenty dollar signs on the window in bright green.

Chadd slid himself between Ari and me, forcing Ari to take several steps backward toward the toilet-shower.

Where he belonged.

"I knew you'd want to hear the truth," Chadd said, his head tilted to the side, his eyes wide with fake sincerity. "Now you can make the best possible decision."

Meaning trust him.

Yeah, right.

Chadd had known about the spell and not told me until it benefited him. They were both con artists.

"The *Olora* Spell doesn't work in your dreams," Ari said around Chadd. "You liked me there too."

"You swore you'd tell me everything," I yelled back.

"You insisted we have boundaries." His voice rose, too, but not as loud as mine. "I don't talk about the *Olora* Spell. Not ever."

"Sasha," Chadd said, pushing sideways between Ari and me again. "The crowd outside is getting impatient. There are notes accumulating on the front seat and—"

"Notes? Are they white?" I rushed to the cab, but the letters weren't from Bob. Ari had left his window cracked and the handlers outside were shoving notes through. I made eye contact with an older man. He called my name and yelled out something involving the word billions. I turned away.

"I trusted you," I said to Ari.

"No, you never really did." Ari shook his head. His lips were a straight line, his brows knit together. "But I'm going to trust you." He raised one hand and murmured with that intense expression on his face that meant spellcasting.

I lunged to pull down his arm, but he snapped his fingers before I could stop him.

Chadd plowed backward as if hit by a giant piston in the center of his chest. He landed against Redfern's dash and immediately leaped forward only to crash into an invisible wall. Ari grabbed my arm, right where Chadd had previously held me.

I jerked free. "That was beyond rude." I turned to Chadd. "Are you okay?"

His mouth moved, but no sound came out. He punched at the invisible wall. No sound there either. In fact, all sound had dropped away. The world had gone eerily silent as if Ari and I were the only two people alive.

"You aren't supposed to put spells on me without permission."

Ari took me by the shoulders, turning me to face him. "Sasha, listen to me. I want to tell you my biggest secret, bigger than the Attraction Spell. The most important truth of my life. Because even if you don't trust me, I trust you."

"Like hell you do."

Ari shook his head. "I'm going to tell you something that wouldn't hurt just me but destroy people I love."

"Then I don't want to know." I tried to pull free of him but he held tight.

"I'm going to give you what it is that Mrs. Valenzuela used to get me to Monterey. How she made me tell her where you were in the Dreamscape. And the real reason I want your Semis."

"You lied about your reason too?" Of course he had. Bob had even tried to warn me. I attempted to step past Ari, but he blocked me.

"I never lied. I left a piece out. For good reason. Look at me." He stepped forward until I was trapped between him and the table. He lowered his voice. "Sasha, I remember what happened to me as a child. I was never abandoned. I know who my real parents are."

"I don't care—"

"It was too dangerous for me to have direct contact with them, so Lord and Lady Montague-Smith-Montague helped me create the Dreamscape Spell to keep them in my life. My father's name is Rohan Fareedi. He's British. My mother's name is Zofia, and she's from Belarus. They met at Oxford. More importantly, I have two younger sisters."

"So?" I tried to push past him.

He blocked me again. "Think, Sasha. Everything to do with magic-handling is genetic." His eyes, his entire being, focused in my direction.

I paused.

My fury paused.

Two sisters. Magic-handling was genetic.

The magic-handlers had tried to recreate Ari's experience. People had died.

"Mrs. Valenzuela knows of my sisters. If she ever let it out that they existed, they'd be hunted, caught, locked up as lab rats, killed." He took a deep breath. "That's what she holds over me. The day I made you drive so I could have a nap? I was telling my parents to take my sisters into hiding. I have to protect them, and to protect them, I need more power than Mrs. Valenzuela. The only way to do that is to infiltrate technology."

Crap.

My anger ebbed even as I fought to hold on to it. I rubbed my eyes. It was a good story, and I believed him. Of course, I believed him. I always believed him. I was a gullible idiot.

But he *was* telling the truth.

Crap again.

"I know I hurt you," he continued. "I should've told you about the Attraction Spell. Especially since you see through it. Not always, I know that. But you see *me* in a way no one else ever has. I was afraid that if you knew there was a spell, you'd reject that, me. Please, you have to believe me."

I wasn't *that* gullible. As Gramps liked to say, *Burnt soup was never going to be edible.*

Nope.

No way.

I wasn't so naive as to hand the Semis over after learning he'd been manipulating me since the first day we met. Absolutely not.

I lifted my maternity shirt, unzipped the fake belly, and took out the Semis. Ari watched, his gaze questioning, apologetic, hopeful. I inched toward him, thinking of just how good it would feel to comb my fingers through his hair, touch my lips to his, bury my face in his shirt, and . . .

Triple crap.

Apparently, it wasn't him I couldn't trust. It was myself. I shook my head. "How much money are you offering me?"

His eyes went wide as if my question had caught him off guard, which it shouldn't have.

"Today?" he finally replied, "None. But someday, sure. Once I have a spellbook written in code, I'll be able to—"

I turned and tossed the Semis to Chadd. It sailed right through Ari's invisible wall.

Chapter Twenty-Eight

Ari's eyes went wide with shock. He took a step backward, the movement half flinching as if I'd physically assaulted him.

"I . . ." He stumbled. "You . . ." Another pause. Longer, and then, "I should go."

"Or you could help me."

He stared at me. Hurt etched his eyes, but then it darkened into something else, something like anger. "I can't do anything about the magic-handlers. You're capable of creating your own diversion so Chadd can try sneaking away. I'm not needed."

He was wrong. I couldn't tell him that, though, since I didn't regret my choice and had no intention of changing it. "Okay."

Ari turned toward Redfern's door and paused with his hand on the handle. "Everything about you is a lie," he said through a clenched jaw. "You and your family, all liars. Even your family's history is a lie. Your grandmother wasn't born Valerie Sterling. She stole the name along with her employer's daughter, her employer's jewelry, and the life savings of all the other housemaids."

"No, she didn't," I said automatically, even though I had no idea what he was talking about.

A slow burn of red climbed his neck. "It's all over the news. Jane Schweigert, that's your grandmother's real name. The whole *Blue Castle* story, she stole it from L. M. Montgomery's book." His jaw ticked, just like the last time he'd totally lost it, only somehow way worse. "You and yours lie constantly. I told one lie. One, and it didn't even start out intentional. You should feel obligated to forgive me." He stared at me as if waiting for a response.

I lowered my gaze to the center of his chest.

He nodded sharply, slammed open the door, and stomped out.

"Now that he's gone," Chadd said, joining me before I could even react to Ari's words, "let's do this."

"Yup," I replied as loud and firm as I could around a sudden lump of loss.

Chadd and I did a quick confer. Then I hollered out the window that if everyone backed up fifty feet to give me some space, I'd come outside. The moment the space was clear, I opened Redfern's door and stepped down to the asphalt.

The view wasn't pretty.

BIMD agents crouched against their vans, doors open, guns drawn, most pointed my way. Those that weren't aimed at me faced the handlers who were gathered in clumps. Half of the handlers had their arms out, fingers spread, intense expressions on their faces, ready to throw spells. Ari hadn't joined the handlers but stood to my right against Redfern.

Which was good. If everything fell apart, he *would* help me.

Mrs. Valenzuela stood next to the French lie detector and Jedda. Jedda wore a bright-yellow sundress, white go-go boots, and a friendly smile. (Yeah, right.)

"Sasha," Agent Thomas called out in his Vader voice. "We've got you. Walk slowly toward—"

Mrs. Valenzuela cut him off. "If you want to protect your family, bring the Semis to me."

I stepped away from Redfern's door to make room for Chadd. "Who wants to start the bidding?" I projected my voice, filling it with a steadiness my family would be proud of.

"You start," Mrs. Valenzuela replied. "Name your price. I'll pay it."

"BIMD will double anything she offers," Agent Thomas said.

"Japan will triple it," someone called out.

"The EU will quadruple Japan," someone else yelled.

"Sasha," Agent Silva said, his voice all chummy, "you know who has your back."

"Don't be an idiot, Sasha," Jedda said, sounding amused.

Whatever that meant.

I was done being an idiot either way.

Chadd exited Redfern and came up next to me. That I could see him and the grocery bag containing the Semis wasn't alarming as he'd been visible to me in Chicago as well.

"I'm real sorry," Chadd whispered. "You don't deserve any of this. Being poor sucks."

So true. I kept my attention on my audience. "So, who wants to—"

A cacophony of high-pitched barking burst from Redfern, and the Brontës blew through the open door. Shoot, I'd forgotten to lock them up.

"The doggos," Jedda said with delight. Emily halted mid-step and pivoted in Jedda's direction. Annie Pup came for me, and I scooped her up. Charlotte went for Chadd, sinking her teeth into the back of his sock. He jumped.

"What the—"

Crap. "Be quiet," I hissed at Chadd. "Let me help before anyone realizes you're here." I tried to grab for Charlotte, but Chadd quick-stepped backward taking her with him. Annie Pup gave a squeaky growl and lunged at him from my arms. Emily came running to join the fray. One moment, we were at the opening stages of bargaining. The next, everything was chaos. Someone in the ranks of handlers laughed.

"She handed it over willingly?" Mrs. Valenzuela called out.

Chadd moved sideways in a failed attempt to avoid Emily who pounced on his shoelaces. I lunged for her but missed.

"She did," Chadd yelled back.

I froze. What?

Mrs. Valenzuela could see him?

Could everyone see him?

Based on the nodding of heads and hands covering laughing mouths, everyone could. I shook my head both to clear it and because this could not be happening. Chadd couldn't have betrayed me mere minutes after I'd picked him over Ari. Absolutely not.

I went hot with rage. Chadd was about to die. With my hands. Around his neck. Slowly.

After, that was, I secured the Semis.

I lunged in his direction, but he jumped sideways dragging the Brontës with him. "You're a thief!" I screamed at him. "I asked you to *hold* it for me. You're supposed to give it back."

"That's a technicality the Semis isn't likely to understand," Jedda said from the crowd.

"I'm super sorry," Chadd said back-pedaling away from me and half-tripping over the riot of dogs still going at his feet. "Agent Silva? Can I get some help?"

"Coming." Agent Silva sauntered forward but then paused, almost as if he couldn't help himself, and turned toward Mrs. Valenzuela. "It's all ours."

"No, it's not," I yelled.

Mrs. Valenzuela balled her fists.

Then suddenly Ari pushed past me, cocked his arm, and landed a fist in Chadd's face. "You don't break deals with friends."

"Hit him again," I said as Chadd fell backward to the ground, barely missing Charlotte. The bag with the Semis landed with a thump at his side. I leaped in that direction to grab it before Ari could, but instead of racing me, Ari turned on his heel and stomped off. "Hit him yourself."

"I will, after—"

A shadow dropped toward us from the sky. A green truedragon the size of a horse arrowed in our direction, neck extended, tail slashing. "We're going to die," I yelped and threw my hands over my head.

The truedragon tilted a wing aiming at Chadd and the grocery bag which unfroze my panic. No way did a dragon get to steal the Semis. I threw myself in the general right direction, landing in a heap on Chadd's chest. All three dogs went crazy with barking. Annie climbed on top of the Semis, snapping and yapping skyward as if to protect it from the approaching dragon's outstretched claws.

"Annie, no." I flung away from Chadd and snatched up Annie, rolling us both sideways so that she was safely underneath me.

The truedragon screamed, flames erupting, the scent of sulfur permeating the air. Both the flames and the dragon smashed into an invisible wall right over Chadd's and my head and bounced upward. Its wings beat a harsh shu-shu-shu as it fled. Ari?

Chadd jumped to his feet, clutching the grocery bag. Emily and Charlotte relaunched their attacks on his feet. He hopped forward, trying to dislodge them and run at the same time.

"Stop him," someone screamed, and there was a rush of magic-handlers in Chadd's direction. BIMD spread out right and left in a military maneuver.

"I trusted you, Chaddwick, you Tall Poppy," Jedda yelled. She was the closest of the handlers. I pushed to my feet and barreled in Chadd's direction, but Jedda beat me and landed a weak fist to his middle. He pushed her off with one hand, holding the Semis as high in the air as he could with the other while still moving toward BIMD.

"Someone, do something," a handler yelled.

The world thrummed. The ground vibrated, making the road pebbles bounce. I ignored it. Just a few more strides to tackle Chadd.

"Now," someone screamed. The thrumming exploded in a rush of energy and sound, like a thousand out-of-tune and inexpertly played concert instruments all going bad at once. Hurricane winds struck from multiple directions, knocking me away from Chadd so that I landed in a half-crouch several feet away. With the wind came a roaring so loud I slammed my hands over my ears. Something not-myself commanded through my skin and muscle and nerves that I bend my knees, shift my weight, back away from Chadd and the Semis.

I fought the feeling, the magic, but it was like fighting an ocean current from a blow-up pool mat with no oars. I took one step backward, then two, three. I couldn't stop my own body.

Agent Silva and his people raced backward, too, tripping and bumping into each other, as did most of the magic-handlers, including Jedda. Those handlers who didn't succumb launched attacks at each other hand-to-hand, wind whipping their clothing and hair. A single magic-handler paced forward, a man in a business suit.

I continued backing until I smashed into Redfern. BIMD and the handlers backed until they, too, either hit vehicles or the front of the store.

Another thunderous boom shook the world. The color in the graphics on Redfern's side drained downward, leaving the advertising images grayscale. And not just Redfern. Everything around me bled their colors like buckets of water with holes in the bottoms.

The ground tipped abruptly to the left, and colorless Redfern was suddenly ten feet above me and the fighting handlers fifty feet below. My stomach roiled with nausea, and I dug my colorless fingers into a crack in the asphalt to keep from plummeting to my death.

Another boom, different this time, like the largest tree on the planet losing a limb. I screamed and ducked, expecting to be crushed by Redfern tumbling downhill. But that didn't happen. Instead, the air thickened with a hazy, tangy, fiery fog that burned my eyes and clogged my nose and mouth with what tasted like vaporized hot sauce. I slammed shut my eyes and coughed so violently my abs cramped. The others hacked and coughed just as forcibly. And a dog too.

The Brontës.

Where were the Brontës???!

Three more booms rocked the air, and I clung harder to the asphalt, trying to clear my lungs and pry my eyes open. "Charlotte? Emily? Annie Pup?"

No answer.

I forced myself to my knees. The air stung and tears rolled down my cheeks, but nothing seemed to be sliding downhill with the horrible tilt of the ground.

The Brontës had been attacking Chadd. Where was Chadd?

I levered myself around so that I faced where I'd last seen him. This put me straight downhill as if I was doing a head-first dive off the side of the planet. My stomach slid up my esophagus to the roof of my upside-down mouth. A body's worth of blood pooled in my head making my ears pound with my pulse. I forced myself to crawl onward anyway.

The haze dissipated enough to see BIMD and the magic-handlers battling around the limo. Black uniforms against suits and saris and this year's top runway selection. Fists flying. Arms raised to cast spells. Yelling. All at a ninety-degree angle as if they brawled while laying down on invisible beds.

At least they were keeping themselves busy.

I crawled on.

Color came back all at once. Then it left just as fast. A barbed wire fence rose from the ground in front of me and then disappeared. I coughed more. A fifty-foot cyclone of insects crossed the tilted pavement, headed toward the fighting. Music started somewhere in the sky, soft but growing. Some kind of edgy pop.

"Charlotte? Emily? Annie?" I screamed as loud as I could manage over the music.

One of the magic-handlers yelled in a language I didn't recognize. A giant lavender tumbleweed appeared out of nowhere, knocking me sideways, scratching my arms and face. Then something I couldn't see crashed and boomed below me as if a magic-handler had lifted and dropped the Buysco building repeatedly. I panicked and hit the ground yet again. The music changed to a mariachi band, and the air started to smell like rancid dog poop.

The spells came faster, so fast I stopped being able to tell them apart. Not knowing what else to do, I curled into a ball, buried my face in my arms, and offered a string of incoherent prayers for the Brontës.

Then, above the magical pandemonium came a voice from the sky, loud, powerful, like the biblical God of the heavens.

"*Para!*"

Mrs. Valenzuela.

The spells evaporated all at once, the world righted itself, the sun and color returned, the oddities disappeared. The silence of the change was deafening and disorienting. I became aware of a rock pressing uncomfortably into my hip.

I took a breath. Then another. No burning. No smells. No sound of fighting.

I forced myself to uncurl, straightening my legs and lifting my head. Blood dripped from a scratch on my arm. My fingertips were raw from digging into the ground. My whole body ached.

Purple pansies with yellow centers bloomed cheerfully in a crack in the asphalt.

I spotted Redfern, or at least the undercarriage. It lay on its side, wheels facing me. The Buysco was still in place but the windows were blown out, the roof shingles scattered in all directions. The other vehicles had been flung about as if they were matchbox cars owned by an angry three-year-old. BIMD was already at work righting their vans.

Half of the magic-handlers were on the ground. The other half had stayed on their feet but swaying and fighting to remain upright.

"Where's the Semis?" someone demanded.

"Where are the Brontës?" I yelled back.

I pushed myself to my feet, every muscle of my body objecting. Jedda sat cross-legged on the ground ten feet away, her hair sticking out as if electrified, her sundress in shreds, and one of her boots missing. She held Emily tight in her arms. Safe, at least for the moment.

A brief relief surged through me. But where were the other two?

"BIMD has the Semis," someone yelled.

Car doors slammed, engines started, and tires squealed as several BIMD vans tore out of the parking lot. From behind me came a shaky yap, and Annie Pup raced out from behind Redfern's upturned bumper, tail between her legs, eyes wide with fear. I scooped her up and pressed her to my neck. We both made whuffling noises of distress. Where was Charlotte?

Mrs. Valenzuela stalked in my direction, her hands on her hips, her outfit and hair a mess.

Chadd sat on the ground, rubbing his head. No sign of the brown paper bag; BIMD really must have taken it. That was a thousand times bad, but I couldn't care just then. Where was Charlotte?

Where was Ari? He'd help. He always helped.

Mrs. Valenzuela stepped in front of me. "Call it back," she demanded.

"Help me find Charlotte."

She grabbed me, shaking me so hard I fought to stay on my feet. "Use your bond to call back the Semis."

I paused, startled by her vehemence. "I can't."

I looked past her, scanning for Ari or Charlotte, but found neither. He wouldn't have just left me. Regardless of how hurt or angry he was, Ari wouldn't do that.

Would he?

The last time I'd seen him was before the craziness started. I spun around, searching in all directions while my throat clogged with an old, familiar prickly feeling of fear.

Ari wasn't here.

It was then that I spotted a small, hairless dog laid out on the ground just past Chadd. Unmoving.

Chapter Twenty-Nine

"No." I dropped to my knees next to Charlotte. She lay on her side, her lip hanging loose, the tip of a canine just showing. I brushed my fingers over her face, gently pulling the longer hairs back and revealing her closed eye and her stubby black lashes. I slid the tip of my index finger down her neck, feeling the soft prickle of shaved fur as I searched for a pulse. Nothing. Was the neck even where I should be searching on a dog?

This was my fault.

People gathered around, talking, their words a blur. Mrs. Valenzuela yelled orders. Jedda replied. I kept my focus on Charlotte, touching her hip, her back, not wanting to disturb her but searching, searching, for any movement, any sign of life.

A weighted numbness flooded my body as if a thousand-pound lead balloon pulled me into the depths of the ocean where frigid water drowned me. "Charlotte . . ."

One of the giant Nordic god magic-handlers grabbed me by the shoulders, ripping me away from Charlotte and to my feet. I fought, but he clamped my arms to my sides. The cold crept up my throat, choking me.

Mrs. Valenzuela grabbed my chin, forcing my attention to her. "The Semis was stolen from Chaddwick, but he didn't have possession of it long enough for it to bond. It's still bonded to you, but it wasn't stolen from you. There's a loophole situation."

I pulled back uselessly against the Nordic giant.

Mrs. Valenzuela dug her nails into my chin. "You have the power to call it back."

"I don't care about the Semis."

"I'm the current owner of all four loans against your family's house as well as your brother's student loans and your father's credit card debt. You do care about the Semis."

"I care about Char—" I started, but Jedda cut me off.

"She's breathing. Charlotte is breathing."

I shoved my shoulder into the chest of the giant to try to break free, but he only made a huff of expelled air and then tightened his grip.

Jedda kneeled next to Charlotte holding a small makeup mirror to her nose. Emily and Annie crouched at her side as if keeping watch. "Moisture," Jedda said angling the mirror to show a small smudge on the glass. "But she needs a vet."

"Please, help her," I cried to Jedda. "I'll forgive you everything if you just help her."

Jedda shook her head. She had worry lines between her flawless brows. "I don't have a healing spell."

Ari had a healing spell. I screamed his name, but of course he didn't answer. He wasn't there.

Mrs. Valenzuela's eyes narrowed with a canny glint. "The McDuffie family has a spellbook for animal husbandry. Call the Semis to me, and I'll make them save your pet."

Hope flared against the cold in my chest. Then it snuffed out just as fast. I'd fail if I tried to call the Semis. I knew it in the gut-deep way I'd always known I needed to get to Bob. "I can't."

"We'll teach you," Mrs. Valenzuela said quickly, her full attention on me.

Jedda covered Charlotte with a leather biker's jacket so that only Charlotte's little head stuck out the top. The fringe of fur had fallen forward over her closed eye again.

I didn't care about the Semis, but I did care about Charlotte.

"Yes," I whispered to Mrs. Valenzuela. "I'll do anything you want."

***

The Nordic giant and an African woman shoved me into a cherry red Ferrari that looked like it had been through ten fender-benders all at once. I wasn't allowed to take Emily and Annie Pup. Jedda kept them, swearing she'd make sure they came to no harm. Hopefully, she was telling the truth because I was helpless to do anything but follow orders.

The Ferrari slammed out of the parking lot in a burst of speed that shoved me backward in my seat. Any other moment, I'd be impressed.

Instead, I stared numbly out the window. I didn't even react when we abruptly passed from the destruction of the parking lot to a completely normal, no-devastation-in-sight Canadian neighborhood.

"Don't call the Semis yet," the Nordic giant commanded from the front passenger seat.

"Not a problem," I whispered.

"We're setting a trap."

A trap. That was good. Hopefully, the trap would take longer for me to fail than the McDuffie family needed to heal Charlotte. Then afterward, Mrs. Valenzuela would destroy me for not producing the Semis. My penance for screwing up.

A penance I deserved.

We stopped in front of a hotel reminiscent of a French castle. Sprawling stone walls were set with balconies and turrets and dormer windows. In the center, a square tower with a copper-green roof reached for the sky. "The Chateau," the Nordic giant said, exiting the Ferrari.

I didn't reply.

The two handlers hustled me through a marble lobby to brass elevators. The room where they finally released me must have been in one of the turrets as it had curved walls to go with more marble flooring, a white bed buried in lace pillows, and a huge crystal chandelier.

"You're to stay here until we're ready," the African woman said. "Someone will come when it's time." The woman muttered a spell over the door and they left.

Not that I had anywhere to go even if I tried to escape. The dogs were gone. Ari was gone. Chances were high even my family would desert me when they learned I'd lost our house and all of their financial futures.

I was alone.

The magic-handlers had taken my phone and the room had no TV. There was no way to find out if what Ari had said about Grams's name was true. But it was probably true. Clemses were liars. It was one of our defining characteristics.

Only there was supposed to be a line we didn't cross. We didn't lie to each other. Or at least not about important stuff.

I slumped onto a window seat, too exhausted and miserable for anything else. Charlotte. The Semis. Ari. My family. I wanted to cry hot, weepy tears. I wanted to scream. I wanted to crumple into a ball and hide. Instead, I stared out the window.

A posse of truedragons the size of large dogs circled the hotel's turrets. Their wings barely beat as they soared and spiraled and dipped. Weird that they were here since I no longer had the Semis. Then again, Canada was known for having lots of truedragons.

I leaned a shoulder against the window and dropped my chin to my chest. Jedda arrived not long after.

"Charlotte?" I asked.

Jedda'd tamed her hair so that it fell in its usual graceful curls down her back. She wore knee-high stiletto boots over skintight jeans and a fussy yellow sweater set. Seemed wrong for her to have cleaned up.

"Broken rib and a punctured lung. Someone kicked her. Chadd swears it was one of the BIMD blokes and not him. A lie-detecting spell said he told the truth, the rat bastard." She snarled the insult. "The McDuffie family is optimistic about fixing Charlotte, but there may be side effects. Their spells are for livestock."

Good news, yet it did nothing to ease my drowning sense of guilt. "Can I see them?"

"Not until the Semis arrives. I'm to help you with that, teach you some visualization techniques. BIMD is batmobile-ing it to the border and Mrs. Valenzuela wants you to stop them."

I turned to watch the circling dragons.

The Semis wouldn't come back. The only time it'd ever listened to me was when I'd yelled at it for keeping Ari and me apart. Even more . . .

I knew what bonding felt like. I was bonded to my family and our home and various cars and Redfern and the Brontës and definitely Ari.

But the Semis?

I hadn't even given it a name.

Jedda took a seat on the edge of the bed, crossing her booted ankles and beaming at me. I was reminded of her pretending to talk like President Bernatella back in the diner in Utah. I had a better relationship with *Jedda* than with the Semis. If the Semis had bonded, it wasn't to me.

"Gonna be honest," Jedda said, flipping a stray curl over her shoulder. "I can't tell you how much I admire you right now."

"Flattery? Seriously?"

"I'm being sincere, not *sheepy*. You're all kinds of brilliant, what my cousins would call *dardy* and that's a high compliment. You nearly made it and against the entire magic-handler's Alliance. No other NoMa has ever done that."

Failing didn't make me special. Besides . . .

"You were so impressed with me that you put your Intentions Spell on Chadd so Mrs. Valenzuela could catch me. That's what happened, right?"

She beamed even wider, not even slightly apologetic. "You would've gotten a boatload of money out of my interference, which is what you said you wanted. Chadd was to get a ten percent cut, and I was to get access to the Chilean library for my grandmother. It would've worked too. Only Chadd's a cow who turned on all of us and then everything went to Hades-in-a-handler-basket."

"So *you're* the victim here?"

Jedda sighed dramatically. "Look, I'm not a horrible person. I admit to playing a part in forcing your hand, and I owe you an apology for that, but I really do admire you and—"

"Enough. What do you want?"

She tucked her lips between her teeth for a moment as if considering how best to answer. Then she shrugged. "Okay, fine, there's one more thing to offer. Not from Mrs. Valenzuela, but from my grandmother." Jedda gave a perky grin.

Exhaustion rolled over me. Mentally, physically, and every bit in between. I needed a bath and a nap. And Charlotte to be healthy. And Ari to come back. And for my family not to hate me. "What does your grandmother want?"

"To help, of course."

I snorted.

"Instead of calling the Semis into Mrs. Valenzuela's trap, stall until my grandmother arrives and then call it to her."

"You have got to be kidding me."

***

After Jedda left, just for the heck of it, I leaned back in the window seat and envisioned the Semis telling Agent Thomas he needed to return it to Quebec City.

Didn't work. My thoughts slipped to Ari. The way he crooked one corner of his mouth to hint at smiling rather than actually doing it. The way he'd teased me. The way he'd always helped me. The way I'd always judged him too quickly.

Next, I pictured the Brontës. I thought back to the first few times I'd walked them for Mrs. Lee and the wild excitement they'd always expressed when I'd returned them to her. I pictured our first night on the road in Dr. Trent, the dogs curled up against the fake belly to keep warm. Then I flashed to all of us on the bed in that horrible motel room in Denver, the TV on, the smell of mold, the dogs sleeping curled around the Semis yet again. They'd slept with it like that the night I'd been so furious with Ari too. And they'd been protecting it, not me, by going all-out after Chadd's socks.

I sat up straight, my eyes snapping open, spooked by a crazy, totally unreal, couldn't-possibly-be-correct thought. No way. But . . .

If I hadn't been the one to bond the Semis, was it possible the Brontës had?

Tiny, imaginary dog paws pitter-pattered in anxious circles around my gut.

I'd obsessed about getting the Brontës back after leaving them with Cronk and Fritzie, even though it was in neither the dogs nor my best interest. I'd even considered backtracking several times to go get them, which made no sense unless the Semis had been influencing me because it wanted them back.

Then when I didn't turn around for them, Ari stole the Brontës, going to excessive lengths to bring us all together. As if *he* were being influenced.

Plus, the Semis had stopped trying to separate Ari and me at the exact same time Charlotte had given up on being jealous.

Holy Daughter of a Dachshund.

It was all so obvious. How could I have missed this?

I started to laugh, a choking, horrified, not-even-slightly-funny laugh. I was *such* an idiot.

With the release of the laughter, my eyes went damp and my throat tightened to a kinked straw. I collapsed forward, pulling my arms into my chest to hold myself together. "I'm so, so sorry," I whispered to the Brontës, the Semis, Ari, The Blue Castle, maybe even the seadragon. "If I'd realized . . . If I'd stopped to consider . . . I would've done everything differently. Somehow."

A sob broke from my lips. Then another. Outside the window, the truedragons circled. "I screwed up," I told them around my sobs. "From one end of this to the other. California to Canada. How could I have screwed up so badly?"

Something white drifted down from the ceiling. I let it go without picking it up, surrendering to the guilt, burying my face in my hands. A second note dropped onto my head. Then a third.

I ignored those too. Bob should've warned me about the dogs. About Chadd. I'd needed him to warn me. (Which was unfair as it seemed unlikely he'd known.)

More notes dropped onto my shoulders, a steady stream of them.

Fine.

I wiped my face on my dirty sleeve and collected the nearest. The salty tang of my tears made my face itch.

Stop sniveling Now is not the time to feel sorry for yourself

No punctuation and the handwriting was worse than usual, as if Bob was so furious with me he could barely form words. Fair enough. I deserved his ire too.

I tossed the note on the floor where it promptly disappeared.

Only . . . How had Bob known I was crying?

"Bob?" I glanced around the empty room. "Can you see me? Also, I deserve to snivel. It's the only thing I deserve."

Another note drifted down from the ceiling. The handwriting was even worse, barely legible in places. Best I could tell, it read:

Yes Youve made a Mess Do Something about it Youre the only One who can Save the Seadragons

It cut abruptly off.

" . . . Semis," I finished for him.

Only I couldn't. "I'm useless," I said toward the window, the universe. "I tried. The Semis won't come to me."

A pearly blue truedragon paused in front of my window, almost as if it was listening.

I startled.

So did the dragon, back-pedaling in the air and then bolting upward out of view.

But . . .

A whole series of thoughts hit me not one by one but as a lump, and not just about how Bob knew what I was doing and how he was sending me messages, but all of it. What was really going on with the Semis.

I held up the last note Bob had sent, the only one that hadn't yet disappeared. I studied the lack of punctuation and terrible writing. He'd sent me a clue.

No, not a clue. He'd sent me something greater. Bob had just made his pitch.

My gut screamed yes so loud it cramped.

First Realization: Bob was spying on me and sending notes through dragons. This was so obvious that I felt foolish again for not getting it before.

Second Realization: I'd read Bob's note wrong. I'd read it as '*You're the only One who can Save the Seadragon's . . .*' and assumed he'd left off a word: Semis. Only there was another possibility: '*You're the only one who can Save the Seadragons.*'

Seadragons as in multiples. As in the entire species. As in my Semis wasn't the last one after all.

As in Bob still had his, and Mrs. Valenzuela has spent the last several decades conning the entire handler world by letting them think she'd purchased it. (At any other moment, I'd have been awed by the sheer magnitude of her lies.)

If I was right, Bob's plan had never been about spellbooks. It'd always been about the ethical thing. The right thing. "Ant would love this."

I pictured my seadragon back on the beach. The sinewy shape of its body, the richness of the black and purple color, the velvety smoothness of the scale in my hands before I'd fallen on my butt. The way it had blinked its eye at me, not with any viciousness even though I'd been terrified in the moment.

I'd told it that it could trust me. That I'd find someone ethical to take its Semis. I'd meant every word. I still did. More so now that I knew what the Semis was.

The truth was that I'd pretty much been trusting Bob wholeheartedly since Day One. I mean, except when I'd ignored him, but that was because I'd gotten distracted over Ari.

And Ari . . .

I'd been so busy seeing him as yet another *faithless schmuck*, that I hadn't let myself accept him as the self-sacrificing hero, the *Barney Snaith*, that he was. Ari had kept his motivations secret, but now that I knew about his sisters, his motivations were about as selfless as possible.

I pictured the seadragon again and then Ari's face as he'd told me I should forgive him for having weaknesses because I had them as well. Then I pictured Ant bent over The Blue Castle's kitchen table, writing out signs for a campaign to save local marine life by banning cruiseships from the Monterey Bay.

Bob's pitch was the ethical one, the *only* ethical one.

My gut gave a gurgle, but that wasn't the reason I straightened and turned to the window. (Come to think of it, I hadn't eaten since a very early breakfast.)

"Bob," I said, speaking loud and clearly. "I'm no longer giving up."

Immediately a white note dropped from the ceiling. I grabbed it, prepared for another angry response.

Lighthouse — Bonavista, Newfoundland

Chapter Thirty

Save the Seadragons, a ToDo List:

- Retrieve the Brontës and our belongings.

- Escape The Chateau and the magic-handlers.

- Find transportation.

- Contact Ant and tell him to pack up everything he needs for a livestream, including our dad and Mrs. Lee, and meet me in Newfoundland.

- Avoid all thoughts or hopes or most-of-all plans for Ari showing up. He wasn't going to.

- (Win back Ari anyway.)

- Change of clothing.

It seemed an impossible list with zero specifics on how I was going to accomplish anything, but I woke the next morning energized. I had a plan. It was a long shot that depended a whole ton on the Semis itself working to reunite itself with the dogs as it had back in Chicago. It also required Bob to go public with why and how he'd stolen the first Semis, which my gut said he wasn't going to like. But if my plan worked, maybe, just maybe, that would be enough to keep Mrs. Valenzuela from destroying my family, prove to Ari I was more than one-moment's-bad-choice, and make us all rich.

First thing to be knocked off the list was clothing. Someone had dropped off a pair of laughing-avocado-print pajamas for me to sleep in, but those wouldn't do for sneaking out of a ritzy hotel unnoticed. I headed to the door. Plan A would be bulldozing whoever was on the other side and running for it. Plan B would be asking for a wardrobe change.

When I tried the door handle, it refused to turn, meaning it'd been spelled shut. "Anyone out there?"

The door cracked open and a stunningly gorgeous woman with short-cropped gray hair leaned her head inside while gripping the edge of the door so tightly the bones of her fingers showed in sharp relief. Her expression was dour and possibly German. "Yes?"

The crack was too narrow for me to bulldoze her, not with her death grip on the edge. I went for Plan B with a Plan C percolating. "I'd like to order some breakfast, please. Plus, I need clothing other than this." I pointed down at my avocado-laden PJs. "And I really want my dogs back." I sent her a charming smile. Plan C, Part One was a room service cart, which would mean she'd have to open the door all the way, allowing me another bulldozing opportunity.

She glared at me and answered in a thick accent. "No dogs until the Semis returns." (Definitely German.)

I winked at her and widened my smile. "When the Semis brought my dogs to me in Chicago, it used Ari to kidnap them and free me from BIMD. Likely it will have to come up with an equally complicated and time-consuming plan now. If you don't believe me, talk to Chadd. He witnessed what happened in Chicago."

The woman's expression didn't change. If anything, her grip on the door tightened.

"How about just clothes and breakfast then? I'd like eggs, please. And hashbrowns. And steak. Ribeye. Medium-Rare. With OJ and pancakes and French toast. All on separate plates. Make sure the syrup is on the side, too, maple, strawberry, and apricot. Did you get all of that?" (With the quantity of plates, a cart would be mandatory.)

She slammed the door in my face, but half an hour later, it clicked open again.

"Take one step in this direction and you go hungry," the German woman said.

I put up my hands to show I wasn't planning on attacking her or anything else crazy-like. She opened the door a crack more, holding onto it as if the world would end if she let go. Down at floor level, a blue-uniformed arm slid a covered platter through the crack, then another and another and another. A chain of nine platters total, plus a linen napkin, utensils, and a steak knife.

No cart, thus no bulldozing opportunities, but Plan C, Part 2 was a go.

"Thank you," I called out.

"No talking," the German woman snapped.

"Where do you want the dog food?" a male voice asked the German woman.

"What dog food?" I quickly asked.

"Next door," the German woman snapped, slamming the door shut and cutting me off.

Next door? The Brontës were next door?!

My door opened yet again, and a large shopping bag stuffed with clothing came flying through. I caught it, noting that the top item was iridescent pink. Great. Magic-handler cast-offs.

I moved all nine platters to the dresser and ate as quickly as possible, sampling everything except the meat. Once done, I sorted through the clothing. The pink outfit turned out to be a corset top with a slinky floor-length skirt. "Way too dressy for a breakout."

Outfit two was a shirt-dress in beige silk, which might have worked except there were no buttons. Instead, it had ties that reached around my waist leaving a line of bare skin from my neck to my navel. "Been-there, done-that on the attracting-icky-guys thing."

Outfit three was a mini-dress made of stuck-together rubber bands. "Just no."

The only two even slightly practical outfits were a white pantsuit covered in a rainbow of paint splatters and a stretchy fitted black dress whose slit-sleeves fell in long drapes to my toes. I went with the dress figuring it was slightly less eye-catching. The draping sleeves slit at my elbows so that my arms were free but then fell to the ground in two pooling trains. I deconstructed the rubber band dress and tied the sleeve-trains together behind my back.

Now I was ready. "Plan C, Part 2."

I dragged the desk chair under the chandelier, climbed up, and used the steak knife to loosen the screws connecting it to the ceiling. Once it was sufficiently wobbly, I grabbed onto the center chain and pushed off the chair.

"I want to swing—" I sang out but then cut off when both the chandelier and I crashed to the ground, me screaming in alarm. (I'd meant to land on my feet, but the draping sleeves came loose and tripped me. Likely sounded better this way, though.)

The door cracked. "What's going on in there?"

"Earthquake," I screamed, leaping to my feet and rushing over to position myself so that the German woman had a limited view of what'd happened. "Ceiling is collapsing. The whole place is going to topple. Help!"

"I felt nothing." She widened the door and stepped forward to get a better look. I pivoted around her, shoved her into the room, and hauled the door shut. I was now alone in an empty hallway. (Yay!)

She immediately pounded on the door, but it remained closed. Plan C, Part 2 had worked. She'd been so weird about holding tight to the door that I'd banked on her not being the owner of the spell locking it from the inside.

No time for self-congratulations, as guaranteed she'd go straight to her phone.

I hurried to the next door down, shoving up my long sleeves as best I could. I didn't have a Plan C, Part 3, so it was time to improvise.

"Room service."

Barking ensued on the other side. Phew.

Only when the door opened, I got Jedda.

Crap. I'd forgotten about Jedda and her stupid Intentions Spell. She was going to ruin everything. (How could I have forgotten about Jedda?!)

I needed a Plan C, Emergency Contingency ASAP. So, of course, nothing came to me.

She looked me up and down. "You look amazing. Is that dress vintage Dior?"

"No idea." I pushed past her, shoving at the sleeves a second time.

Emily and Annie Pup barreled my direction. I fell to my knees to gather them up in a massive hug. Even if everything was about to fall apart, at least I had them back. "Where's Charlotte?"

Jedda pulled the door shut and leaned casually against the wall. She seemed weirdly relaxed, all things considered, pleased even.

"About Charlotte . . ."

A short, shaggy creature waddled out from behind the bed. It was the usual yorkie colors, but the fur fell in chunks so thick and so long that it would've been impossible to tell what was face or tail or body if it weren't for two white horns and a wide black nose sticking out from a tuft of fur on what must be the head.

My mouth fell open in shock. "Holy Mother of a Malti-poo."

Charlotte didn't look like a Maltese. Or a Poodle. She looked like a very small . . .

"The McDuffie's spell is meant for livestock," Jedda said.

. . . Highland cow?

"Mrs. Lee is going to freak."

Jedda shrugged. "As did a good portion of the handlers, which is why I'm here. Magical aberrations are usually euthanized right away, but no way was I letting that happen. She might be a freak, but she's Charlotte. And super cute."

She was. Huggably cute. Charlotte shuffled over to me, awkward in her new body. I brushed the fluff over her eyes to the side so she could see better. "If nothing else," I said to her, "your days of being cold are over."

Charlotte lifted a lip exposing a canine. That was the Brontë I knew and loved.

I turned to Jedda, eyeing her. "The dogs and I are now leaving."

She shook her head, entirely unimpressed. "Not without me."

"Nope," I started, but then the door behind us clicked as if someone was using a keycard to unlock it. I threw myself at it to block them. *Sheesh*, that German woman had gotten reinforcements fast.

"Need some help?" Jedda asked, folding her arms casually across her chest and beaming at me like she was enjoying herself. Annoying.

The handle turned. I braced my back against the door. "Ya think?"

"I've got an Air Pressure Spell that will make that door impregnable." She shrugged all nonchalantly. "Agree to take me with you and I'll cast the spell."

Someone gave the door a shove. I shoved back, barely managing to keep it closed. I wasn't going to be able to hold it for long.

Jedda sighed. "If you refuse to take me, I'll just follow you anyway."

"Fine, you can come, but only because I don't have any other options."

"Knew you'd come around." Jedda threw up her hands and mumbled under her breath.

The door warmed against my back, the feeling growing outward as if there was a huge, invisible balloon spreading between me and the door. I jumped out of the way. The door stayed shut.

Jedda's grin widened.

Great. Except that the room had only the single door and now we had no way to leave.

Time for Plan D.

I scanned the room, hunting for something, anything to trigger an idea for a Plan D. I checked the bathroom in the hope it contained an oversized exhaust vent or something else useful. It didn't, but I did find all the dogs' stuff from Redfern, along with my wallet and cell phone. Nice.

I returned to the room to check the window. Long drop with no balconies or any other way to climb down.

"I've got another useful spell," Jedda commented, still all casual and unhurried-like. "A spell that will create a hole straight through the floor. We could drop down into the room below us, and then I'll seal the hole so no one knows how we left. Admit it, I'm brilliant."

"So brilliant we'll both end up with broken legs." Could work with some adjusting, though. "Let's move the bed. Then you'll make your hole there so that we can fall onto the bed below. And," I continued, warming up to the idea, "We'll move the bed over against the door, along with the rest of the furniture. That way when the handlers break in, the bed being out-of-place won't clue them in as to where we went."

"Look at you being all clever," she said as if this was a lark and she was enjoying herself.

Against all odds, so suddenly was I. I mean, it was crazy. The whole thing. We were stealing dogs and using magic and I was dressed like someone going to a Con as a witch. I chuckled. I couldn't help it.

"You like me," Jedda said. "Admit it."

I shook my head, not willing to go that far.

We rearranged the furniture.

I rounded up the dogs while Jedda worked on her spell. Emily and Annie Pup didn't seem fazed by Charlotte's change in appearance, even if I kept pausing to stare at her.

"All ready," Jedda called. Where once was carpet, was now sliced subfloor, support beams, and then a long drop into open space.

Uh-oh.

"You first," Jedda said. "Then I'll hand the dogs down."

I looked over the edge of the hole. The bed below looked plenty plush enough to catch me, but my stomach rolled and the eggs I'd eaten crept up my throat.

I forced myself to sit and dangle my feet over the edge anyway, digging my fingers into the remains of the carpet and feeling green.

"Are you afraid of heights?" Jedda asked.

"Of course, I'm not, I—"

Jedda shoved me from behind, sending me careening forward. I windmilled my arms, turning the draping sleeves of my outfit into streamers that tangled around my head. I crashed into the bed feet first and then did a face-plant forward.

"Seriously?" I yelled back up at her.

She snickered.

"What the . . ." Someone called out from behind me. A male someone.

Oops . . . We should've verified our landing zone wasn't already occupied. "So sorry." I shoved at the sleeves, trying to untangle my head while also pushing to my feet and praying I'd landed in a businessperson's room rather than a handler's. Once I could see, I turned to face the voice.

Chadd stood just outside the bathroom, naked except for a hotel towel wrapped around his waist, his tanned, muscular chest glistening with water droplets. His gaze traveled from my tennis shoes, up my bare legs, to the skintight dress. "Sasha? Wow, you look totally hot."

So did he. Chad-dwick was gorgeous in a towel.

I grabbed the nearest pillow and launched it at him. "You betrayed me."

"I did not." He started to throw up his hands in defense, but his towel slipped so he grabbed that instead.

I flung another pillow at him, then the room service menu. "You so did." I grabbed a hotel pen. I would've thrown the lamp but it was attached to the nightstand.

"Incoming," Jedda called from above. I looked up just in time for Jedda to drop Charlotte. I caught her, but one of her horns banged my shoulder, which gave me an idea.

"What *is* that?" Chadd asked, staring at her.

"Look, Charlotte," I said, gently putting her down on the floor and pointing her toward Chadd. "You remember Chadd, right? Have at him. Do damage."

She lowered her head, very bull-like, and charged. Good girl!

Chadd ducked into the bathroom, slamming the door. Charlotte rammed into it, pulled back, and hit it again. That would keep both of them occupied for a while.

"We have a problem," I said once the other two dogs, my backpack with our stuff, and Jedda had joined me.

"Don't we always?" Jedda replied after using a spell to close up the hole.

"Whatever it is, I can help you," Chadd hollered from behind the closed bathroom door.

Jedda swung around. "What the—"

"I can sneak us out of the hotel," Chadd continued. "You don't even have to pay me. Just call off your attack-yak and I'll even—"

"Don't call her a yak," I yelled back. Charlotte butted her head against the door again, one of her horns leaving a dent. Annie Pup ran over to join her. Emily plopped down on the remaining pillow, her attention on me.

"What's he doing here?" Jedda asked, all pissy. "Handlers are supposed to be booked onto the upper floors."

Emily yapped as if trying to get my attention.

Chadd cracked the door open enough to look out, but not so wide Charlotte could get him. "If you are escaping, you have to take me with you. The things Mrs. Valenzuela threatened—"

"... are things you deserve," Jedda finished snidely.

"Truth," I added, throwing my draping sleeves over my shoulder in an attempt to figure out how to put on the backpack without strangling myself.

Chadd let out a loud breath. "If you don't take me with you, I'll tell everyone you two are working together. Plus, I have the Invisibility Spell. I can use it to keep the hotel staff and cameras from seeing us leave."

I paused in my wardrobe battle and glared at him. "Last time you promised to use your spell, you lied and didn't actually do so."

He winced.

On the other hand, this all would be easier if we only had to hide from handlers and not the other guests or hotel staff. "Maybe we could . . ."

Jedda glared at me. "Don't you soften."

Emily left her pillow to put a paw on my leg as if trying to tell me something. I looked down at her, cocking my head. She copied the movement. I had a random thought . . .

I let first the backpack and then the sleeves fall so that both draped downward, slowly working out the idea developing in my head. "Doesn't it seem like too much of a coincidence that of all places to land, we ended up in Chadd's room?"

Jedda put her hands on her hips. "You can't seriously be thinking of forgiving him. That would be idiotic. He'll betray us again the first chance he gets."

"No, I won't," Chadd yelled from the bathroom. "Not this time, I swear."

"Hold on a moment," I pursed my lips, still thinking. So very many things had gone right this morning—tricking the German handler, the dogs being next door along with all our belongings, Jedda having just the right spell to get us out of the room, now Chadd. "Do either one of you have a car we could use for several days?"

"I've got a rental," Jedda said, "but Chadd isn't allowed in it."

Emily looked over her shoulder at Jedda and let out a long string of lecturing-ish yapping. Yup, I was on the right track. And had been for a while. No way should I have made such inroads into my ToDo list so easily.

I'd had help.

Semis help. I'd bet anything on it.

Emily rubbed the side of her head against my leg in approval, like a cat might do. Both Annie Pup and Charlotte appeared at my feet, looking up at me as well.

I knew exactly what the Brontës and the Semis wanted me to do. (Even if Chadd's coming along might be less due to his usefulness and more to Charlotte's desire to gut him.)

Plan D² settled into place. "Chadd, I'll give you five percent of the sale price of the Semis in trade for your Invisibility Spell and any other useful spells you have to get me and the Brontës to Robert Minh Quan."

"Ten percent," he replied. "And you don't currently have a Semis."

"Zero percent," Jedda insisted.

"Zero percent," I agreed, "if I don't end up with a Semis at the end of all of this. But in the hopes I do, it's in Chadd's best interest to not betray me again. You, too, Jedda. Because if I do get one, I'll sell it to your grandmother. And in trade, you'll drive the Brontës and me where we need to go and keep Chadd from doing anything stupid. Along the way, you can make him every bit as miserable as he deserves. Charlotte will help."

"You serious?" Jedda said, looking suddenly excited.

"Very. It's Plan D²."

They both gave me blank looks.

"Technically, it should be Plan D, Parts 1 and 2, but you both have double D's in your names so I'm playing with the math. Instead of Plan D, Parts 1 and 2, it's—"

"Got it." Chadd smirked. "Cool, but it should be DD²."

I nodded. "Done, as long as no one brings up bra sizing."

"Gross." Jedda scowled.

I didn't bother to mention that Plan DD² led to Plan XYZ. Which, if it worked, guaranteed I wouldn't end up with a Semis at all.

I'd let Jedda and Chadd figure that out when it happened.

Chapter Thirty-One

Two days until the start of Stanford's Spring Quarter. I should probably give up counting this, but I can't seem to stop.

Total Funds Remaining: $1331.15
Cash: $690.00
Gift Cards: $562.58
Chadd's debit card: $78.57

There would've a been a LOT more money if Jedda hadn't forgotten her freaking wallet and I'd known that prior to ditching both of their phones in a garbage bin.

I missed Ari. I wanted to talk to him and tease him, and once the dogs peed all over a tree that looked just like a place Ari and I had once made out. (Gross, but true.)

Nothing major went wrong during our escape from The Chateau nor on our drive or our ferry ride to Newfoundland. (Turned out Newfoundland was an island, but only in the same sense Ireland was an island.)

Traveling with DD² still sucked. Not only was neither one of them Ari, but idiot Chadd fed Annie Pup his tuna-onion sandwich, making her throw up all over Jedda's rental car. (A brand new, bright-yellow Jeep that I'd immediately named The Wasp since Bumblebee was already taken.)

Jedda talked nonstop. Sometimes about her life in Australia or the magic-handling world, but mostly about why Chadd was armpit sludge. Chadd took this as romantic banter and went all-in flirting back.

The Brontës were no better. Emily yapped anytime she got separated from Jedda. Annie Pup, still feeling unwell, attached herself to me.

Charlotte figured out the best way to use her horns was as twin baseball bats. Chadd had multiple bruises and The Wasp had several tears in the upholstery to prove her speed and agility.

I wanted to tell Ari about it all so badly. And err . . . I also wanted to apologize, do some begging, ask him to forgive me. Instead, I told my brother in a number of rambling voicemails that also included instructions for Plan XYZ.

Ant replied with a thumbs-up emoji.

Forty-eight hours after we left The Chateau, Ant sent me a note through his server telling me to stop at the Gander International Airport in Newfoundland to pick up Grandma George.

Me: *What? Grandma George? Where are you?*
Ant: *Grandma George will explain everything.*

I could just hear the eye-rolling as he typed.

The town of Gander turned out to be on our route to the Bonavista Lighthouse anyway. I waited to tell DD² about Grandma George until we were almost there.

"If your grandmother gets to come along, then mine should too," Jedda said from the driver's seat.

"I could invite my grandmother," Chadd added. At the sound of his voice, Charlotte charged the back of his seat. I wasn't quick enough to stop her, and The Wasp's upholstery tore in yet another spot.

"No room." Which was conveniently true. "And besides, mine isn't a magic-handler. Won't do to freak Bob out by bringing along ten tons of people."

We met Grandma George outside baggage claim. She wore a cotton-candy-pink jogging suit and leaned on her walker.

I threw open the door to The Wasp and rushed over to then slowly and gently give her a hug. She was eight-nine years old after all. "I'm so glad to see you," I said, "But what are you doing here?"

Grandma George handed me a manilla envelope, her expression both stern and smiling at the same time. "There's a phone inside for your friend Bob. And one for you with cell service. Ant wants a safe way for everyone to stay in contact. He wanted to deliver the phones himself, but we decided it would be safer for me to do it. No one would expect me to be gallivanting across the country. The family cavalcade is being followed by the magic-handlers."

"What family cavalcade?" Although I'd figured Ant would be followed. All part of the plan.

Chadd took that moment to join us. "Can I get your luggage, ma'am? Airports have cameras so we should probably be out of here."

Grandma George and I took the backseat with the Brontës. Jedda drove. Chadd took passenger. Definitely no more space for additional grandmothers.

I made the introductions and then turned back to Grandma George.

With Jedda and Chadd present, there was a whole ton we couldn't talk about but one thing I needed to know. "Who all is Ant bringing to Canada?"

"The immediate family, of course. Then there are your friends, Cronk and Fritzie. Nicholas was against inviting them, but Ant had held off on purchasing new camera equipment in the hopes of going high-end once you've been paid. If you want a livestream, he needs help. He promised them that you'd invest in their production company in exchange."

"A livestream," Jedda asked all interested, with a quick glance at Chadd.

"Sounds cool," Chadd said, causing Charlotte to make another leap at the back of his chair. This time I was ready and stopped her in time. (Hopefully, Jedda had paid for the rental insurance.) "I mean," he tried again, "That could get Jedda and I in a lot of trouble."

"A fake livestream," I said quickly. "To trick BIMD into handing over the Semis. You think I want the world to know how much money I'm making?"

Jedda and Chadd exchanged a look as if they both totally got this. Which Jedda at least probably did.

"Plus, Mrs. Lee," Grandma George continued. "And your Gramps. With all the rest of us joining in, it didn't seem fair to leave him home. He's been talking nonstop about asking you for a loan to replace his flagpole. Apparently, the county has a new ordinance allowing him to build five feet taller."

I groaned. But also nodded. All. So. Clems.

"Your dad's being quiet about the money, but Nicholas said he's plastered photos of muscle cars all over The Blue Castle's kitchen."

I groaned a second time, and only part of it was for dramatics.

"But, Sasha," Grandma George said with a quick glance forward to where DD² had continued eavesdropping on our conversation. "There was another reason I insisted on being the one to meet you. I wanted to be the one to tell you the truth about your Grams."

"The criminal grandmother that lied about her name and her birth and turned out to be a kidnapper and thief?" Chadd swiveled around in his seat to face us, his eyes wide with interest.

Grandma George straightened and stared down her nose at him. "Young man, don't be rude."

Chadd shrugged, unbothered. "What? I like true crime podcasts and there are currently twelve of them profiling the infamous Jane Schweigert."

Grandma George's eyes narrowed. "Don't call her that. She hated that name."

Jedda whacked him lightly on the arm. "Respect your elders."

He smiled her direction. "Easy, Babe."

"Don't call me Babe." She said it teasingly, though. As if . . . As if she was starting to soften to him? (Eww . . . gross. Just no.)

"You don't have to tell me," I said to Grandma George. "I already know the whole *Blue Castle* story was a lie. We don't have to relive it."

Grams raised her brows. A wrinkled smile crossed her lips. "You always did have a very black-and-white view of morality, dear. Your Grams lied, but the rest of the story on the so-called podcasts was not particularly accurate." She gave a dark look in Chadd's direction. "For one thing, everything your Grams did, she did to protect me."

What? Attention caught, I turned to face her.

"Your Gram's mother, your great-grandmother, was my family's house-keeper. Your Grams and I grew up together. When my parents announced I would be shuttled off to Europe to marry a fifty-year-old Austrian named Leopold, your Grams devised an elaborate plan to free me. And it worked. Or at least mostly it did, because my family told all kinds of horrible lies about her and placed a price on her head in the hopes of flushing us out."

"Wow, that's awful," Jedda said.

"Horrible," Chadd agreed.

"It's all very Clems," Grandma George said, waving a hand dismissively, as if this happened to us regularly. Which it kinda did.

"So, she wasn't a crook?" I asked softly.

"Oh, she was." Grandma George patted me reassuringly on the knee. "So was I. Together, she and I broke into my father's safe and stole his cash and several of my mother's jewels to finance our escape."

I nodded, weirdly relieved in a way I wouldn't have expected. "Grams really did deserve the name of *Valancy Stirling*."

Grandma George nodded. "Of course she did. Heaven forbid there be any '*colorless nonentities*' in this family."

Chapter Thirty-Two

We pulled into the empty parking lot of the Bonavista Lighthouse in the middle of the afternoon. The landscape was dried grass over rolling hills under a gray sky. The ocean beyond had a choppy, also-gray cast to it, and maybe I was seeing things, but there appeared to be an iceberg floating in the distance.

In contrast, the lighthouse was painted in thick candy-cane-red stripes. Its stout tower jutted cheerfully, daringly even, through the dull grayness of the surroundings. Smaller truedragons circled the tower. That was good.

"No handlers nearby," Chadd said, opening his door to The Wasp and letting in a gust of seriously cold air. Brrrr.

Emily and Annie Pup dove under the seats. Charlotte snarled Chadd's direction. Grandma George tightened her sweater. "I think I'll stay in the car."

A pony-sized red truedragon launched from the lighthouse, heading our way.

I pulled Emily out of her hiding place and tied a pom-pom beanie over her head. Of course, Bob wasn't here. Nor had he contacted me a single time while we'd been traveling. That all would've been way too easy.

As if on cue, a barrel's worth of white notes dropped down on our heads from the ceiling of The Wasp.

"What the . . ." Chadd said, swatting at the falling papers as if they were flies.

Jedda grabbed a handful. "So that's how he contacts you. I was wondering."

"Clever man," Grandma George said. "What do they say? I can't find my glasses."

Jedda held up a white note. "*Sasha and the dogs only. Everyone else leaves. Bob.* Or at least that's what it appears to say. This man has truly horrendous handwriting."

"Yup," I agreed and clipped a leash onto Charlotte's harness. The other two Brontës I'd carry inside my jacket. Even with their sweaters and beanies, it seemed too gray and cold outside for them. (But this was it!) "Go to the nearest town and wait there. I'll handle Bob."

"Fine with me," Grandma George said.

"I'm not leaving," Jedda announced.

"Me either," Chadd agreed with a warm look at Jedda that she returned. (Eww. Gross. Again.)

"It took me three days to catch you after Colorado," Jedda continued, "and now you'll have Bob helping. What if he has a way to counter my Intentions Spell?"

"Is that possible?" Because that would be great. I exited the car and arranged Emily and Annie Pup inside my coat. Jedda followed me out, and the red truedragon shot down, snatching the beanie off her head.

"Not funny," she yelled up at it. "You'll make for an excellent spellbook, if you keep that up."

"Smaller truedragons do make for nice movement spells," Chadd said.

Charlotte charged his leg, head-down. I wasn't ready and got jerked forward by her leash. He leaped back into The Wasp.

"Do not threaten dragons around us." I hauled Charlotte back. "And you," I said, turning to Jedda, "you will not—"

"What's that noise?" Jedda asked, cutting me off and twisting toward the ocean.

I automatically looked too. "I don't hear anything."

Only then I did. A very distinctive shu-shu-shu.

My pulse went into automatic, full-throttle, I'm-going-to-die-mode right as a huge opalescent mustard truedragon rose over the cliff edge behind the lighthouse. A glassy, yellow jewel of a creature against the gray sky.

"What the . . . ?" Chadd grabbed Jedda, shoving her into The Wasp and diving on top of her. I started to dive-bomb the car, too, but Charlotte bolted the other direction, toward the oncoming dragon. Once again, I wasn't prepared for this and she used her newfound muscles to drag me with her.

"Charlotte, no!"

Emily and Annie Pup popped their noses up the neck of my coat.

The shu-shu-shu increased in tempo and volume. The smell of sulfur attacked my nose. The mustard dragon aimed its snout at us. I tackled Charlotte to the ground, covering her while trying to avoid her horns and not squash Emily and Annie.

The sun disappeared as the dragon overshadowed us. I glanced up to see huge, curved talons, each one the size of my arm, stretched our direction. "We're going to die," I whispered, hugging tight to the Brontës. Gravel pressed into my cheek and my heart beat against my ribs.

Then it hit me.

Wait . . .

Hadn't I been here before?

The dragon roared making the ground shake and my lungs collapse from the odiferous assault of rotting eggs.

I *had* been here before.

With a mustard-colored truedragon even.

The *same* mustard-colored truedragon.

It flew past us without killing anyone or maiming The Wasp.

I sat up. Charlotte immediately rushed the end of her leash in the direction of the dragon, as if she wanted to follow.

Jedda and Chadd were still sharing a single seat inside The Wasp, him with his arms wrapped around her. Jedda rolled down the window. "Bob set us up. He's not your friend. We've got to get out of here."

The mustard dragon banked and circled as if preparing for a second go. Which was odd since it totally could've killed us several dozen ways the first time.

Charlotte launched herself again, but this time at me, butting me none too gently in the side.

Got it.

I stayed on the ground but turned back to DD^2 and Grandma George. "Yeah, I think this is Bob enforcing his message that I'm to come alone."

Chapter Thirty-Three

Total Funds Remaining: $297.22
Cash: $140.00
Gift Cards: $157.22

Jedda drove off so fast, I didn't have time to snag Chadd's debit card or say goodbye to Grandma George. Seemed likely I'd see them again soon, though.

Emily started howling the moment Jedda left. Long, despairing doggie howls that made me want to stuff my ears with dirt. Charlotte tugged on her leash toward where the truedragon circled over the road. "I take it we're to follow."

Two hours and thirteen potty breaks later, we still followed the mustard truedragon, who came and went every ten minutes or so, likely annoyed by my slow human pace. Eventually, we ran out of road at the single most desolate place I'd ever been. Short, sparse grass. Rocky soil. Howling wind. Angry ocean. Crumbling cliffs. No people or other signs of civilization. Made me think of a Brontë novel. A good sign?

The truedragon gave out a dying-cow hoot and flew off over the ocean. Apparently, we'd arrived.

I looked down at Charlotte. "Well, at least it didn't try to eat us this time."

"That was an accident," a grouchy male voice announced from somewhere to my right.

I near jumped out of my parka. "Bob?" Apparently, Chadd wasn't the only one with an Invisibility Spell.

"It was supposed to have been a flyby only," the voice, Bob, continued. "And drop you a note once you were in the car. The Brit provoked the attack. Put your hand out and walk fifty feet to your left."

"No, he didn't." There wasn't anything fifty feet to my left but more grass. I turned in that direction anyway. "You don't need an Invisibility Spell against me. We're on the same team."

"No, we're not." He said it in the exact same snarky tone that I'd used. I smiled. I couldn't help it. Bob, even invisible, was exactly as I imagined him. He was going to turn out to be an Asian version of my Gramps maybe. Or an older Ant on one of his I'm-feeling-difficult days.

I walked forward with my hand outstretched until I ran into something solid. Wood.

Then suddenly I could see. A small, clapboard house appeared in front of me, faded blue with a gray metal roof. I'd run into the front door.

"Inside," the voice of Bob snapped. "Before anyone sees you."

I gave a deliberate scan of the barren surroundings. "Who would that be?" I would've been disappointed if Bob hadn't been paranoid, though. He was just so very Clems.

I opened the door and ushered us all inside.

The house had a hum to it, but that was all I got at first because I was blinded by the brightness of the interior. Emily yapped wildly and Annie Pup's butt wiggled so fast she slid down the inside of my parka. I unzipped and set them both down with Charlotte.

My eyes finally adjusted. "Oh. My. Dog."

Rows of giant tech boxes with whirring, flashing lights spread out from the walls like soldiers in formation. Tidily bundled cables ran overhead between the stacks, and the space was huge. A hundred times larger than the exterior of the little house should've allowed.

The only place not filled with servers was a living quarters near the door, and it wasn't much. A steel counter with a sink and metal wall cabinets, a twin-sized bed with a sleeping bag on top, a single wooden chair, and a bookcase filled with what looked like well-worn fantasy novels. Everything else was computers. "You broke the technology barrier," I whispered, not sure if I should be in awe or terrified.

"What?" Bob's disembodied voice demanded from somewhere by the chair.

"Technology," I said, louder this time as what this meant sank into me like a barbell dropped in a bathtub. "You lied. You didn't keep your Semis. You used it to write a spellbook in computer code."

Only . . . Charlotte pulled on her leash toward the disembodied voice, and Emily and Annie Pup both continued to wag their tails as if thrilled to be here. "No way would the Brontës be rooting for you if you were working against the Semis."

"That's what you're judging me on?" he asked sharply.

"Pretty much." I scanned the room again. "Can you at least confirm you didn't use the seadragon Semis to infiltrate the internet?"

Big, irritated sigh from the direction of the chair. Sounded just like my Gramps when someone dissed his cooking. "I didn't use a *Draco marinus* Semis to infiltrate the internet." He said it all snotty-like. "If you must know, I explained the dangers of an unprotected internet to the *Dracos*, and they brought me smaller Semis to build a security system against handlers. The Semis of *Draco porcopiscus* have proven quite effective, and the handlers have yet to figure out why it's so hard for them to get a foothold. Since truedragons loathe *Draco porcopiscus*. They are happy to hunt them."

I stifled a laugh. Not even Ari had figured this one out. "Sounds good for everyone but the *Draco porcopiscus*."

"The deaths were going to happen anyway. *Dracos* have to eat." He said it as if daring me to disagree.

Same logic Jedda had used in killing the magical armadillo. Only Bob's voice was so defensive he clearly knew he didn't have the moral high-ground here. A stance I could respect. "You care about them."

"No, I don't," he snapped back.

He totally did. It was obvious in every grouchy word out of his mouth. A slow, pleased smile slid across my face. He really was a total Clems.

"Don't get all excited," he said, now sounding put-out. "Spells based on *Draco porcopiscus* are no match to one from a *Draco marinus*. The world is still in danger."

"Good to know."

"A lot of danger," he said as if he thought I wasn't taking this seriously enough.

I was, though. I was all-in. I just . . . After everything that had happened, this all felt so incredibly *good*. "Guess it's my turn to tell my story then."

Without waiting for him to respond, I launched into everything that'd happened in the last few days, including not believing Ari, the battle in Quebec City, Charlotte getting hurt and being healed. Come to think of it, he hadn't said a word about Charlotte's appearance. It was also very Clems-like of him to just roll with it.

I told him about the dogs, Chadd, and Jedda and her Intentions Spell, Grandma George, and that I was counting on my Semis working to reunite itself with the Brontës. I put Ant's phone down on the bed and explained Ant's wanting to communicate directly to coordinate between us all.

It was my best telling yet, and the most satisfying. I even dramatized a bit, as if I were telling it to my dad and Gramps and Ant and Nicholas.

Based on the fact that the phone remained on the bed without levitating or anything, Bob did not collect it. "You're right about your Semis," Bob's disembodied voice replied. "BIMD hasn't managed to leave Canada. The agents all lost their passports. Then their vehicles broke down, cellphones batteries died, and President Bernatella fired the head of their department leaving them marooned for help."

"That's perfect!"

"BIMD doesn't think so."

"Exactly." I took a deep breath filled with an excited confidence. "This is going to work. I can get the Semis exactly where we want it, but then you'll need to step in. The Semis is good at controlling where it is location-wise, but it's terrible at determining who has physical custody of it. It let me carry it, and I don't think it ever liked me. Plus, it did a terrible job of protecting itself in Quebec City, for sure. It did nothing to stop Chadd nor BIMD. So I can get it to where we want it, but you're going to have to convince BIMD to hand it over."

Bob said nothing. The Brontës curled into a ball at the foot of the chair, bored with our conversation. I kept going. This was going to work. "When BIMD shows up, my dad and brother livestream it. You hold your Semis up for all to see and explain everything—your story, what a Semis really is, that there are now two of them, what the magic-handlers and BIMD will do if they get hold of them, what happens if you are allowed to reunite the two. The whole planet will then proceed to freak out because nobody wants species extinction. Governments will get involved. With everyone watching, judging, BIMD will have no choice but to turn my Semis over to me. The sheer weight of the planet's social consciousness will win the day."

I paused, facing where Bob'd be in the chair if he was sitting there. Charlotte lifted her head to watch me. "Once I have it, you'll pay me by electronic transfer or something. Then I'll hand over my Semis to you, and right there on camera you'll join the two halves together and save the seadragons. You'll be a hero."

Bob remained silent.

"It's brilliant, right?"

More silence. It lengthened from a pause to awkward to then me getting itchy. When the silence dragged on even more, my excitement drained like a just-flushed toilet. "Why don't you love my plan? Also, this would be easier if I could see you."

"There are three problems." No grouchiness this time. No emotion at all.

"I'm good at solving problems." This would be *so much* easier if I could see him.

"Not like these. First, I don't have the Semis. I threw it into the ocean."

"What?" I glanced wildly around the room as if in search of the nearest water. "Why would you do that?"

"So no one could steal it, of course. The only way to join the two Semis is to throw the other half into the ocean as well and let nature take its course. That means no spectacle showing it off, no filming of the grand moment of reunion, no proof that the livestream isn't a scam to steal the Semis held by BIMD."

"Then we do it without your Semis. Sure, everyone thinks I'm a liar, but not you. You tell your story of the first Semis, maybe even ask a few of your dragon friends to come along to prove your trustworthiness. The whole planet watches and—"

"None of that can happen either."

"Why not?" Frustration tinged my words. It was like he wasn't even trying.

"Second problem. Come here."

I stepped over to the chair.

"Put out your hand. And don't scream."

I did, and my wrist was grabbed by something cold and hard. Not flesh. Not human. Something else.

My vision cleared suddenly just like it had when I'd bumped into the house. One moment the space in front of me was empty, the next a man-shaped dragon filled it. An opalescent, royal blue one.

His face was reptilian and scaled, with oversized eyes, a flat, cartilage-free nose, and a wide, lip-less mouth. His hair was human—straight, dark, long, and tied back from his face. He wore jeans and a twisted, toga-like shirt that left room for wings out the back. Blue leathery wings, folded tight together as if he were trying to make them as small as possible. No obvious tail, though.

He dropped my arm. His hand was also blue-scaled, and instead of fingernails, it had short talons. Bob twisted his misshapen lips into a grimace. "Now can you see why any plan involving me just isn't going to work?"

Chapter Thirty-Four

I stared at Bob, horrified and more than a little freaked-out. Bob wasn't a Clems at all. Bob wasn't even human. How could I have been so totally wrong about someone? Again. (But no wonder he was so unfazed by Charlotte.)

He stared back and then looked pointedly away. "Tea?"

"I . . . what?" He was just so . . . blue. And scaled. He'd looked totally normal in his obituary photo.

"You need tea." He backed away from me, hips and knees bending at weird angles with each step.

"What happened to you?" Only I could answer that. "You flubbed a spell."

"I've never *flubbed* anything in my life." He glared at me all offended-like and then turned toward a steel countertop in the kitchen area to hit a button on the wall. A panel slid out revealing a high-end coffee machine, the type usually found at coffee shops. It gurgled. "Oolong or black? Also, you didn't ask me about the third obstacle."

"I don't actually like tea."

"Chamomile then."

"Tell me what happened."

His shoulders stiffened, making his leathery wings rustle. "Turns out when you cast from a stolen spellbook, things go wrong."

"You stole a spellbook." Holy Piddle of a Poodle. He wasn't just non-human, he was a magic-handler criminal. When I was wrong about someone, I was really wrong. I glanced to the stacks of computers. Had Bob even told me the truth about them?

Out of nowhere, Charlotte headbutted me in the leg. "Hey," I said when she lowered her head to go at me again. Point taken. Once again, I'd let myself dive straight into a pool of personal delusions and the Brontës had saved me from drowning.

So Bob hadn't warned me about his appearance. So what? That didn't mean he'd lied about everything else. I mean, if I were him, I wouldn't exactly be crowing from the rooftops that I'd turned myself into a winged-lizard.

"It was accidental," I said consideringly. "The spell going wrong."

Bob dropped a tea baggie into a mug and held it under the hot water tap of his barista machine. "What it was was idiotic. Foolish. Foolhardy. Naive. Sugar? Cream?"

"Really, I'm not a tea drinker. You don't have to do this for me."

"Lots of both then as you still haven't asked about the third item."

He hit another button, and another panel popped open, this time revealing a well-stocked fridge: broccoli, carrots, eggs, a whole shelf of cheese and deli meats and on and on. (And yes, cream.)

The thing was, he was right about what he'd said before. There was no way Bob could be part of my plan. Putting him on-screen would make me look like a con artist as no one would ever believe he wasn't CGI. The third obstacle no longer mattered because my entire plan stopped here. A lump of something cold and heavy settled in my middle.

"I just wanted to talk to *Dracos*, okay?" Bob walked over to me, mug outstretched. "Is that so wrong? *Dracos* are the most intelligent, most powerful, most overlooked creatures on the planet. I planned to help them, alright? Give them a voice in broader society. It would've succeeded too. The spell I stole worked brilliantly. They now communicate with me, and they have lots to say. Only, the spell also turned me into this."

I accepted the tea and took a sip just to keep from being rude. Yes, chamomile was indeed gross even with the cream and sugar.

Bob continued. "Since the moment you took that Semis, every magical-creature in your vicinity has been listening in on you, passing your words along, making me translate. The *Dracos* heard the promises you made to help the Semis. They believed you. You convinced them that you're going to save the seadragon species."

My first reaction was a massive *Yeah, no*. I'd seen zero evidence of this. I mean, clearly, he was using dragons, and while they were supposed to be smarter than the average animal, never had I heard that they had human intellect or were abstract-concepts-smart. Bob had to be making this up.

Charlotte growled, a low rumbling growl as much from her cow belly as her throat. I threw up my hands. "Fine. I believe him."

"You don't have to believe me. I'll show you." Bob went back to the kitchen area and hit another wall button. There was a whirling of sound and movement above my head. I craned backward just in time to see a sliver of cloudy sky appear in what I had thought was a solid ceiling. The sliver widened until it was three, four times the size of a car sunroof. Just as fast as it appeared, the opening was blocked by a massive, mustard-colored hide and a giant yellow eye.

I jumped backward, my heart racing, my tea sloshing. All three Brontës leaped to their feet and circled excitedly beneath the giant eye as if greeting a friend. The house began to stink of sulfur.

Right. Same dragon as always. No need to panic.

I coughed instead, clearing the odor from my throat.

"See?" Bob said, as several smaller dragon heads pushed in around the eye, scanning back and forth as if searching the house below them. A lavender one dropped down to join the dogs. I started forward to protect them, but then stopped. The *Draco* wasn't much larger than them, and instead of attacking, it slithered out a forked tongue and licked Annie Pup on the nose.

This was just getting weird.

Was it possible that not just me, but the entirety of humanity, were dead wrong in how we viewed *Dracos*?

"Your friends seriously reek," I said.

The odor didn't seem to bother the Brontës. Charlotte snuffled around the little dragon, checking out its snakey tail. The giant eye above us blinked. Bob continued. "The *Dracos* can't touch a Semis themselves or their magic will absorb it. They used me to get the first one hidden from the magic-handlers because they see the survival of the seadragons as linked to the survival of them all. If handlers are allowed to drive one species to extinction in their lust for magic, they'll do it to the next and the next and the next."

"Which they will."

Bob nodded sharply. "Since I clearly couldn't collect the second one, the *Dracos* had to find someone else. You conveniently showed up, and they've been helping you ever since. It's why I contacted you in the first place. They told me to. And it's why I've kept sending you notes and steering you here. Not for me, for them." He paused as a second smaller *Draco* dropped through the hole in the ceiling and landed on the nearest bank of computers. It cocked its head and nodded several times as if joining in our conversation.

"Do the *Dracos* have some kinda plan then?"

"They're counting on you for that."

Great.

"One more thing," Bob continued, "Obstacle number three." He said the last with a whole ton of warning in his voice. "There's no money."

Huh?

The *Draco* perched on the computer stack stretched its wings. The *Draco* on the floor swung around to sniff Charlotte's butt.

"What do you mean there's no money?"

"The *Dracos* think the concept of money is stupid and have universally decided that since you are one of the more intelligent humans, you must as well."

"But *you* have money to pay me." I glanced around at the rows and rows of computers. "You must have money."

"I have seven small-business loans, a line of credit, and five maxed-out credit cards. I've buried myself in debt to protect the internet from magic-handlers and keep myself fed. I don't have a dime to spare. You'll have to give up your Semis out of the grace of your heart."

The giant eye blinked again. One of the smaller *Dracos* gave a moo-caw-shriek. The *Draco* on top of the computers bounced its head up and down.

"Nope," I said automatically. "No way. Not going to happen. You promised me money. Boatloads of it." Only he hadn't. He'd never even mentioned money. It was one of the reasons I'd trusted him. I sat down abruptly on the bed, leaned forward to cradle my forehead in my hands, realized I still held a mug of tea, sat back up, and took a long swig instead. If it was still gross, I didn't notice. "Please tell me you're joking and there are boatloads of money docked just down the cliff waiting for me to come collect."

Bob rolled his eyes, which looked super creepy in his froggy face.

I shook my head back and forth. "But . . ." My single word trailed off into a heart-shrinking, lungs-stalling, ribs-collapsing moment of this-couldn't-be-happening. I was supposed to get rich. That was the whole point. I could make it without the billions promised by the handlers and multiple foreign countries. Or even hundreds of millions. But a couple million . . . I had to get at least a couple million. If not, I was back to square one, living at home, The Blue Castle falling apart, foreclosure notices piling up, multiple jobs to keep my head above water, college and a good future more dream than doable reality. And Mrs. Valenzuela taking her ire out on my family.

My family . . .

It wasn't just my dreams that mattered, but theirs too. Ant and Nicholas and Gramps and my dad.

Charlotte planted her haunches down to stare up at me. Her floppy mop of hair half covered her eyes. Her white horns stuck out, making her look so, so cute. "We're all supposed to end up rich," I said to her.

I could still sell to Mrs. Valenzuela.

No. Never her. But maybe Jedda's grandmother, she might not be that bad. Or Ari, who'd said he didn't have money yet, but I could put him on a payment plan. That could work.

Charlotte cocked her head.

No.

Nope.

None of that would work. Charlotte knew it. Bob knew it. The giant eye still watching from the ceiling knew it.

I knew it. I hated it, but I knew it. The Semis couldn't be put to evil usage. The seadragons had to be saved.

I met Charlotte's gaze. "Fine. I'll do what I can to get the Semis back from BIMD without getting paid. If, big if, I get it back, I'll throw it into the ocean and save the seadragons, again without getting paid. Then I'll go home and get a fifth job. Just know that I'm unlikely to succeed anyway and—"

"Now that we've got that covered, Maur has a question," Bob said right over the top of me, as if worried that if he gave me too much time, I'd change my mind. Which was a fair point. I wanted to change my mind. I should change my mind.

I wasn't going to change my mind. "Who's Maur?"

"The big yellow one. He wants to know if once this is all over, you'd be okay with him eating your friend Aristotle."

Chapter Thirty-Five

The next morning, Grandma George, the Brontës, DD², and I left the Bonavista Motel for Trinity Cove, the place where Bob had thrown his Semis into the ocean. Jedda drove. I couldn't do so. My innards were too busy attempting to discharge everything I'd eaten in the last two weeks out of my nose. This was going to be bad. So, so, so bad. I was going to disappoint the entire planet, my family, Ari, and the *Dracos*. Plus, the world as we knew it might end.

I so, so, so didn't want to do this.

I was doing it anyway.

The drive took about an hour. When we arrived, the GPS coordinates Bob had given didn't lead to an ocean cliff or any kind of beach. Instead, we got a large, rundown, overgrown parking lot.

Chunks of metal and concrete stuck out of clumps of grass and rock with bedraggled trees interspersed. The remains of a rusted, rundown train car sat on one side. Across from it was a half-collapsed small building.

"A dump?" Chadd said incredulously as we stared out The Wasp's windows. "You sure this is the right place? A dump seems a bit disrespectful to the Semis."

"This isn't a dump," Grandma George said. "Ant said it's an amusement park. Closed down in 2004."

As a sign for things to come, I'd have preferred to stick with the dump. Parks were Ari's and my thing, and an abandoned one didn't bode well. Also, where was Ant? He was supposed to be meeting us.

Grandma George continued. "Ant also said we're to follow the old train path down to the cove. We've got maybe fifteen minutes until show time."

"How do you know that?" I asked.

Grandma George held up the phone Ant had sent along. "Ant's been texting."

I'd been too busy holding back burning nose bile to notice.

"Drive on," I said to Jedda, while fighting a sudden need to sneeze.

Jedda took The Wasp down a gravel path to a body of water surrounded by tree-spotted hills. Sticking into the water was a finger of land shaped like a large crochet hook. We stopped at the foot.

Set up on the tip were four different cameras, three lawn chairs, and a huge rainbow pop-up umbrella. My dad, Ant, Nicholas, Gramps, Cronk, Fritzie, and Mrs. Lee were all there too.

Ant and Nicholas blew us kisses. Gramps, Cronk, and Fritzie all waved. My dad gave a thumbs-up. Mrs. Lee folded her arms over her chest.

At the throat of the crochet hook sat a large dog carrier and a sign that read: *Brought to you by C&F Productions in conjunction with John Foster and Antony Clems.* Trust my family to grab a marketing opportunity.

"Ant says you're to stand in front of the sign," Grandma George said, looking at the phone. "The rest of us can either watch from here or join the others at the cameras."

"I'm sticking with Sasha," Jedda insisted. "I need to be close for when she hands me the Semis."

"*We're* sticking with Sasha," Chadd corrected.

"Maybe it'd be better—" I started.

Jedda shot me a steely look, and I gave up. Better to focus on controlling my intestines which were turning boa constrictor against my other organs. "Fine." The word came out half croak. I tried clearing my throat which just moved the lump blocking it further up. I turned to Grandma George anyway. "Can you ask Ant to keep Mrs. Lee quiet? The Brontës can't know she's here yet."

We made it to our spots on the crochet hook without issue. I put the Brontës in the carrier and then picked up a manila packet leaning against the marketing sign with my name on it. Inside was a wearable microphone, a tiny earbud, and a note in my Dad's handwriting: *No risk, no story, no glory. Glory being the ultimate euphemism for money.*

I winced but also clipped the mic to my collar and pushed the earbud into my ear. Immediately, Ant began to talk. "According to Bob, the handlers are going to arrive first with BIMD right behind. You need to—"

"Handlers less than a mile away," Jedda announced.

"You hear that?" I muttered to Ant.

"Got it. Are you nervous?" he asked.

"Of course not."

"You are nervous," Ant said knowingly. "Just think of the money. That should help."

"Yup," I managed.

Just then, a caravan of two Range Rovers, a BMW SUV, a limo, and a Porsche Boxster pulled in behind The Wasp. Following them came a dozen smaller truedragons who landed on nearby trees. Crap, this was it.

"Your dad promised Mrs. Lee a huge donation to the Carmel Rotary Club in her name to get her to wait for your signal," Ant said into my ear.

"Stop already," I whispered back.

"Stream's live," he replied.

Mrs. Valenzuela exited the limo. Both Nordic gods followed her. Then the French woman. (Darn. No lying then.)

"Huge as in mid-six figures," Ant continued. "Also, Fritzie says to remind you not to tell anyone we're livestreaming. Let them think we're just recording and that they can destroy our equipment afterward like they did before."

"I know what to do. This is *my* plan. Stop being all . . ."

I went silent as one of the Nordics turned back to the limo and dragged out another person. Tall, dark hair, jeans, a red hoodie with a tree on the front, handcuffs, and a black gag.

The *Dracos* shot into the air. A lavender one darted at Ari, skimming his head. Ari turned in my direction.

Our gazes met and even at the distance my heart tripped, slid, fell into the depths of his gorgeous, deep, dark eyes. All the blood and electricity and whatever else made a heart a heart condensed to one tiny, wildly beating spot of hope that wanted to race over, grab him, and kiss him so long and so hard all the rest of these people died of old age.

Ari hadn't left me intentionally.

He hadn't been avoiding me.

He'd been kidnapped.

This was good. Very, very good.

Or not. He'd need rescuing, and there was no indication in his expression that he'd forgiven me. Still, my intestines relaxed their camel hold on my stomach. Ari was here.

"We just hit a hundred thousand viewers," Ant whispered into my ear. "Also, Aristotle's even hotter in person than that poster you hung over your bed."

"I was twelve," I muttered back.

"Once this is over, you'll be his financial equal."

"Meaning ridiculously filthy rich," my dad said in the background.

"Forget the boy," Gramps added in. "Stay focused on your bank account balance."

I winced again.

A string of BIMD vans pulled in from three different directions, blocking The Wasp along with the handlers' vehicles. With them came a whole ton more *Dracos*. Larger ones, too, somewhere between horse and elephant-sized.

Maur came in last, his yellow hide catching the sun's rays and scattering the humans. Mrs. Valenzuela, the French woman, and the goons dragging Ari raced in my direction as if for cover. Every other handler raised their hands in the air, preparing spells. BIMD exploded from their vans, half of them holding guns, the other half waving those stapler-devices I'd seen back in Chicago. Chadd leaped sideways to cover Jedda. My family universally hit the dirt. The *Dracos* all scattered back to the trees, except for the small lavender one that chased circles around Ari.

I waved to Maur. "Hey."

He drifted over our heads, bringing with him the loud shu-shu-shu of his wings, a blasting wind, and an overwhelming scent of sulfur.

When nothing additional happened, my family returned to their previous spots looking sheepish.

"You could have warned us you had a friend," Ant mumbled.

I couldn't respond because Mrs. Valenzuela had reached me. I plastered on my most obnoxious pleasing-the-rich-people-smile. Even if this all was going to end in a giant disaster, I could handle this part. "So glad you made it."

Mrs. Valenzuela narrowed her eyes. "I know you're working with Bob."

"Bob who?" I asked, with a glance at the French woman to see if that was vague enough to keep her from coughing. It was.

Mrs. Valenzuela crossed her arms over her chest. "You think this is humorous?"

"No, I—" I started but Maur made another pass above, his head tilted our direction and one sharply-taloned leg hanging loose below his body as if he were considering doing a snatch and grab. Everyone else froze and universally looked up. I raised my fist. "You don't get to eat Ari. I already told Bob that."

Maur gave a popping belch. Sulfur descended on us so thick my throat went all furry and tears stung my eyes. The whole group of us bent over hacking and coughing. "Stop doing that," I yelled at him when I was able to straighten. "It's not helping."

Maur banked and turned toward the open cove. The lavender dragon took this opportunity to land on Ari's head. A Nordic raised a hand as if to punch it off.

"Don't you dare," I yelled at him. I swiveled to face Mrs. Valenzuela and sent her another overly wide smile. "You hurt a dragon, there's no deal."

She leaned my direction, rubbing her hands together, eyes going eagerly wide. "So you're willing to deal then? The Semis for Ari?"

I nodded vigorously.

The French woman coughed.

Crap.

Mrs. Valenzuela dropped her hands, her expression tight and pissed.

"This is amazing," Ant whispered into my ear. "Viewership is over two hundred thousand. Comments are enabled. Majority are teenage girls freaking out about Aristotle and begging you to forget the Semis and save him."

The lavender *Draco* picked through Ari's curls as if grooming him. He flinched, but since he didn't appear to be in danger, I decided not to worry about him for the moment. Also, there was a good chance his reaction was due to germs rather than pain. The *Draco* appeared to be being gentle.

Agent Thomas called out to me through a bullhorn. "Sasha?" His voice lacked its usual deep determination. He sounded quivery instead, confused even. "We're here to protect you. Can you bring the second Semis to us? Please?"

"Sasha is trading the Semis to me for Ari," Mrs. Valenzuela answered back with a renewed tenacity. "Otherwise, I *will* feed him to the dragons."

There was a giant gasp from the direction of my family and BIMD. "Comments just went wild," Ant whispered into my ear.

"Sasha is selling the Semis to my grandmother," Jedda quickly added. "She promised."

Maur roared but had the decency to do it facing the hills.

Ant sighed happily into my ear. "The dollar signs are growing larger and larger."

I gave an exaggerated shrug toward Agent Thomas. "I think we'd better have a group parley to sort it out. Agent Thomas? Bring yourself and my Semis over here."

"I don't have your Semis," Agent Thomas sputtered through his bullhorn. "It's secured in a vault in DC and—"

The French woman coughed. (Not sulfur-related this time.)

Here it was. My first big test.

"Ant, tell Mrs. Lee to call her dogs."

"Come, my darlings." Mrs. Lee's voice rang out weedy and shrill. "Come to me, my sweet babies. I'm over here. It's been like Mary without Joseph while you've been gone."

The Brontës' carrier tilted, all three dogs jumping on the side closest to their beloved owner. Little noses pressed to the airholes. A white horn shoved through a crack. Wild yapping was followed by a long, expressive moo. I turned back to Agent Thomas and the line of vans where my Semis must be waiting. "I'll make you a deal," I hollered to both him and the Semis. "Bring my Semis over here. Give it to me. In trade, I'll release the dogs so that they can go be with their owner, which clearly they want more than anything else in the whole wide world."

"Why would I do that?" Agent Thomas asked, scratching at the side of his head and glancing around as if looking for someone to explain to him what was going on.

"You're an animal lover," I replied.

The French woman coughed, which for once didn't matter. I took a deep breath and held it. Come on, Semis, hear me, take the deal, convince him to do it.

"I'm not, though," Agent Thomas started, "I'm allergic—"

Agent Silva pushed past him. "We'll do it." He sounded thrilled, eager. "Clearly the dogs' happiness is the first step in these vital negotiations."

"No, it's not," Agent Thomas said, although he didn't sound terribly sure of himself.

The French woman coughed again.

Jedda grabbed my arm. "My grandmother is on standby to wire the funds wherever you want. We just need a bank account. You're still going through with your original plan, correct?"

"Absolutely," I replied as enthusiastically as I could.

Jedda glanced at the French woman. When she didn't cough, Jedda got a pleased look on her face. (Joke was on Jedda. The plan she knew about was my secondary or perhaps tertiary one, not my original.)

Then it hit me. A brilliant realization striking the dead center of my skull, sending a jolt of oh-my-Dog through my entire body. A realization so incredibly obvious that I couldn't believe I hadn't thought of it before.

"Ant," I whispered into the mic, my voice thick with excitement. "Every time the French woman coughs it means someone just told a lie. She has a spell that makes her do it. I need you to tell this to everyone watching the livestream so that they know. It's important, okay? Her coughing is how to tell who is lying and who is telling the truth."

So, so, so obvious to use her to my benefit.

"And now everyone knows," Ant replied, "since, you know, anything you say into the mic is live. That's kinda how a livestream works."

"Right." There were still other obstacles. Big ones. But with the French woman there to verify what everyone said . . .

I suddenly had a real chance to pull this off.

The two agents argued for a moment, too low for me to hear from my spot on the crochet hook. Then Agent Thomas threw up his hands and yelled for someone to bring out *The Egg*.

Wait. Had that just actually worked too? Deep down inside, I hadn't been that sure.

Agents Thomas and Silva unloaded a large steel trunk, a high-tech kind with black handles and a huge digital lock on the front. Looked like it might contain a nuclear bomb or ten tons of hundred-dollar bills.

Or a Semis.

I was on a roll.

Chapter Thirty-Six

Success! I grinned while Agents Thomas and Silva walked the trunk our direction. I couldn't help it. I looked to Ari to share my moment.

Only his attention was on an additional BIMD agent following ten paces back from the trunk. The agent pulled off the hood of her SWAT gear, revealing chestnut hair and Bambi eyes. She smiled in Ari's direction all cute and flirty. Ari fluttered his eyelashes at her, too, as if . . .

As if he was flirting?

A knife slid between my ribs. Even if he was mad at me, Ari wasn't supposed to flirt with other girls.

Unless he was doing it *just because* he was mad at me.

Agents Thomas and Silva placed the trunk on the ground in front of the signage.

"Hey," Ant complained into my ear. "They blocked our logo."

Mrs. Valenzuela and the French woman moved in closer so that we formed a line around the trunk holding the Semis. Chadd, Jedda, and I on one side. BIMD, the handlers, and Ari on the other.

Agent Silva bent toward the trunk, but Agent Thomas shoved him aside. "Something's not right here."

So close. But I had a plan for getting that lock open. My biggest gamble of all. The cute BIMD girl latched onto Ari's arm, gazing up at him adoringly. Ari smiled at her. The knife-in-my-chest-feeling twisted to go after my lungs. Wow. Just wow.

"Mainstream news stations just picked us up," Ant whispered. "Influencers are going crazy. So are a bunch of CEOs, Hollywood A-listers, and politicians."

Right. Time to set aside the hurt of Ari being a *Tall Poppy* and get to work. I turned to Mrs. Valenzuela. "If I sell a Semis to you, you'll use it to make a spell to hack the internet. Nothing would be safe. Not people's private records, bank accounts, governments, nothing."

Mrs. Valenzuela dropped her voice. "I'll give you Ari, every penny I have, and the entire lower third of the country of Chile."

There was a long, shocked silence as we all absorbed her words.

"Holy freak," Ant whispered. "No cough."

"Nope, no cough," I murmured back. I turned to Jedda. "If I sell to you—"

"No bargaining," she interrupted. "You already agreed to sell a Semis to my grandmother in trade for my help."

"With a cut for me," Chadd added, placing a hand on Jedda's shoulder.

I raised my voice. "You'll do the same thing as Mrs. Valenzuela. Or some other spell just as disruptive to the life and livelihoods of everyone else."

"We are a peaceful people—" Jedda started.

The French woman coughed.

Ant chuckled in my ear. "Cronk added an exploding bomb emoji to the feed every time that woman hacks. Hilarious."

I turned to BIMD. "If I sell the Semis to you, you'll turn it into the most powerful weapon on the planet."

"No, we wouldn't," Agent Silva replied all eager-like. "We've got a better plan."

No cough. Shoot. If he offered something like electricity for half the North American continent, I was totally screwed. "What's your plan?"

"A superhero." Agent Silva said it all mic drop.

Huh?

Mrs. Valenzuela glanced to Ari and then back to Agent Silva. Ari froze. The BIMD girl now held his hand. His hand which was free from hand-cuffs. His gag had also been removed.

Oh. Got it.

"A Hollywood agent wants to sign the BIMD agent who just freed Aristotle for a screenplay," Ant whispered. "Someone's already selling shirts with her picture."

Well done, Ari. I should've had more faith in him. (Ari'd never have used the Attraction Spell as a tool of manipulation before meeting me.)

"BIMD wants to make another Ari," I said to the camera so that every-one else got what Agent Silva had said. "A stronger one because the two Semis that Ari swallowed were like minnow Semis rather than old and huge ones like mine."

"We'll create a god," Agent Silva said it all mic drop again.

"Holy freak-on-a-stick," Ant said, "The European Union just offered you ten billion dollars to give the Semis to anyone other than the Americans."

Mrs. Valenzuela frowned. "It's a waste of a Semis. The recipient's digestive system will turn to stone and then they'll starve to death. Happens every single time. Plus, you'd need handler help to do the shrinking so that the two Semis are swallowable."

"You offering?" Agent Thomas asked with an engaging smile, totally unfazed by the horrific death scenario.

"No," Mrs. Valenzuela said.

Chadd raised his hand. "My family has a Minimization Spell."

Jedda backhanded him across the chest.

". . . that we'd never share with BIMD," Chadd finished, subdued.

Ant whispered fast into my ear. "A senator from Alabama just called BIMD's plan a victory for Satan. The Catholics, Mormons, and several megachurches are putting together a group offer."

I cleared my throat to bring the attention back to me. "So, basically, BIMD wants world dominion too."

"No, we don't," Agent Thomas said. "BIMD knows nothing about this. BIMD intends—"

I cut him off just in case his offer was actually something honorable. (Apparently Agent Silva really was working for someone other than BIMD.) "Not a single one of you cares about the bigger picture here. Semis are magic, but they're also babies. Or at least they are if two of them get to unite." I explained what Agent Silva had told me about DNA.

"Don't listen to her," Jedda screamed. "She's lying."

"All of it's a lie," Mrs. Valenzuela said.

The French woman launched into a spasm of coughing so violent she doubled forward. (Yay!)

"My Semis, the one I carried across the country, is right here." I motioned to the trunk. "Robert Minh Quan's Semis is somewhere in this cove."

Maur swooped down low, one wing-tip cutting a short line through the water as if confirming my words. Fritzie swung his camera around just in time to capture the motion, whacking Cronk and sending him careening sideways. Maur kept his mouth shut, thank goodness. There was only the faintest whiff of sulfur this time around.

"That's Maur. His offer is that I forget getting rich and throw my Semis into the ocean where its mate is waiting. Then the seadragon species can repopulate, which, if you think about it, is kinda romantic."

"A tech billionaire," Ant whispered, "the famous one, just offered you thirty big ones and stock in his social media company in trade for half ownership of the Semis and a ride on Maur."

I nodded, half at Ant, half at myself. Here it was. My moment of choice. The moment I screwed over my family and went back to being impoverished. I couldn't look in the direction of my family and focused instead on Maur making circles in the distance. "I'm going with Maur's plan of saving the seadragons and giving up my dream of getting paid."

"Wait," Ant started, "What are you—"

Gramps jumped to his feet so suddenly the rainbow umbrella fell over.

"Sasha," my Dad called out in his attempting-to-parent warning voice. "Don't do this."

I winced and avoided eye contact. "But there's a problem. I need BIMD to unlock the trunk and give me my Semis. It's mine by right. They stole it." I tried to scowl at Agents Thomas and Silva, but instead my attention went to Ari. The BIMD girl had draped her arms around Ari's shoulders. He lowered and raised his chin, a slow nod of approval my direction.

Tears of relief that Ari was on my side tried to well up in the corners of my eyes, but there wasn't time for that so I forced them away. Also, since he was free, shouldn't he have escaped the BIMD girl by now?

Dad and Gramps waved frantically in my direction, trying to get my attention. Both looked pissed. Ant whispered furiously into my ear, "You're giving up your future. Our future. Our dreams. Dad had to get another mortgage on The Blue Castle to tide us over until the money came in. Do you know what interest rates are right now? I'm all for doing the right thing, but—"

So much for support. I popped the earbud out and shoved it in my pocket.

"What are you doing?" Ant yelled from the tip of the hook.

"Sasha . . ." Dad tried again.

Nicholas grabbed Ant by the arm, talking fast into his ear. Nicholas was the only family member who might take my side.

It didn't matter. I knew what I had to do. "I call on President Bernatella, the head of the American people and overseer of BIMD, to save the seadragons. I call on not just Americans, but all the people of the world, to ask her to do so. President Bernatella, tell BIMD to unlock that trunk and hand over my Semis so that we can all do the right thing." I widened my eyes, quirked my lips, and gave the most fake-innocent-smile of my life.

The world went still. The ocean lapped against the inner curve of the cove below us. One of the dogs gave a yap. Someone scuffled their shoe in the dirt. Even my family quieted. (They were universally glaring at me instead.)

"Please," I whispered softly, sincerely, into the mic.

"President Bernatella said yes!" Grandma George hollered, sounding thrilled rather than angry.

"I don't care what the President ordered," Agent Silva said. "I'm not letting you throw a seadragon Semis into the ocean."

"Yes, you are." Agent Thomas shoved Agent Silva out of the way and bent to press his thumb to the lock. The top of the trunk rose with a low beeping noise to reveal a black velvet bag nestled in white silk.

"Grab it," Mrs. Valenzuela screamed. Agent Thomas launched himself at Mrs. Valenzuela to block her. Jedda lunged toward the trunk, but Chadd caught her around the waist, trying to push past her. (So much for that relationship.)

I started toward the Semis, too, only something boomed in the sky and the ground under my feet shifted. It was all I could do to keep my balance. A second boom and the world around me turned pink as the sky filled with massive colored clouds.

Crap. Not this again.

Then Ari was at my side sans BIMD girl, his hands up, magic vibrating through him. "My magic will protect you."

"Not me," I yelled over mariachi music so loud it reverberated against my skin. "The Semis." (But seriously, I loved that his first thought had been me.)

"Right." He pivoted around the still-fighting Chadd and Jedda to place himself in front of the trunk and then snapped his fingers. An invisible force hit me in the center of my chest, throwing me backward. I landed on my butt next to the Brontës' carrier. Same thing happened to everyone else, people downed and scattered every direction in a perfect twenty-foot circle around the Semis. I couldn't see Ari's barrier, but it was clear exactly where it was.

"Sorry, Sasha," Ari yelled, barely hearable over the music thrumming the air. The earthquake stopped, though. "Wasn't time to adjust the spell to keep you in."

A bolt of turquoise lightning streaked over the water to smash against Ari's barrier and then fracture in all directions. I hit the ground to avoid being zapped. The world smelled like sulfur again. Maur must be near.

Handlers and BIMD flooded onto the crochet hook from the direction of the cars. My Dad, Ant, Cronk, Fritzie, Gramps, Mrs. Lee, and Grandma George raced from the other direction, Grandma George with her walker. Chadd banged his fists against the invisible barrier. Jedda joined him and then so did Agent Silva on the opposite side.

Ari didn't react. Nor did he move toward the Semis. He stayed in place, frozen, braced, the tendons in his neck and his upraised hands sharp under his skin.

"Throw me the Semis," I yelled at him.

"Can't." His voice was deep with strain. "Can't touch it. It'll go straight to my library. Too much magic in me."

Another bolt of lightning hit the barrier. This time maroon and coming from Mrs. Valenzuela's hands. A wave of water lifted from the ocean from the other direction. It crashed into the barrier, soaking Chadd, Jedda, and the BIMD girl. I crawled forward until the crown of my head hit what felt like six-inch steel. "Ari, let me in."

Ari shook his head, sharp and stressed. "Can't either. Not without dropping the spell entirely."

I looked frantically around, searching for something, anything to solve this impasse other than Ari sending the Semis to his library.

"Come on, come on, come on, I need an idea," I whispered to the world, myself, the Semis.

The Semis . . .

The Brontës . . .

Ari'd said spells were super specific. I'd seen him use his barrier spell against people and Maur but never the dogs, not even Charlotte when she'd been distracting his driving. "Can the Brontës get through?"

"Yes," he yelled back.

I crawled back to the Brontës as spells continued to attack Ari's barrier. "Fetch," I whispered to them as I threw open the door. "Please, please, please, the best way to get us all to safety and to reunite you with Mrs. Lee is to fetch the Semis. It's right there. Next to Ari. Charlotte, you love Ari. He needs your help."

The dogs darted toward the barrier as if they understood.

"What did you do to my dogs?" someone screeched from behind me. Mrs. Lee. My family had arrived from the tip of the crochet hook and were heading my way looking furious. All three Brontës spun in her direction. No.

I jumped to my feet, pushed around my Dad and Ant to grab Mrs. Lee by the hand. I pulled her down next to me as what looked like a military rocket zoomed over our head to hit the barrier. Everyone else hit the ground too.

"Sasha, we need to—" Ant began.

"Later," I yelled and then turned to Mrs. Lee. "Tell the dogs to fetch. Ask Charlotte to fetch. She's strong enough now. She can do it. She needs to bring us the Semis."

Ari shifted, his elbows dropping just a tad as if the weight of holding the barrier spell in place was overwhelming him. Charlotte turned her head back and forth between him and Mrs. Lee.

Mrs. Lee's hand locked around mine, suddenly more vise-grip than handhold. "What did you do to my babies?"

"It's temporary. I'll fix them, but I need the Semis to do it. Please!"

Somewhere to our right, the French lady coughed. Hopefully, Mrs. Lee didn't hear.

"Swear on the Bible you'll fix them," she demanded.

I didn't have a Bible. "I swear I'll do everything in my power to get your dogs back to normal."

No cough. Also not a lie, since my power was all of zero.

Mrs. Lee's eyes narrowed, but then she turned to the Brontës. "Oh, my dear children," she crooned, all soft and loving. "Fetch mommy the pretty black bag. You can do it. Then afterward, we're going to make your babysitter pay."

Charlotte trotted right through the barrier and over to the trunk. She put her front legs on the open edge. She was just barely tall enough to reach it. Emily and Annie Pup followed her through the barrier, Annie

Pup wildly wagging her tail. The Semis had to be helping. They'd never once been this good at Fetch before.

Emily and Charlotte pulled the bag out of the trunk, past Ari, and back to where Mrs. Lee continued to croon.

"Oh no, you don't." Mrs. Valenzuela scrambled our direction. Ant did the same as if he was going to head her off and grab the Semis himself. At the last second, he tackled Mrs. Valenzuela instead. In the same moment, Nicholas took out Chadd, Gramps whacked Jedda with his cane, and my dad shoved Agent Silva backward off of his feet. "Go after one Clems," Dad announced, "go after all Clemses."

"*Just because a guest doesn't eat meat,*" Gramps announced with another swing of his cane Jedda's direction, "*doesn't mean one fails to serve the filet mignon to the rest of the table.*"

Which only kinda made sense, but I didn't care. They were helping me. Tears welled in my eyes. I had the best family ever.

The Brontës pulled the Semis right to Mrs. Lee. I grabbed it as they launched themselves into her arms.

Mrs. Valenzuela, half-underneath Ant, raised her hands in my direction as if preparing to launch a spell. "Sasha Clems, hand over that Semis, or the next lightning bolt takes out you and the dogs."

"I don't think so." Grandma George stood directly behind Mrs. Valenzuela and Ant. In her hand was a small silver cigarette lighter in the shape of a gun. She pressed it to the back of Mrs. Valenzuela's head. "Sasha's going to throw the Semis into the water, and I'm not afraid to pull this trigger if you try to stop her."

Go, Grandma George.

I jumped to my feet, pulling the Semis from the bag and touching it barehanded for the first time ever. No time to be squeamish.

Jedda shoved past Gramps racing in my direction. Agent Silva came around the other side. I hefted the Semis to throw it as far as I could into the water.

Chadd crashed into me from behind, knocking the Semis from my hand and into the dirt. Jedda lunged to grab it, and I did the only thing that I could to beat her. I kicked it as hard as I could, soccer-style. (Yes, Zachary Stultz, *The Faithless Schmuck*, had made me practice with him. So, yes, it was an excellent kick.)

"No," Agent Silva bellowed as the Semis arced away.

"So sorry," I yelled to the Semis as it hit the water thirty feet from the shore. It sank in a gurgle of light and bubbles.

Jedda and Chadd both dove into the water. So did all the handlers and BIMD agents who'd been blocked from getting to us by Ari's barrier.

"Maur!" I screamed.

As if he'd been anticipating this eventuality, Maur did a dive-slide-splash into the ocean and then paddled, wings-spread to where the Semis had sunk. He folded his wings into his body and snorted long and low in our direction. The swimmers all reversed and panic-paddled back to shore. All of us devolved into hacking and coughing as Maur's bad breath struck. I plugged my nose with one hand and shoved my fist into my mouth with the other.

Only Mrs. Lee seemed immune. She held Emily and Annie Pup in her arms. Charlotte leaned against her leg. "What God has joined together," she announced. "Let no man put asunder. Or plunder. And that's that. Now, Sasha Clems, you will fix my dogs."

Sulfur burned my eyes so painfully, I pressed them shut, tears running down my cheeks. I hacked and gagged, trying to clear my lungs. "Sure."

Either way, I'd won.

CHAPTER THIRTY-SEVEN
Two Weeks Later

Total Funds: negative $80.00.
(I borrowed money from Ant for gas and promised him I'd repay it.)

However . . .

After much pushing from my family, I signed with an agent for a true crime documentary. I did it as much to stop Dad and Gramps from being pissed at me as for the money itself.

(Okay, that's a lie, but I'm trying to be a less greedy person.)

The current highball offer is 14.7 million as long as I turn over the video of the seadragon's death. Of those millions, I've pledged five hundred grand each to the Monterey Bay Aquarium on behalf of the seadragon, Monterey Homeless Coalition, Assistance Dogs International, Amtrak Employees' Union Scholarship Fund, the Chicago Un-Homed Center, C&F Productions, the Panamanian Sloth Preservation Foundation, and the Carmel-by-the-Sea Rotary Club.

At 5:31 a.m. on an ordinary Tuesday morning, a white piece of paper floated down from my bedroom ceiling. It crumbled and disappeared before I could grab it. Barkley gave me a droopy-eyed doggie look from my bed.

"Well, that's weird," I said, heading to my closet to dig out my running gear. Plan was to run first, then head to Mrs. Lee's house. No, I hadn't been able to fix the dogs. Yes, Mrs. Lee had used Charlotte's new appearance, which even she'd finally admitted was super cute, to guilt me into walking the Brontës for free until I left for UC Santa Cruz next fall.

The rest of the day I had open because I'd quit my other three jobs. Woohoo!

Another white note drifted down. I did a flying leap to catch it.

If you rec

Huh? Near indecipherable handwriting. Didn't make sense. Crumbled to nothing in my hand. "Gonna have to do better, Bob."

Yay for hearing from him, though. There'd been radio silence since Newfoundland, not even a single congratulations. Not that Bob was a celebratory kinda guy.

I hadn't heard from anyone else, either, although someone anonymously paid off The Blue Castle's mortgages. Whether it was a handler, the US government, or someone like Taylor Swift was unknown. I was rooting for Taylor. Either way, it helped with the whole family forgiveness problem.

According to online gossip sites, Chadd and Jedda had patched things up and fled together to Australia. (Still didn't get that relationship.)

Cronk and Fritzie spent the week after the livestream doing talk-show rounds. The invitations dried up after Cronk argued a little too strongly for making private home ownership illegal. He called me every couple of days to complain.

So far, I'd only given a single interview. My dad's channel. Between that and the livestream, Dad had sponsorship offers from twelve different car companies.

Did my family really have a right to complain about my choices . . . ?

Another note floated down from the ceiling.

You. Me. Train. Park. Yes?

"Ari?"

The paper disintegrated.

"Ari?" I raced to the window, my heart doing a zero-to-one-hundred. It had to be Ari. No one else knew about Dennis the Menace Park.

Things had gotten beyond chaotic on the crochet hook after the Canadian police had arrived. Right before my family had willingly, but unhappily, left with them, Ari pulled me aside to say there was something he needed to take care of and that he'd be in contact in a couple of days, a week at most, and not to worry.

I'd been waiting eagerly, impatiently, ever since. That he was sending floating white notes implied that his "something" had to do with Bob.

"Of course, I'll meet you at the park," I said out of the window in the hopes that whatever *Draco* was working with him could hear. "When?"

No answer.

I waited. "Now?"

Still no answer.

Fifteen minutes later, I pulled Gladys in next to Baby Shark at the park. The fog was in, making the jungle gyms and fake hillsides and other play areas a series of hazy lumps in the distance. Reminded me of our Dreamscape visits.

"Ari?" I headed to where I could just make out the circular front of the steam engine.

"Around back," he called out.

I tingled at the sound of his voice. Totally, completely, tingled. Little bubbles of pure joy flooded my veins. Man, how I'd missed his accent. (And him, of course.)

I hopped the fence surrounding the train and followed the beautiful sound.

I found him perched on the rear of the train car, his feet dangling over the side. He wore dark pants and his usual red Standford hoodie, exactly as I'd imagined him in my daily (hourly) daydreams. The tingles exploded into blooms of euphoria that twined around my chest, through my neck, and across my lips in a massive, couldn't-hold-it-in-if-I-wanted-to grin. "Rule-breaking, are we?"

"I give you full credit."

"Which I deserve." I scaled the ladder built up the back of the train car while envisioning myself ruffling his hair, sliding my fingers over his neck, burying my lips . . .

Stupid Attraction Spell.

Or not.

Could come in useful. And it kept me from thinking too hard about the train's height.

I made it to the top and slid in next to him. Instantly, my butt went cold from the damp steel. (What moment in life is ever perfect . . . ?)

"Apologies for the vague communications." Ari sat stiff and didn't reach out to touch me. He was in tense-Ari-mode. Something was up. "That Messaging Spell is a Gordian knot."

Whatever that meant. "You've been visiting Bob then?"

Ari tangled his hands in his lap, fidgeting his fingers as he did so, and stared out at what would be a baseball field if the fog weren't in the way. We hadn't yet made eye contact. "I dropped out of school."

I turned to stare at him. "You. Did. What?"

He shrugged, his face flushing with embarrassment, his attention still straight ahead. "Not permanently. Just for the quarter."

"You. Dropped. School?" I put a hand on each side of his face and forced him to look at me.

He turned even redder and kept his eyes downcast rather than meet mine. "I needed to stay where I was."

"With Bob?"

"It's a long story." He lifted his hand as if to cover mine, hesitated a moment, and then dropped it.

I released his face, the chill of the train suddenly way too cold on my butt.

Until this exact moment, my assumption had been that we'd leap straight into mushy, romantic declarations, then start kissing. Only Ari wasn't giving out a relationship, romantic, kiss-me-now vibe at all. Wariness edged in on my happiness. "What's going on?"

"Mr. Quan sent me a note. Back in Newfoundland. He wanted me to visit, said it was urgent, and that the only way to get to him was to walk."

Which was so very Bob. "He told you he solved the technology problems?"

"Yes, but he was more interested in the corrupted spellbook that turned him into . . . well . . . what he is. You saw him, correct?"

"I did."

Ari twisted his hands together in his lap again. He still hadn't looked at me, and his whole body was tense. Kinda like how he acted when he was freaking out because some flirty girl was hitting on him.

Oh.

Oh, no.

No.

The remains of my heart's happiness turned to coal. The chill of the train car seemed to drop another twenty degrees. I shivered. Ari was here to dump me.

"The spellbook Bob stole used to belong to Lady Montague-Smith-Montague. Since I'm a member of her family with full access to the family library, Bob hoped I might be able to undo the spell. We haven't figured it out yet, but we're trying."

"You're going back." I managed to keep a quiver of impending hurt from my voice, barely.

"He wants me to, but I can't. Newfoundland's been shut down to outsiders, especially handlers. Since I'd already missed so much school, I thought I might take some time off instead. Go visit my parents. Both sets even. Mrs. Valenzuela told everyone about my bio family, but after all the things she lied about on the livestream, no one believes her, not even when her French friend doesn't cough." The corners of his lips tipped up in the barest edge of a smile as if I should find that funny.

Which I didn't.

It did make me want to jump him. I *adored* his secretive little half-smiles.

An ocean-deep sadness swept through me at the thought that after today, this moment, I'd never again get to see one of his smiles in person. I'd have to hang a poster of him in the back of my dorm room closet just so I could remember. "I'm sorry I didn't trust you in Quebec City and that I gave the Semis to Chadd. I was wrong. And stupid. And short-sighted. And . . . well . . . if it were me, I would've kept the Attraction Spell a secret too. Me being me, I probably would've lied about it even after Chadd explained."

"About that—"

"You don't need to apologize. I get it. I really do." My eyes prickled with stupid tears and I placed my hand on the sleeve of his hoodie just so I could touch him one last time. "I should've trusted you. You were great to me in every way, and you were right about everything. I *was* scared. I *did* hold back. You're the best, most amazing person I've ever met, and I regret not choosing you wholeheartedly when I had the chance."

Ari's mouth fell open. His eyes went wide. He cocked his head to stare right at me for the first time since I'd arrived. "Still?"

"You think I'm incapable of apologizing?"

He shook his head, but it wasn't a shake of denial, more a working-through-something-unexpected. "Hold on a second." He shifted sideways to dig around in his front pocket and pulled out two black disks stuck together. He pulled them apart and handed one to me. "Do you remember what you said about magnets? It was in a Dreamscape. I'd kissed you and Maur had attacked and I wanted to know why you were so angry. We sat on the swings."

"Fine, I was wrong then too. And I apologize for it."

"You said that attraction is like a magnetic force. But that it doesn't guarantee that the attraction is right or correct, it just means two magnets are near each other with nothing stronger to attract them."

Oh.

This was the moment he dumped me. I cleared my throat around a painful lump. "You found someone else you like better than me."

Ari's eyes went wide with horror. "No. Sasha, never."

"I'm in the way of you working with Bob."

Ari shook his head, violently this time. "Not at all. Don't ever think that." His voice sped up. "I'm trying to say that attraction doesn't have to mean everything. I know you're no longer attracted to me. I was hoping . . . I hope that—"

Now it was my turn to let my mouth fall open. "What?"

"Bob helped me undo the Attraction Spell. He knows everything there is to know about reversing spells. It's gone. I'm now entirely ordinary. I get that you no longer find me attractive, but as you said back in the Dreamscape, attraction doesn't have to mean everything. Maybe we can still—"

I stared at him as he rambled, letting his words sink in. Then I shoved him on the shoulder. "You think I'm no longer attracted to you?" I yelled. "That's what this is all about?"

His shoulders slumped forward. He stared down at his hands, refusing to look at me again. "I know you aren't. I traveled commercial to get here and not a single girl looked in my direction."

I shoved him again. "I thought you were dumping me."

He shook his head, finally meeting my gaze. "I'd never. You're the best, most determined, most loyal, funniest, prettiest, most generous—"

A pleased warmth spread under my skin bringing the tingles-times-a-thousand with it. He was just so . . .

Ari was just so very Ari.

He'd been stressed and suffering, possibly for days, because he'd been afraid that I might not like him anymore. How did one capture the perfection of such an idea?

He took my hand in his. His deep, dark, gorgeous eyes brimmed with sincerity and his own brand of determination. "Sasha, you're the best thing that's ever happened to me. And I am so very sorry that I didn't initially trust you, that I called you a liar, and that when you needed me the most, I wasn't there."

An overwhelming urge to wrap my arms and my legs and every other part of me around him built inside my chest. "I totally am a liar. But I'm telling the truth when I say that I am still utterly and absolutely attracted to you. I've wanted to throw myself at you from the moment I got that nearly indecipherable white note this morning."

He looked me up and down, the surprised expression returning. "Truly?"

I reached for his face a second time, happy to prove just how truthful I was. His lips twitched upward and his face lit with a warm happiness that equaled my own, but he also grabbed my wrists, halting me. "We have to do this right. Where's your magnet?"

I leaned in to kiss him. "I don't need a magnet to know I'm attracted to you."

"Hold on. This is important." He released me and held up his magnet. "Next fall, I'll be at Stanford and you'll be at Santa Cruz. That's only one hour and a coastal mountain range between us."

"Plus, a ton of traffic." I sighed and reached my magnet toward his since it seemed important to him.

He pulled his backward. "Not so much traffic that we can't make it work. And once I've visited my family, I can spend the summer in Monterey with you. Do you want to make it work, Sasha?"

"Duh." I reached forward with my magnet a second time.

He pulled back a second time. "Then you need to say it."

"'Duh' in American sarcasm means 'Yes' in English."

He chuckled. "You need to say your grandmother's words. The ones about Greece, from her *Blue Castle* book. The words that have so much meaning to your family."

"My grandmother stole those words, that story."

"Which doesn't change their meaning for you."

Which was true.

That he understood it felt important.

Ari got me. And I got him. My gut gurgled its approval, and the words of the cross-stitch that had hung over Gramps's bed my entire life tingled their way up my throat. *"The glory that is Greece and the grandeur that is Rome—Lure of the ageless Nile—Glamour of the Riviera—Mosque and palace and minaret—I know perfectly well that no spot or place or home in the world could ever possess the sorcery of you."*

"Perfect," he whispered as if something truly awe-inspiring had just occurred. Which it had. "Next, we should—"

I grabbed him, attacking his gorgeous, delectable, still-too-gorgeous-face. I kissed him with nothing held back, every last bit of me attracted to every last bit of him. In the same moment, entirely unintentionally, our magnets came together with a satisfying click.

(Yes, my butt was still cold.)

CHAPTER THIRTY-EIGHT

Six Weeks Later

Crap. I was running late. I slipped on my new shoes and snatched my month-old iPhone from The Blue Castle's kitchen counter while stuffing the last of a veggie wrap in my mouth. I raced through the family room, leaped over Barkley, and grabbed the remote from the coffee table to turn off the TV for a sleeping Gramps. Just as I swung into the hallway, my phone vibrated with a special three-beat rhythm to tell me exactly who was texting. (Man, I loved new technology!)

Ari: *Do I have to do this?*
Me: *I'm not dignifying that with a reply.*
Ari: *What if I beg?*
Me: *Does that mean you're here?*

The door chimes went off.

"Ari's here," Ant called out as if he'd been sitting in the front window watching, which he probably had been.

"Don't you dare embarrass him," I said as Ant and Nicholas exited the living room, Dad came down the stairs, and Gramps and Barkley wandered in from the family room. "You were asleep," I said accusingly to Gramps.

"You think I'd miss this?" Gramps replied, a huge smile splitting his face. "It's an important life moment."

"A character-building moment," my dad agreed.

I shook my head in mock disgust. "You guys are so going to embarrass him."

"Actually," Ant replied. "We like Ari. We're hoping to embarrass you."

"Family privilege," Dad agreed.

Nicholas gave me a nudge on the shoulder. "Don't listen to them. You look great, smart and sassy and all the things we love about you. Who wouldn't think you are the dog's bow-wow?"

"Uh, no, Nicky," Ant said, "that just doesn't work as a metaphor."

"Idiom, not metaphor." Gramps hollered.

The house creaked as if it found us amusing.

Glad someone did, because in truth I was a tad nervous myself. I'd spent an extra amount of time on my appearance. My hair was down for once and spritzed with a high-end product that gave me both volume and shine. My lips were tinged with gloss, my lashes with mascara. I'd even worn little dangly dragon earrings. Ari had better appreciate my efforts.

My phone buzzed in the special three-beat rhythm again.

Ari: Since the door remains shut, can I assume no one is home and leave?

"No," I said out loud and pushed past my obnoxious family to let him in. They followed on my heels. Of course, they did.

"You are so going to embarrass him." I swung open the door anyway.

Gramps pushed past me to get the first look. "Not bad, for an English-man."

"You look great, Ari," Nicholas said.

"Distinguished," My dad added.

Ant nodded. "Gotta love a man in a uniform."

I grinned in a sloppy he's-here-and-I-can't-stop-staring grin. Attraction Spell or none, Ari was still the hottest guy I'd ever laid eyes on. (Or at this point, hands, lips, elbows, etc.)

Ari nodded back at us, his expression carefully neutral, so neutral that it was clear he was freaking out.

"Stand together so I can take your picture," Ant said.

"Under my new flagpole," Gramps insisted.

Ari winced.

"Photos are a requirement," my dad said. "Today you are building an entire floor of the edifice that is your character. You want that commemorated."

"Just one," I said, my nervousness evaporating now that he was here. Besides, I'd been through this myself plenty of times.

Ari and I took our places next to the flagpole, him stiff and silent, me with my hand on his arm. Barkley planted his rump on Ari's Oxford shoe. (I wore shiny white sneakers. $150 on sale.)

Other than the shoes, we were dressed identically. Khaki pants, white long-sleeved polos. Navy vests. I reached over to pin one more detail to Ari's vest.

"Will it cause an international incident if I request we not include the Irish flag in our photo?" Ari murmured as I finished up. "Lord and Lady Montague-Smith-Montague have asked that should I be unable to extricate myself from this unenviable situation, I send them proof that it occurred." He sounded deeply British.

"They know?" I asked, surprised he'd told them since he'd been so adamantly against my plan.

"They are amused." He sighed as if disappointed. "My sisters as well."

"I'll tell Ant to make sure nothing but the pole shows."

Ari nodded, still stiff.

The thing was, though . . . as much as he didn't want to do this and had objected in every way possible, he'd also caved and agreed. For me. Because I'd said it was important. That's the kind of guy I'd won in Aristotle Montague-Smith-Montague. (Also, this really was going to be good for him.)

Ant lifted his camera. "Smile pretty. It's not every day that the famous—"

"—Not so famous anymore," I said, wrapping my arms around Ari's waist.

"Fine," Ant corrected, "The previously famous—"

"But still famous to me," I added.

Ant wrinkled his nose at me. Nicholas snorted.

"Just take the picture," Ari said through gritted teeth.

As Ant started snapping photos, I reached up and kissed Ari on the cheek. His shoulders relaxed, the tension draining. Then I pointed at the shiny new nametag I'd pinned to his uniform. It sat right over the logo for the Monterey Bay Aquarium and the words "Guest Experience Representative."

Today, with me at his side, for the first time ever, Aristotle Montague-Smith-Montague got a job.

****

Thank you so much for reading *Sasha vs the Whole Wide World (and Dragons)*. If you have a moment to help out a newbie author, please consider leaving an honest review in one of the usual spots. It really does help.

My next book, *Partridge Up a Pear Tree (and Dragons)* is set to release summer 2025. To receive notices for that and my other releases plus a free novella set in the world of my high fantasy series, come join my monthly newsletter: https://tinyurl.com/354z8rh

Happy Reading!
~Rachel

Acknowledgements

A huge thank you and shout to my two critique partners, Al Stegall and Kathleen Dougherty. The three of us met weekly via zoom for two and half years going through each other's books chapter-by-chapter. Both the book and I as a writer are so much better because of their pushing, prodding, questions, and reminders to get-out-of-my-characters'-heads-and-into-their-bodies. I can't say enough good things about working with Al and Kathleen.

A second (and just as big) thank you to Venessa Giunta, the fearless leader of TWT - The Writers' Troupe along with the Troupe itself. I started Sasha at my very first TWT zoom co-working and proceeded to write Sasha through more co-workings, twitch streams, and Sunday night chats. I don't know if the book would've happened without Venessa and TWT. (And...err...if anyone is looking for a fantastic, supportive, open-to-all writers group, go find TWT on Facebook. I attend as many group events as I can.)

And then many, many thanks to editor Stephanie Shiftlett of WhiteRabbitEditing and all the beta readers, ARC readers, friends, family, and other supporters that gave of their time/expertise and cheered me on. I couldn't have done it without you.

About the author

Rachel Taylor Thompson lives in the central coast area of California with her husband, daughters, and a truly ridiculous number of animals (including but not limited to horses, rabbits, chickens, cats, a guinea pig, a bearded dragon, bees, and various wild animals that endlessly steal everyone else's food). She started storytelling many years ago after she and a group of friends played the game Two Truths and a Lie and not a single person guessed that "I'm writing a book" was her lie. Since her friends had so much faith in her, she decided to go for it. To hear more about her books (and animals) head over to her website: www.racheltaylorthompson.com.